The Ugly Sister

JANE FALLON

PENGUIN BOOKS

PENGUIN BOOKS

Published by the Penguin Group
Penguin Books Ltd, 80 Strand, London WC2R ORL, England
Penguin Group (USA) Inc., 375 Hudson Street, New York, New York 10014, USA
Penguin Group (Canada), 90 Eglinton Avenue East, Suite 700, Toronto, Ontario, Canada M4P 2Y3
(a division of Pearson Penguin Canada Inc.)
Penguin Ireland, 25 St Stephen's Green, Dublin 2, Ireland (a division of Penguin Books Ltd)
Penguin Group (Australia), 250 Camberwell Road, Camberwell, Victoria 3124, Australia
(a division of Pearson Australia Group Pty Ltd)
Penguin Books India Pvt Ltd, 11 Community Centre, Panchsheel Park, New Delhi – 110 017, India
Penguin Group (NZ), 67 Apollo Drive, Rosedale, Auckland 0632, New Zealand
(a division of Pearson New Zealand Ltd)
Penguin Books (South Africa) (Pty) Ltd, 24 Sturdee Avenue, Rosebank,
Johannesburg 2196, South Africa

Penguin Books Ltd, Registered Offices: 80 Strand, London WC2R ORL, England

www.penguin.com

First published 2011
4

Set in Garamond MT Std 13/15.25 pt
Typeset by Palimpsest Book Production Limited, Falkirk, Stirlingshire
Printed in Great Britain by Clays Ltd, St Ives plc

A CIP catalogue record for this book is available from the British Library

ISBN: 978–0–141–04725–6

www.greenpenguin.co.uk

Penguin Books is committed to a sustainable
future for our business, our readers and our
planet. This book is made from paper certified
by the Forest Stewardship Council.

I

Genetics is a strange science. It's imprecise. A jumble of random combinations that make a unique whole. It's basically a lottery. So you can inherit the beautiful turned-up nose of your mother, but the fact that it's so big it takes up half your face from your paternal grandfather. Or your long legs from one side, but their tree-trunk-like appearance from the opposite. Or sometimes, cruelly, one sibling can inherit all the available beauty, leaving nothing for the other except the cast-off bits that didn't quite make the grade. It's as if there's only so much good stuff to go round. Or at least that's how it has always seemed to Abi. But then you could say her perspective is a little warped.

It's a subject that's close to her heart. One that pre-occupies her from time to time. The unfairness of it. The way that your inherited characteristics can determine the course of your whole life. Or, to be more exact, the way someone who shares more than their fair share of DNA with you can have such a different experience of the world simply because of the few small dissimilarities in the chain.

She knows too that the universe always appears to be a different place to siblings just by virtue of their place in line. The oldest – used to being the entire focus of their parents' adoration for as many years as they remain alone – entitled and imperious, convinced the planets revolve around them. The younger destined to grow up in the shadows, eager to please, aware that their very arrival has destroyed the idyll of the indulged first born and so prone to apology and self-sabotage.

In a large family you can get away from the endless comparisons or, at least, you can manipulate them to make yourself feel good. If measuring yourself against one of your siblings is making you feel bad, pick another. There's always someone you can feel superior to. When there are only two of you, though, there's no escape. Your every feature, every ability, every quality is held up for scrutiny and direct comparison. And the sad truth is that some people are simply handed a bigger deck, a shinier, sharper set of tools. Some people, as the saying goes, have all the luck.

She's contemplating this – for the millionth time, or so it seems to her – as she stands on the doorstep of her sister's palatial Primrose Hill home, gazing up at the sheer magnificence of the architecture, suitcases at her feet, wondering why no one is answering the door. Actually it's an exaggeration to say she has suitcases; she hasn't been on a proper holiday for years – why would she even own a suitcase? What she has is a large green nylon rucksack, an oversized Debenhams carrier bag stuffed full of last-minute bits and pieces, and a smaller Nicolas one containing a bottle of cheap (ish) champagne by way of a thank-you gift. Looking around the upmarket neighbourhood, she has no doubt that house prices in the area must be dropping by the minute the longer she stands there.

In fact, for the past month or so, ever since the email pinged into her inbox reminding her that she had a sister in the first place, Abi has thought about little else. It wasn't so much the fact that she received a communication from Caroline that set her off. Well, in part it was: Caroline doesn't often get in touch outside of birthdays and Christmases and then only in a sort of formal and disinterested way. A duty call. The real surprise was what was in the email. The fact that it was an invitation to go and stay. And not just for a night either, for the whole two months of the summer holidays. Abi can't remember the last time she and Caroline spent eight days together let alone eight weeks. Or seven for that matter. Or even six. Three, maybe, and that would have been a few years ago. A strained Christmas at their mum and dad's, probably.

Abi had to read the email four times to make sure that was really what it said:

It's been so long since we've spent any time together. I really regret that we've grown so far apart, and I miss having you in my life. Go on. You never know, it might be fun!

She had called Phoebe away from the TV to come and verify that she hadn't lost her mind.

'What do you make of this?'

Phoebe read it quickly, bending over Abi's computer, holding her too-long dark-brown fringe away from her eyes as she did so.

'Wow,' she said, 'are you going to go?'

'I don't know. What do you think?'

'She's right – it might be fun. After all, I'm not going to be here,' Phoebe said hesitantly, and Abi instantly felt guilty about being the only family Phoebe had that she really knew.

'Why do you think she's invited me?' Abi asked. Her daughter, all of eighteen years old, usually had an opinion on everything.

Phoebe shrugged. 'She's your sister.'

Phoebe would love to have a sister, so in her mind it's straightforward: if you have a sister, they must want to spend time with you – that's how it works. She's young – she'll learn.

Abi scanned the email again. 'I suppose it's true. It would save me having to rent a flat. And if you're not going to be around anyway . . .'

Abi, painfully aware that her only child was about to leave home, had recently sold the small cottage, two streets away from the seafront, where Phoebe had grown up. She was downsizing, moving into a shoebox-sized flat with views across the town from the tiny balcony, and a minuscule spare room with a sidelong glimpse of the sea that would be Phoebe's whenever she came home for a visit. She had got her timings all wrong, though, and was going to have to vacate the cottage weeks before she could take possession of the new place. She had been planning to rent in the interim, something she could ill afford to do, and it was when she had told Caroline this in a routinely small-talky email, of the kind Abi regularly sent but to which she seldom received a response, that the invitation had come. Now she could put all her belongings into storage at a fraction of the cost and spend the summer in London with her only sibling. It was a terrifying thought, but it was a solution. More than that – much more if she were being honest – there was the hint of a reconnection with her sister. For the first time since, well, for as long as Abi could remember really, Caroline seemed to be reaching out to her and, if that was the case, she didn't see how she could pass the opportunity up.

'Maybe.'

'What have you got to lose?'

'I suppose it might be good to spend some time with Caroline. I never see her these days.'

'You mean Cleo,' Phoebe said. 'Don't call her Caroline, whatever you do.'

'Yes,' Abi said quickly. 'Of course I do. I mean Cleo.'

2

Caroline is Cleo. Or, to be more precise, Caroline became Cleo on the day in 1985 when a scout from West End Model Management spotted her in Covent Garden and told her she had a big future. She and Abigail were out shopping, having caught the ten-fifteen train up to Charing Cross. Caroline at sixteen: tall and rangy, the winning combination of the all-you-can-eat skinniness of their father and their mother's delicate catlike face. Abigail, thirteen: short, round and soft courtesy of her maternal genes, while her father's side had kindly donated their blunt, no-nonsense, do-what-they-say-on-the-tin facial features. No one ever said that life was fair.

In actual fact, Abigail was prettier than she ever imagined. Her eyes, which were big and a nutty brown, softened her face and drew attention away from her nose, which was just a little too prominent. She'd grow into it later, but that was precious little comfort then. Her hair made up for what it lacked in colour – mousy brown not being about to turn any heads – in texture. Thick and shiny, grown long enough to hide behind. Her curves, disastrous for a thirteen-year-old who wanted to be able to wear cropped tops and pedal pushers, would in later life appeal more to the average man in the street than Caroline's bony angles, even if they wouldn't always admit to it in public. In any other family she might well have been handed the compliments, but being forced to stand next to Caroline for most of her young life ensured that she rarely got much attention.

They were having a good time. The summer holidays had just started and it was hot and sunny and the world was full of possibility. The grown-up Abi sometimes – no, often – looked back on this day, the day that changed everything, and thought that it was the last time she ever felt that way. The last morning she wasn't yet really aware of the different hands she and Caroline had been dealt in life. The last minute when she truly believed that looks weren't everything. However much she may have protested since, underneath it all she knows better now.

The woman, tall, skinny, pale and black-haired like one of the living dead, had been following them for more than a few minutes. When she finally approached them outside French Connection both girls jumped, shrieked, giggled in quick succession. She introduced herself, holding out a card in her clawlike hand. Vampyra, Morticia, something like that – Abi has never been able to remember. It's as if the shock of what happened afterwards blotted out the details. Then she asked them, looking around, if their mother was with them. Abigail, always the more grounded of the two, had tried to communicate to Caroline not to give too much away, with a shake of her head, but too late.

'No,' Caroline was saying already. 'She's at home. In Ashford. That's in Kent,' she'd added, as if that mattered.

The woman indicated the card that was now hanging limply in Abigail's hand. 'I'm from a company called West End Model Management. Have you heard of them?'

Caroline and Abigail looked at her blankly. Shook their heads.

'We're an agency for models. We get them jobs. Does that make sense?'

Abigail looked at Caroline. It seemed like a light had suddenly gone on in her sister's eyes. She quite literally lit up. Apparently she had guessed where this was going. Abigail, finally, looked at the card, took in what it said, remained clueless.

'We're always looking for girls with potential. How old are you?'

Caroline told her and the woman smiled as if being sixteen was a very good thing. Abigail tugged at Caroline's sleeve.

'Come on. We should go . . .' Caroline didn't budge.

'Maybe you could ask your mother to call me,' Vampyra said. 'We could set up a test shoot. No guarantees, of course. We need to find out how photogenic you are before we can promise anything.'

'OK,' Caroline said, pulling herself up to her full height – already five foot nine. Abigail was nearly five foot two. Five foot one and three quarters, thanks to her mother's mother. 'Thank you.'

Vampyra smiled her undead smile, wafted her hand and disappeared into the crowd. It was only after she had gone that Abigail realized the woman had never even looked her way. It was as if she had a firewall built in that screened out anyone less than five foot eight or with anything other than perfect bone structure. Turned them into white noise. Short, soft, pretty Abigail simply hadn't appeared on her radar.

'What was all that about? Madwoman,' Abigail said, pulling a face and hoping that Caroline would laugh, they could just agree that it had all been a big joke and then forget about it. She felt uneasy although she couldn't have said quite why. Caroline, usually so chatty, ignored her, gazing off into the distance as if she could see her whole future opening up.

'You should throw that away,' Abigail said, slightly desperately, reaching for the card that Caroline had snatched out of her hand at some point and that now seemed welded to her fingers. Caroline held on to it tightly.

'Mum'll be furious if she thinks we've been talking to strangers.'

'I'm going to be a model,' Caroline said, a smile creeping over her face. 'I'm going to be a model.'

'Don't be stupid,' was the best Abigail could come up with. Something wasn't right. 'As if.'

Caroline had tucked the card in the pocket of her jeans, checking out her reflection in the shop's window as she did so, in a way that Abigail had never seen her do before, and Abigail knew that she had lost her. What hurt the most, what Abigail spent hours dwelling on in the months to come, was that Caroline had never expressed an interest in modelling. Never. She was going to be a hairdresser and Abigail was going to go away to study to become a teacher. Then she'd move back to Ashford once she'd qualified and they would live near each other, their husbands would be best friends, their kids would go to Abigail's school. They had even got as far as planning that they would each have a boy and a girl and what their names might be. They had picked out their ideal houses, walking distance to their parents but not too close, and speculated on the initials of their future husbands. They were ordinary people and they had mapped out an ordinary life for themselves. Happily, or so Abigail had always thought. She'd had no idea that Caroline was harbouring secret ambitions to get away and leave her — and their plans — behind. She'd had no idea that Caroline had just been humouring her all those years.

Back at home, their day out cut short by Caroline whose heart no longer seemed to be in it, the girls' mother, Philippa, was as dizzy and excited as if she had been plucked from obscurity herself. Picture a pair of hysterical schoolgirls looking forward to their first date, only one of them was forty-seven and had been married to the other one's father for nineteen years.

'Margaret Wilson's Julie did modelling,' Philippa said, talking about one of her friends from the WI. 'I saw her picture in the *Sun* once. I think she was going out with one of Haircut 100.'

'I need a new name,' Caroline had suddenly announced out of nowhere. 'I can't be a famous model with a name like Caroline Attwood. It doesn't work. I need to stand out. I mean no one who's any-one needs to use their surname these days.'

'Well, what's wrong with just Caroline?' the girls' dad, Andrew, said, trying to be helpful. Caroline gave him a look that could freeze water.

'It's so . . . ordinary. So . . . suburban.'

Philippa looked a bit disappointed. No doubt she was thinking that if Caroline ever did become famous then it would be harder to make sure all the neigh-bours remembered that she was actually a member of the Attwood family if she changed her name. Philippa wanted to be given her due credit for having successfully passed on half her genes. The good ones obviously.

'Julie Wilson was always Julie Wilson,' she'd said hopefully.

'And who's ever heard of her?' Caroline snapped back. As usual, Philippa gave in immediately to Caroline's wishes.

'I know,' she said, fingering Caroline's long dark fringe (so like her not-yet-born granddaughter Phoebe's), 'how about Cleopatra? You look like Cleopatra with your hair like that.'

'Cleopatra,' Caroline said, trying out the sound of the word. 'Cleo. I like it. It's perfect.'

'Cleo Attwood?' Philippa said hopefully.

'No. Just Cleo,' Caroline/Cleo said.

So, at nine thirty and fifteen seconds on the Monday morning Philippa had called West End Model Management and arranged for 'Cleo' to go in for a test shoot. Philippa was so excited that she hadn't even bothered to check whether they were a real modelling agency and not some kind of paedophile ring. The fact that it had been a woman who had approached Caroline was good enough for her. Actually, by then the fever had reached such a pitch that, Abigail thought, Philippa probably wouldn't have cared if it had been a dirty old man in a grimy mac offering to let the girls stroke the puppies he had in his pocket, so long as he had access to a nice camera. By three o'clock on the following Thursday, West End Model Management had decided that they wanted Cleo for a client and less than six weeks later, by the time Abigail returned to Ashford Girls'

Grammar School to begin her third year, Cleo had been hailed as 'the face of 1985' in one of the national newspapers after some famous photographer or other had tipped them off. Abigail didn't see her much after that.

Cleo moved up to London just a few weeks later to share a dingy flat on the Brompton Road with two other girls she had met on a shoot somewhere, leaving Abigail to deal with all the envy and spite that her sister's success had brought out in their school friends. Abigail tried to be pleased for her, and she actually managed it for a while, but the ease with which Cleo shrugged off her old life – her sister, her mum and dad, her friends, her beloved cat, George – left Abigail reeling. One minute Caroline was there, best friend, partner in crime, confidante, and the next she had gone from her sister's life so completely that Abigail sometimes felt like she was an only child. At least she might have thought so if it hadn't been for the constant refrain of 'You're Cleo's sister?' that would rise up to taunt her whenever anyone new found out about her celebrity connections. Always accompanied by a look up and down her five-foot-one-and-three-quarters frame of course. Not that she ever told anyone about it herself. She avoided mentioning she had a sister at all if possible, but word always seemed to get around somehow wherever she went.

It wasn't that Abigail wasn't proud of her. She was the younger by three years – it was a given. Caroline had been her role model and brightly shining example since the day Abigail was old enough to toddle around behind her. She just found it hard to believe that the gorgeous enigmatic creature she saw in the magazines, so different from the gangly awkward sibling she had grown up with, shared her genetic material. She spent hours in front of the mirror trying to spot Cleo in her own less feline features. And sometimes she was there fleetingly, in an expression or a flick of the hair, but she never stayed for long.

At first Cleo and Abigail used to write to each other quite often, although Abigail always struggled to find anything interesting to say — went to school, had the wart on my finger frozen off, George brought a frog in from the garden, that kind of thing. Cleo's responses, which started off short and grew shorter with time, nevertheless glittered with the glamour of a world that was so alien to Abigail's own that sometimes she wondered if her sister was making it all up. There were parties with celebrities, clubs, boys — no, make that men — hints of drugs. In the early days Abigail used to look forward to studying the letters on her walk to school but before long she barely recognized the person she found in them. It was only a matter of weeks before Caroline seemingly completely disappeared and Cleo was left in her place. And Abigail didn't much like Cleo she had decided. Cleo was a show-off, full of stories of the hearts she was breaking and the fabulous doors her looks were opening.

Abigail responded by never mentioning anything contained in the letters in her replies. If she acted like that person didn't exist, then maybe she didn't.

One half-term Abigail went up to stay in the flat on Brompton Road but Cleo was always busy and the other girls seemed only to be interested in talking about themselves or how rich and successful their boyfriends were. She moped around London on her own for a couple of days, with no money to do anything and no one to do it with. On the third day she had asked Cleo if she could go along to her shoot with her – Cleo had recently snagged a contract with Miss Selfridge and was spending two days being photographed in the new autumn/winter collection for outsize posters that would adorn shopfronts everywhere from the following August onwards – and then had wished she hadn't. Not only was the whole experience deathly boring after the first hour or so, but she felt in the way, the only person there without a seemingly life-threateningly important job to do. Cleo, surrounded by fawning stylists and make-up artists, spent the morning scowling and rolling her eyes whenever the photographer asked for her outfit to be tweaked or her hair teased.

'Oh, for fuck's sake,' she said when he called for a belt he had previously rejected to be returned. 'Make up your mind.'

Abigail, pre-programmed to be polite to adults and unused to hearing anyone swear in their company, waited for the explosion but none came. The photographer merely smiled indulgently and called out, 'Sorry, love,' apologetically. When Cleo snapped, 'Ow. For god's sake be careful,' at the hairdresser in front of the whole crew, Abigail blushed. When she followed it by saying 'silly bitch' in an overly loud stage whisper as the hairdresser sloped off, tail between her legs, Abigail decided it was time to call it a day and took herself off to the National Gallery instead.

The final straw came one night when she was in bed, having spent the evening alone while Cleo went to a party to which Abigail was firmly not invited, and she was woken up by her sister's urgent insisting that she decamp next door to the sofa.

'I need the room to myself,' Cleo had hissed. She smelt of alcohol and cigarettes and something else – musty, musky, manly.

'What? No. I'm asleep.'

Cleo had pulled the covers off with a theatrical flourish, holding them out of Abigail's reach.

'Now.'

Abigail, still befuddled with sleep, dragged herself out of bed.

'Here,' Cleo said, handing her the stiff scratchy bedspread and keeping the duvet for herself.

'What's going on?' Abigail protested as Cleo bundled her towards the door. In the hall she was dimly aware of a man in an expensive-looking camel-coloured coat, a ring glinting on the third finger of his left hand as he swept his hair back from his face. In the half light he looked almost as old as their father.

'Good girl,' he said as she passed him, and Abigail shuddered. In the living room she lay on the sofa and pulled the bedspread up over her head, her hands over her ears. At about three o'clock she heard the bedroom door open and the man's heavy footsteps as he gathered up his things and left.

Next morning Cleo was full of 'Geoff' this and 'Geoff' that.

'You do know he's married?' Abigail had said.

Cleo laughed. 'So? That's his problem.'

'Not to mention that he's old. And gross.'

'He's only forty. And he's very rich,' Cleo said. 'You're just jealous.'

Over time both Cleo's letters and her visits home became increasingly rare. Every now and then she would telephone her mother and feed her enough tit-bits about her glorious life so that Philippa could pass them around town and have everyone believing that she and her famous daughter lived in each other's pockets. The truth was that most of what the family came to know about Cleo's new life came from what they would read in the papers.

Abigail had left home herself eventually and gone to use the family brains – almost exclusively inherited by her – at Kent University in Canterbury. She became Abi to her friends although her parents never got used to the idea. She cut her hair and wore a lot of black and smoked foul-smelling French cigarettes. By then she had given up her teaching ambition – she never asked, but for some reason she suspected Cleo might have forgotten all about hairdressing too – and she had new dreams of having a glittering career in publishing, but then suddenly she was pregnant with Phoebe and that was that really. So she had replaced those dreams with visions of playing happy families with the baby and her boyfriend of not very long, Dave, but it turned out he had visions of being single and child-free for a few more years, so he ran a mile when Abi told him she was pregnant. She sent him a photo of Phoebe when the baby was born and he sent her a solicitor's letter asking her to leave him alone.

It's hard to resurrect a non-existent career when you're a single mum so eventually Abi gave up trying and got a part-time job in the local library. She's still there. Eighteen years later. It suits her. The hours are flexible. The work unchallenging and pleasant enough. The library has its regulars, the old people, the nerdy kids, the homeless. Abi and her colleagues (a random collection of the most timid and unassuming members of society coupled with a smattering of part-timers who are more interested in the hours than the work) chat to them all and sometimes even offer them a cup of tea. Abi earns next to nothing, but she doesn't really care. She gets by. Officially, of course, she is 'a disappointment'. So much untapped potential. There was never anything Philippa could boast about: unwed single mum with badly paid part-time job not sounding quite so grandiose as international supermodel apparently.

After her sister married Jonty – an advertising executive with his own agency, as she never tired of telling the family – Abigail saw her even less often. Once a year, if she was lucky. And then usually only for a day or two. Abi has never stopped missing Cleo, though – or, more specifically, Caroline. Abi and Cleo have never really been close. She has never grown out of that feeling of excitement whenever she gets a letter or an email or – very rarely – a phone call. There is always that moment, that split second, when she can allow herself to think that it might be Caroline and not Cleo getting in touch. Like they might fall back into their sixteen- and thirteen-year-old easy way of being. The running jokes and confidences. It hasn't happened in a long time. Phoebe was Abi's family now. But Phoebe was about to go off for her gap year, travelling around the world with her two best friends before she took up her place at the London College of Fashion, and Abi was at a loose end. Single Mother, One Not-so-careful Owner. Anything Considered.

The house is grandiose grey stucco, identical to its twin next door. The mouldings picked out in white give it the look of every little girl's dream doll's house. It sits right on the edge of the neat green rolling park that

Abi presumes – from the large grassy mound rising up in the middle – is Primrose Hill itself. Dog walkers slog up the steep slope to the top where people flying kites rub shoulders with those who have made the climb just to admire the view. The house itself is picture perfect. At least five stories high and of giant proportions. There is only one bell; no one has attempted to destroy the eighteenth-century character by dividing it up into flats.

Abi smoothes down her hair – grown long again since her rebellious student days and now fairer, streaked with a white blonde – as if her subconscious knows that she needs to smarten up to match her surroundings. She leans back, taking in the vast majesty of the place and her nerve leaves her. She suddenly has no idea why she had thought this would be a good idea. If she hotfoots it back to Charing Cross station now she could be back home in Deal in a couple of hours. Except, of course, that home is packed up in boxes and sitting in a dank musty-smelling storage facility in Dover.

3

The only thing that Abi knows about Primrose Hill beyond the fact that her sister lives here, is that it is – or, at least, once was – home to all sorts of glamorous celebrities who were famous for not very much other than thinking that they looked good and partying a lot. When Cleo had first said that she and Jonty were moving there, Abi had thought, Perfect. It made sense for them to live among the self-anointed beautiful people, all style over substance. She remembers thinking that Primrose Hill must be like a kind of Rodeo Drive in Beverly Hills (not that she has ever been) with a bit of *Footballers' Wives* Cheshire (again, ditto, but she has seen it on TV) thrown in. All McMansions and bling. In actual fact, Abi thinks, looking around now, it all looks rather pretty. The houses are stately and dripping with features that are both original and tasteful. The little shopping street is stuffed full of one-off shops and restaurants. There are normal-looking people walking their dogs and going about their non-celebrity business. She decides to have a look around the area and try again in a few minutes.

She's halfway down the steps when she hears someone walking across the hall. She freezes and stands rigidly to attention, waiting for the door to open. She has been assuming that one of Cleo's staff would let her in. That's right. Cleo has staff. 'My people' she calls them. As in 'I'll get one of my people to call you back', which is what she said to Abi when Abi called to try to persuade her to go to their dad's seventy-fifth birthday party a few years back: 'I'm not sure where I'll be.' One of her people did indeed phone back and thanked Abi very formally for the invitation but unfortunately Cleo had a prior engagement and would not be able to attend. 'Thank you for thinking of her,' he'd added insincerely.

'Do you know I'm her sister?' Abi had said, not being able to hide her irritation. 'Do you know that this is an invitation to our dad's birthday party not some show-business lunch or the opening of a new art gallery?' To be fair he had been very apologetic and had completely dropped the sanctimonious tone and Abi had known that this was in no way his fault. Cleo had obviously just given him a bunch of requests to turn down and hadn't even thought it worthy of a mention that one of them was from family.

Anyway, Abi is standing there rigid, holding her breath, still thinking of leaving rather than waiting for one of the 'people', when the door opens and there she is. Cleo. Abi's big sister Caroline, aka Cleo the supermodel. Abi is momentarily dazzled by the five-thousand-watt welcoming smile. The smile that always makes you feel you're the person Cleo most wants to see in the world. Until you know better, that is.

'Abigail! Come in. It's so good to see you.'

Abi feels the breath squeezed out of her as Cleo sweeps her up in a big embrace. She savours the moment, hugging her sister back, which is a bit awkward what with the Debenhams bag and the champagne. She inhales Cleo's signature 'Exotica' scent and marvels, as she always does, about the fact that Cleo still has some left, it having been discontinued years ago. Then she allows herself to be led inside and into the enormous hallway, which is easily twice as big as Abi's whole house and probably four times as expensive. She has never been to this house before – even though Cleo, Jonty and their two girls have lived here for the best part of six years – and she struggles, trying to find the words in her head to describe it. Palatial, opulent, lavish, regal (although that last one is more or less covered by palatial and so doesn't really count). Lush, Phoebe might say, Abi thinks fondly. Fierce.

If the outside is intimidating, then the inside is its scarier bigger brother. All marble and dark wood and classic, ornately framed works of art and antique vases and that's just the hallway. Abi doesn't really have time to take it all in though because she is trying to take in her sister. Every time they see each other these days it has been so long since the last time, and Abi's vision has been so clouded by the airbrushed images of Cleo that pop up in the most unlikely places (her face was on one of the best-selling posters of the 1980s, every boy student had it and you still see it for sale everywhere. A gaunt faun's face peering out from under that fringe, her long hair just-got-out-of-bed sexy, endless bare legs emerging from the volume of her oversized thigh-skimming sweat top, which had cheekily slipped off one tanned shoulder; you know the one. That's her. That's Cleo) that she has to adjust her mental picture to take account of the real live woman. Cleo is still beautiful, there's no doubt about that. Still tall (obviously, Abi doesn't know why that one always surprises her), still slim although, thankfully, not the emaciated stick that she was in her twenties. Still groomed to within an inch of her life. Still, to be honest, scary.

When she stopped modelling about five years ago, Cleo had allowed herself to relax just a little after an adult lifetime of a strict self-enforced dieting regime. To Abi's eyes she looked even more beautiful, more natural, more like a real person, but some of the papers had been a little unkind. One of the glossy magazines printed a blow-up of a photo of Cleo on the beach with a red circle highlighting a microscopic area of cellulite. Several times journalists had insinuated that she didn't quit of her own volition as she has always stated, but that her looks simply hadn't stood the test of time like Naomi's and Cindy's had, and that she had pissed off so many people with her attitude on the way up that they were positively queuing to push her back down again and then stamp all over her when they got the chance. Abi has no idea what the true story is. It isn't something she's ever felt she can ask.

Cleo's trademark hair is still dark brown, nearly black, although she has grown out her thick fringe and trimmed the whole thing to a stylish shoulder length. The sleepy upward tilt of her eyes is as pronounced as ever. Maybe more pronounced – can that be possible? Her skin is ridiculous. Smooth and glowing and healthy. Actually, Abi thinks, maybe it's a little too smooth. She catches herself wondering, not for the first time, if Cleo has had Botox. Or worse.

'You look great,' Cleo says, holding Abi at arm's length. Her smile doesn't quite meet her eyes. Not because it isn't sincere necessarily, but because her face is refusing to move to accommodate it.

'You too.' Abi feels herself blush a little and realizes that she has come over all shy and clumsy. Straight back to adolescence. This happens to her pretty much every time she sees Cleo. It's like their relationship, from Abi's point of view, halted at the point where Cleo left home, and whenever they spend any time together she is instantly transported back to her awkward thirteen-year-old self, wanting approbation from her big sister.

'This house is incredible.'

Cleo smiles graciously again and says yes, they love it and that she'll show Abigail straight up to her room if she'd like so that she can get settled in. Abi latches on to this as if it is the most profound statement she's ever heard.

'Great. Perfect. How are you?' she asks and even she is stunned by her own banality.

'I'm well,' Cleo says. 'Busy.'

Abi thinks about asking her what she is busy with since she no longer works, but that might sound rude so she says nothing. It's always like this when they haven't seen each other for a while. It takes a few minutes to warm up. They have to feel their way around each other, both conscious that their relationship is held together by a few fragile threads and neither wanting to be the one responsible for breaking them irreparably. She follows Cleo across the hall and up the stairs, looking around in awe. There are ornate mirrors and sculptures everywhere you look. Everything, right down to the handles on the doors, is exquisite. It's like a show home, something from the pages of *Country Life*. There is no obvious evidence that a family lives here. It's perfect. Sterile. Abi assumes that some of Cleo's people, the ones who do the housekeeping, must spend all day tidying and polishing. It's intimidating. Abi finds herself wondering all over again if this is such a good idea. She and Cleo hardly know each other. Caroline is long gone. Abi isn't sure any longer what she was hoping to achieve by spending the next two months in a house of near strangers. Part of her, she knows, has been fantasizing that the sisters can somehow recapture some of what they once had. That Cleo's mask will fall and there will be the old Caroline, funny and clumsy and, above all, Abi's friend. But, actually, now that she's here, she really isn't sure Caroline could be alive and well living in a house like this.

When Caroline and Abigail were fourteen and eleven they took a vow that they would be each other's best friend forever. They were too squeamish to swear in blood so they used tomato ketchup instead, smearing it on their thumbs and rubbing them together, laughing at the gory mess they'd created. Abigail felt safe and secure knowing her big sister had her back, and about a week later, when a boy in Caroline's class who Abigail had liked for ages asked her if she wanted to meet him in town on Saturday morning, Caroline had proved her worth as protector.

Gary Parsons had a haircut like Ian McCulloch from Echo & the Bunnymen and Abigail had often seen him smoking in the alleyway beside the school and thought he looked very big and very clever. She'd taken to hanging around outside Caroline's classroom at break time (cue much shouting of 'Why are you hanging around me all the time? It's embarrassing') in the hopes of reaching the dizzy heights of him one day saying 'all right?' and her being able to say 'yeah, you?' in a cool and insouciant way. She'd been practising. Anyway, to cut a long story short, they had all righted and yeah, you'd? successfully a couple of times and then one day they exchanged a couple of other scintillating words and then Gary had dropped his bombshell of asking Abigail to meet him upstairs at McDonald's in town at eleven o'clock that Saturday.

It was her first date. She was nearly faint with excitement. She couldn't wait to tell Caroline. Caroline got asked on dates all the time. Sometimes she went, sometimes she didn't. She didn't seem that bothered. But she'd mirrored Abigail's excitement when Abigail blurted out her news, she'd indulged her in her trauma about what to wear and how to do her hair. She'd coached her in the art of captivating conversation based on her observations in class of what Gary's interests might be.

Then, on the Thursday, just as Abigail's excitement peaked, with the watershed that was the coming weekend – the transitional step between her childhood and the fabulous, glamorous life of an adult – set firmly in her sights, Caroline had come home from school, taken Abigail up to her tiny attic bedroom and told her that Gary was not the boy Abigail thought he was. He had betrayed her already without ever really giving their love a chance.

Caroline had found herself sitting next to him in double Biology and somewhere along the life cycle of the frog, between amplexus and the metamorphosis, he had admitted to her that it was she, Caroline, that he was really interested in and not Abigail. In fact,

Caroline had said in a half whisper to emphasize how awful she felt for having to tell Abigail this, he had said that he had only got friendly with Abigail in the first place to get closer to Caroline. Then he'd asked Caroline to meet him in McDonald's and to tell Abigail not to bother, Caroline told Abigail, a look of horror mixed with concern clouding her face. Could she believe that? The cheek of it. Caroline had turned him down, obviously, telling him exactly what she thought of him. He wasn't good enough for either of them she'd said, so loudly that the teacher had asked her what was going on.

Abigail had cried from the sheer shame of it and Caroline had mopped up her tears and comforted her with the fact that it was far better for Abigail to have found out what kind of person Gary really was now rather than later. Rather pitifully, devastated though she was, Abigail had still wondered whether she should turn up on Saturday as arranged. That maybe she and Gary could pretend nothing had happened and he might still agree to become her boyfriend. But Caroline had talked her out of it. She wouldn't let her sister show herself up like that, she'd said. Abigail had to keep her dignity and not go chasing a boy who was clearly far more interested in Caroline's looks than anything Abigail's own personality might have to offer. There must be a boy out there somewhere who valued brains over beauty and Abigail should wait for him to come along and announce himself. Despite her misery Abigail had known that she was lucky to have an older sister looking out for her.

'The girls are at their friends',' Cleo says as she leads Abi up several flights of stairs. Abi nods, panting. She's out of breath by floor two and she knows there are still more to come. It's beyond her why you would ever need to go to the gym if you lived in a house this size. Just going up to bed at night would constitute a workout.

'They should be home any minute. They're dying to see you.'

Abi finds it hard to imagine that the arrival of an aunt they hardly know is going to be the highlight in the girls' social calendar. The girls, by the way, are Tara and Megan. Ten and seven. The family Christmas newsletter that always accompanies the card generally makes it sound as if the girls are accomplished in ways you couldn't even begin to imagine – tennis, dancing, languages, polo, international diplomacy, you name it. No doubt they're also well versed in etiquette and could ace an exam in their sleep on which forks go where and which way to pass the port.

Abi is intimidated by the very idea of them. She hasn't seen either girl in the flesh for a couple of years – apart from in the pictures on the aforementioned Christmas cards, which are always happy family portraits like the ones the queen sends out, only with less tartan. They had still seemed like normal little girls then, a bit overconfident, but when has that ever been a bad thing? Now their list of skills mastered and engagements attended threatens to eclipse the curriculum vitae of Abi's entire thirty-eight-year life. To put it bluntly, they scare her.

Abi follows Cleo into a very pretty top-floor bedroom with its own bathroom next door, taking in her sister's running commentary as they go. Mostly it seems to be about where things are from with big hints as to how much they cost. The important stuff. Even four floors above the ground, the opulence is staggering. There's art on the walls and adorning little side tables — works of art in themselves — by people whose signatures Abi recognizes. Not old masters, not twenties of millions of pounds' worth, but the Stella Vines and the Grayson Perrys. There's a small scene of carnage in a Perspex box on the landing that she could swear is a Jake and Dinos Chapman. Art — modern art in particular — is a passion of Abi's, but one which she can only indulge by traipsing up to London to the Saatchi Gallery or Tate Modern a couple of times a year. It has never crossed her mind that you could own any of it, let alone display it in what she assumes is the second-tier guest bedroom.

The bath has claw feet and stands in the middle of the room under a huge skylight. There are candles everywhere and little bottles of body lotion and shower gel like you would get in a smart hotel except that these look as if they have been bought and paid for rather than sneaked out in the bottom of a suit-case. To Abi the idea that her sister lives like this is awe-inspiring to say the least. And the fact that she can be so impressed by someone she's related to actually buying small matching containers of toiletries, she thinks, says everything anyone needs to know about how her life has turned out.

Cleo leaves her to 'settle in'. 'You must treat this as your house,' she says as she heads downstairs. Abi thinks of her tiny two-up, two-down little cottage and the even tinier flat she's about to move into and has to stop herself from saying 'Why? Does your ceiling leak too?' or asking whether they should keep a plunger handy for when the toilet blocks. Both sisters are all too aware of the difference between their circumstances, there's no point trying to make an issue of it.

Abi suddenly remembers that she has forgotten to mention the leak to her purchasers. Oh well, they must have had a survey done. She doesn't feel it was her duty to take them round the place pointing out its flaws. She's not even sure if they are moving in straight away or having work done first because, to be honest, the house desperately needs some TLC. If the leak in the kitchen ceiling bothers them, then she can't imagine what they'll make of the damp patch under the stairs or the crack in the bathroom wall. Abi, on the other hand, after fifteen years of watching her home crumble around her ears – with a few feeble attempts to stem the tide with self-taught DIY – can hardly wait to move into somewhere that has a management company you can phone and make demands of when things go wrong.

She lies down on the bed to recover her breath and to take in the expensive-looking rococo-style wall-paper. Silvery blue floral swirls on a silvery blue background. Tiny exquisite birds scattered here and there. The bed which, even up in the attic, is bigger than her one at home, is covered with throws in a variety of opulent fabrics. There are so many bolsters and cushions that she can hardly find a space to stretch out on. There's a classic French-style chair, painted white and covered in a cool icy blue silk, a white distressed dressing table with a complementing stool and a giant white-and-gold armoire that Abi thinks she could live in if she had to, let alone use to store her pitiful wardrobe. Not for the first time she wishes Phoebe had been able to come with her. She wonders what Phoebe's reaction to this room would have been. 'Awesome', probably.

Phoebe has only met her famous aunt a handful of times in her life and is therefore able to be far more forgiving than her mother. In fact, just thinking about the fact that her sister is downstairs now makes Abi's stomach lurch. She's about to spend more time with Caroline – Cleo, she must remember to call her Cleo, she hates Caroline – than she has spent with her since Abi was thirteen years old, since Abi was Abigail. She can't imagine how they are going to be with each other, what they're going to talk about. She wishes her daughter was here to back her up. Funny, confident, couldn't-care-less Phoebe. Someone to have a debrief with in the evenings and a laugh about Cleo's over-the-topness. She feels out of her depth, doggy-paddling nervously, head only just above water. She's tempted to pack everything up again, rent a flat, move into a B 'n' B, anything. She isn't sure she's ready to reconnect with her sister just yet.

She's thinking that maybe she'll just have a soak in the big roll-top bath before she goes when she hears voices downstairs that tell her that her nieces are home. She has no choice but to go down and say hello. They're only children, nothing to be scared of.

Standing in the living room she finds two little girls who nearly make her heart skip a beat. In the two years since she has seen them last Tara has shot up and slimmed down into a carbon copy of her mother at the same age. She has the same rich dark-brown/black poker-straight hair, the same long skinny legs, the same green cat's eyes. Next to her, Megan looks short even for her age, plump and nondescript. Her hair neither blonde nor brown, but somewhere muddy in between, her eyes, looking at Abi warily from beneath her fringe, are a hazelnut brown. She's the image of her aunt at the same age.

Both girls smile politely.

'Hey, girls,' Abi says. 'Remember me?'

'Hi, Auntie Abigail,' they reply in unison.

They're dressed near identically in what look suspiciously like Juicy Couture tracksuit bottoms and Ugg boots. Just because Abi can't afford to buy designer clothes doesn't mean she doesn't recognize them when she sees them. She likes to read all the magazines at work. It's one of the perks of working in a library. When she can wrestle them away from the homeless clientele who like to stay all day and read everything, that is. It never ceases to amaze her how long a fifty-five-year-old down-and-out with piss stains on his trousers and wearing Special Brew cologne can spend studying *Grazia*.

Megan fiddles uncomfortably with the hem of her T-shirt, tugging it down to try to cover her tummy. Abi flashes her a smile and Megan looks at the floor, mortified to be caught out.

'Do you want to see my room?' Tara says, and Abi says yes, of course, she'd love to, even though she finds the prospect alarming, but then Cleo interrupts. 'Let Auntie Abigail have a rest first – she's only been here five minutes.'

'I'll come up later,' Abi calls to a sulky-looking Tara as she stomps off into the hall. Megan follows. Abi assumes Megan follows Tara everywhere, caught up in the thrall of big-sister hero worship. She wants to tell her not to, that big sisters don't always turn out to be what you think they are, but she knows it would be pointless. Megan will have to learn the hard way.

An image flashes into her mind. Herself at Megan's age, crying because her first-communion dress – Caroline's cast off from a few years before – was too tight and too flouncy and too old-fashioned and she felt stupid and self-conscious, mutton dressed up as lampshade.

'Take it off a minute,' Caroline had said.

'Mum said she has to pin the hem up,' Abigail sniffled. She had tried to protest to Philippa that something that had once fitted her sister was unlikely to fit her, but Philippa was having none of it.

'Just do it,' Caroline insisted. Abigail did what she was told and then sat on the bed shivering in her vest and pants.

Caroline had laid the dress out on the floor. Then she had walked over to her bedside table and picked up the glass of Ribena that was sitting there. Abigail watched open-mouthed, knowing and not knowing what was about to happen. Unable to stop it. Not wanting to.

'Whoops,' Caroline said, laughing as she threw the contents of the glass over the dress. A reddish purple stain oozed its way across the bodice and down onto the frilly skirt. 'Now she'll have to buy you a new one.'

'She'll kill me,' Abigail had said. She felt sick but she felt triumphant too. Whatever happened there was no way she was going to have to wear the dress now.

Five minutes later, once she was sure that the black-currants had well and truly worked their way into the fabric, Caroline had called their mother. Philippa, see-ing the dress, flushed the same violet shade as the ugly stain.

'What on earth . . .?'

Abigail had looked at the floor, gulped noisily. Said nothing.

'I'm so sorry, Mummy. I didn't mean to. I was just playing and then . . .' Caroline was looking at her mother with Bambi eyes. Wet tears were working their way down her cheeks. 'It was all my fault.'

Philippa's time bomb had defused almost immedi-ately. 'Maybe it'll come out,' she'd said, and taken the dress off to the bathroom to soak. Caroline, behind her mother's back, had winked at her sister, tears for-gotten, and at that moment Abigail would have done anything for her. It didn't matter that in the end their mother had declared the dress fit for church and that Abigail had ended up slightly worse off, dressed in the offending frills and trying to ignore the faint pink hue that made them stand out even more against the other girls' virgin white. Caroline had risked life and limb and probably several weeks' pocket money in an effort to make her happy. She couldn't have cared less about the dress any more.

'I just got a new Ralph Lauren duvet cover,' Tara shouts as the girls head up the stairs. 'It's totally cool.'

Abi looks at Cleo who gives her a slightly apolo-getic eye roll.

'She's her mother's daughter, what can I say?'

Well, you could say no you can't have bed linen made by Ralph Lauren when you're ten years old – it's a total waste of money, Abi thinks, but of course she doesn't say it. Instead she opts for, 'Where's Jonty?'

'Work,' Cleo says. 'He'll be home about six.'

'Oh.' Abi can't think of anything else to say so she just sits on one of the cream leather Barcelona chairs and looks out of the patio doors. 'Nice garden.'

'Thanks,' Cleo says, and then she sits down in the other chair across the room and settles back, in for the long haul. 'It really is good to see you.'

Abi makes herself mirror Cleo's smile, hoping it's genuine, knowing the odds are against it. 'You too.'

She reminds herself why she is here. Now that Phoebe is all grown up Abi needs the rest of her family, however flawed they may be. And there aren't many of them to go round. She's sure there must be uncles and aunts, cousins somewhere. Neither their mum nor dad had been an only child. But Abi has never really got to know them. She can hardly turn up on their doorsteps now and throw herself into their arms and expect them to love her unconditionally. Besides, there's something about a relationship with someone you grew up with – shared a bedroom with, in fact, until they were twelve and you were nine – that you can't recreate with anyone else. Someone who knew you before you became whatever you became, who remembers the raw material. Someone who looked out for you, protected you, whatever they later turned into. She knows it's important; she just isn't sure why.

4

Abi stares vacantly out of the window while Cleo fetches two vast glasses of a red wine that Abi's sure must have cost a fortune but that tastes like chalk dust. She noticed that her own champagne went straight in the cupboard after Cleo had had a cursory glance at the label. She isn't bothered. She doesn't like champagne that much anyway. She only bought it because she assumed that it would be Cleo and Jonty's drink of choice, although now she realizes they probably only ever drink the really expensive stuff. She's not keen on red wine either. She'd rather have an icy cold glass of Pinot Grigio any day. Still, needs must, so she swigs it back and tries not to dwell on how foul she thinks it is. While they make small talk, Abi tries to remember the last time they did this, just chatted, the two of them, like normal siblings. And then it comes to her. Their mum's funeral. While all the friends and relations were eating pizza slices and chicken legs downstairs, Abi and Cleo sat in Abi's old bedroom and reminisced, not just about their memories of Philippa but about when they were little and growing up in the house. Funny how funerals will do that to you; it's as if they open the gate a fraction to let out all your remembrances of the person who's died, but then the flood takes over and everything else comes cascading behind: having tea with Grandma before tap class on a Wednesday, hanging around the park trying to pretend they were ignoring the boys on a Saturday afternoon, Cleo still very much Caroline languishing in bed with chicken pox and crying because she thought her face might be disfigured by the spots. Actually, maybe Abi should have realized then that Caroline's looks meant an awful lot to her.

She remembers being touched that it was all still in there somewhere. Cleo hadn't completely erased her family history from her thoughts. Her official story of her upbringing had been somewhat eroded over the years through misquotation and embellishment both by her and by journalists too lazy or uninterested to check the facts. Just being an average girl from an average family clearly hadn't been exciting enough for the papers so Cleo had been edged closer and closer to coming from poverty and lack of a future until her home life had started to sound like something out of Dickens. It used to drive Philippa to distraction. She'd spent so long bragging to her friends that her oldest daughter was a top model, that even though she was calling herself Cleo she really was our Caroline, so every time an article came out, chronicling Cleo's rise to fame from almost Third World deprivation to glory, she would die a thousand mortified deaths at the thought of those same friends reading it. She used to beg Cleo to put it right next time she did an interview, but, Abi has always believed, Cleo had secretly liked the street credibility she thought it brought her. So it had been good to know that she still remembered the fun they had had as children and the way that their mum and dad had worked hard to make sure they'd had everything they wanted.

They had sat up there for about an hour that day reminiscing. And then Cleo had said that she felt bad that she'd hardly been home in recent years. It wasn't that she had meant to cut herself adrift, it was just that commitments and time had conspired to make it difficult. Now that their dad was on his own she fully intended to shoulder her share of the burden. Be a dutiful daughter. Abi remembers that they'd hugged and promised to be there for each other from then on. Of course, it hadn't quite worked out like that. Cleo had been no more present in their lives than before. Abi, unable to bear the thought of their father sitting in his house alone, had had to beg days off work and favours from friends to collect Phoebe from school or drop her off at netball practice, so that she could do his shopping and clean his house and just make sure he didn't crumble under the weight of the loneliness. She had tried bombarding Cleo with emails laden with non-accusatory but nonetheless pointed remarks about how much time she was spending with their bereaved parent, but it had made no difference. Eventually she had called and asked her sister outright if she would do her share, but all Cleo had said was: 'Abigail, I don't have the kind of job where I can just take a day off – you know that.'

'And I do?'

'Well . . . yes, I suppose you do. If you can't work one day, you don't lose a contract, do you? Or let an important client down?'

'Cleo, I just . . . I can't do this on my own. It's not fair.'

'Is it a national tragedy if Mabel from number seven can't check out a new Catherine Cookson because the library's shorthanded?'

'Wow. That's low even for you.'

'Point taken. I'll see what I can do. Let me look at my diary.'

Cleo may indeed have looked at her diary, but she never reported back on the findings. Rather than have to go through the whole uncomfortable conversation again, Abi had continued on her solo care mission, travelling backwards and forwards to Ashford and listening in resentful silence when her father sang Cleo's praises on the rare occasions she remembered to call him.

At Andrew's funeral, eleven months later, Cleo had turned up at the service with Jonty and the girls, and sniffled into a tissue, but then they'd cried off going back to the house for drinks afterwards because they had to be somewhere else. Not that Abi is bitter. Not that she's still annoyed two years on.

So it feels a bit awkward just to pick up where they left off. Or, in fact, more that where they left off is not a place that Abi would necessarily want to pick up from. Of course they have emailed since. How are you doing? How are the kids? Happy birthday. That kind of thing. Hardly in-depth. They've never even come close to addressing the issue head-on just like they have never addressed any of their issues head-on. Still, this is meant to be a clean slate, a new start. Abi is determined to leave everything that has gone on in the past in the past and to see if they can forge a proper grown-up relationship from here on in. She just needs to think of what there is for them to talk about that isn't too controversial, some common ground to get them started. Of course, the children. Fallback position number one. If in doubt about what to say to someone else who also happens to be a mother, ask about their offspring. It's a guaranteed crowd pleaser. It works every time.

'I can't believe how grown-up Tara is.' Abi cringes at her genius opening line.

'Ten going on twenty,' Cleo says, and that seems to be that topic done with.

'So.' Cleo leans forward in her chair, her glass swinging between two fingers. 'Tell me what's going on with you.'

It's a typical Cleo question. Generic enough to cover the fact that she really has no clue what might be happening in Abi's life, but said in a conspiratorial tone that hints at the possibility that, whatever it is, she might just find it fascinating and exotic. Abi hesitates. Surely Cleo has known her long enough by now to know that this is never going to be the case.

'Oh, you know, the usual,' she says. She dredges around in the depths of her brain, trying to find something worthy of adding, some little event that will make a story, but all she can come up with is that they are thinking about starting pottery classes at the library or that the local town council has announced a war on litter on the beach. Neither of these fascinating stories can, she knows, compete with the sheer glamour of life in Primrose Hill, so she opts to say nothing. They sit there quietly for a moment.

'Oh, how about you? How's things?' Abi suddenly remembers that the polite thing to do is to reciprocate the question.

'Good,' Cleo says. 'We're well.'

The momentum has gone. If indeed there had ever been any. Usually their visits are so short they barely have time to find some safe and neutral common ground before it's time to say goodbye again for another seven or eight months. Or, on this occasion, two years. Now, of course, they have all the time in the world to work out a way of communicating. There's no need to hope for a miracle breakthrough on day one. Still, it would have been nice not to have ground to a complete halt this early on.

'Oh,' Abi says suddenly, remembering that she

does have one momentous event – to her, at least – to share. 'Phoebe got away OK.'

Cleo knows about Phoebe's trip because her original invitation had been for both of them and Abi had had to explain, by email, that she would be coming alone.

'Where has she gone first again?' It's a comfortable middle ground. There are no hidden agendas lurking in their discussion of Phoebe's travels, no poorly disguised accusations or barely concealed jealousies. Abi tells her the whole plan, such as it is. It doesn't really stretch beyond Phoebe making her way to Greece and then looking for a job before moving on to India. Abi feels herself go weak at the knees the way she does every time she says it out loud, because, try as she might, she can't stop herself picturing all kinds of dangers and horrors lurking out in the big wide world just waiting to ensnare her daughter. Cleo, to give her credit, picks up on this.

'She'll be fine. She's her mother's daughter.'

Abi scans the last sentence for any implied criticism. Phoebe's her mother's daughter so . . . what? She's too dull to get herself in trouble? Too uninteresting? Too unattractive, unimportant, unadventurous? She counts to ten, forces herself to look for the positive. Maybe Cleo meant too clever? Too sensible – which in itself could be either a compliment or a criticism? Too mature? Abi decides to give her the benefit of the doubt. She's come here to give Cleo the second chance she seems to be asking for so best not to jump down her throat on day one. She nods.

'She's got a lot of common sense. They grow up so fast these days.'

'They do,' Cleo says, nodding back.

'Although to be fair you'd been gone for two years by the time you were Phoebe's age.' The chat lurches straight into controversial waters. Abi attempts to qualify her comment, to make it sound less pointed. 'Although you were only up in London, I suppose, not halfway across the other side of the world.'

'Exactly.' Cleo sips her drink. 'Even so, I was probably a little young to be on my own.'

Abi thinks about Phoebe at sixteen, half child, half woman. Staying out far too late at a party with the lad from next door one night and then wanting to curl up in her mother's bed with her the next, because she was still scared of the dark. If it's hard to imagine her freewheeling around Asia with her friends now, it's impossible to picture her taking care of herself in one of the biggest cities in the world back then. Let alone coping with the particular pressures and pitfalls of the modelling world. 'I guess you did have to mature overnight.'

'I'd never have made it otherwise. I'd have been eaten alive.' Cleo laughs so Abi will know she's joking, although she doesn't pull it off entirely convincingly. Abi decides to take a risk. They seem to be getting on OK, what the hell?

'Do you ever wish that it hadn't happened, that you hadn't been spotted that day?'

'Honestly, I never really admit this, but sometimes I do. Not that it hadn't happened at all. After all, I wouldn't have all this . . .' Cleo waves a hand around the room. 'I know how lucky I am. Just maybe that it had happened a few years later when I would have been old enough to have handled it all better.'

It's hardly a classified revelation, but Abi isn't sure she can remember Cleo being this open in a long time. Usually she is sharply protective of her decisions and the life she's had. Not for the first time Abi wonders why Cleo has invited her up, whether Cleo's desire to reconnect now the family has dwindled down to just the two of them might be as great as her own. Maybe Cleo misses Abigail as much as Abi misses Caroline. She fills the glasses again, throwing caution to the wind. If being a bit tipsy on rancid chalky red wine is what they need to be upfront and honest with each other, then she can do that for the cause.

'Mum should never have really let you go off like that. Moving up to London on your own, sixteen . . .'

Cleo shrugs. But Abi isn't going to let it go that easily. She's determined that one of these days they are going to have the conversation she's been waiting to have for twenty-five years and why not today? And then she hears the click of the front door and the moment has gone.

'That'll be Jonty,' Cleo says, signifying that the subject is closed. Abi knocks back the rest of her glass. She's feeling quite pissed, she realizes, as she stands up to greet her brother-in-law. Probably not a good idea given that where family are concerned she can go from happy to crying in under thirty seconds when drunk. Not much more when sober, if she's being honest.

Abi is always slightly taken aback by Jonty in the flesh. He's very good-looking in a too-perfect, groomed-to-within-an-inch-of-his-life, catalogue-model way. He is obviously a man who is on first-name terms with product because his hair is always just so, thick, glossy, swept back to show that there is not even a hint of recession. His clothes have an air of nonchalance, as if he merely picked up any old things off the floor in the morning and put them on, but somehow they all happen to fit perfectly, with the creases in all the right places, as if someone has spent all night and a great deal of money making sure they will give off just the right laid-back-chic vibe.

He is carrying a painstakingly battered brown leather bag – a man bag, Abi believes they are called. He's a metrosexual through and through. She can't stand him. Not because he has good hair and a man bag, although ownership of the latter does make her predisposed to dislike pretty much any bloke, but because she has always found him to be a bit pleased with himself, a bit smug, as if he thinks he's better than them, the run-of-the-mill Attwoods.

Even his name is annoying. Jonty. It's as contrived as his appearance. Pretentious masquerading as one of the lads. Cleo is always banging on about how successful he is, how he has his own agency and he earns this much and he drives that car. To be fair, Abi has never heard him brag about his achievements himself, but that is probably because he never really talks about anything, just prefers to sit in a corner and read a book or the paper until it's time for them to go home again. When Philippa and Andrew were alive, that is. She doesn't think she's even clapped eyes on him since, apart from across a graveyard, which has never seemed like an appropriate venue for a get-to-know-you-better session.

So it's fair to say they're not great friends, Jonty and Abi. Barely even acquaintances. Plus she is feeling more than a little resentful that he's come in at this exact moment, just as she had decided it was time for her and Cleo to have the conversation of their lives.

'Abigail!' Jonty says, and to give him credit he does look genuinely quite pleased to see her. They do that awkward-hug/kiss-on-the-cheek thing that is neither one nor the other.

'Hi,' Abi says. 'I haven't been here long.'

Jonty walks over to where Cleo is sitting and drops a kiss on her head. 'Well, you look great,' he says to Abi. 'Doesn't she, Cleo? Look great?'

'I already told her that,' Cleo replies.

'I've never had so many compliments,' Abi says, forcing a laugh. 'I'll come again.'

She waits for Jonty to sit and join them, but instead he says, 'Salmon OK? I got some samphire from the market on the way home.'

'Lovely.' Cleo turns to Abi. 'You eat fish, don't you?'

Abi, a little taken aback, nods.

'Great, I'll get dinner started,' Jonty says, and heads off in what, Abi assumes, is the direction of the kitchen. She's a little confused to say the least. Last she heard, Cleo and Jonty had a chef who came each evening to cook up perfectly balanced, non-fattening nutritious meals for the whole family. She remembers spluttering into her vodka when Cleo had told her – Abi had coerced her into meeting for a quick drink on one of her art-fix trips up to London, the Courtauld she thinks it was – it sounded like such a ludicrous extravagance. Cleo wasn't even really working by then and both the girls were at school or nursery all day – how hard would it have been for her to knock up a quick dinner for four? Abi had pretended something had gone down the wrong way, though. She knew Cleo wouldn't have seen the funny side if Abi had laughed in her face about it. She assumes it must be the chef's night off. That's if Cleo's 'people' ever get nights off. And, if they do, don't some other people have to come in and cover for them? It's hard to imagine her sister fending for herself.

'No chef?' She tries her hardest not to make it sound like she's having a go.

Cleo rolls her eyes. 'Jonty got rid of him. He decided he wanted to get into cooking himself.'

'Oh. Good for him.'

'I've never eaten so much salmon,' Cleo says, and then she laughs and for a split second Abi thinks she can almost see Caroline peeking out from behind her perfectly made-up face.

Dinner is absolutely delicious, the salmon cooked for just long enough and not a second more, the salty samphire, the Jersey royal potatoes buttery and sweet. Jonty clearly has a hidden talent. Abi is grateful to Tara for prattling on about herself and her friends incessantly, because she isn't sure what they would have talked about otherwise. She loves her niece, it goes without saying, but Tara is relentlessly self-obsessed. Just like her mother. On this occasion, though, she is just what's required. Abi is feeling exhausted already from the strain of spending time with people she doesn't feel entirely comfortable with. She can't wait to get up to her little attic room, just her. Tired as she may be, she's also feeling optimistic. Cautiously optimistic. There's no question in her mind that Cleo was about to open up to her a little before Jonty came home. She isn't stupid; she knows they aren't going to go from polite exchanges to full-on sisterly bonding overnight, but she's here for eight weeks. And if today was anything to go by they're already moving in the right direction.

It's still light when she heads upstairs and, even though she's exhausted, she sits in the armchair by the window for a few minutes soaking up the view across the city, the stretch of Regent's Park a green barrier between her and the high rises of the square mile on the one side and the stately mansion blocks of the West End on the other. She has two whole months to explore. She feels elated. If she and Cleo can reconcile, then anything is possible.

5

Abi is up by half past seven the next morning, before anyone else except Jonty, who is already on his way out of the front door when she gets downstairs. She's pleased to note there's no sign of the man bag.

'The coffee machine's on,' he calls by way of a goodbye. 'Just press the big button on the front.'

'Bye,' Abi says to his retreating back. She goes through to the huge chrome-and-white Corian kitchen that at this hour on a sunny morning is nearly blinding it's so shiny. She finds a mug on the third attempt – actually it takes her about five minutes just to work out how to open the cupboards, which are flush with the walls and have no discernable fittings. She presses the appropriate knob and the coffee machine grinds and whirrs, making a noise like an enraged lion. No wonder Cleo and Jonty need such a big house, she thinks. If it were any smaller, there would be no chance that anyone could sleep through anyone else getting themselves a hot drink in the mornings.

She gazes out into the garden. There's a small patio out the back with olive trees in terracotta pots and then a slightly larger lawned area. Tiny by country standards, but spacious for central London, Abi assumes. Picture-book roses line the perimeter with rows of pleached hornbeams above them to ensure that none of the neighbours can invade Cleo and Jonty's privacy. At this time of year, at least.

Abi hunts around for a key to let herself out, but then she feels bad about rooting around in someone else's drawers so she gives up and goes to sit at the big white wooden table looking out through the patio doors instead. She's starving as she always is when she first gets up, but she doesn't feel at home enough to help herself to stuff yet. It's a perfect morning and she tries to think of things to suggest the family might do today. She's sure Cleo will have ideas of her own, but she wants to be able to chip in with suggestions too.

Although she grew up in fairly close proximity to London, it never really felt like anything other than living in the sticks. The fateful shopping trip to Covent Garden was only the third time she can remember coming up to the big city in her life (the previous two occasions having been a trip to see the Oxford Street Christmas lights with her mum and dad when she and Caroline were six and nine and a family day out at Madame Tussaud's and the Planetarium a couple of years later). The whole idea of the capital was tainted for her after Caroline was whisked away to her new life. It was a place where bad things happened. A place that ripped families apart. The visit to the Brompton Road flat only compounded that feeling.

Since she had Phoebe she has tried to bring her up to London whenever she can, not wanting her daughter to feel the parochial burden she grew up with herself, and, of course, there are her solitary gallery visits, but she's still very much a tourist here and is actually quite excited to finally have the time to do all the touristy things: Kew Gardens, the Tower, the South Bank. And then, once she's ticked a few of the more obvious contenders off the list, she intends to live like a local, absorbing the pace and the feel of the city. She decides on the Eye first, the slow-moving big wheel that dominates the south bank of the river. Who knows, this might be the only clear sky they get all summer – they should make the most of it.

Spurred on, she decides to start getting breakfast ready for when everyone surfaces, but as she is hunting through the fridge for the butter she hears a key in the back door and she jumps as if she's been caught shoplifting. A small tired-looking woman, white-haired, in her late sixties, lets herself in. She smiles at Abi hesitantly as if to apologize for startling her. Abi smiles back.

'You gave me a fright. I wasn't expecting anybody. I assume you're the housekeeper? I'm Abi.' The woman still says nothing, just smiles again and nods so Abi holds her hand out and says 'Abi' again. The woman shakes the proffered hand then says something unintelligible in a language Abi can't place.

'Do you speak English?' Abi says slowly. 'English?'

The woman shakes her head. 'No English.' She makes herself busy and Abi takes it that their conversation is over, but also that she's redundant as a breakfast chef because the woman is already assembling foodstuffs on the kitchen table with practised ease.

'I'll get out of your way,' Abi says pointlessly, because, of course, the woman has no idea what she is saying. Abi waves her hand in the direction of the living room and the woman smiles and nods, and so Abi does the same before she backs out.

She tries to sit and relax. It's always strange being in someone else's house. However much they tell you to make yourself at home it's almost impossible to do so. Abi is hyper aware of the imprint she is making on the sofa, the small dent her arm is carving out in one of the cushions. She reminds herself to shake it out when she stands up. Then she starts stressing about it so she gets up and smooths it over, removing any trace of her ever having sat there. She sits back down, perching on the edge, minimizing the impact. She wishes she'd brought her book down from upstairs because now she doesn't know what to do with herself. She doesn't want to go up and get it in case she wakes everyone. She could turn the TV on, but it isn't even nine in the morning so that doesn't feel right. She doesn't want the nodding smiling woman to think she's some kind of waster while she's beavering away next door herself. She considers going to offer to help make breakfast, but she doesn't know how she'd manage to convey that with just hand gestures and, besides, the woman might take offence, might think Abi was implying she couldn't manage or something.

In the end Abi opts to just sit and wait, praying that the noddy smiler doesn't decide to come in and dust the living room, because then she really wouldn't know where to go, and it's out of the question that she could just sit there while someone cleaned around her. She looks at the clock on the wall. Still only twenty past eight. She has no idea what time Cleo usually drags herself out of bed. For all she knows she could end up sitting there for two hours doing nothing before anyone even surfaces. Apart from anything else she probably will have starved to death by then.

Maybe she could pop out to a café. She noticed all kinds of interesting-looking shops on the way here from Chalk Farm tube last night. She could buy herself a pastry and a newspaper and then amble back slowly by which time, hopefully, at least the kids might be up and about. It's the best idea she has come up with so far, but then it occurs to her that she doesn't have a set of keys yet and she has no way of knowing whether the smiler would understand to let her in if she rang the doorbell. For all she knows the woman might think she's a friendlier than average burglar and is just waiting for Abi to leave of her own accord before she calls the police. She's desperate for another cup of coffee; she doesn't usually move until she's had at least three at home. But in the end she decides that doing nothing is the best and safest option. She sits down again and goes back to staring out of the window.

After about ten minutes of twiddling her thumbs, she decides that she really has to do something. There's a little antique desk in a corner of the room so she risks looking inside to find a pen (Mont Blanc, of course, no Bic biros here) and some paper (Smythson's finest). She doodles for a while but it feels criminal to waste the notepad that probably cost two weeks' wages, so she starts to make a list of all the places she has come up with for them to visit. At least that way when Cleo finally does appear she can present her with a plan.

She has just finished when she hears footsteps on the stairs and then voices in the kitchen. Cleo. Abi waits for a moment to see if Cleo brings a morning coffee into the living room, but everything goes quiet, so she decides to brave the kitchen once again. She's surprised by what she finds there. Cleo, fully dressed and made-up, is halfway through eating a bowl of what looks like muesli, yoghurt and berries, sitting at the table, reading the paper. Abi feels a little stab of hurt. She has been sitting in the other room listening to her stomach rumbling for what seems like hours because she assumed that they would all eat breakfast together. She tells herself not to say anything negative, not to ruin the good atmosphere that was created last night. Cleo looks up, coffee cup halfway to her lips.

'Oh, hi,' she smiles. 'I didn't realize you were up. Did you have breakfast?'

'No, I was waiting . . .'

'What do you want? Orange juice? Toast? Cereal? Elena will get it for you.' She waves her cup at the smiler in a gesture that seems to mean another one of these for my friend, please. 'Did you meet Elena?'

'Um . . . Kind of . . .'

'She doesn't speak much English, but she's very reliable,' Cleo says cheerfully, and Abi cringes at the idea that they are talking about Elena as if she wasn't there when she is, in fact, standing right in front of them. Never mind that she can't understand, it still doesn't seem right.

'Once she gets an idea of what you like, she'll just have it ready for you whenever you get up. Don't start waiting for everyone to come down or you'll wait forever. Tara's like a teenager already; I can hardly get her out of bed in the mornings.'

'Where's she from?' Abi asks, trying not to make it obvious to Elena that she's talking about her.

'Oh. I'm not sure. Somewhere in Eastern Europe.'

Abi manages to communicate toast to Elena by waving the bread and pointing at the toaster. She can't help thinking it would be quicker and less humiliating to simply do it herself.

'She's here every weekday from eight till one. If you're around later, she'll make you some lunch before she goes . . .'

'Oh, OK. I . . . um . . . I assumed we'd all be doing something today. I made a list . . .'

Cleo drains the last of her coffee, looks at Abi triumphantly. 'Not today, I'm afraid. I've got a hair appointment in town and then I've got a go see . . .'

Abi stops in her tracks, list in hand. It isn't so much that Cleo has plans, after all Abi wasn't expecting her to put her entire life on hold for the whole eight-week visit (although maybe the first day . . . Abi stops herself pursuing that potentially poisonous train of thought), it's the fact that she's going on a casting. As far as Abi is aware Cleo announced she was hanging up her modelling boots five years ago, conveniently right about the time the modelling industry decided it was done with her for good. Time to move over, there's a new girl in town. A hundred new girls, probably. A hundred new girls not just younger and fresher-faced, but still eager and polite, still not demanding limos and Cristal, still not insisting on keeping the diamonds they were showcasing or asking for £25,000 just to get out of bed (inflation hit the modelling world just like any other). Still not shouting at the stylists and telling them they were fucking halfwits and what do you know about anything, you dried-up frumpy old hag?

Abi had read about this last one in one of the tabloids. A well-known stylist for one of the top women's magazines had sold the story of how her editor out and out refused to work with Cleo any more, because her bad behaviour far outweighed any added value she brought to the magazine. It was all a balancing act, she'd said. If Cleo had been vile but her presence on the cover had meant thousands more magazines sold, then it would have been worth it. As it was her cachet was down, her popularity at an all-time low. Pain in the arse plus no extra sales equals no future bookings.

And come to think of it, even when Cleo was still working, when had she ever gone on a go see in the past twenty years? She thought they were demeaning. Everyone knew who she was – if they wanted her to do a job for them, they should just make an offer. None of this lining up with fifty other hopefuls for Cleo. That was for the B-listers.

Abi doesn't know where to start so all she says is, 'Oh . . .'

'I've decided to go back to modelling,' Cleo says. 'After all, Kate and Naomi still work, so why shouldn't I? It's just that I've been away for a while so I need to get my face out there, show people that I've still got it. And if that means having to endure a few go sees then . . .'

'Gosh. Good for you.'

'Surprised? I am myself a bit. I hadn't really ever imagined I'd want to go back to it, but here I am.'

'That's great,' Abi says, not really sure whether she believes it even as she says it.

'So, sorry about today, but – I hope you don't mind – I thought maybe you could still take the girls somewhere? And there's plenty of time for us all to do stuff together.'

Abi knows she's right. There's no rush. And, if Cleo wants to try to pick up the threads of her career, then why shouldn't she? Abi gives her a smile to show she isn't upset. 'Of course.'

'Great,' Cleo says matter-of-factly. She stands up, leaving her bowl, spoon and cup on the table. 'I'd better run – see you tonight. After I've been to the gym. I've got a session booked with my new trainer. I'm trying to go every day.'

'See you later.'

Abi picks up her plate, along with Cleo's things, and takes them over to the sink where Elena is fussing around cleaning. She puts them on the draining board and Elena taps her hand away as if to say she shouldn't be clearing up after herself.

'Sorry.' Abi wants to ask if she is allowed to put the Marmite away, but she doesn't know the international hand signal for that so she doesn't bother.

In the brief period between Caroline becoming Cleo and her subsequently being crowned the 'face of 1985', it had looked like everything might turn out OK after all. Abigail knew that much had changed, that their cosy family unit was never going to be quite the same again, but she had no idea, at that point, of the extent to which things would be different. After the initial excitement, there was a lull – the calm before the storm as Abi now sees it – when, despite Philippa's attempts to ensure there was no one in Kent who didn't know that her eldest daughter had been spotted and was now officially a model, nothing much seemed to happen. Cleo had her head shots done and then they waited, breath held, for the job offers to come flooding in. For a couple of weeks there was silence, nothing, and life more or less returned to normal. Even better than normal, maybe.

Caroline, it seemed to Abigail, had started to feel a bit guilty that she was stealing the limelight so completely from her sister. She went out of her way to include Abigail in whatever she was doing, inviting her to parties – where Abigail, grateful to be there but struck dumb through social ineptitude, stood in a corner nursing a lemonade and watched her sister and her contemporaries get drunk on cheap lager – trips to the cinema on wet evenings and to the shops in Maidstone in the afternoons. She had insisted to her friends that Abigail was now a fully paid-up member of their gang. Abigail had never felt so socially plugged in even if in her heart she knew at the time that Caroline's friends were really only including her on sufferance. Abigail became the gang's official lookout, watching out for parents when they passed round cigarettes in the park, waiting outside the off-licence in case anyone they knew caught them in the act of attempting to buy cider, and on more than one occasion causing a diversion outside Woolworths so that no one would notice a line of girls leaving the store with make-up-shaped bulges under their tops. She never shared in the spoils – no one ever offered – but she felt needed, part of a clique for the first time in her life. And then, of course, the famous newspaper article had appeared and life as she now knows it began.

There's nothing else for Abi to do but to go upstairs and have a bath as noisily as she can in the hope that the girls will decide they might as well get up. She manages to wrestle Elena at the coffee machine and makes two large cups, taking them both upstairs fully intending to drink the pair of them herself. She turns the taps on full and, because the house is old, everything begins to creak and bang so then she hotfoots it down to Tara's room just in time to hear her niece saying could Auntie Abigail please shut up because she isn't awake yet. Abi is in there like a shot, opening curtains, plonking herself down on the bed. She hates to do it to her, really; Tara looks like a giant contented dormouse, huddled up beneath the covers. She stirs.

'Auntie Abigail!'

'You need to get up. We're going out.

'What time is it?'

'It's half past nine,' Abi lies. Actually it's not quite nine o'clock, but she knows that if she tells Tara that she'll just roll over and go back to sleep.

'Your mum's going on a casting,' Abi says. 'So I guess we'll have to do something without her. What do you fancy?'

'Well, sleeping would be nice,' Tara replies, doing her best impression of a fourteen-year-old. Abi can hear the bathwater chuntering on upstairs. She wonders how long it takes to fill that outsize bath. Tara pulls the covers up over her head just as the door opens and Megan comes in fully dressed and ready to go.

'I'm bored,' she says, yawning as if to prove her point.

'Me too,' Abi says, and Megan smiles. Abi pats the bed next to her and Megan sits down. 'If I can get your sister up, we can all go somewhere. You can show me the sights.'

'Where's Mum?' Megan asks, and Abi tells her what she knows. 'Lucky I was here,' she says. 'I suppose Elena would have looked after you otherwise.'

Megan pulls a face. 'You're better than Elena. Mum said at least you could take us places. Elena doesn't even drive.'

'Well, neither do I. At least, I do, but I don't have a car so . . .' Abi says. 'Don't you have a nanny, though? I'm sure your mum said . . .'

'She left. About a month ago. Mum was panicking

66

because she couldn't find anyone new, but then she thought of you.'

'She . . .?' Abi doesn't trust herself to say anything. She reminds herself that Megan is only a child; she's probably got the wrong end of the stick, explained the situation badly. It's probably just a coincidence. The nanny left and Cleo invited Abi to stay at around the same time. One did not lead to the other.

Megan is still talking. 'Mum says that at least this way she has a couple of months to find someone else and everyone knows it's easier to find someone outside of the summer holidays. All the good people have jobs for the summer.'

Abi stands up abruptly. 'My bath's going to overrun,' she says by way of explanation.

She had been looking forward to wallowing in the colossal bath so much, but now she's here she's finding it hard to enjoy it. The nanny walked out and then Cleo thought of her — that was definitely the way round Megan had been insisting it had happened. Abi tries to consider the options calmly. Her instinct is telling her that she should just pack up and go. She pictures herself challenging Cleo, confronting her with this new information, telling her that she has no right to treat her sister as an unpaid babysitter, accusing her of being selfish and thoughtless and a user. She thinks she would enjoy it. She could flounce out in a cloud of self-righteousness and go . . . where?

The owners of the flat she's buying insisted on completion in September – they wanted one last summer in their old home they'd said – and Abi had agreed because the flat, though far from perfect, was the best thing she had seen so far. Plus she could afford it, which made it seem all the more appealing. And what about Tara and Megan? Although they give off an air of thirty-year-old sophistication she couldn't in all conscience just walk out and leave her seven-year-old niece in the care of her ten-year-old sister. She decides to do nothing in a hurry, nothing she'll regret. She needs to think this one through.

By the time she's dressed and downstairs, the girls are being served breakfast by Elena and Abi is managing to do a fairly good impression of someone who isn't a seething mix of furious and heartbroken.

'I thought we might go on the wheel today. That might be fun.' She hates herself for sounding like a primary-school teacher. Tara and Megan look at her blankly.

'We've been on it before,' Megan says.

'It's lame,' Tara adds. 'It's what tourists do.'

'Well, I am a tourist,' Abi says. If she is going to be forced to be Mary Poppins, she certainly isn't taking any more crap from her charges. 'We'll leave in an hour, OK?' She gives the girls a look that says she is not to be messed with. They take absolutely no notice.

Tara yawns and stretches. 'Mum said we could go shopping. I need to get a dress for Tamsin's party . . .'

'Yes, well, your mum says a lot of things.' Most of them bullshit, Abi nearly adds, but she stops herself. Cleo is their mother, after all. 'We can go shopping another day, OK? Now, this is my first whole day in London and so it's either the Eye or the Tower, you choose.'

6

In the end Abi doesn't have a bad day, as days go, where you stand in a queue for two and a half hours while your precocious niece complains loudly that anyone who was anyone would have booked VIP tickets in advance to avoid queuing, where you are unable to enjoy the sights because of the seething resentment bubbling just under your surface and your feet hurt. It costs her a fortune too, because, of course, she has to pay for everyone and provide lunch on top of that, somewhere sitting down because Tara refuses to eat a sandwich in the street ('too chavvy'). While she is very happy to treat her nieces in theory, in practice she's flat broke so, while she would never accept Cleo paying her way, she hadn't anticipated having to fork out for the three of them. If this keeps up, she'll actually go home at the end of the summer worse off. She briefly wonders if she should bill Cleo for her nannying services. No. Definitely not. That would officially make her the hired help.

Despite being only ten years old, Tara, it seems, lives in hope of being spotted just as her mother was. She's obviously heard the story of Cleo's discovery many times so being out and about is one big showcase to her, because apparently you never know who might be watching. She doesn't relax all day, sitting up straight, standing rigid like a ballet dancer, practised pout on her lips. And actually Abi finds herself feeling a bit sorry for her. She's a beautiful girl, there's no doubt about that, but somewhere along the line Cleo's feline features, so unique, have been rendered more ordinary by having been blended with Jonty's perfect symmetry. Tara is stunning, but she's not her mother. Maybe she will get work as a model one day if that's what she really wants to do. She has the height, the natural skinniness. But she's never going to reach the dizzy heights of Cleo at her peak. She's never going to be a household name. And sadly, it seems, that is all she aspires to.

Megan on the other hand has plans to be a nurse and to get married and have three children and a large dog. Tara rolls her eyes as Megan tells Abi this, so Abi makes a big show of admiring her choices.

'Just because you know you couldn't be a model even if you wanted to be,' Tara says, and Abi says, '*Tara . . .*' and gives her what she hopes is a warning look, which she follows by making apologetic faces at the horrified mothers with their well-behaved children who are sharing the pod with them. She wants to say, 'She's not my child and I have had nothing to do with her upbringing,' but there's no easy way to use that as a conversation opener so she tries to change the subject. Megan's having none of it, though.

'Well, I don't want to be, do I? So it doesn't matter if I could or not, does it, stupid?'

Although Megan is clearly in awe of her big sister, Abi is pleased to see that she is able to stand up for herself when she needs to. She's blessed with a lot more confidence than Abi had at her age. Not that Abigail had had to stand up to Caroline. In fact, she relied on Caroline to stand up for her. She used to hide behind her confident older sister, secure in the knowledge that Caroline had her back. She can clearly remember that summer when she was thirteen when some of Caroline's more catty friends were laughing at her attempt to look trendy in her stone-washed jeans and a jacket with shoulder pads the size of Big Macs. Caroline had given them a piece of her mind and then taken Megan aside and they had shopped in Miss Selfridge for matching leggings, leg warmers and stretchy tube dresses. Caroline had crimped Abigail's hair the way she was currently doing her own and lent her a pair of big hooped earrings. It wasn't so much the outfit that had made Abigail so happy – if the truth be told she felt a little uncomfortable in it, a bit like a sausage bursting its skin – it was the fact that Caroline was willing to go to these lengths for her, to be seen to be dressed near identically, surely potential social death for a sixteen-year-old, just to make her sister feel better. To be fair, it didn't really seem to stop the other girls sniggering at her, but Abigail felt that if she was being poked fun at then so was Caroline, and knowing how popular her sister was, how much she was the envy of their friends now she had been singled out for greater things, that had made all the difference. She finds herself hoping that, when pushed, Tara would go to the same lengths for Megan.

It's a glorious day and London is looking its best, sprawled out glinting provocatively in the sun. It's overwhelming how many recognizable landmarks there are. Everywhere Abi turns there's an icon looking back up at her, waiting to be admired. She points out the obvious – Hyde Park, St Paul's, the Gherkin – and the less obvious – the Thames Barrier, the NatWest Tower, the rapidly rising skeleton of the Shard. Most of these buildings she's never even seen in the flesh before, but they're as familiar to her from photographs as if she walked past them every day. Megan at least pretends to pay attention, oohing and aahing in all the right places while Tara strikes a nonchalant couldn't-care-less pose that she almost certainly learned from *America's Next Top Model* and, perversely, looks anywhere but where Abi is pointing in her best tour-guide fashion.

By the time they get home Jonty is already there, sleeves rolled up, doing something delicious-smelling in the kitchen. The girls go off upstairs, Abi assumes to their separate rooms because they had a fight about something or other on the way home and there's definitely still a frosty air. She herself is desperate for a cup of tea, but she doesn't really want to have to hang around in the kitchen while the kettle boils, so she just flops on one of the sofas, exhausted. Her legs ache. The three of them walked back from the South Bank, all the way to Primrose Hill, which was a mistake probably, because it was twice as far as Abi had anticipated, but she couldn't work out the buses and Tara flat out refused to get back on the tube. Plus they got lost in Soho somewhere and doubled back on themselves several times. And then again trying to find the entrance to Regent's Park so that they could enjoy the scenic route home rather than the somewhat frightening depths of Somers Town that they ended up experiencing. All in all it took nearly two hours. Two hours of whinging and complaining about sore feet and blisters and that was just Abi. She knows she should go upstairs and change, but she can't quite face it at the moment. She leans back, eyes closed, feet propped up on the arm of the settee.

'You look like you had a hard day.'

Abi jumps and sits up straight hurriedly. Visions of teachers asking if she'd sit like that in her own home flash through her head. Her answer to that one was always yes, by the way. Yes, she did sit at home with her elbows on the table/feet up/shoes on and no one ever seemed to mind that much.

Jonty is standing over her, mug in hand.

'What? Oh . . . yes . . .'

'I thought you might like a cup of tea. You look shattered.'

She almost bites his hand off for it. 'I'd love one, thank you.' There's no way she can deny that was thoughtful of him.

'Did you have a good time at least?' he asks, and Abi nods.

'Lovely. Well, me and Megan did. I'm not so sure about Tara.'

They haven't really got their small talk worked out yet, so Jonty just stands there for a second then says, 'Well, I'd better get on. Dinner.'

'Oh. Right. Do you need any help?' She crosses her fingers and hopes that he says no.

'No. It's fine. Thanks, though. Cleo should be back any minute.'

Abi thinks about saying something about the nanny situation – she assumes it must have been Jonty's idea as much as Cleo's, but it seems mean-spirited to raise it when he's in the middle of cooking dinner for everyone.

'Do you cook every night?' It seems so unlikely somehow.

'Perk of having your own business,' he says. 'There's no one to tell me I can't leave early.'

'Well, I'll do my share, obviously, while I'm here. I mean if that's OK . . .'

'Great,' he says, and another scintillating exchange

draws to a close. She makes a mental note that she really must go on a social-skills course.

Cleo, when she breezes through the door, is full of the great meeting she's had with someone or other who is clearly desperate to work with her, and how much they loved her at the casting and she's almost certain to get the job because they told her she was looking incredible. Abi waits for her to finish, for Cleo to ask her how her day has been. She waits quite a long time and the longer it goes on the more irritated she becomes. Cleo it seems is like an unstoppable train when she is telling a story about herself. Eventually she apparently feels the need to take a breath so Abi says, 'Caroline,' because she knows that will get her sister's attention. It does the trick – Cleo practically double takes. It's doubtful anyone has called her Caroline for a few years. Even Philippa and Andrew, so resistant to 'Abi', got used to 'Cleo' almost immediately, because they knew their eldest would have made their lives hell if they didn't. Abi hesitates for a moment, unsure what to say. Does she really want to start a fight?

'It's just . . . well, I was a bit surprised that . . .' She stops because she realizes that what she is about to say actually sounds a bit stupid, a bit too needy. You didn't come out with us today. I resent the fact that I had to take your two daughters, my nieces, out for the day without you. Why won't you play with me?

'Is everything OK?'

'Yes . . . no, actually. Well, the girls mentioned

something about the nanny leaving suddenly and that being why you'd invited me and, well, I just wondered if that was true?' Abi finds she can hardly look her sister in the eye it sounds so pitiful spoken out loud.

Cleo laughs. 'Well, it's true the nanny left, but that's not why I asked you to stay for the summer. God, Abigail, you must really think I'm an awful person if you believe that. I asked you up because I wanted to spend time with you. It was just coincidence that idiot girl walked out without giving any notice, but did I get you here to replace her? No. Of course not.'

Abi colours, feels stupid. Thirteen years old and scared of being abandoned all over again. 'I suppose it's just that I was hoping we would do stuff together, you and I . . .'

'Of course we will. But I can't just drop everything I have in my diary. I've got a few meetings this week and next, but I'll be here in the evenings. I've been really looking forward to us spending some time together. Reconnecting. I just won't be around during the days, that's all. And if you don't want to have to amuse the girls – and, believe me, I'd understand if you didn't – then Jonty can take some time off work. It's really not a problem.'

Now Abi just feels like a fool. 'No. I'm really happy to keep an eye on them. I just got the wrong end of the stick, that's all. You do what you have to do. Forget I even said anything.'

'You analyse things too much,' Cleo says. 'You

always did.' She gives Abi a quick hug, disarming her completely. 'I need to get changed. And then we can chat over dinner. I'm starving.'

She goes off and Abi slumps in her chair feeling like an idiot. Cleo's right. That's always been Abi's problem, over-thinking things. She was the family worrier. Well, she figured someone had to be. Philippa and Andrew were just too naive, too parochial, to ever really realize there was anything in the world to worry about. Abigail was the one saying maybe Caroline shouldn't just leave school and move up to London, that she could still live at home and pursue a modelling career from there, but she was always regarded as the family killjoy.

Abi tells herself she needs to just try to relax and enjoy the summer and, if she and Cleo emerge closer than they have been, then all to the good, but if they don't then that will have to be OK too. You can't force a relationship with someone just because they share your DNA. She decides to wait and see how things develop naturally, although that totally goes against her nature. She's a planner, a list maker, a what-if type of person. It's one of those qualities that it's good to have in small amounts, but when every decision you make is preceded by days of analysis of the pros and cons it can become a bit of a handicap. Going with the flow means nothing to Abi, but she determines to give it a try.

7

She spends the next few days in a haze of sightseeing, moaning reluctant pre-teenage girls and home-cooked dinners round the kitchen table in the evenings. Cleo is busy every day with either go sees, meetings or some kind of grooming or other, which takes up an inordinate amount of time. She is getting everything extended it seems to Abi – hair, eyelashes, fingernails. Every time she comes home there is a little bit more of her. It's like the world's slowest takeover bid. She returns in time for dinner and regales the assembled family with tales of her day. Abi can only assume from the lack of any information to the contrary that she's not getting any of the jobs she's going for. She seems a little hyper, a little too desperate to have them all believe how well it's working out.

Abi finds herself wondering if all the beauty treatments are in response to less than entirely positive comments Cleo's been receiving. She knows that the modelling world is a harsh one. If you look less than perfect, someone is bound to remind you of your faults sooner or later. Personally she's not sure she could spend all day with someone pointing out her spots or her cellulite. She can do that perfectly well herself in front of the bathroom mirror, thank you very much. Cleo is barely eating anything either. For all she's always claiming to be starving, she only ever picks at the food that Jonty cooks. She pushes it around her plate as she talks. No one else seems to notice or, if they do, they don't comment on it.

Abi has settled into a routine without really intending to. She tried getting up ridiculously early so she could help herself to three cups of coffee and some toast in an Elena-free kitchen, but on the second morning Elena caught her and gave her such a long and heartfelt lecture – not that Abi could understand any of it, but she could swear Elena's eyes filled with tears at one point – that she gave that strategy up pretty quickly. But she's never been any good at sleeping in. As soon as she's awake, she has to get up no matter how little sleep she's had. Otherwise she just lies there and broods on all the things she has to do and the time she's wasting by lying in bed. Not that she does have anything at all to do at the moment. Elena won't even let her wash a glass. So she still rises early, but she takes her time lying in the bath, pottering around her private domain before she heads downstairs.

The days are starting to feel quite long and Abi knows she could do with losing a few more hours to sleep in the mornings, but she's still usually heading for the coffee machine just as Jonty is hurtling out of the door. Most days he leaves for work at seven forty-five, which seems needlessly early, but he says he likes to be in the office by eight fifteen because then he doesn't feel so bad leaving at half five to get home and cook. So they have a brief exchange as he goes – bye, have a nice day at work, that thrilling – and that's usually all the human interaction Abi has until either Cleo or the girls deign to rise at about half past nine. Cleo no doubt will have been up for a couple of hours, beautifying in the enormous dressing room off the master suite. Abi can hear Elena taking coffee up to her sometimes although it's a mystery how she knows when the right time is to do so. Maybe Cleo calls her on her mobile or perhaps there's a bell she can ring like they used to in *Upstairs, Downstairs*. By the time Cleo comes down she's dressed, made-up and ready to go out after a hurried bowl of cereal, berries and yoghurt, barking out orders to Elena – 'The kitchen cupboards need cleaning out. They're filthy,' or, 'Make sure you put the duvet on the bed the right way round, will you? I kept getting tangled up in the buttons all night.' – that Abi then feels she has to try to interpret, because otherwise Elena won't have a clue and will undoubtedly just get shouted at again later on – and generally leaving Abi and the girls to fend for themselves.

Tara and Megan have a convoluted and not-up-for-negotiation social life that means that, most days, sightseeing or doing something fun as a family is out: Abi is reduced to ferrying them around from one engagement to the next. Cleo is letting Abi use her car since the walking home from the Eye debacle, so basically she has become the chauffeur. She tries to do something fun in between dropping Megan at her piano lesson and Tara at Carluccio's in Hampstead for lunch with her friend's family and picking them up again, but time is tight. This is hardly turning out to be the summer she'd promised herself.

Abi and Elena have come to enough of an understanding now so that Abi feels she can go out in the mornings before anyone else has surfaced, safe in the knowledge that Elena will let her in again. She still hasn't got a key to the house, something that makes her feel even more like one of the staff. Tara and Megan have a set each and Abi believes that Cleo just assumes that because she will always be running about after them she doesn't need one of her own. She has taken to going for a long walk just for the sake of it, just for a bit of me time.

If it's a nice day – which it often seems to be, it's turned out to be a lovely summer, which feels a little wasted on London; Kent would appreciate it so much better – then she walks across the hill, or down past the canal into Regent's Park. If it's not so nice, then she potters around the local shops, which have lived up to her first impression and are surprisingly charming. One of the last bastions of the small independent outfits in the city, probably because everyone around here is hideously rich and can afford to pay £28.75 for half a litre of hand-pressed virgin olive oil in a fancy bottle rather than give Waitrose £5.50 for something that tastes the same. There's a baker's; a candle shop; several vintage-furniture outfits that almost make Abi cry with frustration, so badly does she want to own their contents; a few clothes stores with beautiful one-off pieces that cost the same as her whole wardrobe; and a little independent bookshop where she can happily kill half an hour if it's not so sunny outside. In truth, she could kill the whole day there if she had to. It's tempting.

It's while she's mooching about in there on about the fifth morning of her stay that she notices a sign by the till: PART-TIME HELP WANTED. She has been looking for a way to make her point to Cleo – the point that she can't be taken for granted, that is, that she is not just a free home help. Before she really thinks through what she is doing (does she really want to take a job just to get back at her sister? And, if she does, does she really want to put herself up for one where they are almost certainly expecting a sixth-former to apply and will be paying accordingly?) she is halfway up to the counter. Over the past few days she's reached nodding-acquaintance status with the owner and they've exchanged anodyne pleasantries each time she's bought something– she's averaging a book every other day so much time does she spend hiding out in her room – so he smiles as he sees her approach.

'Hi. How are you this morning?'

Abi launches straight in. 'Look, I know this might

sound a bit ridiculous and I'm sure I'm far too old, and I'm only here for a few weeks and you're probably looking for a permanent Saturday girl or something, but I was wondering about the position . . . the job . . .'

'Oh. Well, let's see . . .' the man says. 'It's actually for two days a week, while my regular lady has to look after her grandchildren.' Oh the irony. 'She's sixty-one, so I think you just about qualify on age terms.' He smiles so Abi knows he's joking. He's incredibly self-assured, smooth and flirtatious in that louche 1950s rat-pack way. What he lacks in conventional good looks, he more than makes up for in confidence and attitude. It's easy to imagine him propping up a bar with a shot of whisky in one hand and a cigarette in the other (yes, Abi does still think smoking is big and clever – she just doesn't do it herself any more). It's not really a look that appeals to her, it's a bit too knowing, a bit too studied, but she imagines he's used to turning the bored rich ladies of Primrose Hill into quivering messes.

'Do you have any experience?'

'Well, I read a lot. I work in a library at home . . .'

'That's a good start.'

'And I've worked in shops before, but years ago, when I was a teenager.' She waits for him to say something crass like 'that can't have been long ago', because that's just the kind of comment she imagines he thinks middle-aged women crave, but, to give him credit, he doesn't.

'And you're only here till . . .'

She feels stupid. She doesn't know why she's doing this suddenly. 'I leave at the beginning of September so I don't suppose that's any good. It was a stupid idea, really. Never mind.'

She's already backing out of the door when he says, 'That should give Wendy's daughter time to sort out some proper childcare. Tuesdays and Thursdays. We open at nine thirty, as you know. The shop closes at six and it's £7.50 an hour. How does that sound?'

To Abi it doesn't sound too bad, actually. She was expecting minimum wage. She wouldn't pay herself any more than that.

'Cash if that's OK with you. It's just that it's easier as you'll be here for such a short time . . .'

Abi nods. Has she just taken a job?

'And you get a discount on books, of course. Twenty per cent.'

That does it. 'OK,' she says before she has time to change her mind. She needs to at least give Cleo a bit of notice that things are going to change. 'I could start next Tuesday. I just have a few things to sort out.'

'Great.' He holds out a hand for her to shake. 'Richard,' he twinkles.

'Abi,' she says in a way that she hopes says, 'Don't even think about it. It really is the job I want, not you,' but she's not sure she carries it off.

It's not that she's not interested in men. She's had

85

a few relationships since Phoebe's father, but none of them have lasted that long because someone would have to be pretty special for her to allow them into her daughter's life. And the flirty chancer has never been her type of choice. Not since Phoebe's dad has she been attracted to someone who she thought might mess her around. In fact, she's gone so far the other way that she has ended up in relationships with men who almost bored her to tears in their slow steadiness.

In the end she has come to the conclusion that she's fine as she is. She doesn't need a man to feel complete, although a good one would be a nice bonus and occasionally she scares herself by imagining her future when Phoebe has gone off to the bright lights to do great things and she's shuffling around on her own except for the cat. In fact, that future is now although she doesn't even have a cat. She'll have to get one specially. She's not sure she even likes cats. But she reminds herself that she has to stay true to what she believes in. It's not about being with anyone, however far removed they are from your ideal bookend. It's about waiting for the right person to come along and if they don't then they don't. Lots of women – and men for that matter – live on their own and are perfectly happy thank you very much. Abi has lots of good friends in her little community. It's not an issue. Anyway, the point is that Jack the Lads like Richard do nothing for her so don't go thinking there's romance on the horizon because there isn't. It's the last thing she's looking for.

Cleo can barely contain her irritation when Abi makes her announcement at dinner (baked monk-fish wrapped in Parma ham with butternut squash and broad beans).

'I have a go see on Tuesday,' she says. 'I told you I had all sorts of appointments over the next couple of weeks.'

'And I'm telling you I can't look after the girls on Tuesday. Sorry. Maybe you should have made sure that I was going to be free every day before you made all of those appointments?' Abi doesn't want to get into a fight in front of the girls, but she doesn't want to let Cleo walk all over her either. She hardly thinks she's being unreasonable.

Tara pulls a disgusted face. 'I don't know why we need anybody to look after us. I'm ten. None of my friends have to be babysat.'

'That's not true and you know it,' Jonty pipes up. 'Plus, even if it was, Megan is only seven. And someone has to ferry you both around. Maybe Elena could do a few more hours until we sort ourselves out?'

'Oh god. Not Elena,' Tara says, and shoots Abi a filthy look. 'She can't even drive.' Abi realizes that Tara has said this before and that's, no doubt, where Megan got it from.

'She can take you places on the tube,' Jonty says. 'And I'm sure she could do with the extra money.'

'I don't want them going on the tube,' Cleo says. 'Not with anyone.'

'Well, maybe I could take those days off. It might be fun.'

This isn't what Abi wanted. 'Look, forget about it. It was a stupid idea. I'll tell Richard tomorrow that I can't do it after all –'

'No,' Jonty interrupts. 'That's not fair. If you want to go to work, then that's what you should do. You're our guest here, after all. You're not here to be an unpaid babysitter. We should have sorted something out before you came.' He gives Cleo a look which tells Abi that this is not the first time this subject has come up between them. 'Cleo and I can work it out between us. She can move some of her engagements and I can move a few meetings and it'll be fine. Don't worry about it, Abigail, OK?'

'Well, I can't move the go see on Tuesday. I have a really good feeling about this one. They specifically asked to see me. And it's editorial. *Harper's*,' Cleo says petulantly. Abi knows enough to know that editorial, rather than commercial, is the Holy Grail. Only the most unique models, the elite, the striking one-offs rather than the ten-a-penny pretty-pretty girls, get to do editorial for the top-end fashion magazines.

'Fine,' Jonty says. 'So I'll take Tuesday off and you

can move whatever you've got on Thursday. We should be grateful that Abigail's happy to do the other days. You are, aren't you?' he adds as an afterthought. 'Just until we find someone.'

'Of course,' Abi says. 'And I didn't mean to cause a problem.' Now she's had her little victory she feels a bit mean-spirited. So she's shown Cleo that she can't be taken for granted. Big deal. She doesn't feel any better for it. Actually, though, she is rather looking forward to going out to work. It feels very grown-up and cosmopolitan having a job of her own to go to in the big city.

8

Guilt makes her go into overdrive and she sets out to prove that she is the best all-round sister/aunt/sister-in-law that anyone could wish for. She cheerfully drives the girls around all day and even takes them down to Portobello Road market when they have a spare couple of hours, which is really a treat for herself, but which everyone seems to enjoy. Tara is convinced that wannabe models are spotted in its shabby chic environs all the time, and so does her best runway walk between stalls, while Megan seems to love the vintage-clothes shops almost as much as her aunt does. Real vintage proves to be too expensive but Abi spots an Oxfam shop and steers the girls towards it. Tara stops dead in her tracks like a reluctant mule.

'You're not really going to buy clothes from there?' she says, eyes wide. Megan, who was happily going along with her aunt's plans, stops too, unsure which way to jump.

'Why not?' Abi says brightly. 'They've all been cleaned. What's the difference?'

Tara pulls a face. 'Because . . . they're, like, other people's . . .'

'You know that dress Jessica Alba was wearing in *Heat* last week? That was vintage.'

'So?'

'That's what vintage means. Old. Used to belong to someone else.'

Tara colours, annoyed with herself for not knowing such a basic fashion fact. 'But this is Oxfam.'

'So it's cheap vintage, that's all. Things that belonged to other people, but that weren't made by Chanel or Gucci.'

Tara's not having it. Now she's made her point she's not backing down. 'Mum says she won't give her clothes to Oxfam because she doesn't want to see some tramp begging outside the tube station wearing her Louboutins. She takes them to the second-hand designer shop and they sell them for her. That way she gets money for them too.'

'Of course. God forbid she'd just give them away for nothing. And to a charity at that.'

'Well, I'm not going in there. What if one of my friends walked past? I'd die. I'd literally die.'

'Well, we can't have that. Do you mind waiting out here while I go in? Just don't talk to anyone. Megan, are you coming with me?'

Megan looks nervously between her sister and her aunt. Tara shrugs.

'Go on if you want to.'

'We won't be long,' Abi says, grabbing Megan's hand before she can change her mind.

Back at home Abi insists on helping Jonty with dinner. He's a little reluctant – probably, like her, he's wondering what on earth they'll talk about while they shell the peas – but she tells him that now she is going to be out working two days a week she'd like to feel she was contributing to the household in some other way.

They manoeuvre around each other cautiously at first. Abi tells him about her job in the library, which, she realizes as the words are coming out of her mouth, couldn't sound more dull if it tried.

'Sounds like fun,' he says, and Abi tries, and fails, to work out if he's being sarcastic.

'It really isn't. But the hours suit me and I get to read all the books.'

'I'm serious. Ask anyone who runs their own company and I bet they'd tell you the same thing. The idea of set hours, no disgruntled employees, no hustling for the next contract. It sounds like heaven.'

She can't decide if he's patronizing her or not, but she tries not to rise to the bait if indeed there is one. 'Like I said, it suits me fine. In fact, no. It's perfect, if I'm being really honest.'

She asks him what his agency, MacMahon Fairchild Advertising and Media, is working on at the moment and he tells her they've just started on a new TV campaign for one of their biggest clients. Abi asks who and Jonty just says, 'Oh, you probably wouldn't have heard of them,' passes her a paper bag of very knob-bly carrots with the green bits still on them that definitely didn't come from Lidl, and says, 'Could you wash those?'

She assumes he's trying not to show off in the face of hearing about her own lowly position. 'Try me.'

He laughs. 'One-hit Comparison dot com.'

'One-hit what?' He's right – she doesn't know what he's talking about. She's not even sure he's talking English.

'Comparison.com. They're a website. You know, where you go and look at the prices of different things and they tell you which one is the best bargain. This one is aimed at housewives. School uniforms, kids' shoes, tins of beans, nappies. It'll tell you who has the cheapest of anything at any given moment.'

'Sounds right up my street.' She's a little taken aback. At the very least she'd expected one of Mac-Mahon Fairchild Advertising and Media's best clients to be a cosmetics range or maybe a car manufacturer. 'And they're one of your best clients?'

He nods. 'Glamorous, eh?'

'I had no idea those websites made so much money.'

'Advertising,' he says, and then adds, 'I don't mean them advertising. I mean people paying to advertise on their site. If they're successful, they can make a fortune – they've got a captive audience of millions of housewives looking on there every day. If you were Pampers or Palmolive, wouldn't you want to tap into that?'

'And easywhatsit.com is raking it in? I've never heard of them.'

'Ah, but you will have by the time I've finished with them – that's the point. They've just got a big investment and they're spending it all on saturation advertising: TV, radio, billboards, print. You'll be singing their theme tune in your sleep.'

Abi laughs. 'And how does it go?'

'I don't know. I haven't found anyone to write it yet. We've been working on the slogan for the past couple of days. You know, that iconic one line that will pop into your head every time someone says "onehitcomparison.com".'

'Like "Beanz means Heinz"? Or "The best a man can get"?'

'Exactly. It's earth-shattering stuff.'

The vegetables are all chopped into neat piles. Abi panics a bit about whether or not she's supposed to include the green bits that came on top of the carrots. It seems like a waste to throw them all away so she hedges her bets and leaves them next to the chopping board. Jonty is carefully stuffing big organic chicken breasts with a mixture of cream cheese and herbs. Thin slices of streaky bacon are laid out like a row of pink coffins to wrap round the outside.

'Anything else I can do?'

Jonty shakes his head. 'It's all under control. You could pour the wine, though.' Abi looks at her watch.

It's quarter to six, a little before her self-imposed six o'clock watershed, but what the hell. 'OK.'

She's hit with a sudden inspiration: '"One-hit the one-hit wonder".' She looks at him triumphantly.

'Thought of it already. It's on the shortlist. How about "your one-stop comparison shop"?' he says, and Abi says, 'Not catchy enough. And it makes it sound like it's for car insurance or something. How about "one hit for cheap shit".'

When she's finished laughing at how hilarious she is, she says, 'How come you have to worry about this, anyway? Don't you have a team of creatives sitting around on bean bags coming up with the ideas?'

'Of course. But this is the fun bit. The rest is just admin.'

Abi puts down her wine glass. She's drinking way too fast. 'Jonty,' she says. 'Why do you come home and cook dinner every night? I mean it's great that you do and I know Cleo said you got rid of the chef because you love cooking, but isn't it a bit of a bind having to leave work early every day? Surely Cleo could do it sometimes?'

'Have you seen her cooking?'

Abi laughs like she's meant to, but then she says, 'Really, though?'

'Well, it's true that I like to cook, but that's not the real reason I got rid of the chef. Cleo hasn't worked for a few years as you know and I do OK, but, to be honest, it seemed like a ridiculous expense when there are

95

two adults living here who are perfectly capable of rustling something up for themselves. Cleo'll do her share, I'm sure she will, but she's so wrapped up in trying to get back out there at the moment that I'm happy to do it all myself for a few weeks till things calm down. She's giving it a couple of months by the end of which she'll either have got herself an agent or a major new campaign or she'll stop trying and become a full-time mum. That's what she says anyway.'

'Makes sense, I suppose.'

'Besides, if I cook the meals myself, I can make sure they're so laden with calories that even if she just eats a quarter of it it'll be enough. Have you noticed how little she eats?'

Abi nods.

'She's been half starving herself since she decided to try and get back into modelling. So I hide calories. Full-fat cream cheese, butter, olive oil. I wouldn't eat a whole one of my meals if I were you, or you'll leave here the size of a house.'

'I'll bear that in mind. Are you worried about her?'

He puts down the cloth he's been wiping the surfaces with. 'I think she'll snap out of it. Between you and me, I think she's going to find it harder than she imagines to pick up where she left off. A few more weeks of this and she'll probably find that she's up against a brick wall. It's an unforgiving world. Do you know the awful thing? I hope that is what happens. She's a nicer person when she's not modelling.'

'She was certainly a nicer person before she ever started,' Abi says, and then she regrets it. 'Sorry, I didn't mean it to come out like that.'

'The whole job is about self-obsession. It comes with the territory. The industry expects the girls to think of nothing but themselves and how they look and then turns on them when that's what they do.'

'I suppose.' She drains the last of her wine just as the sound of the front door indicates that Cleo is back from the gym.

'Hey,' she says, slinging her gym bag on a chair. She looks thin and tired. 'Good day?'

'Not bad,' Abi says. 'You?'

'Oh, you know. More of the same. I'm going up to get changed.'

'Jonty,' Abi says when Cleo has gone. 'Do you think she's glad I'm here?'

'Of course she is. You're her sister.'

'I don't even know if you have siblings,' Abi says, realizing that Jonty has been her brother-in-law for nearly twelve years but she knows precious little about who he was before that.

He nods. 'Two brothers. Both younger.'

Abi smiles. 'And you still think it's that straightforward? I'm her sister so she must want me around?'

Jonty shrugs. 'Why not?'

There is no point trying to explain. Clearly the MacMahon family come with less complications than the Attwoods. She gets up to go. 'I promised Megan

I'd go up before dinner to see how her new charity wardrobe was shaping up.'

'Oh, and, Abigail,' Jonty says as she goes. 'Do me a favour and call me Jon. It's only Cleo who calls me Jonty. It's not even my name and I hate it, but she's always thought Jon is too suburban. Not glamorous enough.'

Abi laughs. 'OK, but only if you call me Abi. Only Cleo calls me Abigail. She once told me Abi sounded like someone off *EastEnders*.'

Jon raises his glass. 'Deal.'

Upstairs Megan is dressed in some cut-off jeans that she has decorated with sparkly bits, over black tights, and a boat-neck top that she has made out of a man's T-shirt belted in at the waist. She looks cute. Very 1980s.

'God, what do you look like?' Tara says when she comes in. 'You need to lose some weight.'

'You look cool,' Abi says to Megan. 'Actually, Tara, I think cut-off jeans are in, especially when you bling them up.' She's bluffing, obviously, although she thinks she vaguely remembers seeing a photo shoot in *Red* that featured customized denims.

'I don't think so,' Tara says.

'You wait,' Abi says, leaving the room while she's (just about) ahead. 'It's the next big thing. I read about it in *Vogue*.'

*

Tuesday comes round way too quickly. Abi actually has quite a nice weekend mainly because she sleeps most of Saturday morning and then she takes herself off to the National Gallery in the afternoon for some kind of Spanish old-master retrospective. Old masters aren't really her thing, but it passes the time and allows her a few hours of culture righteousness. It's like a workout. It might not be the most enjoyable thing at the time, but the feeling of self-satisfaction afterwards, the knowledge that you have done something worthy, something good for you, makes it all worthwhile. Not that Abi would ever dream of working out, she still gets out of breath climbing up to her attic room, but she imagines that's how she might feel if she did.

Then in the evening Cleo and Jon take their two girls to the theatre to see some new musical or other. The show has been booked up for months and they bought their tickets back in April so there's no chance Abi can go along with them, which she thinks is a bit of a relief because she really, really needs some more time on her own, and she slouches on the sofa in a way she never feels she can when Cleo and Jon are there, and watches bad TV and eats take-out Indian from the restaurant round the corner. She spends five minutes tidying the place and spraying away the mushroom balti smells with air freshener before the others get back. She's still not that at home.

On Sunday there's no Elena so Abi sneaks down

and makes herself a big pot of coffee before anyone else is up, takes it back upstairs and sits reading in the stately Louis armchair in her room. The prospect of a whole long day with the five of them all together fills her with horror slightly, but in the end it's a beautiful morning so they go for a long walk in Regent's Park – Megan in her 80s get-up, Tara and Cleo both perfectly groomed and made-up, teetering on their heels and Abi slouching along in sweatpants and trainers.

They walk round in circles trying to find the rose garden that Abi has read about and which she cannot believe none of the family seem to know anything about despite the fact that they live only fifteen minutes' walk away. In the event, it's a bit of an anticlimax because most of the roses are past their best, so they walk to Marylebone High Street and sit down to a huge pub lunch (well, those of them who eat do; Cleo picks around her roast beef and Yorkshire pudding and in the end just nibbles on some carrots while Tara, eyes always on her mother, flirts with some lamb chops but never gets fully acquainted).

Abi feels much more relaxed around the brother-in-law formerly known as Jonty now, but when they get home she still claims she has things to do upstairs and sneaks off for a nap. She hadn't realized how exhausted she is running around after two kids all day. It's hard work. At home when she's not at the library and Phoebe's at school (*was* at school, she reminds herself. Those days are over) she spends her

100

days pottering about, a bit of housework here, some laundry there, a quick fix of *Loose Women*. It's hardly taxing. She ends up sleeping for nearly two hours. At this rate her job in the bookshop is starting to look like a holiday.

Monday: Tara to street-dance class, Megan to French tuition, pick up Tara, pick up Megan, lunch, Tara to a drama workshop, Megan to violin, pick up Tara, pick up Megan, home. In between engagements Abi drives around London getting lost and failing to find anywhere to park.

At five thirty when Jon sticks his head round the door and says, 'Salmon en croute, want to help?' she's so exhausted she wants to say no, but she's also keen for any more insights Jon might offer up into her sister, so she drags herself off the sofa and follows him into the kitchen. They chat about their days for a bit (latest suggestions for onehitcomparison.com: 'get your life back with onehitcomparison.com' from him and 'lazy mothers swear by onehitcomparison.com' from her) although Abi struggles to make hers sound like anything other than a day of drudgery.

'So, new job tomorrow,' he says as he's rolling out the freshly defrosted pastry. 'Looking forward to it?'

'I am, actually. I'm a bit nervous too, which is stupid but, you know . . .'

'It'll be just like the library except people'll be handing over cash instead of library cards.'

'I know,' she says. 'That's the bit I'm worried about.

That I'll forget the taking-the-cash part. Someone'll get done for shoplifting, but it'll be my fault.'

He laughs. 'You'll be fine. I'll bring the girls in when I can and buy something so you can practise on us.'

'And then tell the boss how brilliant I was. I was wondering . . . don't the girls ever help you with this, by the way?' Abi says, waving the knife she's using to chop courgettes around the kitchen. 'I mean . . . not that it's any of my business.' She has noticed that Tara and Megan are only too happy to be waited on. Neither of them has lifted a finger since she got here.

'I'm ashamed to say my girls have no concept of housework. They take after their mother.' Jon smiles ruefully.

'She was always like that,' Abi says, laughing. 'Even before all the . . . you know. She had such a sense of entitlement even then that she used to lie around watching TV and Mum'd be running about getting her stuff. It's mad now I think about it.'

'Well, just substitute your mum for Elena. Or me. Nothing's changed.'

It's funny, Abi had forgotten about that. Queen Caroline, their dad used to call her because she just had the knack of getting other people to do everything for her. No one ever argued, no one ever said 'get it yourself'. Not even Abigail. It was just sort of accepted that she wouldn't.

'That's part of what this is too, if I'm being honest.'

Jon indicates the food. 'When they were little, I was just too busy working to spend much time with them, and Cleo was still modelling, so they were brought up by nannies and housekeepers. They think it's normal to have help. To just snap your fingers and have everything done for you because someone's being paid to do it. So it's not just a love of cooking that makes me leave work early every night – it's guilt. I want them to get a bit more of a sense of how normal people live.'

'Good for you. Although I'm not sure most normal people live in a house like this, but still . . .'

'Or have a housekeeper who comes in every day, I know. But it's better than nothing. Maybe not normal, but more normal. I'm not sure it's working, though.'

'I'm going to go and get them,' Abi says, suddenly inspired by the idea of bringing her spoilt nieces back from the brink.

Jon laughs. 'Good luck with that. Believe me, I've tried.'

Upstairs Megan and Tara are watching a *High School Musical* DVD in Tara's palatial bedroom, which has its own en-suite bathroom and dressing room. Both the girls' rooms do.

'Who's going to come and set the table?' Abi says breezily.

Megan looks like she's about to get up when Tara says, 'You're already helping. It doesn't take three of us.' Megan sits back down again, caught in the crossfire.

'There are other things you can do. Your dad's down there slaving away, wouldn't it be nice to go and offer to help him?'

'I'm watching a film,' Tara says. 'Sorry.'

Abi is momentarily stumped. She's not used to children who flat out refuse to do what you tell them and, as these two aren't her own, she doesn't really feel she has much leverage. 'Well, if you change your minds, you know where we are,' she says, trying to pretend she couldn't care less as she turns and leaves the room.

'I see that went well,' Jon says when she arrives back at the kitchen alone.

It's amazing how many people go into a bookshop just to mooch around reading the books for free. It seems to Abi that it really is a lot like being in the library except that occasionally someone comes up to pay and there are no tramps asleep in the corners. Richard shows her how the till works and then gives her a box of books with which to restock the tables. It's hardly rocket science, but that's good because if it was then she'd be lost. As it is she feels at home almost straight away. Once they've topped up all the piles of books and opened a few boxes of new deliveries, Richard seems happy for her just to sit and read or chat so long as she springs into action when there's a sniff of a customer.

He tells her that he's divorced with two grown-up children. Abi tries to work out how old he is. She would probably put him in his mid-forties because he has a few lines round his eyes, but not yet deep valleys either side of his mouth. She can't imagine that he would have been a teenage dad, so with a twenty- and a twenty-two-year-old she would put him at forty-five at the youngest. It's hard to tell if his hair is greying because he has it cropped very short, presumably because it was thinning or receding. It suits him. The severe haircut forces people – women anyway – to concentrate on his eyes, which are an icy blue and which, against a background of tanned skin, remind Abi of a wolf's. He's definitely aware of the fact that he's attractive and he plays his role as the local heartthrob to perfection. From about eleven o'clock onwards the shop is full of designer-clad Primrose Hill mothers with their designer-clad preschool offspring hanging on his every word. Their kids run riot in the tiny children's section and it's Abi's job to keep an eye on them while he flirts away.

'It's good for custom,' he says laughing when she accuses him of being a Lothario. And he's right. Almost all of the mums buy something, as if that might fool anyone into thinking that the real reason they have come in is for the books. The place is a hotbed of seething hormones all day. It's like living in a Jackie Collins novel. Abi is relieved that Richard doesn't try his twinkle on her. Or at least that, when he does, he gets the message pretty quickly that she's not up for playing.

'I can't believe you're old enough to have a daughter who's about to go off to university,' he had said in the first hour they worked together.

Abi smiled. 'Yeah, yeah. I've heard it all before.'

Richard acted affronted. 'I mean it. You look great.'

'Well, I'll accept the compliment, but I should tell you I don't respond well to flattery. I have a state-of-the-art bullshit detector built in.'

'Oh, thank god,' Richard said, laughing. 'One less person to have to flirt with. It's exhausting.'

She decides that he's funny. After each of the blushing ladies leaves, convinced that his attentions are all hers, he gives Abi the lowdown on their life – most have rich absent husbands, many are trophy wives; all exterior and no substance. One is frustrated that her husband is rich but not famous, so while he can buy her whatever she wants he can't get her into the pages of *OK!*. Another told Richard outright when her husband was going to be away and that she would leave the back door open for him after the children were in bed.

'You didn't!' Abi asks, horrified.

'I'll never tell,' he says archly, which makes her laugh. It's fun and the day goes by before she's even noticed what the time is. When she leaves him locking up for the night, she finds herself looking forward to Thursday.

Cleo is already home when Abi gets there, having apparently skipped the gym, and she's sitting in the kitchen with Jon sipping a glass of what looks like champagne. She's looking very pleased with herself. In fact, she looks better than Abi has seen her since she arrived. She looks happy, waving her glass around as she talks animatedly. The stress, always present in her face, seems to be gone.

'Get a glass and then you can toast me,' she says when Abi stops by on her way upstairs to change.

'Why? What's happened? Quick,' Abi says. She can never wait to be told good news.

'She's got a new agent,' Jon says.

'That's fantastic.' Abi gives Cleo a hug, and Cleo's in such a good mood that she hugs her back. Not the usual slightly stiff hug of someone you don't really know very well, but a warmer, softer version. It feels nice. Her hair smells of coconut and mint. When she was young, it always smelt like bubblegum, as did Abi's, courtesy of the Co-op's own brand.

'I'm back,' she says, and they clink glasses. Abi smiles at Jon and he smiles back, although there's a hint of it being forced. She knows he's worried about Cleo entering that whole insane world again, and who can blame him? Still, it's hard not to be happy for her when she's so clearly elated. Whatever this new agent turns out to be like, for her this is a vindication that she was right to keep trying.

'You'll be fighting off the contracts in no time,' Abi says.

Cleo smiles as if she knows this to be true. 'We

should go out and celebrate. How about Marcus Wareing?'

'It's a bit short notice,' Jon says. 'And I've already started dinner.'

'If you tell them it's for me, they'll fit us in. Go on. Ring them.'

Jon sighs and picks up the phone. Abi jumps up with excitement. She has always wanted to go to a Marcus Wareing restaurant, let alone the exclusive eponymous Berkeley Square one, but she has to confess to feeling a bit bad about the organic chicken that's already roasting away in the oven. It smells delicious. She mentally runs through her wardrobe. She has no idea what the dress code is.

'You don't mind keeping an eye on the girls, do you, Abigail?'

Ah. Of course. She's the help.

She smiles weakly. 'No, that's fine. Have a great time.'

9

While Jon and Cleo celebrate at Marcus Wareing, Abi feeds the girls the chicken that she has somehow allowed to dry out, hassles them into their baths and bed and then sits wondering how she is going to entertain herself this evening. The truth is that she's feeling lonely. She feels like she felt when she was a seventeen-year-old au pair living, for a summer, in Rome. Happy enough to be distracted by the needs of the children and the excitement of being in a strange city during the day, but adrift and alone in the evenings. Not quite part of the family. She thinks again about leaving, giving up and going home, turfing the Carvers out onto the street and insisting that she wants the flat now, that she can't wait till the end of the summer, or going back to her old house and somehow managing to persuade the new owners that it was all a dream.

Of course she knows that neither of these options is a remote possibility; she's not stupid. And she also knows that even if she could miraculously sort out the practicalities then that would be it. She would have officially given up on Cleo and there would be no going back. And she doesn't really think she can allow that to happen while there's still a glimmer of hope, however faint.

She hasn't spoken to Phoebe in a few days and, even though she knows that by this time – eight thirty in the evening – Phoebe is bound to be out somewhere with her friends, enjoying herself, Abi can't resist calling. She's feeling down. This isn't her usual state of mind. She's happy enough being on her own, really she is. She just misses her daughter, that's all.

'Mum!' Phoebe shouts when she answers. Abi can hear music and laughter in the background. She can practically feel the heat and smell the sea. She forgot, of course, when she dialled, that it's more like half ten or even later wherever Phoebe is.

'Hi, darling.' Abi finds herself shouting to match Phoebe's pitch. 'Where are you?'

'At a beach party.'

'No,' Abi laughs. 'I mean where in the world.'

'Oh. Naxos. We got here a couple of days ago. It's fab.'

'Are you all OK?' Abi can tell that this isn't the time to have the cosy catch-up she wanted. She reminds herself not to burden her daughter with her neediness.

'We're great, we're all great. Don't worry about us.'

There's no way Abi will be heeding that advice, but she just says, 'Well, I just wanted to say hi and that I love you.'

'Love you too, Mum. How's it going with Auntie Cleo?'

'Fantastic,' Abi says in what she hopes is a convincing voice. Now is not the time. 'Really good.'

She says goodbye and Phoebe promises to call her back at a more sociable hour. Abi just manages to stop herself asking too many questions about who her daughter is with and exactly where they are staying and whether she is remembering all the lectures Abi gave her about rohypnol and STDs and always sticking with her two friends. She'll save those for another day. She looks at her watch: eight thirty-seven. She decides to go to bed with her book and a big glass of wine. Actually, she thinks, she might as well take the rest of the bottle with her, save her coming downstairs again.

She has already hunted for a bottle of anything she recognizes the name of – a Pinot Grigio or a Sauvignon Blanc – that she might feel comfortable opening because she could safely assume that it isn't worth a small fortune (although, who knows, maybe you do need a mortgage to purchase a certain fine year of Sauvignon Blanc – she wouldn't have a clue truthfully – but she figures the names of any wines she has ever drunk before are probably the best bets). She's thought about asking which ones it's OK to help herself to, but that seems like saying she expects Cleo and Jon to provide her with drinks. She could bring a bottle home from the off-licence up the road, of course, but she worries that makes her look a bit desperate and, anyway, on each occasion she has, they are put in the cupboard, not even the fridge, so unworthy are they, so she would have to drink them warm, which even she is loath to do. Consequently she is in the process of educating her palate to appreciate the many bottles with unpronounceable names that are languishing in the wine fridge. This evening, left to her own devices, she tries to pick one that looks familiar, that they have all shared before, reasoning that if that's the case it's unlikely to be priceless.

At about five past ten she hears Jon and Cleo come in much earlier than she'd anticipated. She considers going down in her pyjamas to ask if they had a good time, to get the low-down on the restaurant, but as she's pulling on a hoody over her little vest top she hears footsteps on the stairs and Cleo saying, 'I'm going to bed,' in a voice that contains no hint of an invitation, and then slamming the bedroom door. The evening obviously went well, then.

Abi starts to climb back into bed, but then curiosity and, surprisingly, a genuine concern for Jon's wellbeing take over and she creeps down past their bedroom door and into the kitchen to find him. He's pouring himself a glass of red and looking, it's fair to say, miserable. He jumps when Abi comes in, and then looks at her hopefully, giving away for a fleeting moment that he thought she might be Cleo come to make up.

'Oh,' he says. 'Hi.'

Abi decides not to give away that she's heard anything. 'Good night?'

'Yes. Thanks.'

'Where's Cleo?'

Jon takes a long sip of his drink. 'Gone to bed. She's got an early start . . . you know.'

'Right,' Abi says.

He obviously doesn't want to confide in her, and why should he? Just because they've spent a couple of fairly pleasant early evenings together doesn't mean he is about to start treating her like family. They just don't know each other well enough for that however long they've been related on paper. She makes a move to go. It's obvious that Jon doesn't want company.

'Actually,' he says as she's turning away, 'it was a disaster. We had a fight in the cab on the way and it was all downhill from there. We never even got to dessert.'

Abi looks back. Jon has slumped down onto one of the kitchen chairs and is rubbing his eyes with one hand as if he has a headache. She sits down opposite him.

'Sorry to hear that.'

'It's my fault,' he says. 'I was trying to be pleased for her, but, to be honest, it scares me to death the idea that she's taking up modelling again and I guess she picked up on that. She was furious that I was being so unsupportive. I shouldn't really be telling you this . . .'

'You don't have to.'

'It's just . . . I don't want you to think that I'm not behind her, of course I am if that's what she really

113

wants to do. I'm just not sure it's the best thing for her . . . for us both, if I'm being honest.'

Abi doesn't really know what to say to that. In some ways she's always thought that modelling was the worst thing that ever happened to her sister. That Caroline had always been a better person than Cleo ever could be. But she also knows that for Cleo it was everything. And Abi desperately wants her sister to be happy because maybe, if she was, she could afford to be nicer to those around her.

'It's hard work,' is all Abi says, which she knows doesn't really mean anything, but she's struggling.

'It's not that. Well, that's part of it. She was always exhausted when she was working and, of course, she never ate properly . . . but it's more the whole package, the need for her to always look perfect, to go out and be seen in the right places, the paparazzi and the gossip columns. Everything has to revolve round it. I'm aware that I sound like a sulky child, by the way,' he says, smiling. 'Like I'm worried I won't get enough attention or something. I just don't want the girls to have to get involved in all that. To get used to having photographers following them around and their friends reading nasty comments about their mum in the papers. And, honestly, the bottom line is that she's been a nicer person since she gave up, like I said before. A kinder person . . .'

Abi can certainly believe that. Jon looks abjectly miserable. She feels sorry for him. Being her sister's sister is hard enough. It's difficult to imagine what being her husband must be like.

'But I also know that if it's what she really wants to do then I have to support her. It's not up to me to tell her how to live her life. I should have told her it was fantastic and just left it at that.'

'She was modelling when you first met her. What's changed?'

Jon sighs. 'It was before I set up MacMahon Fairchild. I was working for one of the big agencies and we were doing some flashy campaign – a car or a perfume, I don't even remember. Cleo was the model. I thought she was beautiful, obviously, but she was horribly rude to everyone, a real nightmare. Then in the middle of the afternoon I came across her hiding out in the kitchen in floods of tears. She said she thought everyone hated her and I said she was probably right because of how high-handed she was being. I'd had enough by then and I didn't really care if she walked out at that point.'

'Brave man.'

'Anyway, she smiled. Said she knew I was right and that was part of why she was upset. She was trying to change, but it was like everyone expected her to be a diva now and so she couldn't help slipping into the role. She seemed so vulnerable, like she really was a sweet person and the whole prima donna thing was an act. She was always like that with me. For a long time, anyway.'

'I get the impression the diva won out in the end, though.'

He nods, sadly. 'I don't think she ever mastered being gracious at work. And that gradually became her whole personality. Until she stopped modelling, that is. Then she was like she was when we first met. But I still should have acted like I was pleased for her tonight, though. I'm her husband; I'm meant to be head of her cheerleading team.'

'That I'd like to see.'

He gives her a half smile, but Abi can tell his heart's not really in it.

'Don't beat yourself up. She'll probably have forgotten all about it in the morning.'

Jon doesn't seem to be listening to her platitudes, though. He's got something on his mind and he wants to say it. 'The honest truth is for the five years since she stopped modelling until she suddenly decided she wanted to give it another try we were closer than we've ever been. We had the girls and we were a family and I really thought that things had changed.' He exhales noisily. 'OK,' he says abruptly, draining the last of his wine. 'Too much information. I should go to bed.'

'If we're being honest . . .' Abi says. 'Just because she's got a new agent that doesn't mean she's going to be inundated with work. It's not going to be like it was . . .'

She feels bad, trying to make the fact that her sister is unlikely to ever rekindle her former glorious career a positive, but she understands his uneasiness. Cleo in the full flush of success was never a pleasant person to be around. She's touched by his concern for his wife. Abi can't imagine she's easy to live with at the best of times and Jon clearly genuinely cares about her. She's a little surprised too, truthfully, by Jon's unease about Cleo's return to modelling. She always assumed he got off on having a supermodel for a wife, that he liked the status and attention it brought them as a couple. That and the money and the fame by proxy that came his way courtesy of her job. She'd felt sure he revelled in being with a woman every other man in the world thought was gorgeous. She figured Cleo was a prize, a trophy. Apparently not.

It seems that she is often being surprised by Jon these days. He's not at all the person she'd had him down as.

Cleo is sitting frostily at the breakfast table when Abi comes down a little later than usual the next morning. She assumes that Jon has gone to work. The girls are squabbling over the remote in the living room and Abi can hear Elena chastising them. Either that or she's part of the argument and she's trying to turn over to *Loose Women* while they're watching *Cash in the Attic*. It's hard to tell.

'How was dinner?' she asks as innocently as she can.

Cleo takes a sip of her coffee. Elena, clearly having

given up on whatever it was she was trying to achieve, comes into the kitchen and slips some toast into the toaster for Abi. She actually feels like granola today, but it seems like too much hard work to convey that.

'For god's sake, Elena, this is way too weak,' Cleo says, angrily waving her coffee cup around. Abi cringes at her imperious tone.

'I'll get you another one,' Abi says, jumping up. She smiles at Elena who looks as if she knows something is wrong, but not quite what.

'No. She's got to learn. She's been here three years and she still can't work the bloody coffee machine properly.' Cleo goes back to reading the paper, giving Abi the chance to hand her cup to Elena and make furious miming motions trying to convey the word 'stronger'. But she only ends up looking like she's practising for a weight-lifting competition. She looks at the machine, which couldn't appear more complicated if it tried.

'Maybe there's a button somewhere . . .'

'Oh, leave it,' Cleo says. 'I'll go without.'

Abi touches Elena's arm to try to reassure her everything's OK. Elena gives her a wary smile. Abi resolves to hunt around for the instruction manual the next time Cleo is safely out of the house.

'So . . . dinner?' she says as she sits back down.

'Fine. The food was good.' Abi waits in case there are any Jon-like revelations to come, but Cleo isn't telling.

'Are you busy today?' She's not giving up on her happy family summer scenario despite her rational self telling her she should, but, as always seems to happen, nervousness makes her blather on.

'I mean I'm sure you are, you usually are and now that you have a new agent I guess things will get crazy, but, if you're not, then maybe we could all do something together. Us and the girls,' she adds, just in case Cleo's not sure who she means by 'all'. Elena puts the toast in front of her and Abi smiles her thanks, waiting for a response from Cleo.

'I'm going out for lunch,' Cleo says. 'And then I must go to the gym because, of course, I won't be able to go tomorrow.' Tomorrow being the one day in the week when she is being expected to entertain her two daughters herself because Abi will be working. Abi doesn't rise to the bait.

'Right,' Abi says. 'Another day, maybe.' The sight of Cleo, reading glasses perched on the end of her nose, suddenly reminds Abi of something, some forgotten memory of when they were young, and she says, 'Hey, do you remember the time Mum left her glasses in that café in Leamington Spa and we had to read everything aloud to her for days . . .?'

Cleo sighs. 'Not now, Abigail. I'm exhausted.'

The atmosphere in the house is tense to say the least, so on Thursday Abi can't wait to get out of there and get to work. She's so early that she has to walk round the park for twenty minutes while she waits for Richard to open up.

The previous night pretty much went to script. Abi helped Jon cook dinner although their chat was not quite as relaxed as it has been lately, because, she thinks, he was regretting having confided in her in the kitchen the night before. They talked about work mostly and Abi tried to make him laugh by offering up some new suggestions for onehitcomparison.com ('Too fat and lazy to walk round the shops? Let us do the work for you' and 'Looking for the cheapest place to buy crack? Take the stress out of your addiction with onehitcomparison.com), but even though he smiled she could tell his heart wasn't really in it. Neither of them mentioned Cleo at all.

Her sister got home from the gym at about six thirty and they all had dinner together in the kitchen with the welcome distraction of Tara talking nonstop as usual. Jon made a few attempts to engage Cleo about her day, but she wasn't having it. Her commitment to being in a bad mood is impressive to say the least. Then, while the girls played on their DSes, Abi loaded the dishwasher, then claimed a migraine and went and hid in her room upstairs where she watched bad TV and swigged the rest of last night's wine warm and straight from the bottle. Anything rather than sit with the happy couple in the frosty wasteland of the living room.

She's a bit more confident at work today. She

doesn't make any mistakes on the till and she finds it easier to make conversation with the customers. She actually enjoys the mindless chit-chat after the *Sturm und Drang* going on at home. Most of the swooning ladies come in again and Abi teases Richard by encouraging them ('Richard will be SO pleased to see you! He was just saying he wondered if you were going to be in today') which both horrifies him and then makes him laugh when she re-enacts the expression of pure joy that comes over each of his admirers' faces when she gives them hope. At about twelve o'clock she's just wondering what she can have for lunch, and when she can reasonably ask to go and get it, when the door opens and three familiar figures walk in. Megan bowls straight up to the counter, Jon and Tara trailing behind.

'Hi, girls.' Abi comes round to the front to give them a hug and a kiss before she turns to Jon. 'What are you doing here? I thought Cleo was at home today.'

'She has a casting,' Jon says with the slightest roll of his eyes.

'It's lucky you own the company,' Abi says, 'or you'd be using up all your holiday.'

'Anyway, the girls wanted to come and see where you worked. So here we are.'

Abi assumes by 'the girls' he means Megan. She's not sure visiting her aunt in the local bookstore would have been top of Tara's agenda. The Regent's Park Road Bookshop is not often awash with model scouts.

'Well, here it is.' Abi suddenly notices Richard hovering around curious to see who her visitors are. 'Oh, this is Richard. He owns the shop,' she says. 'And this is Tara and Megan, and Jon, my brother-in-law.'

Jon and Richard shake hands in a matey manly way. For some reason Abi feels the colour rise up in her face. Surely she's way too young to be having hot flushes.

'So, girls, this is the kids' section here. See anything you like?' The shop is pretty quiet so Abi spends five minutes sorting through shelves with Tara and Megan. She's gratified to find they have read half the books in the shop, which makes Abi think Tara has inherited something from her after all. She lets them pick one each and tells them she will buy them with her discount and bring them home this evening. Richard, clearly a natural with children, makes a big fuss of them, praising their choices.

'How about me?' Jon says. 'Can I choose a book too?'

'Of course. But I can't give you a discount. Richard would fire me,' Abi says in front of Richard, who laughs like he's meant to.

'In that case, I'll take my custom elsewhere,' Jon says, and Abi is glad to see he's back to his usual self. A usual self she has realized she actually rather likes. She feels herself blush again as she thinks this. What is going on?

'Good-looking bloke,' Richard says when they leave.

'He's OK,' Abi says. 'Not my type really.'

'Yeah, right.'

'Plus he's married to my sister.'

'Ah yes, I'd forgotten that.' He raises an eyebrow at her and she says, 'Not funny, Richard,' and goes off to tidy the travel section.

In truth, she is a little disconcerted by her own reaction, though. There's no doubting she was pleased to see Jon. Why shouldn't she be? She hardly knows anyone up here and they have discovered they get on well, despite all the odds. But was she a little too pleased? Did she feel a little jolt of something extra when she looked up and saw him? It's true that she has stopped thinking of him as an over-groomed mannequin and come to acknowledge that he is, in fact, just naturally very well put together. Attractive you might even say. He has cracks in his perfect façade – the odd laugh line here, a grey hair there – which, if you ask Abi, actually add to his appeal. He always looks the same morning and night, and he doesn't seem to spend an inordinate amount of time in the bathroom, so, she supposes, he's just blessed with good looks. Plus, she feels she should acknowledge, she has never seen the man bag again since that first day so she has allowed herself to believe that he had something important to carry on that one occasion and nothing else available to carry it in. Anyway, it's no big deal.

Suffice to say, she has accepted that Jon is an

attractive man. But that doesn't mean anything. She reminds herself that Richard's default setting seems to be to tease everyone about fancying everyone else. He loves a bit of sexual intrigue. He was just pushing her buttons, although it makes her uneasy that he seems to have found a button she didn't even know she had to push.

Abi keeps her head down all afternoon, and by the time they're locking up she has convinced herself that she's being ridiculous. It's so long since she's fancied anyone that she's misreading her own signals. She's confused the fact that she was surprised to find herself liking her brother-in-law with it meaning something more. She's just impressed with the way he's trying his hardest to give his kids a stable upbringing. She just feels a little sorry for him the way that Cleo treats him sometimes. She just needs to get a grip, that's all.

'Fancy a quick beer on the way home?' Richard says, and then he nearly jumps in the face of Abi's overenthusiastic reaction. She'll let Jon cook dinner on his own tonight.

They walk for about five minutes in a direction she hasn't yet explored, past rows of stately five-story terraces and out onto a main road. The tables outside The Hill are packed with office workers soaking up a bit of sun before they can face their journeys home, but Richard and Abi luck out by arriving just as two people are leaving so she grabs their seats while

Richard goes to the bar. He takes ages, because, as he tells her when he finally returns, two large glasses of wine in hand, he bumped into a few people he knew and had to stop and say hi. He knows everyone. The shop, he tells Abi, has been open for nine years and because he's always had a policy of letting people browse and read for hours without hassling them to buy anything, he's ended up with a large and loyal clientele who are so far resisting the urge to go to the Waterstone's in Camden.

She asks him why he's single when all the local ladies seem to love him so much and he laughs and says that if he got married he'd lose half of his customers in one fell swoop. Actually, he tells her, he has been seeing someone recently and it's going well. She's a single mother with two small children and they met jogging round Regent's Park one day. He'd noticed her a couple of times before and then a sudden rainstorm and the need to take shelter in the little stone archway at the southern end of the gardens had afforded him the chance to strike up a conversation. Apparently it was hard work persuading her to take it to the next level from idle chats in the park to dinner.

'I've never run so much in my life. It was the only way I knew how to get in touch with her for weeks. She runs every morning at half past seven with the kids in a buggy. I had to keep turning up like it was a coincidence.'

'You're such a cliché,' Abi says, but in what she hopes is a nice way. 'It's all about the chase.'

'Well, to be fair, we've been out to dinner a few times now and I still really like her, so while I think the chase was a big part of the attraction it can't be everything.'

'And it doesn't bother you that she's got two kids?'

He looks at her like he barely even registers what she means. 'No. Why should it? I love kids.'

'It shouldn't, but you'd be amazed how often it does. Good for you,' she says, and she means it. She's got nothing but admiration for the men who are prepared to take on single mothers. They're rarer than one might imagine. She likes that there's a more substantial, more thoughtful side to Richard underneath all the flirtation. She'd like to think they could become friends.

10

When Abi gets home, slightly tipsy from knocking back two supersize wines in very quick succession, dinner is half over and there's nothing to do but sit down and eat the meal that has been keeping warm in the oven. She feels a bit like a wayward thirteen-year-old when she realizes that both Jon and Cleo have been worrying about where she's been. Even though it's only just gone seven fifteen, they know she has no life to speak of, no friends here. There is no rational conclusion they could have drawn from her absence other than that something horrendous had befallen her. She apologizes profusely, promises to keep them abreast of her movements in future.

'I missed my sous chef,' Jon says. Abi is having trouble looking at him. Something has shifted and it's making her very uncomfortable. It's a bit like bumping into a co-worker the morning after you have had a completely random erotic dream about them. It's impossible to catch their eye without looking guilty. Plus her heart seems to be trying to beat its way out of her ears. It must be the wine.

'Sorry,' she says, looking at the floor. 'I should have called . . .'

Before she can go on to tell them where she was or how her day went or any of the other riveting facts she could share about her new life, Cleo launches in about her casting. At least her bad mood seems to have lifted.

'The photographer is Falco,' she says, speaking to Jon and not Abi, because she knows Abi wouldn't have a clue about photographers. 'Remember him?'

Jon shakes his head. 'Not really.'

'He did that Citroën commercial I was in. You remember. Anyway, he said he's always wanted to work with me again and he's so glad I'm going back to work. Honestly, I'll be amazed if I don't get it. It's for a moisturizer, so you have to have really flawless skin, but then I've always been lucky with my complexion.'

'That's great,' Jon says. 'The girls and I went to Abi's shop today.'

'Oh yes,' Abi says, turning to Tara and Megan, 'I've got your books.' She produces them from her bag with a flourish and the girls effuse their thanks.

'That's nice,' Cleo says. 'Linda – that's my new agent – says we'll definitely hear by Tuesday afternoon. Obviously Falco will want who he wants, but the clients have to at least think they're having a say and their meeting is on Monday morning. The shoot's the following week. New York. It's been ages since we went to New York.'

'We?' Jon says. 'I can't go to New York. Not at the moment.'

Oh god. Abi can feel another row brewing. She sits there unable to think what to say to divert it.

'Of course you can. You're the boss. Just tell them you're taking a couple of weeks off.'

'A couple of weeks?'

Cleo's face assumes a frosty expression. 'I have to get there a few days early to give me time to get over the jet lag and for my skin to fully recover and then they're shooting a commercial and some print stuff as well, so that's going to take a week –'

Jon interrupts. 'I'm too busy. We're right in the middle of a big campaign and I'm already having to take days off when I can't really afford to . . .'

Abi sinks down in her chair. That'll be because of her, then. 'Sorry . . .'

'I didn't mean it like that. Sorry, Abi.' Jon smiles a quick smile at her and her heart skips a couple of beats. Get a grip.

Jon turns back to Cleo. 'Besides, what about the girls? Are you thinking of taking them with you?'

'Yay,' Tara says. 'I've always wanted to go to New York.'

'Of course not,' Cleo hisses. 'I'll be working.' For which read: I want to go out on the town and be fabulous every night and you have to accompany me. 'Abigail's here. She can look after them. It'll only be for ten days or so. A fortnight, maybe. You don't mind, do you, Abigail?'

Abi does mind, actually. She minds a lot. She shakes

her head slightly. She doesn't want to get caught up in their fight and, besides, if she did she knows whose side she'd want to take. 'Um . . .'

Luckily Jon butts in. 'We are not going to ask Abi to look after our children for a couple of weeks while we swan off to New York. And I am not going to take two weeks off work. By all means go and do your job if you get it, but don't expect me to drop everything and come with you . . .'

Tara and Megan's heads flip round from one parent to the other like they're watching a tennis match.

'Why not? I'll probably get paid twice as much as you'd earn in that week . . .'

OK, enough. Abi decides that her nieces really don't need to hear the rest of this. Wherever it's headed is not a good place.

'Right,' she says, standing up and leaving her half-eaten cod and butter-bean stew, which she was really enjoying, by the way. 'Who wants to play on the Wii Fit?'

Luckily the girls jump at the chance, and so they go into the family room and box each other for half an hour, by which time Abi thinks she needs a heart transplant and Tara and Megan seem to have forgotten all about their parents' argument. She's heartened to see that Tara can let herself go a bit and join in. It seems she knows that even the most ubiquitous model scouts are unlikely to be spying through the front windows. Abi still catches her standing on the coffee table to check her hair in the mirror over the fireplace whenever it's not her go, though, and she steadfastly refuses to take off the uncomfortable-looking strappy wedges she's wearing even though she keeps stumbling in them.

Rather than face the icy atmosphere seeping out of the living room, Abi takes the two girls upstairs to get ready for bed once they've all had enough. And then spends the rest of the evening sitting miserably in her pretty little room yet again, only this time without even any wine for company. It's hard not to feel like you're intruding when couples start bickering in front of you. Abi could tell that Cleo and Jon were spoiling for a full-on fight, but that they couldn't get into it with her and the kids there. Well, she hopes it was both her and the kids they were concerned about. She would hate to think that they would argue in front of the girls unchecked if she wasn't around. Cleo, Abi suspects, is blind to who she might be upsetting once she gets into one of her self-obsessed moods. Either everything goes according to how she wants it, or she's going to make a fuss. If you provoke her in front of the children, then tough; she's still going to say whatever it is she wants to say. It's not that she does this not caring if it upsets the girls, it's more that she believes they will think she's in the right and that it's perfectly OK for her to put her foot down. She probably thinks she's teaching them a valuable life lesson. You have to be selfish to get on. A woman deserves to be treated like a queen. If your man doesn't treat you like you're the most important person in the world, then you have to stand up for your rights, or some other Oprah-worthy mantra.

The new chilly atmosphere persists right into the weekend. Cleo huffily cries off going out for a family trip on Saturday – a day which everyone had agreed to spend together pottering around the South Bank, primarily so Abi could go to the Tate Modern and then down to the Tower, which, she has discovered, the girls have also never been to. Not that they have shown the slightest interest in going there, but anyway. Despite Abi's protestations that she could still go alone or with Tara and Megan, whichever suited everyone best, Jon insists that he come too, so that she can slope off to the upstairs galleries in the Tate while he amuses the girls on the interactive giant wooden sculptures, made for climbing on, which are currently in the Turbine Hall.

'Otherwise you won't get to do anything you want to do,' he says.

On the one hand he's right. Abi really doesn't want to spend yet another day amusing two small girls on her own. It's exhausting. Especially when all they really want to do is go clothes shopping. But the idea of spending a whole day playing happy families with Jon makes her feel anxious. Will he pick up on her ridiculous crush? Which is what she's decided it is, the reason for her blushes and palpitations whenever Jon is around. Will she forget herself and flirt with her sister's husband? No, she thinks, definitely not the latter. She is loyal to her sister no matter what, never mind that she has always run from married or even just attached men like they had the Plague. She would never go there. But what she might well do is colour up like a complete idiot every time Jon speaks to her.

She can't decide what to do, but, while she dithers around arguing with herself in her own head, Jon makes the decision for her and before she knows it they're out the door and in a taxi.

Abi is ridiculously self-conscious of where and how she sits in the cab, making a big deal to Megan of how much fun it would be to sit on the pull-down seats and go backwards, and then keeping her legs tucked under her just in case there's a jolt and her foot brushes Jon's.

She is all too aware that she has had crushes like this before. That's how she knows it will pass. In fact, she seems to have them all the time, blushing inappropriately when the postman rings the doorbell, or, for a while, stumbling over her words whenever she was in the local seafront café and the ancient owner's son served her. After a few days she usually snaps out of it and then spends weeks thanking every deity she can conjure up that she didn't do anything about it. Not only does her infatuation disappear as quickly as it arrived, but generally she can see nothing – nothing – attractive about the person she has spent hours fantasizing about once it has gone. In fact, having twinkled and batted her eyelashes in their presence for weeks, she can barely even look at them until she knows that if they ever did receive the message that she was flirting with them they have now definitely received the follow-up that it's all over and they're never to mention it again. There must be some seriously confused men in Deal.

She attributes her adolescent behaviour to the fact that she has been on her own for way too long. Since she had Phoebe – eighteen years ago now – she has barely had what could be described as a relationship, because whenever it came down to it and she had to ask herself the question 'Could I ever see this man being a father for my child?' the answer has always been no. So there was never any point in carrying on.

After a couple of years she decided there wasn't really much point even starting a relationship because she was only going to end it fairly rapidly once she had to decide whether to introduce them to her daughter or not. Consequently Phoebe has never met any man Abi has been involved with. Abi has never even told her daughter about them. None of them ever felt 'Phoebe worthy'. At least, this is the spin she has always put on the situation when she is torturing herself with her aloneness. Deep down she suspects that she actually rejects all men before they have a chance to reject her so that she doesn't have to relive the whole Phoebe's-father humiliation, but she has no intention of acknowledging that fact, even to herself.

Anyway, whatever the psychology behind it, the bottom line is that lack of real male companionship equals indiscriminate schoolgirl crushes, which she now knows count for nothing but which pass the time. So far none has been as screamingly inappropriate as the current one on her brother-in-law, but she puts that down to the fact that they're living in very close proximity and he's being nice to her in a time of emotional stress (i.e. her need for a proper sisterly relationship with Cleo and Cleo's apparent indifference). She's fully aware of how pitiful that sounds. It's that easy – be in her immediate surroundings and be kind to her and you will be rewarded by being her crush object of the day. It's funny but, however much she can rationalize about the whole situation, she still can't control her blushes and stutters and stupid girly nervous laughter. Her head knows that this is meaningless and pointless, but her body is still bent on shaming her. Maybe she'll tell him that she's having an early menopause. That would explain the redness at least.

Luckily Jon seems entirely oblivious to her state of mind. He hardly knows her, after all. He probably thinks she's always this socially inept. He's a little pre-occupied at the moment anyway with Tara's moaning that she doesn't want to waste a day going to an art gallery and the stupid Tower that's for tourists and the under-fives.

'You never know, you might enjoy yourself,' Abi says, and Tara rolls her eyes. 'At least do me a favour and give it a chance,' Abi tries as Jon and Megan walk on ahead, 'for your dad's sake. He's giving up his day off, so, you know, it'd be nice if he thought you'd had a good time.' Tara acts like a teenager so Abi figures that trying to talk to her in a mature way might just work.

'It's for little kids,' she whines, and Abi has to stop herself from saying, 'You're ten! What is that if it's not a little kid?'

'Listen,' she says, trying to adopt a calm and conspiratorial tone. 'You know that modelling is all about pretending, right? Pretending you're really enjoying standing knee-deep in freezing water in a bikini in February, pretending you're in love with the male model you're shooting with when his breath smells like onions and old socks, pretending you don't think you look stupid in some ridiculous haute couture concoction with a hat that looks like a lobster on your head. It's acting. It's just acting without the words.' This has definitely got Tara's attention now; she's looking at her aunt with interest. 'So look on this as your first modelling job. I'm the client and I want you to pretend you're having a great time climbing up those wooden sculptures. How about it?'

'OK,' she shrugs. 'But I'm still not going to enjoy it.'

'Doesn't matter,' Abi says. 'In fact, even better. Gives you a chance to show how good you really are.'

When they get to the Tate, she makes for the stairs, arranging to meet the others for lunch at twelve o'clock – in an hour's time. Not long enough really to explore all the delights the Tate has to offer, but Jon, quite rightly, is worried that he won't be able to keep the girls entertained for any longer than that. So she heads straight for Level Three and the room where they keep the Francis Bacons along with a few other favourites of hers, knowing that an hour is perfect to do justice to that one section of the gallery only. She's finding it hard to lose herself in the paintings, though, so she wanders around aimlessly, stopping here and there. After fifteen minutes she's waltzed round three sides and not really experienced anything, so she decides to take herself in hand and go back and start again from the beginning and do it properly. She hasn't been here for what seems like years – who knows when she might be here again – she owes it to herself to make the most of it. She forces herself to concentrate and after a few more minutes she's so absorbed in what she's seeing that she doesn't even notice the time go by.

When she gets back down to the ground floor, expecting to see Jon and the two girls already waiting impatiently for her beside the fire exit they agreed on as their meeting point, she's surprised to see there's no sign of them. She checks her watch. She's a couple of minutes late. She wonders if they got impatient and headed outside already, and she's about to go and check when she hears a voice shouting, 'Auntie Abigail, look!'

Abi tries to see where the voice is coming from. The ground-floor exhibit is of oversize wooden sculptures, smooth as hazelnuts, with a complex arrangement of stairs carved up the sides of them and through the middle of each one. There are branch-like structures joining them high up with tunnelling through the centre and along the top, and these serve as walkways, probably forty feet up. A hole at the bottom of one nut seems to be spilling people out of it, so she guesses there's some kind of slide inside. As an art exhibit it leaves her cold, but as a climbing frame it's fantastic. People are lining up to climb them, many of them with kids. Abi hears her name being called again and she looks up at the highest branch and there are Tara and Megan waving down at her.

'Come up!' Tara shouts. She looks like she's got her brief nailed down to a T. Something about her strikes Abi as a bit strange, though, a bit unusual, and then she realizes what it is: Tara really is behaving like a child. She's not putting it on to make Abi or her father happy. She actually looks as if she's enjoying herself. Her hair is all messed up and one leg of her (designer) skinny jeans has come untucked from her Uggs. She's not worrying about what she looks like or whether she's being sophisticated enough – she's just having fun.

'OK,' Abi shouts back. She looks at the queue. There's probably a ten- or fifteen-minute wait – they are clearly rationing the amount of people allowed to scale the heights at any one time both, she imagines, to enhance your experience once you do get there and for health-and-safety reasons. Abi can't imagine how much the insurance must cost on something like this – but she doesn't want to lose the moment. So, head down, she works her way along to the front of the queue muttering to people that she's really sorry, but her children have gone up without her and she needs to get up there quick to make sure they don't do anything stupid.

She waves to the girls as she goes as if to prove that there really are children up there who might belong to her. She keeps her fingers crossed that Jon doesn't appear behind them because she wants to keep up the myth that they are alone and in danger of falling off, at least until she's on her way up herself. People roll their eyes, some empathetic, some irri-tated, but no one tells her to stop, so she pushes her way on through and waits to be given the go-ahead to climb on up. Actually, it's fun negotiating the stairs and tunnels – although she still feels none the wiser about what it's saying. She rushes through, not really able to take the time to appreciate it, because something inside her says that this is an important moment. Even with their evening on the Wii, she hasn't seen Tara properly let her guard down and behave like the ten-year-old she is since she arrived, and she wants to encourage her as much as she can.

It takes her a few minutes to find them – there are false starts and wrong turns to go down, all part of the fun – but when she does it's just the two girls who start jumping up and down enthusiastically when they see her.

'Where's your dad?' Abi asks. She's slightly out of breath. She tells herself she really must do some exercise one of these days. She tries not to look over the edge, vertigo rushing up to meet her.

'He went down to take a picture,' Megan says. 'Come on.'

They take a hand each before Abi can object, and pull her towards a large hole that she assumes – at least she's hoping – contains the slide.

'Jump,' Tara commands, so Abi does what she's told and the next thing she knows the three of them are hurtling down the curved wooden surface, round and round the inside of the giant hazelnut, like an inside-out helter-skelter. Both girls are screaming and it's impossible for Abi not to join in. After what seems like an age, they spill out onto the floor laughing, terrified and exhilarated. Jon appears, waving his camera.

'I got it,' he says excitedly, and he shows them on

the screen a picture of the three of them at the moment of exit, mouths open, hair on end. Abi looks like . . . well, she couldn't even begin to explain what she looks like it's so bad. But she doesn't really care – it was fun. Tara and Megan are in fits over the photo and they make Jon scroll back to show Abi the earlier ones they have taken; Jon with Megan, Jon with Tara, the two girls together. They've definitely been having fun while she was gone.

'They've been up there five times,' Jon says as they walk towards the exit on their way to lunch, the girls running on ahead. 'They didn't even complain about having to wait. This was a great idea.'

Lunch is pizza on the river. Abi watches how Jon manages to coax Tara into eating more by ordering side dishes he knows she won't be able to resist and she can't help but think how good a father he is and how it must be alarming to be bringing up two little girls whose mother is trying to teach them by example that all that matters is being skinny and beautiful. Already Tara pays far too much attention to the way she looks. At least Abi, queen of the five-minute-hair-comb, dab-of-concealer-on-the-worst-offenders and mascara routine, thinks so. But today she seems to be staying in her new ten-year-old mode, and she happily wolfs down everything that's put in front of her. Megan, who definitely gets her genes more from her aunt than from her mother, orders way too much and sets about eating it all.

Abi wonders briefly how different life would have been for Phoebe if she had had a father around. Any father, not even one as attentive and caring as Jon. Even Dave's initial rejection of his daughter didn't have to be final. It didn't have to mean the door was shut on him ever having a relationship with her. Deep down Abi had understood. They were young. It was never meant to happen. He'd panicked. So she had always kept tabs on where he was, just in case, and, sure enough, one day when Phoebe was fifteen she had announced that she wanted to know more about her father. It was important to find out everything you could about your ancestry, after all. What if she had a congenital disease that she didn't even know she'd been born with?

Abi had told her all she could and eventually, after much soul searching, Phoebe had written Dave a letter addressed to his work (he still lived and worked in Canterbury; he had turned out not to be very adventurous at all). She had enclosed a potted history of her life along with photographs. 'I don't want anything,' she'd written in her neatest writing. 'I'd just like to get to know you.' A week or so later Abi had received a letter from Dave. He hadn't even had the guts to reply to Phoebe directly. The gist of it was: 'I have my own family now. I don't even know this girl. I can't suddenly start acting like she's my daughter. Please tell her not to contact me again.'

Abi had agonized for days, had finally decided she

had to be honest with her daughter, to let her know what kind of a man her father really was. Phoebe had been devastated. Abi had never forgiven him for that.

'So what did you see?' Jon asks when they've ordered. 'I want to hear all about it.'

'Just the Francis Bacons and the Picassos, really. I like to go for quality not quantity.'

'Is the *Triptych* still there?' he asks, naming one of Abi's favourites. She's impressed. He's obviously been there before.

'It is. That's half the reason I wanted to come.'

They talk about Francis Bacon for a couple of minutes while the girls' eyes glaze over a little. It's obvious Jon has a real love of art. Oops, time for Abi to experience another self-conscious blush. She'd been having so much fun she'd forgotten her newfound awkwardness. She searches around for something else to say, but all her conversation has left the building. Then she remembers the vase that is on her bedside table.

'By the way, is that a Grayson Perry in my room?' Now there's a question she never imagined herself asking anyone.

Jon's face lights up. 'It is! Bought long before he won the Turner, of course. You recognized it . . .'

'I'd recognize his style anywhere.' Abi had assumed that all the art in Jon and Cleo's house was trophy art. Look-at-us-we're-rich art. Maybe she was wrong.

'And I'm guessing that sculpture on the landing is the Chapmans'?'

Jon holds his hands up as if to say, You've got me. 'Again, bought before they were successful. I don't want you thinking we go around spending millions on this stuff.'

'To be honest, if I had millions – which I don't and never will – that's exactly what I'd spend it on.'

'You may have noticed that all the modern stuff is tucked away on the top floor. That's because Cleo hates them. She calls them my monstrosities.'

'So . . . what? You go and sit up there and look at them sometimes?' It breaks her heart to think of all those works of art that she would die for languishing away unvisited. Although the thought of Jon sitting alone on what she has now come to think of as her bed admiring them gives her a shiver of excitement.

That's enough, she tells herself. Focus.

'Sometimes,' he laughs. 'Does that make me sad?'

'I like the vase,' Megan pipes up. 'I've seen a photo of the man who made it. He was wearing a dress.'

'It's a woman, stupid,' Tara says dismissively, safe in the knowledge that as the eldest she must be right. Jon catches Abi's eye and smiles and so, of course, she flushes an attractive bright scarlet. She looks away.

'And what about the stuff downstairs? All those sculptures and paintings in the hall and the living room?'

'Those we agree on. Our taste does meet in the middle sometimes.' He says this with no hint of sarcasm or discontent. Jon is never anything other than

144

loyal where Cleo is concerned. That's one of the reasons Abi has decided that she likes him so much. Perversely she has begun to fantasize about a man largely because she knows he would never reciprocate. And if he ever did then he wouldn't be the man she had been fantasizing about any more, so she'd no longer be interested. Don't ask her to try to analyse what that's all about. She knows it doesn't paint her in the best, most rational light.

Lunch over, they hop on a boat to the Tower and manage to get seats up at the front for the short journey, where both the girls and Abi ooh and aah over the views. To Abi's surprise, every few seconds one of the girls starts yelling out 'spaniel' or 'Jack Russell' and pointing manically at someone walking a dog on the embankment. She looks between them quizzically. She's about to ask what's going on when Jon suddenly shouts, 'Labrador. I win,' and does a kind of victory salute. The girls groan.

Abi laughs. 'What . . .?'

'Top Dog Trumps,' he says, as if that should mean something.

'Right . . .'

Tara and Megan are giggling at her confusion. 'A Jack Russell beats a spaniel because it's cleverer, but a Labrador wins because it's clever *and* gentle,' Megan says by way of explanation.

Abi is none the wiser. 'Who says?'

'We do,' Tara laughs.

'Don't ask,' Jon says. 'We've been playing it ever since these two were little. I think Tara may have made it up. It makes no sense to anyone but us.'

'Alsatian,' Megan shouts, pointing.

Jon smiles at Abi. 'Be my guest.'

She looks around. 'Um . . .'

There's a woman walking a large black thing, but she doesn't know what the breed is.

'There,' Tara says, pointing to a gathering of about five owners and their mutts.

Abi has no idea what she is meant to say. 'Staffy?'

Megan rolls her eyes. 'A Staffy doesn't beat an Alsatian. Only a Border collie beats an Alsatian.'

'Of course,' Abi says, clueless.

'Everyone knows that,' Jon says, laughing.

'Everyone,' Abi says, nodding sagely.

'So do you get it now?' Megan demands.

'No. Definitely not.'

The girls fall about laughing, and Abi joins in. She doesn't know why it's so funny but soon they're all helpless and tears are pouring down her cheeks. She looks at Jon who seems to be finding it as amusing as the rest of them, one arm round each of his girls, unashamedly revelling in a carefree moment with his daughters. She feels a warm rush of something, an overwhelming feeling of family and rituals and in jokes and belonging. She takes a deep breath, looks out at the river, afraid that if she's not careful she might cry for real.

The Tower is packed to the rafters, but Abi still loves it. They go round in a big group with a guide, which ordinarily would drive her crazy, but when it's so busy it seems like the best way to get close to anything. Tara and Megan get caught up in all the gory tales, as does she, and they seem to have completely forgotten that being a tourist is uncool. On the way back, on the bus, Abi gamely shouts out the name of every other dog she sees, generally to a chorus of 'no's and gales of laughter. She still has no idea what the rules are, if indeed there are any – she has an inkling there may not really be rules, that the whole thing might be an elaborate practical joke – but it's fun trying.

By the time they get home, Abi is exhausted. She can't face helping Jon to cook because she's not sure she can keep up the pretence that everything is normal between them for much longer, so she disappears off to lie in her big bath while she waits for dinner to be ready. Thankfully a bit of distance has thawed relations once again and Cleo seems happy to hear all about their day.

'I wish I could have gone with you,' she says at one point, conveniently forgetting that it was her decision not to.

'We can go again – we've got weeks,' Abi says, although she has a sneaking suspicion that had Cleo been there the excursion might not have been such a success.

'Lovely.'

'We tried to teach Auntie Abi Top Dog Trumps,' Megan says excitedly, wanting to recreate the fun atmosphere of the afternoon.

'Oh lord, that stupid game.' Cleo pulls a face. 'It drives me to distraction when they all start shouting out that nonsense.'

Abi had completely forgotten that Jon had promised to go over to see his brother in Shepherd's Bush tonight and that that would mean once the kids had gone to bed it would just be her and Cleo for the rest of the evening. The thought of a long stretch of time alone with her sister fills her with unease. What are they going to talk about? This will be the first time they've been alone together since Abi got there, apart from about twenty minutes the day she arrived and the odd snatched breakfast here and there. She reminds herself that this is what she came for, this is why she's here. It's all about rebuilding her relationship with her sister. Nevertheless she tries to keep Tara and Megan from going off to bed for as long as she can. It should be easy – they always want to stay up longer than they're allowed – but they've worn themselves out and by half past eight they're falling asleep and demanding to be said goodnight to. Well, if all else fails, maybe she can just suggest that she and Cleo watch Ant and Dec together.

She gets hugs from both girls as they head off, and

they both tell her they had a fun day and can we do it again? Abi feels as if she's made real progress with them, and she hugs them back, kisses the tops of their heads and promises them that they will. Now that just leaves her and Cleo. They chat about not much for a while and Cleo asks more about what they did today and whether Abi is having fun and it actually seems like she means it.

Abi tells her again how much the girls loved the Tate and Cleo smiles and says, 'Tara's growing up way too quickly. My fault, I suppose.'

Abi refrains from agreeing out loud, although, of course, she does so in her head. It's an insight that Cleo's even aware of it.

'Jon's very good with her,' Abi says, and then thinks, Oh no. I've got crush symptom number three: mentionitis. I want to say his name out loud. (Number one is the blushing, by the way, and number two the tongue-tiedness, the lack of ability to say anything remotely intelligent. Reaching Mach three is a worry. There's a number four, but don't even ask what that is. There's no way Abi is going to reach number four.)

Remember he's your sister's husband. Don't keep talking about him.

'He's a good father all round –' Oh good, she thinks, I stuck to the plan, then – 'at least, he seems to be.'

'He is. Jonty's very good with the girls,' Cleo says in a way that implies that he's not so good in other ways. Abi can't stop herself.

149

'I've never really got to know him before, I suppose,' she says. 'I mean we never saw much of him and everything . . . but he's a really nice bloke. You're lucky. Both of you, I mean.'

Cleo knocks back the contents of her wine glass. 'We are.'

Don't ask. 'You don't sound entirely convinced. Is something wrong?'

Cleo looks at her. 'No . . . it's all me . . . I just . . .' Abi waits with bated breath. Cleo smiles. 'He's not very exciting sometimes. He's a very devoted father and he's loyal and kind, but . . . well, he used to be more dynamic, more ambitious . . . more fun.'

Abi can't believe what she's hearing. It's so typically Cleo. 'Things have to move on, though, don't they? You have kids now. It's amazing to find a man who's happy to come home and cook for them every night so you don't have to.'

'Amazing, yes, just not very . . . thrilling.'

Abi honestly can't imagine much that would be more thrilling than having a man who she loved who was prepared to leave work early to wait on her and Phoebe every evening. She's not going to say that, though, so she tries to make a joke of it. 'I'm not sure thrilling and having kids can ever go together.'

Cleo takes her at face value, nodding. 'And, between you and me, his business has never turned out quite like I imagined it would. When we first met, he had all these plans, he was chasing all the big campaigns. Now he seems content to make adverts for small-time compensation lawyers and people who buy up your old gold.'

'What's the difference? They all pay, don't they?'

'Well, not so much, actually. He's doing fine financially, though, but that's not the point . . .'

Can Cleo really be this shallow? Abi knows she's self-obsessed and narcissistic and a whole host of other negatives, but she's always believed that there was still a real person under there somewhere. Maybe not. Maybe Caroline is well and truly dead.

'Things change,' Abi says. 'People's priorities shift as they get older . . .'

'I just feel like my life has become very ordinary,' Cleo says, lighting up a cigarette. Me me me.

Well, at least she's opened up. That was what Abi wanted, after all. There was never any guarantee she'd like what was in there. She feels as if she should seize the moment so eventually she says, 'What we were talking about before . . . you being too young to go off like that? I always wonder what Mum was thinking.'

Cleo bristles. 'She wanted to give me the best chance in life. She knew it was what I wanted.'

'I wouldn't have let Phoebe, though. I mean sixteen, it's so young, whatever you think at the time.'

'Well, it paid off, didn't it?'

Abi can feel Cleo's getting irritated, somehow interpreting Abi's comments as a criticism. She has to backtrack. As always happens when they get onto shaky ground, she has to resort to flattery to placate her sister. 'You've had an amazing life, really. You've achieved so much.'

And, as always, when Abi gives a little so does Cleo. 'It's not always been easy. You're right – those early years were tough. Being on my own, away from home . . .'

Abi refrains from saying that moving out was Cleo's choice. We all make bad choices at sixteen. Abi's sure she did, although she can't think what they were, because she spent most of her time trying to be the perfect daughter to make up for the one who had gone off and pretty much forgotten all about their parents. She blew that, obviously, when she became a single mother and jacked in her degree.

Cleo goes through her well-rehearsed and often repeated monologue about her struggles and sacrifices to make it as a top model and Abi says nothing. She's heard it all before. It's a masterpiece in self-justification. In fact, she's heard it many times before, whenever she's tried to steer the conversation round to something more fundamental, more real. It's a revisionist's attempt to paint herself as as much of a victim as the rest of the family and, every time Abi hears it, it makes her angry. This is not what she's here for. She interrupts.

'Cleo, why did you invite me up for the summer? I mean really.'

Cleo stops in her tracks. She is not used to being interrupted. 'I told you, I thought it would be fun . . .'

'What? Me looking after the girls while you run around trying to relaunch your career?'

'Oh, come on, Abi. Not this again. I thought it would be nice to spend some more time with you and then, when the nanny unfortunately walked out, yes, at that point I did think you might be able to help us out of a crisis. Isn't that what families do?'

'Like you'd know anything about family duty,' Abi says before she can help herself, and then immediately wishes she could take it back. Too far too soon.

'Ah, the old "you abandoned us" routine. I wondered when we'd get round to that one.'

Abi takes a deep breath. Counts to ten. Twenty. Sod it, goes for twenty-five. 'No,' she says evenly, once her pulse has slowed a little. 'I didn't mean that. It's just that you say it would be nice to spend some time together, but what time have we spent together since I've been here? You're always out or busy or . . . something.'

She's all too aware that she sounds sulky and immature. Here we go, she's thirteen again.

Cleo gives her a look that could freeze water. 'We're spending the evening together now, aren't we? And look how well it's going.'

Abi blinks back tears. This always happens. Don't cry, for god's sake. 'That's low,' she says.

'Let's face it,' Cleo says, in her stride now. 'You still can't move on. You still can't get over the fact that I made a success of my life and . . . well, you haven't, to put it bluntly. It's easier for you to think you were hard done by somehow than to admit you might have messed up. Is it my fault that you dropped out of college? That you never had a proper job?'

Abi wants to say, 'Actually, maybe it is, because whatever I had done would never have been impressive enough for Mum and Dad. I would never have lived up to their firstborn's greatness. I was young when I had Phoebe. I could have gone back to studying or found myself a rung on the bottom ladder of some career or other — I know that. Other single mums manage. But there never really seemed any point. What was I going to do that could possibly have made an impact?'

She bites her tongue, though. She doesn't want to give Cleo any more ammunition.

'You were the one with the brains. You could have done anything you wanted, but you chose not to bother. That's not my fault.'

'Whereas all you had to do was look pretty and it just all fell into your lap.'

Cleo smiles patronizingly. 'Yes, aren't I lucky? Of course, I never had to get out of bed at four a.m. or half starve myself to be thin enough or shoot for seventeen hours in my underwear in the snow? I just sat around looking pretty and everything, as you say, fell into my lap.'

'You know what I mean.' Abi can see that this argument is pointless. She should just get up and go to bed. It's better all round if they go back to how they usually are, burying their grievances in the sand.

'What? Would you rather I'd said, "No, I can't take you up on your offer — my little sister might be jealous?"'

'I wasn't jealous. It's not like I ever wanted to do what you were doing . . .' She waits for Cleo to say, 'Just as well,' but she doesn't, which, Abi grudgingly supposes, is something. 'I just . . . it was hard, that's all, you going off like that, watching the way Mum boasted about you to everyone . . .' She's run out of steam.

Cleo looks at her pityingly. 'Don't blame me for taking an opportunity, for making something of my life.' She stands up. 'I'm tired. I'm going to have an early night.'

Abi doesn't want the evening to end like this. Despite the fact that she has done nothing wrong except to be a bit needy, a bit sorry for herself — which she would be the first to admit is irritating, but it's hardly a hanging offence — she knows that she has to be the one to try to put things right. She always is.

'I'm sorry, Cleo,' Abi says as Cleo moves towards the door. 'I'm just being stupid. Stay and have another drink. I'll shut up, honest.'

'I'm going to bed. I'll see you in the morning,' Cleo says, and she goes, no doubt to sleep peacefully, secure in the knowledge that it's not her who has ruined everything all over again. Abi feels a desperate need to know that it's all going to be OK or at least to know how bad the damage is. 'Would you rather I went back to Kent?' she says rather pitifully to Cleo's retreating back.

Cleo turns round. 'For god's sake, Abigail, stop being so melodramatic.'

She struts off to plant her flag in the middle of the moral high ground and Abi dissolves into predictable but no less real tears. She hardly ever cries and then only really when she's angry – either at someone else or at herself. This time it's herself. Not because she deserves it more; she's not blind to Cleo's faults. Cleo is rude and self-obsessed and mean. She has no hesitation in saying the most hurtful, most cutting thing she can conjure up at any one time. But it's Abi's fault they had the conversation at all. She pushed it and then she didn't like the result. She has the whole summer to try to rebuild her relationship with her sister and she pushed all Cleo's buttons in one night. Not only that but she made herself look pathetic in the process. Poor old Abi, still envious after twenty-five years. This wasn't how it was meant to go.

11

She's still sitting in the living room, in the same spot, only now in the half dark, when she hears the front door open and close, and she realizes that Jon is home. There's no way she can get to the stairs and out of the way before he spots her so she sits quietly and hopes he'll go straight through to the kitchen or up to the bedroom without noticing that she's there. No such luck. He strides right into the room, switching on all the lights, and then jumps when he sees Abi. She dabs at the creases underneath her eyes as if she can rub out the red marks she knows must be there.

'Jesus, Abi. You scared me. What are you doing sitting here in the dark?'

Abi tries to say something, but it just comes out as a grunt and then she feels the traitorous tears welling up again. She doesn't know what to do to stop them.

Jon looks at her. 'Are you all right? What's wrong? There isn't . . . Something hasn't happened to Phoebe?'

She actually manages a laugh, which, as she's now crying again for real, she's all too aware must look a bit insane. 'No. Everything's fine. I'm fine.'

He sits down on the sofa, near her but thankfully not too close. She's not sure she could handle that at the moment at all.

'Well, clearly you're not. Or is this what passes for fine in Kent these days?'

She sniffs pitifully. Even if she wanted to she doesn't know how she could explain what has happened without it sounding like she was having a go at Cleo. She can't do it. 'I just miss her, that's all. I worry about her.'

He looks relieved. He was clearly worried that it might be something closer to home. 'Of course you do. I can't imagine what I'll feel like when the girls leave home.'

'I should just go to bed. I'll be OK in the morning.' Abi feels as if she should just get out of there. Jon being nice to her is more than she can take right now.

'It's not even ten o'clock,' he says. 'I'll make some tea and then I want you to tell me all about her trip. I want all the details – who she's going with, what her itinerary is. I always think of Phoebe as being such an individual, so independent. I've got no doubts she can look after herself. I'm sure she must be having a great time.'

Abi never really thought Jon had taken any notice of Phoebe at all the few times he's met her, but he's hit the nail right on the head. She's an individual. A strong-minded, independent one-off. If it really was Phoebe she was upset about, then hearing him say this would have made her feel so much better. 'I know,' she says.

'Wait here. I'll put the kettle on.'

She feels like such a fraud. This kind man is putting himself out for her on entirely false pretences. There's no way she can tell him that actually the reason she is crying is because his wife is such an insensitive cow. She'll have to keep up the myth that it's thinking about Phoebe that's got her upset, although, to be honest, she does miss Phoebe desperately, so it won't be too much of a stretch.

A few minutes later Jon brings the tea in and sits back down. 'Right,' he says. 'Start at the beginning. When did she leave?'

Abi doesn't need much of an excuse to talk about Phoebe, so she does as she's told and he asks questions and actually seems to be genuinely interested. The whole thing is quite cathartic, because by the time she has bored him to death with every detail of her teenager's life she's entirely forgotten to be upset about her fight with Cleo.

'It must have been hard,' Jon says, 'bringing her up on your own.'

'We're used to it,' Abi says, a little defensively. 'I had no choice.'

'No. I know. I wasn't criticizing. God, no. Please don't think that. I just mean it's hard enough with two of us. I can't imagine . . .'

'And now she's gone I have literally no idea what

I'm going to do with the rest of my life.' She doesn't know where that came from, but as she says it she realizes it's true. Phoebe will be going to the London College of Fashion once her gap year is over. Working in a library three days a week and then going home to feed the not-yet-existent cat is not going to be enough to keep Abi fully occupied for the next twenty-five years.

'She'll be home. There's the holidays . . .'

She nods. He really must think she's a pitiful specimen. She thinks that and she's her own biggest fan.

'Anyway, there's loads of things you could do. You're still young. You could retrain. Or finish your degree. Or you could go backpacking round the world yourself. Or, I don't know, take up . . . carpentry. The world's your oyster. You'll only have yourself to please and you can do whatever you like.' He says it like it's a positive, a great opportunity, but it just sounds sad to Abi. She doesn't want to be on her own. Even with Phoebe, she's been on her own in one way or another for most of her adult life.

'You could move to London. Cleo would love that.'

Abi can't help it. She snorts.

'What?' Jon says.

She says nothing. This, in itself, seems to be enough of a giveaway.

'Ah. I get it. You and Cleo have had a fight. That's what the tears were really all about.'

Abi gives him ten out of ten for observation. She

doesn't want him to be pissed off that she let him think it was all about Phoebe, though, so she just shrugs and says, 'No. Having a fight with Cleo just made me realize how much I was missing Phoebe, that's all.'

'Nice try,' he says. Abi looks up and he's looking straight at her. She suddenly realizes that lying to him is not as easy as it should be.

'OK. Yes. I had a row with Cleo. But I do miss Phoebe too. I mean it could just as well have been that. I wouldn't want you to think I was making it up . . .'

Jon laughs. 'Calm down. I appreciate that you were trying not to put me in an awkward position by telling me about Cleo. I also know you genuinely miss Phoebe. So let's start from the beginning. Pretend I just came in. Hi, Abi. Oh no, you're crying. What's the matter?'

She can't help but smile. 'I've had a fight with Cleo.'

'Good. Right. What was it about?'

This is the bit she doesn't really want to share. Besides the fact that it will make her sound like a pathetic sap, she really doesn't think it's fair on Jon for her to moan on about Cleo. It's not like he can join in. 'Oh, you know, the usual . . .'

And, of course, she knows it's his sworn duty to defend his wife. 'She's got a lot on her plate at the moment.'

'None of it food probably,' Abi says, and he's polite

enough to laugh. She knows he doesn't want the details and she doesn't want to tell him them, so she just says, 'I don't know why she invited me up, really. I don't feel like she wants me here.'

'She does. She's just not very good at showing it.'

If you can't say something nice then don't say anything, Philippa used to say. 'Mmm . . .'

'She really does care about you, Abi. I know she has a funny way of demonstrating it. And you're good for her. You remind her of . . . I don't know. She's been in her own world since she was sixteen and I guess you remind her that it wasn't always all about her.'

'Except that it was, though. Everything was always about her. What Caroline wanted, what would make her happy. Or at least what wouldn't put her in a strop.'

'Yes, well, she's good at that, I grant you. But it does mean a lot to her that you're here.'

He's bluffing, she can tell. To give him credit, he's trying to say things that he thinks will cheer her up. 'What I'm attempting to say, I think, is that even if Cleo doesn't know it yet having you here will still be good for her.'

Abi grunts. 'Beyond me having solved the nanny crisis, I'm not sure she cares if I'm here or not.'

'Even if she didn't invite you for all the right reasons in the first place . . .'

Ah, so she *is* the unpaid babysitter. She lets it pass.

'. . . she'll soon start to appreciate what she's been missing. Just give her time.'

'I don't know. Maybe I should go home . . . or somewhere,' she adds, remembering that technically speaking she doesn't really have a home at the moment.

'No. It's great having you here.'

He's trying so hard to make her feel wanted that she feels bad. She'd like to be able to tell him that everything is going to be OK, but she just doesn't believe it herself. Not for the first time she finds herself wondering how Cleo can fail to appreciate what a lovely man she's married to. 'It's nice of you to say so, Jon. I appreciate it, I really do, but I'm not sure it's going to work.'

'Give it a chance,' he says. 'I really want you to stay.'

Abi feels a hollow in the pit of her stomach. She knows that the reason Jon wants her to stay so much is because he thinks that somehow a reconciliation with Abi might help keep Cleo grounded if her career takes off again, and might help cushion the fall if – the more likely scenario, let's face it – it doesn't. But just for a moment she allows herself to believe that he's saying those words to her because of her, because he wants her to stay for him.

She looks at him and he's looking at her hopefully. There's nothing flirtatious or inappropriate about his look – of course not, she thinks, this is Jon we're talking about – it's just open and warm and friendly. She notices he has a little patch of freckles underneath his right eye that she's never seen before. They look unbearably cute and it's all Abi can do to stop herself reaching out her hand and tracing them with her finger.

She suddenly realizes that she's spent about an hour talking to him without once blushing or falling over her words. Oh god, that's not healthy. It means she's moved on. She's admitted there was a stage four and it really wasn't good. Well, she thinks, she's there. She thinks she's reached stage four. This is no longer a random trifling crush that makes her colour up and stutter and behave like a giggly schoolgirl. This has moved on from an infatuation that will burn itself out in a few days or weeks. This is serious.

She thinks this might be love.

12

As news goes, Cleo's could not really have been more alarming or come at a worse time. She has got the job. Of course Abi is pleased for her on one level. Hooray. Good for her. Let's celebrate! Oh? It means you're going to New York for two weeks and leaving me – if I don't mind, and how can I refuse? – to look after the girls because although Jon can take a couple of days off he is, of course, right in the middle of a big campaign so naturally it wouldn't be fair to ask him to drop everything. Great! The best part of a fortnight of me and Jon in the house on our own (well, near enough). Jon, your husband, who I have just decided I have fallen headlong in love with. Perfect!

She has been avoiding him since Saturday night. Right after she had her eureka moment, she claimed tiredness and told him she really felt much better now, thank you, and went to bed. He, of course, is oblivious to her inner torment, so he just said goodnight and he was glad she had cheered up a bit and that he'd see her in the morning. Abi barely slept because every time she got close she would drift into half-conscious fantasies that would give Dr Phil a field day, and she had to pull herself together and force more anodyne, less provocative thoughts into her head. Every now and again she chastised herself – he's your brother-in-law, your sister's husband, your nieces' father, grow up, snap out of it. Never mind that her feelings are entirely unreciprocated, that nothing would – or should – ever come of them even if she did allow them to flourish, it's still wrong to be giving them space in her head. They deserve to be shut out.

Sunday she woke up late because, of course, she had been awake for half the night, so she spent the day hiding in her room, feigning exhaustion, venturing down to the kitchen only when she heard the family go out. At dinnertime she dragged herself downstairs before anyone (Jon) could appear at her door with a tray, made uninspired conversation for just long enough for them all to accept that she was fine, nothing wrong, just knackered, and then disappeared back upstairs with her plate.

This morning she still crept downstairs like a commando, determined to ensure that Jon had already left for work before she showed her face. She managed to grab her toast and some coffee from Elena and get back upstairs before Cleo emerged too, and then she waited to hear her sister go out before she came back down. She didn't want to have to see her yet either. Not until Cleo had had a chance to think about the things she'd said.

The summer seemed to have vanished suddenly, to

be replaced by something altogether more wet and windy, so the girls and Abi stayed at home all day and had fun making more outfits from the charity-store bargains and some of Cleo's cast-offs, which were destined for the second-hand shop, and doing fashion shows for each other. Even Tara seemingly enjoyed herself because Megan and Abi both realized early on that the way to keep her happy was to let her tell them what to do. Abi found it surprisingly relaxing, actually.

It's important to her that the girls don't pick up on any kind of atmosphere, so when it gets close to home time she makes sure they're in the living room playing Twister like they don't have a care in the world. When she hears the front door close, she tries to forget how undignified she looks with her backside in the air and her face smushed against the floor, and she laughs extra loudly at nothing. Look at me. I'm just fine. Everything is normal. She waits for Jon to stick his head round the door to announce his arrival and what he's intending to cook for dinner. Instead she is hit by a rush of long-discontinued 'Exotica by Cleo' and then Cleo herself breezes in and, not even acknowledging that they're clearly in the middle of a game, says, 'So, I got the job.'

In the rush of the hysterical little-girly excitement and Cleo's self-congratulation that follows, Abi has only one thought in her head. Cleo is going away for two weeks and leaving her and Jon together. That can't be a good thing. Hold on, when did she become such a master of understatement? That's a fucking disaster.

Cleo has obviously decided that her good news cancels out any memory of their having had a row. She needs an appreciative and envious audience. Allowing Abi to sulk would ruin her moment, so she just acts as if everything is normal, and as if her sister will naturally be as thrilled for her as anyone else.

Abi has realized now that this is another way of her controlling things, of being in charge. Cleo is the one who decides when rows are forgotten and everything is back to normal. It's all in her gift. She never says sorry or even refers back to the bad atmosphere at all, she just switches to all's-fine mode and expects everyone else to do the same.

Abi tries to play along. Cleo is full of New York and where she's going to stay – The Mercer, she hopes, that's where she usually likes to be, opulent but discreet, downtown where all the hip people like to hang out, although there's also a case for saying it's been ruined by the hordes of tourists thronging the streets on a weekend, but still, on balance, it's her preferred haunt – and how Falco told her agent that he picked her first of the five women who are going to be in the ads. Abi asks her what the product is and it seems to her Cleo is a bit vague, telling her it's a moisturizer without actually naming the brand. Maybe she thinks Abi won't have heard of it, living in the sticks and taking as little care of her appearance as she apparently does. As Cleo suspected, there are going to be both TV and print ads, which the girls get very excited about until Cleo tells them that the campaign is just for America so they'll probably never even see it. Several times Cleo refers to herself as the 'face' of the product.

Abi is thankful for the distraction when Jon gets home. All the talk is of Cleo's success. She has to leave for New York next Tuesday week and then she shoots from the following Monday until the Saturday inclusive and flies back overnight arriving home on the Sunday. Nearly two whole weeks for Abi and Jon to play happy families. Well, thirteen days and let's not forget twelve long nights too. Abi has to come up with some things for them all to do, places she can go in the evenings. Displacement activities. At all costs she has to avoid spending long periods alone with Jon, because she's not sure she can trust herself. She flinches when she acknowledges this to herself. However annoying Cleo can be, Abi is certainly not proud of herself for having these thoughts about her sister's husband.

'What's the product again?' Jon says as they sit down to eat. He is making a big show of being delighted for his wife although Abi knows he has mixed feelings.

'Oh, it's a moisturizer,' Cleo says, once again avoiding saying the brand, which strikes Abi as even more odd. Jon is not a stranger to product although happily not the slave to it she once thought he was. He would surely recognize the name even if she wouldn't.

'Yes, but which one?' Jon persists. 'I want to know so that I can boast to people. 'My wife's the face of . . .'

'I can't remember the exact name,' Cleo says. 'It's new.'

OK, Abi's gut tells her something's not quite right. Cleo has told them that the product is a moisturizer so why would she be so deliberately avoiding saying the brand? She shoots a glance at Jon and he studiously avoids looking at her. Both of them have the sense not to push it, though, and Jon skilfully changes the subject. They talk about New York – somewhere Abi has never been and has always wanted to go to – for long enough that the atmosphere shifts and the question of the name of the brand Cleo is promoting is no longer hovering over their heads. She tries to think what the issue might be, but she's stumped. She and Jon, both ambivalent, to say the least, about Cleo the supermodel's rebirth, and, speaking for herself at least, completely traumatized by the idea of Cleo going away and leaving them more or less alone, couldn't be acting with more enthusiasm about her trip if they tried. Abi has no doubt Cleo is aware that they're patronizing her, but so long as none of them say what they're actually thinking it'll all be OK.

A memory comes flooding back. Caroline, aged fifteen or so, defiantly bright-eyed and with a smile plastered on that, even to Abi's twelve-year-old self, looked fake, insisting that the reason she wasn't performing the lead solo in the dancing-school annual show — as she had almost every year Abi could remember — was because she had chosen not to. She had told the teacher to give someone else a chance, she said. Preferably one of the less talented, often overlooked girls with thick ankles and no sense of rhythm. She was blissfully happy to be part of the ensemble.

Philippa had been all over her, telling her she was such a kind and thoughtful girl and that it was wonderful to see that even with all her natural advantages she could still think of others before herself. Caroline accepted the praise graciously, but Abi knew her heart was breaking and, while it annoyed her that Caroline was getting credit where it most definitely wasn't due, she had also felt desperately sorry for her. Why couldn't she just admit to failure, have a good cry about the fact that she'd been passed over and accept the sympathy that would have come flooding her way? What was so wrong with admitting you weren't perfect?

It's a relief that Abi has work on Tuesday because there are just too many strange vibes buzzing round the house for her to feel comfortable there. Not that she's a big believer in vibes, but there's something almost tangible filling up the atmosphere and making it hard to breathe. Richard, witch that he is, says, 'How's things with the handsome brother-in-law?' almost as soon as she walks through the door, so to pay him back she phones Anita, the hormonal Primrose Hill mum who left her back door open for him that time, and tells her that Richard found a pair of sunglasses in the shop that he thinks might be hers and does she want to come in and have a look?

Obviously there are no sunglasses and Abi has simply looked up Anita's number on the shop's computer, because, like all the hormonal mums, she orders things from time to time as an opportunity to remind Richard that he has her details should he ever choose to call. Anita undoubtedly knows that she hasn't lost a pair of glasses, but she's not going to pass up the chance to come into the shop and is no doubt interpreting Abi's call as Richard sending her some kind of coded message. She'll be in at about twelve, she laughs breathlessly.

Round one to Abi.

Does she feel bad that she's misleading Anita like this? Honestly, no. She's a married woman who's trying to cop off with someone on the side. Abi isn't trying to be judgemental – it's more that Anita's willing enough to make a fool of herself whether Abi helps her or not. And to be honest it will have made Anita's day to have been given an excuse to come in.

Abi is really into her work routine now. She buys

coffees and home-made pastries from the little local bakery on her way in (for which Richard thankfully insists she pay herself back out of petty cash, because otherwise she'd be broke) and they catch up with the gossip while they mooch about tidying half-heartedly. The shop is always quiet for the first twenty minutes or so. Abi makes Richard tell her all about the adoring ladies and he quizzes her about Cleo. He's fascinated by Cleo. Although he has never met her, he knows everything about her from the press and he's always asking Abi is this true or did she really do that? He should be gay, really, with his love of gossip magazines. He's desperate for Abi to get her to come into the shop, but she tells him it's unlikely Cleo's going to be looking for a way to spend any extra time with her. She tells Richard Cleo has a job in New York, but when he asks who it's for Abi is as vague about the details as her sister was.

At lunchtime, if it's fine, she takes her sandwich to the park, usually climbing to the top of the picture-book hill to take in the breathtaking views across London. Elena has taken to shoving a packed lunch in her hand on workday mornings, as, Abi imagines, she does for the girls when they're at school.

Abi never knows what's going to be in there and, despite her trying to explain to Elena that she doesn't really eat meat – apart from a very occasional piece of chicken and anything bacon related, oh, and pepperoni and Parma ham and chorizo, anyway, it's complicated – she often finds some kind of bloody-looking scary thing in there. No doubt it's Kobe beef and cost a fortune, but it ends up in the bin either way.

Abi thinks Elena likes her now because, despite her protestations whenever Abi tries to do anything, Elena seems to appreciate the fact that she does try. Unlike half the household who never even remember to say thank you. Not forgetting that Abi has mastered the coffee machine and taken Elena wordlessly step by step through its advanced options. She has also been teaching her English whenever she gets the chance and Elena can already identify most of the objects in the kitchen when Abi points them out. Sometimes Abi can hear her pottering about in there on her own: 'Plate!' 'Knifes!' 'Freege!'

If, like today, Abi remembers to check the sandwich contents before she goes out for lunch and they're not for her (today looks suspiciously like foie gras. It's some kind of pâté anyway and she's not taking the chance) then she has taken to offering to swap with whatever Richard has brought. Richard, in turn, very sweetly, has taken to bringing only veggie or fishy sandwiches on the days when Abi is in, so that she is guaranteed a nutritious lunch and he will be able to enjoy the super-gourmet offering.

Today, of course, there is the added excitement of Anita's visit before lunchtime, and that makes the morning fly by. At five to twelve she breezes in, trying to look nonchalant although she has obviously spent most of the morning doing her hair and make-up.

'Oh god,' Richard mutters when he sees her. Abi smiles at him triumphantly and he says, 'What have you done?'

'Oh, just playing Cupid,' she says innocently.

'I'll deal with you later,' he says as Anita approaches the counter.

Obviously Abi doesn't want Anita to know it was all a ruse because, while Anita's an idiot, Abi doesn't want her to feel as if she's trying to make a fool of her so, before Anita can say anything, Abi jumps in and says, 'Oh, Anita, I'm so sorry. I meant to ring you back to say that the owner of the sunglasses came back for them, so they obviously weren't yours. I'm sorry.'

Richard is looking half confused, half amused. Anita, of course, couldn't give a damn if they had been her glasses and Abi had fed them to a passing dog. She's here for one reason and one reason alone. She twinkles at Richard who smiles back with his best fake charm. Got to keep the customers happy.

'I'm going to go and tidy the reference section,' Abi says, picking the department furthest away from the counter, and moves off, leaving them alone. She's far enough away not to be able to hear what they're saying, but Anita seems to be doing most of the talking. She almost feels sorry for Richard. Anita stays for about twenty minutes, hanging around the till and on to his every word. Abi's starting to think the joke must be wearing a bit thin, so she decides to go to the rescue.

'Don't forget you've got that lunch.'

Richard grabs at the lifeline as if his life depended on it. 'Oh god, yes, the lunch. I'd forgotten. I'd better not be late.' He looks at his watch as if to make the point. Luckily Anita is not so thick-skinned that she doesn't take the hint.

'I should go. Miles is going away on business for a few days and there are all sorts of things I need to sort out. He won't be back till Saturday,' she says pointedly. Richard doesn't leap at that opportunity; he just says goodbye and see you soon, so Anita adds, 'Maybe I'll come in again before the end of the week. After all, I'm going to be so lonely on my own.'

Once she's gone, Abi dissolves into fits. She's taken a bit of a gamble — Richard is her boss, after all — but the one thing she knows above all else about Richard by now is that he can take as good as he gets. He tries to pretend he's cross for about a millisecond and then cracks a smile and says, 'You are so dead.'

He has his lunch hiding out in the stock room at the back because he's so scared he'll bump into Anita on the street and Abi leaves him in peace, but when he comes back in she says, 'Where have you been? I've been so lonely on my own,' in her best Anita voice, which cracks them up again.

Apparently it's all going well with Mrs Baby-buggy

Jogger and Abi has to admit she's pleased for him. If he settled down with a nice woman – she's assuming Mrs BBJ is nice, although she has nothing but Richard's word to go on – and lost the cringy twinkling that he seems to feel obliged to do around any women, he would be perfect new-best-friend material. In fact, scrub that, he *is* new-best-friend material, because he doesn't mind if she laughs in his face when he tries to twinkle at her. Not forgetting there are no other candidates for the role. She loves that he's almost impossible to offend, and that as a boss he's laid back to the point of being almost comatose. Plus she has such a good time at the shop that she forgets about all the drama at the house. And without a doubt she really needs to be able to have a break from it, even if it's just for a few hours a week.

She and Richard have also made the post-work two fishbowls of wine a routine. That is to say they've done it twice now so that counts as a tradition in Abi's book. She feels so proud of herself that she has a little London social life all of her own – well, if you can call two Pinot Grigios with the boss twice a week a social life. Phoebe would be proud, although in a way Abi is glad she's not around to witness it, because any woman over the age of about sixteen is fair game to Richard and she's not sure she could face seeing her daughter fall for his wolfish charms.

This evening he is meeting Stella – Abi has finally discovered this is Mrs BBJ's name – and she's both honoured that he's decided to introduce her and curious to meet the woman who Richard thinks is so special.

She knows Stella the minute she walks in. She looks exactly right to be a match for Richard. Slim, pretty, long straight blonde hair pulled back into a ponytail, casual clothes that scream of money but not in an ostentatious way: 7 For All Mankind jeans and a tight but not too tight cashmere cardigan. She's smiley. She looks nice.

'Hi! You must be Abi.' Stella greets her warmly and sticks out a hand for her to shake. Other women never think Abi is a threat, something she has decided is a response to the way she looks, but which, in actual fact, owes more to her approachable, welcoming demeanour. And, of course, in this case she's most definitely not. In fact, she never is. She would never knowingly steal another woman's man – most importantly her sister's, she reminds herself, as she does now several times a day. Don't flirt with him; don't let him guess how you feel – but just once in a while she wishes everyone wouldn't write her off so quickly. Stella has all the confidence of knowing that she has won the looks lottery, but she's so open and friendly that it's impossible not to like her. While Richard gets the drinks, the women chat away happily. Abi asks Stella about her kids (yet again the trusty old default conversation with women she knows are mothers) and Stella tells her about her two little boys who are three and eighteen months.

'You're a single mum too, aren't you?' she says, so Abi is able to bang on about Phoebe, her favourite topic, but she tries not to bore Stella to death. Stella asks about Phoebe's dad, so Abi gives her the short version and Stella tells her that her boys' dad buggered off with the au pair a year ago.

'How can you . . . I mean isn't it hard . . .' Luckily Stella realizes where Abi is going and puts her out of her misery.

'Trusting another man?'

Abi nods.

'Definitely, but the way I figure it is that if I don't give someone else a chance, then I'll end up on my own forever.'

'Tell me about it,' Abi says, and she tells Stella how she has been single pretty much for the past eighteen years. Stella is gobsmacked as everyone always is when Abi admits to that. 'I've been out with people,' Abi tells her. 'I'm not that sad. I just haven't had what you'd call a real relationship.'

'Oh god,' Richard says when he appears with the drinks and catches the tail end of their conversation. 'Slagging off men already – that's not a good sign.'

Abi has hardly been able to look at Jon since she found out that Cleo was going away. She's sure he must think he's done something terribly wrong. He probably assumes that she resents him for pushing her to admit that she and Cleo aren't getting on. She hopes that's what it is anyway, and not that he thinks she has taken a dislike to him for some random reason. Since Phoebe's dad Abi has only reached stage four once before – at least she thought she had for a while although it didn't turn out to be the case – and that was with someone she knew through the library.

He worked in social services and he used to bring a party of OAPs from a local home for the elderly down to browse around every few weeks. Abi used to make him coffee and chat to him while he waited. Of course she blushed and stuttered for a few weeks and then, just as with Jon, one day that all miraculously went away and in its place was something far more real and scary. He was divorced, he seemed to like her, there was nothing stopping her making a move, really, except fear of rejection and the fact that Phoebe was about eleven at the time and she couldn't imagine taking someone home and introducing him as her boyfriend. And what if she did and Phoebe got to like him and then it all went wrong? So she did nothing about it except palpitate a bit dramatically every time he came in.

Eventually her infatuation disappeared as quickly as it had arrived – Abi thinks around the day when he happened to mention that he was a member of the local church choir at the exact same moment she noticed he was wearing novelty socks with Bart Simpson's face on them. She was horrified that she might have made a huge mistake, might have somehow given away her feelings and that he might actually have realized she fancied him. So she dealt with it in the most mature way that she knew how. She started avoiding him and more or less blanking him if they did come face to face. She can still remember the confused look he gave her the first time she told him she was really busy and didn't have time to chat. She's the first to admit she has all the emotional maturity of a fifteen-year-old when it comes to relationships.

Luckily the focus is all on Cleo's trip for the moment. The girls want to hear the details of where she is going and what she's going to be doing over and over again and that suits Abi just fine. Let her have her moment. Abi is assuming that while Cleo is away Jon will take the days off work to do his fatherly duty when she is otherwise engaged at the bookshop, but she doesn't like to ask. She can't even begin to think about what they'll do in the evenings and at the weekends.

The house seems to breathe a bit of a sigh of relief when Cleo leaves to catch her plane late on the following Tuesday morning, and although the kids get caught up in a teary goodbye they're fine five minutes after she's gone. Abi has swapped her days, working yesterday in lieu of today to allow her to do childcare once Cleo has left and she ferries them to their self-improving classes (Megan: French conversation; Tara: drama and improvisation) and then she has a delicious afternoon all to herself pottering around doing not much and hoping that the evening won't come round too soon. If at all.

If she had any friends up here, she could arrange a night out and then just tell Jon he is on his own. But there's only Richard and he would interpret an invitation to anything more formal than two drinks in the pub as Abi asking him out on a date. Maybe she could go out with him and Stella. She's decided she really likes her. For all her intimidating good looks she seems down to earth and funny. Easy to talk to. When Abi left them to it in the pub the other night, they made all the right 'we must do this again' noises, but she knows that with her two children Stella doesn't get to go out that much so it would feel like an imposition to muscle in on one of her and Richard's evenings together.

She could take herself off to the cinema, but she'd feel like a bit of a saddo on her own and, even if she did, that would still only be one night out of twelve. She just needs to get a grip, keep her head down and her emotions in check, and try to get through the next two weeks unscathed.

13

So here they all are. Abi, Jon, Tara and Megan, sitting round the kitchen table, all chatting away as if it's the most normal thing in the world, which Abi imagines it is to the other three. Actually it's really just the kids who are chatting. Jon and Abi are interjecting occasionally, but there's not much that would pass as conversation flowing between the two of them. Abi doesn't mind. As well as feeling relieved that they are filling the silence, she has come to love her nieces' ceaseless banter. Tonight Tara is trying to fill them in on an incident that happened at her drama class involving the teacher and the mother of one of the other girls who had insisted on staying to watch the lesson.

'So she just sat down on one of the chairs in the corner even though Mrs McClusky never lets anyone stay and watch.'

'Which one is she again?' Megan chips in.

'I told you. She's Tamara's mum.'

'Which one's Tamara?'

Tara rolls her eyes. 'You don't know her. Anyway, she's sitting there then –'

'Is she the one who broke her wrist?' Megan always likes to know the details.

'No. Shut up, I'm trying to tell a story.'

'Sorry. But is she? Or was that Ruby?'

Tara ignores her. 'And then her mobile rings right in the middle of Amy reciting her monologue that she's got to do for her Guildhall exam. Can you imagine? Mrs McClusky nearly exploded.' Tara pauses, waiting for a reaction. Abi sees a smile creep across Jon's face.

'Which one is Amy?'

'Dad!' Tara says, but she smiles as Jon had clearly known she would.

He tries to keep a straight face. 'Is she the one with the cross eyes or the one with thirteen fingers?'

Tara can't help herself, she bursts out laughing. 'Stupid,' she says.

Abi watches them happily, loving the easy atmosphere despite her own anxieties. She is dreading the moment when the girls go to bed, and she's tempted to tell them they can stay up all evening and watch DVDs. They'd love her for it, there's no doubt, but she has a feeling Jon might overrule her.

Before she knows what she's doing, she finds herself wondering what her and Jon's children would look like and she realizes that actually Tara and Megan could be them. She must have the genes buried inside her somewhere that would pass on long legs and skinniness to Tara just as they somehow have circumvented Cleo and Jon and passed her own looks straight down to Megan. Just as Phoebe has inherited her physicality from her aunt. Actually it makes Abi wonder what Phoebe's dad brought to the table. He was tall, but she had tall in her family anyway. He was dark, but so is Cleo; funny, but Abi firmly believes Phoebe gets her sense of humour from her. She doesn't remember him having much to contribute in the brain department despite the fact that he went to university.

And then it hits her: the kink in her nose. Phoebe has this tiny bump on the bridge of her nose that lifts her face from picture-perfect pretty to – in Abi's humble opinion – strikingly beautiful. She scans through her family in her head – Mum, Dad, Cleo, random aunts and uncles she might have met once. Not a nose bump between them. Her own nose is straight and blunt. Not bad, not a horror, just ordinary once she grew into it. Jon's is similar, although longer and more masculine, of course. There, she tells herself, if you had children with Jon, they wouldn't be as adorable as Phoebe. There's no way they would have the nose bump. She tries to hang on to this inane piece of rationale, as if remembering that might save her from making a fool of herself by taking off all her clothes and throwing herself at him.

When they finish eating, she asks the girls to help her fill the dishwasher and to her surprise they don't complain – they just do it – and then they demand that they all play on the Wii Fit, which seems like a fairly harmless way to pass the time, so she agrees readily. Actually, boxing the life out of the object of your unrequited crush is quite a fun way to spend an evening. They box, they bowl, they play tennis and then Abi insists they box some more. In the end Tara and Megan actually volunteer to go to bed they're so exhausted, so Jon goes and tucks them in, and Abi decides, what the hell, and breaks out the Pouilly-Fumé.

She's still out of breath when he comes back in and sweating a little, not her best ever look. She hands him a glass of wine.

'One more match?' he says. 'I was holding back before. Now I'm really going to thrash you.'

They are ridiculously competitive. After each bout, the victor parades around the room, hands aloft, rubbing their triumph in the face of the loser. It's the most tiring thing Abi has ever done. If ever there was a perfect displacement activity, this is it, because she has no energy left to think about how much she thinks she is in love with Jon; she just wants to win.

Five matches later (Abi having lost three to two) she is lying on the floor in need of oxygen and laughing so much she's making herself cough. Jon flops on the sofa, panting.

'Bowling,' Abi says. 'Best of five.'

He groans and drags himself back up. 'You're worse than the girls.'

They play till at least eleven o'clock. Abi barely even notices the time go by. Just as they're packing up, Jon's mobile rings and she gathers it's Cleo letting him know that she's there safely and, by the sounds of it, not very happy with her hotel which is clearly not The Mercer. She half listens in for a few moments, but then it seems like a good time to make her escape, so she waves goodnight at Jon and practically runs up the stairs and shuts herself in away from temptation.

OK. One evening down. Eleven to go. She gets into bed and turns out the light, but she can't get to sleep for ages because her head is filled with all sorts of thoughts that it ought to be illegal to have about your brother-in-law. She tries to replace him with her default fantasy objects: George Clooney, Johnny Depp, that bloke off *Top Gear* who's not even the one everyone else thinks is good-looking, but it's hopeless. Every time the fantasy Abi in her head (the one with no stretch marks, much longer legs and unerring self-confidence) turns round there's Jon beating a path to her door. In the end she just succumbs. Sod it. Why fight what you can't change?

Wednesday starts off quite well. Abi keeps out of the way till Jon has left for work and then she ferries the girls around in the car. She's getting quite good at driving in London now. She can be as aggressive as the rest of them, although when Megan shouts 'bastard' at an old man who nips into a parking space just before them Abi realizes that she should probably try to rein herself in a bit. And, of course, she laughs when she asks Megan not to use language like that again, which completely cancels out any authority she might have earned.

'Bastard,' Megan shouts happily to someone who cuts them up on Regent's Park Road.

'Megan,' Abi says, 'it's not funny, really. Don't.'

'You do,' Megan says, and of course she has a point.

'Yes, but I'm a grown-up. I'm allowed. Please don't use language like that or your mum and dad will be really cross with me.'

'What if she doesn't ever say it in front of them?' Tara pipes up.

Is this acceptable? Negotiating about how and when to swear with a seven- and a ten-year-old? It must be better than nothing. 'Or anyone else. No teachers, no parents of your friends.'

Megan contemplates this. 'OK. I'll only ever say it in front of you and Tara.'

'What about me?' Tara whines. 'I want my own word.'

Great. 'Fine. Which word do you want?'

She thinks. 'Shit-head. That's what dad always calls people when they annoy him.'

Abi can't help it; she laughs.

'That's two words,' Megan is saying. 'That's not fair, is it, Auntie Abi?'

'It's one phrase – it counts. OK, here's the rules. Megan may call people bastards, Tara may call people shit-heads, but only in this car and only in front of me and each other. And not so loud that the people in the other cars hear and I get beaten up. Agreed?'

'Agreed,' they both say, and then they all spend the rest of the day arguing about whether everyone they come across is a bastard or a shit-head. Abi is glad she's teaching them valuable life skills. She has found herself warming more and more to Tara. Of course she loves her, Tara is her niece, her flesh and blood, but she hasn't always found spending time with her that easy. She's usually so busy worrying about what she looks like or what the socially acceptable thing to say is that she's not actually much . . . fun. It might just be that she's relaxing with Abi because they're together all day, but she seems to be loosening up a bit, becoming more like a normal child all the time. Maybe this time away from watching her mother pretending to eat and discussing everyone's weight and dress sense as if that was the only thing about them that mattered might do her the world of good. And if allowing her to call all their near neighbours shit-heads can help her down that path then maybe Abi is a marvellous auntie after all.

There's no avoiding it. There's another evening coming up. With her newfound feeling of solidarity with the girls giving her courage, Abi dares to suggest that they might actually help with the preparations for dinner and, miracle of miracles, they agree. Tara MacMahon

Attwood doing manual labour. Where will it end? So they all spend an hour in the kitchen together chopping and stirring and generally, honestly, having a good time.

At one point Abi looks at Jon showing Megan how to make the dressing for the salad and she feels a lump the size of an orange well up in her throat. He's so patient with her – because, truthfully, she's not that interested – and he somehow manages to make mixing oil, soy sauce, mustard, honey and sesame seeds fun. Megan is obviously the daddy's girl of the two, but even Tara insists on having a go at making her own version and, in the end, they have a salad-dressing-off in which Abi is the judge. They're actually both pretty rank because the girls insist on adding their own special ingredients, which, Abi suspects, are Marmite in Megan's case and half a bottle of vinegar in Tara's (Abi has been banished from the room for five minutes while they finesse their offerings), but she exclaims over their deliciousness and then suggests they mix the two together because there's no way to choose between them.

Jon looks at her, eyebrows raised. 'Really?'

'Why not?' she says, smiling. 'But, I know, let's have it on the side like they do in America.' She's basing her knowledge of the way they eat in America on *When Harry Met Sally*, by the way. Everything on the side. 'That's how your mum'll be having it, if she's having a salad.'

Jon grabs that idea quickly before it can be vetoed. 'Great idea. I'll get a jug.'

Just as they're about to sit down his mobile rings.

'It's Mum,' he says, and Tara grabs it and answers.

While she and Megan take turns to burble away, Abi says to Jon, 'Have you spoken to her today?'

He nods. 'Only for a couple of minutes. She was in the middle of a make-up test. It seemed to be going OK.'

She makes the appropriate face. Neither Jon nor Abi have mentioned the anonymous-moisturizer issue since it first raised its ugly head, but she's pretty sure they both know there's a strong possibility this is not the dream job Cleo was trying to make out it is. Abi has decided it must be a downmarket brand. A cheap, supermarket-available face cream that only Cleo would care didn't have a designer label or cost £200 a jar. Made from actual chemically proven ingredients rather than enhanced with acai berries or sea water or puppy's tears. It'll be an overblown sense of her own importance that's preventing her from owning up to the brand. Abi wonders how honest Cleo is being with Jon, whether she can really admit even to him what the real story is. She doubts it some-how. Or, even if she is, Abi isn't sure she and Jon will make it real by acknowledging it to each other. She waits to see what he'll say next.

'She's feeling better about the hotel, by the sound of it. It's somewhere in Midtown. Not exactly The Mercer, but at least it's close to where they'll be shooting. There are four other models, all British. She didn't really say much about them.'

'Right.' She doesn't really know what else to say. Maybe that's the issue. Maybe Cleo is not *the* face of whatever it is, but she's *one* of the faces. That would certainly damage her ego.

They both sit there in silence for a moment listening to the girls gabbling on about what they've been up to. Then Tara hands the phone over to Jon.

'She wants to talk to you.'

'Hi, love.' The tender tone he adopts gives Abi a jolt and a much-needed reality check. He loves her. Of course he does. She's his wife and even if she is a bit of a nightmare she's the woman he chose. Out of all the women in the world, he wanted her, faults and all. And he still does. And, anyway, so what if he didn't love her any more, she chastises herself. He's still married to her, he's still Abi's sister's husband. She's never stolen a man off anyone. She's hardly going to start with her own sister. She reminds herself: I am starved of male company, I am lonely because my only daughter has just left home, of course I would fall for the first man to be nice to me, it's textbook. It means nothing. Get a grip, she tells herself for the twentieth time.

Jon takes the phone into the living room and Abi's relieved. She doesn't want to hear him whispering sweet nothings. She wraps his plate in foil and puts it in the still-warm oven then gets on with eating with the girls while they tell her what Cleo has been up to. She's glad to hear Cleo is giving them a rosy picture of the trip and she lets them witter on excitedly about how she can see the Empire State Building from her hotel window and how it's nearly a hundred degrees outside, but inside she's shivering because the air-conditioning is so strong. By the time Jon's off the phone they've pretty much finished eating.

'How's she getting on?' Abi asks him as she starts clearing away. Megan jumps up to help her and then, completely unbidden, Tara joins her. Abi double takes.

'Great,' he says. 'She's having a good time.'

She can't tell whether this is really the case or whether he is just saying so for the sake of the kids, so she just says, 'I'm glad,' and leaves it at that.

The kids are full of questions about what else Cleo said and has she bought them any presents yet, so Abi sneaks off to the living room and watches *The One Show* although she's only half concentrating. She needs a plan for this evening. She's not sure she can insist they play on the Wii again; he'll think she's some kind of arrested-development overage teenager. Maybe they could watch a DVD. That's got to be harmless. She hunts around a bit, but she can't find evidence of any and then she remembers that Cleo and Jon have a 'cinema room' in the basement. She hasn't been down to see it, but the idea of the two of them closeted away in a tiny dark room suddenly doesn't seem like such a good idea. She's just planning her escape upstairs – she can claim she wants to write a long email to Phoebe – when the three of them pile in and the girls sit either side of her on the sofa and insist that they all watch last night's *EastEnders* together. They fill her in on all the plot points, half of which contain situations she's not entirely sure a ten- and a seven-year-old should even know about, let alone be watching, but at least it fills both the time and the silence and, to be honest, by the end of the episode she wants to know what happens next. She finds herself asking when it's on again. It's like crack.

When it's over, Jon starts making noises about baths and bed, and Tara and Megan whinge and complain as usual. Sometimes Abi thinks they just do it because they think they should. Phoebe was the same. She would fight to stay up past her bedtime even when Abi could see she was falling asleep standing up. She finds herself starting to wonder what Phoebe is up to now and, as always, that makes her start to panic about all the awful things that might have befallen her, so she decides that she will go and write an email, after all, in the hopes of getting a swift and happy response.

But when she stands up to go Jon says, 'You're not going up yet, are you?' and when she tells him that she is he says, 'Stay and have a glass of wine first. I feel like a saddo drinking on my own,' and Abi finds herself agreeing to have 'just the one'.

'I'm a bit worried about Cleo,' he says once the girls

have gone upstairs and they have a full glass each. 'She's saying she's having a great time, but I'm not sure I believe her. She sounds a bit manic, like she's a bit too keen for me to think it sounds amazing.'

Abi doesn't want to be the one to bring up the fact that the job sounds a bit rubbish, so she just says, 'Well, it must be a bit strange getting back into it after all these years. She probably just needs some time to adjust.'

'Honestly, though,' he says, 'she still hasn't said what the brand is. I mean . . .'

He tails off, never quite saying what he does mean.

'I know. But it's a moisturizer, they're shooting in New York, how bad can it be?'

'I just hope she's not heading for a massive disappointment. I knew I should have tried to talk her out of it.'

'No one could have done that, I don't think. When Cleo wants something, she's going to have it no matter what anyone else says. She's always been the same.'

Jon fills her glass up again. There goes her 'just the one' resolution. 'What was it like for you growing up?' he asks. 'It must have been strange . . .'

Abi has never really unloaded all her angst and resentment about her and Cleo's shared past onto anyone. Philippa and Andrew, of course, wouldn't have wanted to hear it and, anyway, they share as much of the blame as Cleo does, really. She's told friends some of it, but because none of them know Cleo they can never really understand, and Abi usually ends up sounding as if she's feeling sorry for herself because her sister became a big success and she didn't.

She can remember droning on to an ex-boyfriend once when she'd had too much to drink, but, after he got over the initial excitement that the great Cleo was actually her sister, his eyes glazed over and, to be honest, it was just as well, because when she sobered up she was mortified about the things she'd been saying. It seemed incredibly disloyal to be slagging her sister off to someone she didn't even know that well. Thinking about it, that might have been the reason she stopped calling him and turned her phone off for a few weeks. She wasn't that keen on him anyway. He was another one of her safe but dull options.

But Jon would understand. He knows Cleo even better than Abi does. No, make that much better than she does, these days. He knows how she turned her back on her family. He must have witnessed it. And he knows exactly how annoying and selfish and hurtful she can be. On the other hand, he loves her, despite all those things. He's her husband. It's his job to be loyal to her. Still, she can't stop herself. Maybe it's the wine but it suddenly seems really important to Abi that Jon understands things from her point of view.

'It was,' she says. 'Cleo, well, Caroline, was the focus of everyone's world. It was hard to compete.'

'That must have been tough when you were a teenager.'

'You could say that.' Before she can even stop herself she's telling him how close she and Caroline were before Caroline got spotted and how much it hurt when she just disappeared out of Abigail's life one day. She tells him how Philippa and Andrew thought the sun shone out of Caroline and, despite the fact that she barely even remembered to phone them from one week to the next, they always acted as if she was the perfect daughter. How there didn't seem much point Abi even attempting to do anything interesting with her life because she couldn't hope to impress.

Jon listens to it all intently, head on one side. (Abi loves how he does that head-on-one-side thing. It makes you feel as if he thinks you're the most interesting person he's ever met and he wants to be sure he's heard every word. God help him if she is. He needs to get out more.)

'You'd have been doing it for you, though. It's not a competition.'

She knows he's right. She realized when it already seemed to be too late that the only person she was punishing by not pursuing a career was herself. OK, so Philippa and Andrew wouldn't have thought that whatever she did was as boast-worthy as Caroline's career, but so what. It was nothing to do with them. On the other hand, Abi can't bear to be reminded of the fact that she is the architect of her own un-remarkableness. She can think it about herself, but she definitely doesn't want anyone else to think it about her.

'You wouldn't understand,' she says a little petulantly. 'You had to be there.'

'It wasn't meant as a criticism.' Abi can see that he's nervous he's upset her. 'And you're right. I can't possibly understand what it was really like. Ignore me.'

'No. It's me. I get all defensive when I feel put on the spot. It's stupid. And the truth is I can't blame Cleo for the way my life has turned out . . .'

'Is it really that bad, though?' Jon says. 'I mean you've got Phoebe. You've got a job you like. Not everyone has to fight their way to the top of a career ladder. There are other things that are just as important.'

'That's easy for you to say. Mr Successful Advertising Agency.'

'It's a middling run-of-the-mill agency that does pretty well with very unexciting clients. Onehitcomparison.com is about as glamorous as we get. And I may be the boss, but we don't exactly rake in a fortune. And, honestly, these days it's just a job. It's not exciting, it's not particularly challenging, but it's what I do. I'm just grateful we're still afloat and that we might actually manage to see out the recession. If we're lucky. We're not exactly McCann's.'

'Cleo always made it sound like you were.'

Jon rubs his temples with his right hand. He sighs. 'I know.'

'I thought you were a big shot,' she says, and she smiles.

Luckily he laughs. 'I do OK. I mean by a lot of people's standards I do really well. Just not so well as she likes people to think, I guess. Honestly, it gets a bit embarrassing when I hear her talk about my business. It sounds like she's talking about someone else. She doesn't do it with our friends, obviously, because they'd know she was exaggerating, but people like your mum and dad . . .'

Now it all starts to make sense. 'Is that why you hardly ever used to visit with her?'

He nods. 'I didn't know how to deal with it. So I thought that if I wasn't there then she could boast about me as much as she liked and I wouldn't have to know about it. Actually, I used to feel like I was a bit of a letdown to her, because she obviously needed you all to think I was something I wasn't.'

'Well, the good news is that if she didn't marry you for your money and status it must have been love. Either that or you're a con artist and she thought you were something you weren't.'

'I think she thought I was going to be the next Charles Saatchi.'

'Well, you do like modern art and you don't seem to go out much.'

He gives her a look that says 'very funny'.

'Honestly, I probably told her that was my plan. I can't remember. I just know that then we had the kids and she was still working all the time and other things started to seem more important.'

'I'm sure she appreciated you being such a hands-on dad.' (Abi knows she would have. Oh god, she would have found a million ways to show him her appreciation.) 'After all, it would have been much harder for her to work if you hadn't been.'

'Mmm. Maybe.' He doesn't sound convinced and he's right. His success or the lack of it must have been of crucial importance to Cleo, otherwise why did she go on about it so much? Abi feels bad for him. She wonders if Cleo has been making him feel how she's made Abi feel all these years: inadequate and unworthy. And suddenly the best thing to do to rid herself of her guilty crush seems to be to make sure that he is as secure in his relationship with Cleo as he can be. The happier they are the less likely it is that she is going to keep fantasizing about him and her. At least that's the plan.

'Well, she was always saying she did,' she lies. Rather convincingly if she says so herself.

Jon smiles at her. He has a kind of lopsided closed-mouth smile that always makes him look as if he's thinking of something funny and maybe just a bit naughty. Not that it's important. Not that it makes her want to throw herself across the room at him. 'Nice try,' he says. OK so maybe her lying skills aren't quite as accomplished as she'd thought.

She decides it's not fair to patronize him too much.

'All right, she didn't, but she should have.' She actually blushes when she says this. Great, so the blushes are back. She doesn't know what that means. Maybe this is Mach five. A level never before attained. A level Abi didn't even know existed.

'You're way too nice to be an Attwood,' he says, and she doesn't know if she's imagining it, but she thinks he holds her gaze just a fraction longer than is strictly necessary (according to the brother-/sister-in-law etiquette code as just devised by her). His eyes, in case anyone was wondering, are a dark soulful brown, which, Abi feels, is a surprising and not unattractive contrast to his dirty-blond hair. Just in case you wanted to know. Which you might. She forces herself to look away.

'I'm exhausted,' she says, nearly leaping out of her seat. 'I should go to bed.'

14

Despite the fact that the shop doesn't open till nine thirty she is sitting on the step with two coffees and a bag of pastries at quarter to. It's not even a nice enough day to go for a walk in the park, but there's a tiny stripy awning she can shelter under and it's preferable to being at home as she now laughingly refers to Jon and Cleo's house. Jon has taken a day off work to look after the two girls and it's best Abi is well out of the way.

She couldn't get to sleep for what seemed like hours last night thinking about that look that he gave her. On the one hand thrilled, excited, her heart pounding: he likes me. On the other horrified and a bit sickened. Has she given off way more signals than she ever intended and unwittingly pushed him into feeling something he most definitely shouldn't be feeling?

Or maybe it was just the wine. She's getting quite a taste for wine these days. She's thinking maybe she might become an alcoholic when she grows up. That'd give her life some purpose. They'd had three big glasses each, about a bottle and a half between them, by the time Abi realized she had to get out of there fast or live to regret the consequences. She still finds it unlikely, though. Jon doesn't strike her as the kind of man who would just randomly flirt once he's had a few. He takes his marriage too seriously.

His marriage TO MY SISTER, she says to herself over and over again.

Oh god, she's hoping he hasn't picked up on the vibes or the hormones or whatever it is that must be positively oozing out of her whenever she's around him. Please let it just be the drink or a moment of madness or a complete misinterpretation by her of what was meant as an ordinary run-of-the-mill glance.

That's it, she tries to convince herself. She's so besotted that she's reading meaning into things where there was none intended. She's transferring her feelings onto him and imagining that a look must mean something because if she had gazed at him for that long it certainly would. That comforts her for about five seconds and then she pulls up the video of that look from her memory bank and plays it back to herself in slow motion and she knows, she just knows, that however much she might wish she was, she's not making it up.

After work, Stella joins Richard and Abi in the pub for their usual two drinks. Abi's glad. She likes having Stella around. She tries to make her drinks last as long as possible, which results in the other two sitting there for ages with empty glasses while they wait for her to finish her second. They're about to call it a night and leave when Stella suggests they might as well have another one because they don't have plans and, although Abi doesn't want to be a gooseberry, she accepts without hesitation.

'I don't feel like going home yet, to be honest. It's a bit awkward.'

'Ah,' Richard says, sitting back in his seat.

'No, not "ah". There's no "ah" about it. It just isn't my house and sometimes I feel a bit in the way.'

'Isn't Cleo in the States this week?' Richard remembers every piece of Cleo news Abi tells him. She really must learn to keep her mouth shut.

'Yes, but . . .'

'Ah.'

'OK, what am I missing?' Stella says, looking from one to the other. 'I'm clearly not getting the subtext.'

'Nothing,' Abi says defensively.

'Abi has the hots for her brother-in-law,' Richard announces triumphantly.

'No –' Abi starts to say, but he's not finished.

'You only have to mention his name and she blushes.'

'You don't even remember his name.'

'And this week her sister is away working, so I imagine it's a bit like a Tennessee Williams play in their household at the moment. All meaningful looks and the air full of simmering passion.'

If only he knew how right he was.

'Abi!' Stella says, and Abi says, 'He's talking rub-bish. Just for a change.'

'And, actually, I do remember his name. It's Jon. And do you know why I do? Because you never stop talking about him.' He smiles at her. Got you.

'Honestly, Stella,' Abi says, ignoring Richard, 'he's exaggerating. I'm just surprised to find I like Jon, that's all. I thought I didn't.'

'But you're not about to jump him while your sister is out of the picture?'

'No! Of course not!'

'Good,' Stella says. 'I didn't have you down as a husband stealer.'

'Absolutely, a hundred per cent not,' Abi says, and she means it.

Richard smirks. 'But you wish you could, don't you?'

'OK, you. Enough,' Stella says. 'Go and get us another drink.'

'Don't mind him,' she says once he's out of ear-shot and on his way to the bar. 'You know what he's like. He's only teasing.'

Abi forces a laugh. 'Oh, I know. It takes more than that to wind me up.' In fact, she feels a real need to confide in someone, to talk over how she's feeling and what she's going to do about it, but, much as she likes Stella, this is only the second time she's met her, so she thinks that would count as too much too soon. There's no one she can talk to who would understand.

She doesn't understand herself. So she tells Stella how she gets her own back on Richard by giving the hormonal ladies hope, and Stella's laughing so much that when he comes back from the bar he asks what's so funny.

'Nothing,' Stella says innocently.

'You,' Abi says to him, and gives him a big cheesy grin.

In the Ladies she rattles off a quick text to Jon – 'Out for the evening so eat without me' – and then agonizes about whether or not to put a kiss on the end. She puts a kiss on the end of pretty much every communication she sends. It's just a habit and she never even thinks about whether the person on the receiving end even registers it or not. It comes from having a teenage daughter who covers everything, including her homework and probably her A-level exam papers, with hearts and kisses. This time, though, the innocent little x seems to be laden with subtext. Abi puts one on, takes it off again, puts it on, takes it off. Eventually she decides it's better without. She can't imagine Jon sprinkles kisses liberally on his texts and she doesn't want him trying to analyse her meaning.

In the end the three of them have such a good time that she forgets about Jon. The five glasses of wine help. Both Richard and Stella are such good company that Abi's cheeks ache from laughing by the time they get up to go. She doesn't realize how drunk she is feeling until she gets out into the fresh air and starts to totter round the corner to the house. She offers up a quick thank you that they went to the closest pub to the house and not the one they usually frequent all the way up Haverstock Hill. It's a nice drunk, though. A happy, how-bad-can-it-be drunk.

Luckily she finally got around to getting herself a key cut, so she doesn't have to ring the bell and disturb everyone, but she can see the light in the living room is on, which means that Jon must still be up. She fannies around trying to get the key in the lock quietly, which takes her about four attempts, and then she tiptoes heavily through the hall and bumps straight into a table, knocking a lamp – a very expensive lamp, she has no doubt – onto the floor. She scrabbles around trying to pick it up, cursing her lack of coordination. She's not so drunk that she's unaware of her state, unfortunately, so she is completely conscious of how ridiculous she looks, flailing around on the floor, when she looks up and sees Jon standing in the living-room doorway, watching her with an amused look on his face.

'Good night?' he says, and he picks up the lamp, which has, thankfully, not broken. Abi scrambles to her feet.

'Lovely,' she says. 'We went to the pub.'

He laughs. 'Now, how did I guess that?' He takes her arm and steers her into the living room. This isn't right. She's not meant to be sitting in here with him late at night, five glasses of wine down. That seems like asking for trouble.

'Nightcap or coffee?'

'Oh no. Neither.' She needs to get up to bed, fast. Alone. 'Thank you,' she adds as an afterthought.

'Jon,' she hears herself saying as she turns to go. She has no idea why. She should just get the hell out of there, but the words tumble out before she can stop them. There's something she needs to know. Suddenly it's vital. It's a defining moment; if he gives her the answer she's most hoping for, it might kill her infatuation stone dead. 'Why did you have a handbag — I mean a man bag — the first day I was here?'

Jon laughs. 'A man bag?'

'Yes. A brown leather thing. Like a handbag only a little bit . . . manlier.'

'Ah,' he says. 'That'd be my camera bag. Not quite a handbag, but I can see where the confusion might lie. I'd taken my camera in to be repaired.'

Shit. 'Good. I'm glad. I didn't want to think you were the sort to carry a handbag. Goodnight.' Actually, she realizes as she's saying this that she wouldn't care any more. Man bag, church choir, Simpsons' socks, he could have the lot, all at once, and it wouldn't sway her feelings. She tries to conjure up a picture. Jon, singing his heart out in church, man bag dangling saucily off one shoulder, trousers rolled up to show his comedy socks off to best advantage. Nope. She still wants to jump him.

She heaves.

'Are you going to be OK?' he asks as she stumbles towards the stairs.

'Yes. Fine.' She is suddenly hit by a wave of nausea. Oh god. Not now. Not on the cream stair carpet. She veers round and tries to head towards the downstairs toilet.

'Abi?'

'I feel a little bit sick,' she says. 'I'll be fine. Don't worry.' All this would sound a little more convincing if it wasn't for the fact that she doesn't even have time to shut the door before she's doubled over the toilet throwing her insides up. This is so shaming. So undignified. She hates being sick. Not that she assumes anyone actually enjoys it. Well, maybe bulimics get a certain satisfaction, but anyway. It frightens her. She feels out of control. There is nothing she can do to stop it so she doesn't even try; she just collapses onto her knees and hopes that it's over soon. She can't remember the last time she was properly drunk. Tipsy quite often, probably, but so drunk that she was sick? Probably fifteen, no, twenty years ago. Not since Phoebe's been around, anyway, and she's eighteen. She's not used to drinking all evening and those glasses of wine they give you in pubs are so huge these days. Plus she hasn't had anything to eat since lunch. Anyway, even as she is throwing said lunch up into the toilet she is telling herself never again. She'll take a vow of abstinence. Just make it stop.

As she's thinking this, promising herself that this is a one-off and it will all be all right in a minute, she becomes aware of a strange sensation. She can't feel her hair on her neck. In fact, there's definitely a breeze there where her hair should be. Resting her head on the bowl she looks down, suddenly conscious that there is a foot next to her and it definitely isn't hers. Not unless she's taken to wearing Converse All Stars and she's become a contortionist. She makes a silent plea. Please tell me Jon isn't in here with me. She hears a voice, very close, saying, 'You'll be OK now,' and she realizes that not only is he in the tiny cloakroom with her, but he's holding her hair. Jon is holding her hair. Not only has he been witness to a scene from *The Exorcist* playing out in front of him, he's been holding her hair out of the way while it happened. That is hands down the nicest thing anyone has ever done for her. Ever.

She nearly flattens him trying to get away and upstairs.

'Thanks,' she calls back down as she goes. 'Sorry.'

As she lies in bed, she tries to think who she would do that for. Who she cares about enough that she would stand in a tiny enclosed space with them while they heaved their guts up and hold their hair out of the way. Phoebe obviously, but she doesn't count. She's Abi's child; Abi would do anything for her. Carol, her best friend from school who she still emails and meets up with a couple of times a year? No way. Juliet from the library who she sometimes goes for a drink with after work? Out of the question. Cleo? Forget it.

There's no one to whom Abi feels close enough that she would even think of doing that for, but Jon was prepared to risk life and limb and permanent damage to his olfactory system doing it for her.

Would I do the same for him? she wonders, and then she gets a bit distracted by thinking that if she needed to that would be because he had long girly hair and then she has to factor that in with the bag, socks and choir just to make sure her devotion is as rock steady as she's afraid it is. But would she do something fairly gross because she thought it might make him feel better? Absolutely she would. Bring it on.

Everything hurts. Her head. Her eyes. Her ears. She knows that strictly speaking her eyes and ears are part of her head, but they're hurting so much in their own right at the moment that they deserve their own mention. Her tongue is surely too big for her mouth, and furry, as if someone's replaced it with a guinea pig in the night. Her stomach aches. She opens her eyes and then closes them again. It's too much effort. Snapshots keep popping up in her head. She's in the pub, she's fine, she's funny and fabulous and on form. She's knocking over a lamp. She's crouching on the floor of the downstairs toilet. Jon is holding her hair back. Oh god. She forces her eyes open. She is most definitely in her own bed and most definitely alone.

She can't really remember getting here, though. It's all a bit of a blur. She couldn't have . . . she wouldn't . . .

A half-formed picture takes shape – her stumbling around her bedroom getting changed. She is definitely taking her own clothes off. No one else is helping. She peers under the covers. She has her pyjamas on: pink bottoms dotted with little white flowers, a white vest top. There's no way she could have had a drunken night of passion and ended up in her PJs.

Of course I didn't have a drunken night of passion, she tells herself. This is Jon we're talking about.

Even if she lost all sense of reason and threw herself naked at him – which, thankfully, she's now pretty certain she didn't – there's no way in a million years he would have gone along with it. OK, keep calm. She may have made a drunken fool of herself, but, compared to what might have happened, that now seems like model behaviour. It's just a bit embarrassing; it's not the end of life as we know it. By the time Jon gets back from work this evening she might even be able to laugh at herself with him. OK, maybe not.

She turns her aching head round to look at the clock. If Jon has gone to work by now, she needs to get up and see what the girls are up to. Elena will have made them breakfast, but Abi thinks Tara has gymnastics at half past ten and she needs a lift. There's something in the way of the clock. A glass of water. Abi doesn't remember bringing that up with her. Leaning in front of it is a sachet of Resolve and stuck on the side of that a Post-it note, which reads, 'Drink me!'

It can only be Jon. He's the only one who knew the state she was in and how bad she'd be feeling this morning. He must have crept up here before he went out this morning, while she was doing what? Sleeping like a baby? Lying on her back with her mouth open, snoring? Breathing out fumes that could kill a small child? It doesn't bear thinking about. If ever there had been a chance that he might be feeling the same about her as she does about him, then that will have cooled his ardour. Which she knows would be a good thing. Obviously.

She mixes up the Resolve and drinks it gratefully, then has to resist the urge to lie straight back down and pull the covers up over her head. She has the world's quickest shower, which basically involves her turning on the water and walking in and straight out again. Actual washing feels like too much effort. She ties her wet hair back off her face, shoves herself into comfort clothing – sweat pants and a baggy T-shirt – and makes her way downstairs reluctantly. She can hear the girls chatting away in the kitchen and smell the coffee and toast and suddenly breakfast seems like a great idea. So long as no one expects her to speak. She practises looking awake as she walks towards the kitchen, but then she catches sight of herself in the hall mirror, hair on end, eyes wide, face white. She looks like a blonde Morticia Adams. On a bad day. One glimpse of her will probably screw up Tara and Megan for life. Oh well, it'll be good for them. A lesson on the perils of drink. If Tara thought it made you look like this, Abi doesn't think she'd ever touch a drop.

She can hear Elena gabbling away in what she's decided is Hungarian as she shuffles in. You've got to admire Elena; she's persistent even though no one ever understands a word she says. And then, just as it's too late, just as Megan has caught sight of Abi and said, 'Hi, Auntie Abi,' loudly, she hears a man's voice, Jon's voice, saying something to Tara, but she's missed her moment to turn back. Great.

'She's alive!' he says in a hammy tone as he catches sight of her. The girls fall about laughing and even Abi reluctantly cracks a smile.

'Barely.'

Elena places a coffee in front of her and then briefly strokes her head as she walks off. It's such a comforting motherly gesture that, emotional wreck that she is, Abi almost cries. 'Thank you,' she says and gives her best attempt at a smile.

'What time is it?' Why hasn't Jon gone to work yet?

Jon points at the huge clock on the wall. 'Twenty past nine.'

'You got drunk,' Megan says helpfully, and Abi says, 'Yes, I'm afraid I did a bit.'

'Dad says you were funny.'

Abi raises one eyebrow at Jon. 'I'm not sure about

that.' What has he told them? Surely not about her throwing-up-all-over-the-place routine? She briefly wonders if anyone has cleaned it up and then thinking about it makes her feel sick again, so she pushes the thought out of her mind.

'I told them you knocked the lamp over,' he says, clearly aware of what she's thinking.

'And he did an impression of your walk,' Megan adds helpfully. 'Like this.' She gets up and does a comedy drunken stagger. Tara and Jon nearly wet themselves. Abi momentarily feels a bit picked on; it's hard to laugh at yourself when you are in the throes of a rampaging hangover.

But then Tara says, 'Dad got drunk on sangria on holiday once. He fell over and then tried to go to sleep on the beach, because he thought he was in bed. He was like this . . .' she says, and then does an impression, a noisy stumble that Abi sincerely hopes is exaggerated.

She can't help it – she laughs. No one's picking on her; this is what families do – normal families – they tease each other and no one takes offence.

'Well, if that's how it is, then I'm going to show Auntie Abi what you looked like when you tripped over that bit of pavement in the middle of Oxford Street,' Jon retaliates. He performs an elaborate pratfall, which has Megan banging on the table she's laughing so much and even Elena's joining in.

Abi is relieved and heartened to see that Tara is

laughing along with the rest of them. Teasing wasn't encouraged when she was young. If you had told Caroline she looked ridiculous doing something, then she would have stormed off in a huff, Philippa following closely behind, and there would have been a black cloud over the house all day. Funny that. Abi can remember laughing and laughing with Caroline until they were breathless about pretty much nothing. In jokes and bad puns. But, now she comes to think about it, none of the jokes were ever at Caroline's expense. She had a sense of humour, she definitely did. Just maybe not about herself. Abi wonders if she's changed or if Jon, Tara and Megan save these moments for when she's not around.

When they've laughed themselves out, she realizes she's starting to feel more human. 'Why aren't you at work?' she asks Jon accusingly. She's hoping he didn't feel he had to stay home and take care of the girls because she was incapable and not to be trusted.

'Well,' he says slowly. 'I thought it might be nice for us to all do something together.'

Really? 'Tara has gymnastics,' Abi hears herself saying.

'I'm not going,' Tara says. 'Dad said I didn't have to.'

'I thought you loved gymnastics,' Abi says, clutching at straws, and Tara shrugs her shoulders and says, 'It's OK.'

'We don't have to,' Jon says hastily. 'I mean, if you don't feel up to it . . .'

216

'Because you got drunk,' Megan chimes in.

Jon laughs. '. . . because you got drunk – that's exactly what I was going to say – then we can do something on our own. I just wanted to say thank you for all the time you've spent with the girls . . .'

Actually, the thought of being able to crawl back up to bed and sleep it off is almost irresistible. She should protest. She should come up with an excuse why she can't go with them – an appointment with the doctor or a promise to Richard to go in and cover for him for a couple of hours over lunchtime – but her brain is too fuzzy to be able to offer up anything coherent. Why is she going to the doctor? For that matter, what doctor? Why would she have a doctor in London? And where is Richard's regular Friday assistant? If they're away, how come he only needs Abi to be there for a couple of hours conveniently timed so that she could run the girls to their classes and pick them up again? It's too complicated. She's too hung over. She knows that spending the day playing mummy and daddy with Jon, especially when she's feeling so off her guard, is a terrible idea, but he and the girls are looking at her so hopefully and it's so thoughtful of him to have planned something that before she knows it she is going along with it.

'Excellent. So, what's the plan?'

'We thought we could get the train down to Richmond, have a walk along the river, lunch at the Gaucho there, maybe a boat trip . . .'

'Lovely.' She does think it sounds lovely, as it goes. It's a beautiful day and, being away from home, she misses the water. In the summer she usually goes down to the beach every morning, even on days when she's working because she doesn't start till ten. Admittedly the Thames isn't quite the same, but it's the closest thing she's got at the moment. And she'd be lying if she said the idea of a day with Jon didn't appeal.

'I'll get ready,' she says, and she picks up the toast that Elena has given her and heads upstairs before she can change her mind.

15

If you saw them out, you could be forgiven for thinking they were just a normal nuclear family on a day trip. Husband, wife and their two adorable-looking (and surprisingly well-behaved) girls. You would never imagine that she was in love with him, but he was married to someone else, and that that someone else was her sister with whom she has a complex and not entirely healthy relationship. Well, maybe you would if you were Barbara Cartland and you had a deadline coming up.

Hangover and hormones aside, they actually have a brilliant time. Richmond is beautiful and, once they get the girls past the shops, they walk along the river for miles admiring the stately Georgian houses and the ducks. They stop at a little truck in a field and buy coffees and Abi sits on the grass while Jon chases Tara and Megan around screaming. Tara and Megan that is, not Jon. Abi doesn't think she's ever seen Tara run before. At one point she comes over and drags Abi up by the hand and makes her join in. Generally Abi doesn't do running either (she and Tara have that one thing in common, she thinks). She's not built for it. But she doesn't want to put a damper on the occasion so she has a half-hearted go and then collapses breathless on the grass. After a couple of minutes, Jon joins her and suddenly, there they are, on their own together for the first time today. Abi racks her brain for something to say, but before she can come up with anything Jon speaks:

'How are you feeling?'

'Good, actually.' Abi takes a deep breath. 'I'm sorry for all that last night. I'm not used to drinking.'

He laughs. 'It's fine. I've got kids; you become immune to the horror of the sight of people being sick after a while.'

'I mean it. It was immature and frankly pretty gross. What I can remember of it, anyway.'

'We're all allowed to let off steam once in a while. I imagine it's been quite stressful for you the past few weeks.'

'Mmm . . . well anyway . . .'

She can't think of anything else to say so she flops back on the grass and lets the sun wash over her. Jon does the same. Every now and then one of the girls runs past them giggling.

'I've never seen Tara like this,' Abi says, half to herself.

'Me neither,' Jon says. 'Not for years anyway. Having you around is doing her good.'

She feels herself blush. 'I don't know about that.'

'It's true,' he says and Abi can't look at him. 'She looks up to you and that's a really good thing. At least *I* think it's a good thing.'

She can't think what to say in reply. They lie there in silence for what seems like an age and then, much to Abi's relief, the girls throw themselves down next to them, panting heavily. For the rest of the afternoon Abi makes sure she sticks to them like glue.

By the time they get off the train at Waterloo it's gone six, they're all starving and, although no one says anything to confirm it, it's clear that none of them want the day to end. Instead of peeling off towards the tube or heading for the taxi rank, Jon strides purposefully towards the street and the rest of them follow.

'Who wants to eat out?' he says in such a way that it sounds rhetorical. He takes the cut through that brings them out by the Royal Festival Hall. The area is buzzing with after-work drinkers steadfastly refusing to miss one second of the sun by embarking on their journeys home before it goes down. They head towards the river, each with one eye open for a free table outside one of the many cafés and restaurants that line the way.

'I want pizza,' Megan says, and Jon says, 'I don't think we can be that choosy. Let's just find a table and then see what they have. There's bound to be something you like.'

Abi waits for a whine of protest, after all, it's been a long day, but Megan just says, 'OK,' cheerily, and that's that. As they're approaching the last restaurant in the row, the one closest to the river, where the tables outside have an unadulterated view of the water and the boats going past, not to mention the full floor-show of the pedestrians parading up and down the river walk – the holy grail in 'locations to eat outside on the South Bank' terms – a couple stands up to leave, and Tara is over there like a whippet, sliding into one of the four seats before they've even had a chance to pick up their change. Abi, used to polite Kent seaside society, where even the tourists would stand and wait until hunger overtook them completely before they would rush a table that still had occupants, thinks about chastising her, but, she has to admit, she's impressed by her niece's skills and, more than that, she really wants to sit down.

'Sorry,' she mouths to the couple, but they just smile and move off.

The restaurant turns out to be Neapolitan, much to Megan's delight. The waiter is like a rent-an-Italian, all over-the-top accent and flamboyant hand gestures. Even though he's probably never been across the Channel, let alone to Naples, Abi is pleased to see that he has certainly mastered the art of Latin hospitality and he makes a big fuss of the children who, in turn, bask in his attention.

'I think we deserve a glass of wine,' Jon says, and then thinks better of it, 'or we don't have to if you know, you still feel . . .'

Abi knows she should say no. That she should just go on the wagon until Cleo gets back. But they've had such a gorgeous day and she just wants to relish being in the moment: the sun, the view, the feeling of belonging. 'I'd love one. Just the one, though. Let's order by the glass. Not a bottle . . .' She's blathering. Shut up, she tells herself.

The wine is ice cold and delicious, her linguine al pesto flavoured perfectly, although she does get green oily basil sauce down her chin, and a couple of times she's left with straggly strands of pasta dangling becomingly from her mouth after she takes her fork out. She finds she doesn't mind, though. It all feels so . . . comfortable. This is family, after all, just a slightly distorted version.

'Your daughters are beautiful,' the waiter says as she passes him on her way to the Ladies. She thinks about correcting him, but she doesn't, she doesn't know why.

'Just like their mother,' he calls to her retreating back, laughing.

If only you knew how right you are, she thinks, but she still just smiles over her shoulder and accepts the compliment.

The week rolls into the weekend. There's been tension, there's no doubt about it, moments when she thinks she's given herself away, moments when for a fleeting second she wonders, heart lurching, if Jon has feelings that reciprocate her own – the too-long gaze, the awkward but sweet exchange on the riverbank in

Richmond, the night he held her hair while she was sick – but, on the whole, they're getting through it. Once safe in her room at night Abi locks the door and hides the key at the bottom of the drawer in her bedside cabinet, as if that might prevent her from going back downstairs if her subconscious self decides to act out her suppressed fantasies while she's sleeping. Nothing untoward has happened; no one has admitted to anything. There's nothing that would stand up in court.

Saturday and Sunday loom large and Abi works out a schedule with military precision. At all costs she has to avoid long hours spent with Jon, with or without the children. Hours in which they'd get to know each other better, inch their way closer. She insists that now is the time to tick all the rest of the touristy things off her list and that, because she knows there's nothing worse for native Londoners than being forced to visit their doorstep cultural treasures on hot summer weekend afternoons, she announces that she will happily entertain herself if Jon doesn't mind. He smiles quizzically when she says this, one eyebrow raised as if to say, 'I know what you're doing,' but he doesn't object.

Abi blows all her available cash tearing backwards and forwards across town in a random fashion seeing Kew Gardens then St Paul's, Westminster Abbey then the V&A.

On Sunday she wanders around the deserted echoey

streets of the City, down cobbled alleys, past medieval pubs nestled up against twentieth-century metal and glass. She walks across the flimsy Millennium Bridge and treats herself to a sandwich from an overpriced concession, which she eats sitting on a bench. By the time she gets home she's exhausted, but she feels as if she's achieved something if only that the weekend is pretty much over without incident. The rest of the week is charted waters, days spent apart, dinner with the girls as human shields, minimal alcohol and early nights.

Oh god. Shit, fuck, bollocks. How did she not know that this was happening? Once she got home she had a leisurely bath with a large glass of lime and lemonade and then headed downstairs to see what needed doing for dinner, safe in the knowledge that the new Tara and Megan would be there to help both with the food and the air of tension. Now, as she gets to the hall, she is stopped in her tracks by the sight of her two nieces carrying their backpacks and being ushered out of the front door by the father of one of their friends.

'Where are you going?' Abi almost shouts, giving away far too much panic in her voice. Don't go out. Don't leave me alone with your father.

'Sleepover,' Megan says casually, and the dad introduces himself. Abi shakes his hand and tries to pretend that everything is fine. It's too late for her to claim she is going out for the evening herself, even if she could think of somewhere to go. She is clearly not dressed for anything other than slobbing around at home. She even said earlier that she was glad she had no plans because she was knackered. Jon even checked that she was going to be home for dinner and she said yes.

They're out of the door before she can think of a way to stop them. She's about to turn round and creep back up the stairs (and then what? Call Jon from her mobile and say she has a highly contagious disease, don't come anywhere near her?) when he suddenly appears from the kitchen brandishing an open bottle of wine.

'Peace at last,' he says, and Abi smiles weakly, but refuses his offering.

'I'm on the wagon.'

She has no choice but to follow him into the kitchen. He hands her a knife and a bag of courgettes and they just get on with it like they always do. Everything will be fine so long as she acts normal. Whatever signals she's thought Jon might have been giving off in the past couple of days are all in her imagination. She's incapable of making conversation, though. Suddenly she can't think of a thing to say. Luckily Jon seems oblivious to her monosyllabic answers.

'I took them swimming in the ponds in Hampstead,' he says, and Abi grunts. 'Don't tell Cleo, though. She thinks the bathing ponds are full of bacteria and paedophiles.

'I don't mean that to sound disloyal,' he adds hurriedly, afraid that Abi will be offended by the apparent slight to her sister. 'Just that she's very overprotective. Which is a good thing, obviously.'

'How's she getting on, by the way?' Talk about Cleo, that's a good plan. Keep reminding both him and herself (especially herself) that Jon is married to her sister. Her sister who may be difficult and demanding, but who has never done anything to deserve Abi making a play for her husband. Abi's nervousness strikes her as ridiculous. She and Jon often prepare food together while the girls are off doing other things. It's no big deal. But there's something about knowing they are alone in the house. All night. And knowing that he knows it too.

'She actually seems to be having a good time. They love what she's doing or at least they keep telling her they do, which amounts to the same thing.'

Abi is sceptical. She thinks he is too loyal to be honest, but neither of them is going to admit it. 'That's great.'

They eat in silence for a few minutes. Abi can't think of anything to say. She looks at Jon's hand holding the fork, pushing food around his plate. She thinks he has nice hands. Tanned. Long slim fingers, but with a strength about them. Neat short nails, not too manicured. She looks away. In her head she sees the outline of his brown fingers on her paler skin. She could imagine those hands getting up to all sorts. In fact, she has. Several times.

'What do you see yourself doing in ten years' time?' Jon says out of the blue.

This is not a subject Abi feels very comfortable with now that Phoebe's left home. She has no idea what the answer is. Work in the library part time and hope some grandchildren who need her come along eventually? Girls these days don't even think about having kids until their late thirties so she might have to wait a long time.

'Honestly?' He nods. 'I haven't got a clue. Get a cat?'

'You must have a dream tucked away in there somewhere. Round the world trip? Write a novel? Move to the country?'

'I already live in the country. Well, more or less.'

'Oh yes. So you do. Anything else?'

'I'm trying not to think about it.'

He sighs. 'Me too.'

She can sense that he's waiting for her to react. She doesn't know how. She doesn't know what he is trying to hint at. She concentrates on her food. There's an atmosphere tonight that hasn't been there before. It's making her feel uncomfortable. She wishes the girls would come home. Maybe one of them will feel unwell and insist on being brought back to the house. Or they might have an accident. Not a bad one, just break something minor. Then they'd all have to rush off to A and E and the excitement of the moment would dissipate whatever it is that's going on here.

That would work. Great, so now she's wishing pain and trauma on her nieces. And just when they were beginning to like her.

She can't bear the loaded silence, so in the end she says 'Well . . .' in a way that she hopes implies she's about to launch into a new topic but then she can't think of one so she leaves it at that.

Jon sighs. 'I'm not sure how the future's going to pan out for me and Cleo,' he says, and all of a sudden there it is out in the open. The admission that he's clearly been building up to. Half of her leaps up in joy. He doesn't love Cleo any more! He's telling her that their marriage might not last! Maybe there could be a future where Jon and Abi get together! And then the other half – the sober, sensible, loyal half – puts its foot down. The marriage that he's hinting might be in trouble is to her sister. The woman he might be falling out of love with is the mother of her nieces. Would she really wish that on them? Or Cleo for that matter?

'Oh, come on,' she says in what she hopes is a breezily dismissive way. She doesn't want to be seen to be taking him too seriously. 'You're just having a rough patch. Trying to adjust to her going back to modelling and all that. Things'll be OK.'

He tries to make eye contact and Abi looks at anything else but him. Oooh, that's a nice clock. Why haven't I noticed that before? Look at that chopping board! It's amazing!

'I don't know. I love her, but things haven't been great for a while. Cleo going back to work is just a symptom of that. It's not the problem. And if I thought it would make her happy, make her more content when she is here, then I'd be all for it. But it won't. I really want my marriage to work more than anything, but the truth is I sometimes think the only thing that's been keeping us together for a long time now is the girls.'

'But . . .' Abi says. 'Really?' She's finding this hard to believe. 'Does she feel the same?'

He shrugs. 'I don't know. We haven't really talked about it. That's part of the problem. We don't really talk about anything these days. Or at least anything real, anything about us, you know.'

She thinks about the way Cleo was speaking about him the other day. Even though she was being a bit disparaging Abi never doubted for a moment that she still loved him. 'I think she's just a bit preoccupied with what's happening to her at the moment.'

'We're still friends, don't get me wrong. I mean it's not like it's hard living together or anything. At least it wasn't . . .'

She's about to say, 'What's changed?' but then she thinks better of it. She's scared that she already knows.

'I wouldn't want you to think I've ever acted on those feelings. I mean . . .' Abi nods her head quickly to show him she understands what he's getting at.

'I never would. That is, I never would have before.'

She can feel him staring at her. She gets up and starts clearing the table, clattering the plates and dishes, trying to break the moment. They say be careful what you wish for and now she knows why. As she goes to pick up his plate, Jon reaches out and clasps her hand. She nearly jumps through the roof. This isn't right. Unless she knows with absolute certainty that Cleo has fallen out of love with Jon, then she can't do this. However much she wants to.

'Don't . . .' she says quietly.

'Abi,' he says in a voice that literally makes her go weak at the knees. She has to sit down on the chair next to him before she falls over. Now he has her hand he's not letting it go, massaging her fingers with his. She knows she should pull it away, but she seems to have forgotten how to move it. He puts out his other hand and gently strokes her face. This is it. This is the point of no return. There's no way that what he is about to propose will be a quickie while the kids are away. If she goes along with this, then Jon and Cleo's marriage will be over. Megan and Tara will be the product of a broken home. She's paralysed. He's looking at her so intently that she can't seem to look away. He leans in. He's going to kiss her, she knows he is, but she feels powerless to stop him. No, scrub that. It's not that she can't – she doesn't *want* to stop him. She feels herself edge forward to meet his kiss head-on. It's indescribably amazing. It only lasts for about ten seconds, but afterwards she'd swear she saw fire-works and heard an orchestra.

An image flashes into her head. Cleo teaching her how to kiss a boy, using a pillow to demonstrate. The two of them laughing about how they'd read some-where you were supposed to stick your tongue in, and how disgusting it was.

She comes to her senses all at once. This isn't right.

'No!' She pulls herself and her hand away from him and stands up, nearly knocking over her chair in the process. 'We can't.'

Jon stands up too and he puts his hand on her arm. 'We can. Abi, I think I've fallen in love with you. I didn't mean to — it's the last thing I ever would have wanted to happen — I just . . . I'll talk to Cleo when she gets back. We can work out a way to make it as painless as possible for the girls. If it's what you want too. I mean . . . I think it is, isn't it?'

Yes. Absolutely one hundred per cent yes. Please. She tries to force her foggy brain to see clearly.

'No.'

'No?'

'What I mean is . . . I can't.'

OK, she'd better come up with something quick.

'That is . . . I'm seeing someone else already.' It's the only thing she can think of. In retrospect she'll realize it wasn't such a good idea, but at the time it seems inspired.

Jon drops his hand. 'What? Who?'

Who indeed? She only knows one person. 'Richard.' Oh good, she thinks, I'm glad I said that.

Jon looks devastated. 'Richard? Since when?'

'Since . . . well, not very long, but I really like him and I want to give it a go so, you see . . .'

'Yes,' he says before she can finish. 'I see. I'm really sorry, Abi. It looks like I got things all wrong.'

He starts to clear away the rest of the stuff from the table. 'Let's just forget this ever happened, shall we?'

'Of course,' she says, not meaning it. How can she ever forget that he admitted he was in love with her? How can she forget that he kissed her? Or that it was the sweetest, most sensual, most loaded kiss of her entire life?

'It's forgotten.'

Fifteen minutes later she's lying on her bed thinking about the mess she's got herself in when there's a knock on the door. Abi freezes. She knows without having to ask that it's Jon. And not just because he's the only other person home. Maybe if she lies very still he'll think she's dozed off and go away again. She holds her breath and he knocks again and then calls her name softly. She stays silent. Even though she owes it to him, the last thing she and Jon need at the moment is an intimate heart to heart in her bedroom. She couldn't answer for her actions. She watches as the door knob turns. Thank god she thought to lock the door. She waits a few moments till she hears him retreat quietly down the stairs and only then does she allow herself to cry.

16

So there are a few things in Abi's life that need attention, even if she doesn't count her screwed-up relationship with her sister:

Her brother-in-law, Jon, has just told her he is in love with her.

She is in love with her brother-in-law, Jon.

She is going to have to tell her boss, Richard, that they have to pretend to be going out.

She is going to have to tell her new friend Stella that she and Stella's boyfriend, Richard, are going to have to pretend to be going out.

She is going to have to find somewhere to stay and get the hell out of there.

Abi puts her mind to the last first. The others are too traumatic to even think about.

If she moved out, she wouldn't be able to afford to stay in London, not on two days a week in the shop. She could go back to Kent and leave Jon, Cleo, Richard, Stella, the whole mess behind, but she wouldn't have anywhere to live for the next few weeks or a job for that matter, because a vacationing student is already covering her position during their summer break. She's sure her boss would be only too happy to ditch her temporary replacement and have her back, but that would just mean that she was causing a whole different set of problems for a whole different set of people.

She could find a full-time job either in London or at home and rent a tiny bedsit, but, who is she kidding, there's a recession on and she's qualified to do precisely nothing. Besides, none of that could happen overnight.

Realistically the immediate problem she has to face is how to get through the next twenty-four hours without hurting anyone or doing anything she shouldn't.

Once she'd let Jon down not so gently last night she retreated up here, to her little bedroom. She didn't even offer to help clear up. She just had to get out of there. After he knocked on her door she could hear him moving around downstairs late into the night and the temptation to go down, to put her arms round him and tell him that she was faking before, that she loved him too, was almost overwhelming. Knowing he was lying in the bed two floors below her, almost certainly feeling as wretched and miserable as she was, and that the girls were away and it was just the two of them in the house meant that there was no chance of her sleeping. But she didn't want him to hear she was awake in case he decided to come up to her door again, so she just lay there rigid, afraid to move, torturing herself with the details of their conversation. In the end she must have fallen asleep in the early hours of the morning.

The girls are due to be dropped off at about ten so Abi decides that the safest thing to do is to stay in her room till then, just in case Jon is late going into work. If they have another sleepover planned for tonight, she fully intends to ground them. Or go with them. Jon, no doubt feeling humiliated and embarrassed by what he must see as his misreading of the situation, will probably want to keep out of Abi's way as much as she does his.

Actually, she can't think about how Jon must be feeling. The awful thing is that he's right – there clearly is something between them – and she's sure she must have been giving off signals left, right and centre even as she was trying her hardest not to, which allowed him to think that if he spoke up his feelings would be reciprocated. She's let him down – she knows that. Knowing Jon as she does now, she can't imagine he goes around all the time propositioning women who aren't his wife. In fact, she'd put money on her having been the first. And he wouldn't have done it unless he truly believed Abi felt as strongly as he did. Oh god. She has no idea how she's even going to look him in the eye. And then it hits her that, of course, he may want her to leave. And who could blame him? She needs to do the grown-up thing and offer to go. When she can get the courage up to head downstairs, that is.

After what seems like hours, she finally hears Tara and Megan chattering away, so she plasters a smile onto her face, steels herself and heads down to meet them. Out of the corner of her eye she can see Jon in the kitchen as she greets the girls in the hall.

'We stayed up till half past twelve,' Megan says as soon as she sees Abi. 'And then we still didn't go to sleep – we talked. All night.'

'Good for you,' Abi says, giving her a hug.

'She's exaggerating, obviously,' Tara says, offering herself up to be hugged as well. 'As usual.'

Megan's eyelids are drooping. Jon comes out of the kitchen, not looking at Abi. Gives his daughter a kiss. 'Do you want to go back to bed for an hour?'

Megan nods sleepily.

'Why aren't you at work?' Tara eyes her father suspiciously. Abi looks anywhere but at him.

'I'm not going in. I wanted to see my girls when they got home. And then later I thought we could go to the zoo – how would you like that? Give Auntie Abi a bit of peace for once.' Tara allows herself to be hugged. Abi forces herself to breathe again. Not too long and he'll be out of the house.

'Do we have to?' Megan says. She looks dead on her feet, big dark droopy circles round her eyes.

'Not if you don't want to,' Jon says. 'Or we could do it this afternoon once you've had a bit more sleep.'

'I'm going to have a bath,' Abi says, anxious not to be left alone with him even for a moment. Now she's going to have to find something to do with her day just to get out of Jon's way.

'Hold on,' Jon says, and she freezes. 'Go on up, girls, and I'll get Elena to bring you toast in bed in a bit.' He waits until the two of them have shuffled off, asleep on their feet.

'I . . .' Abi starts to say at exactly the same moment as Jon says, 'Abi . . .' Ever polite he adds, 'You first.'

'I was just going to say that I'll leave if you want. I don't want to make it awkward for you, me being here . . .'

'God, no,' he says. 'Don't leave on my account. I was just about to apologize for being so stupid. Cleo's your sister and I should never have said the things I said to you. I'd like to be able to put it behind us. I promise you won't keep catching me gazing at you adoringly every time you look round.' He's attempting a joke and Abi obliges by attempting a faint laugh in return.

'I'm sorry too,' she says, meaning of course that she's sorry she has given him every reason to suspect she wants him as much as he says he wants her, but she leaves him to interpret her apology any way he likes.

'Cleo would kill me if I'd driven you out while she was away,' he says, all forced jollity.

'Yeah right. Nice try,' Abi says, smiling at him to let him know it'll all be OK. As long as they both just pretend that there isn't an atmosphere, that everything is fine between them, business as usual, then it might as well be. Only they will know differently.

'Friends?' he says, and there's a moment when she nearly thinks sod it and throws herself at him after all.

She holds herself back. 'Of course.'

'What the hell did you do that for?' Richard is looking at her with wide-eyed amusement.

'It's a long story,' she says. 'And I'm really sorry. But could you kind of go along with it if you see Jon?'

'Well, well, well,' he says. 'What kind of a mess have you got yourself into?'

She doesn't really have any choice but to tell him the whole story, or at least an edited version. Just enough for him to understand why what she's asking him to do is important, but not enough to incriminate the people involved. She puts all the blame on herself, making it sound as if she lost her mind and launched herself at Jon and then had to come up with something quick to convince him she was joking when it was obvious he wasn't going to reciprocate. Although he's a little concerned about whether Stella will see the funny side, he still finds the whole thing highly amusing.

'What's Cleo going to say when she finds out?'

'Nothing because she won't. And because there's nothing to find out. I just made a bit of a fool of myself, that's all. Please, Richard.'

'I don't even know her. I'm hardly going to say anything, am I?'

'Even if you ever meet her . . .' Abi knows she's

going on too much. She's entrusted him with a secret and now she's acting as if she doesn't have faith in him to keep it. Which she doesn't, for the record, but she has no choice.

'Of course not. Although I must say my ego is destroyed. How could you throw yourself at that man when we're so in love?'

'Very funny.' He does make her laugh, though. That's the thing with Richard, it's impossible not to find him funny even when you don't want to.

She hangs around the shop for a while watching Richard amuse himself at her expense. She doesn't really know what to do with herself all day so when he suggests she join him and Stella for an early lunch at the pub — where she can explain to Stella herself the 'hysterical' situation she's got them all into, as he puts it — she accepts even though she's not really sure she wants to be the one to tell Stella the good news.

Luckily Stella, being an all-round reasonable and rational kind of a woman, seems to take it in her stride. Abi promises her that she will only be keeping up the pretence for a week or so and then, once she thinks everything's calmed down and gone back to normal, she can claim that Richard has dumped her to go back to Stella, his true love, and that she, Abi, is broken-hearted.

'We could have a slanging match in the street outside their house,' Stella says, warming to her role as Abi's rival. 'I could slap you. Or the other way round,' she adds when she sees Abi's less than enthusiastic expression.

'It's funny,' Richard says, 'it looked to me like he had as much of a thing for you as you did for him.'

Abi rolls her eyes theatrically. 'In the five minutes you actually saw us together. The only five minutes you've ever met him, I should add.'

'You forget, I'm an expert.'

'Well, you're wrong this time.'

She looks at her watch. Good fun as Richard and Stella are, she doesn't want to stay and be grilled by them. She knows that she'd cave in under questioning. She's always been crap at keeping secrets. Especially ones about herself.

She makes her excuses and goes, and then gets the tube to Westfield to kill a few hours before she has to go home. After about fifteen minutes she's bored, though. Window shopping when it's completely out of the question that you could actually purchase anything, even in a mall which seemingly has one of everything you might ever desire, is duller than you might imagine. She looks at the people sitting at the champagne bar with envy. How lovely to have nothing to worry about in the world, to have the money, the friends, the time to sit around drinking champagne and laughing all afternoon.

She gets a bus back, intending to sit in the park, but it's a dreary day, dark and damp. Reluctantly she drags herself back towards the house. It's half past two. There's a chance that Jon will have persuaded the girls to go out somewhere or other by now. If not, she'll just have to face the music. She can't spend the next few days wandering aimlessly around northwest London.

The house is quiet so she spends the rest of the afternoon holed up in her bedroom, emerging only when she thinks it would be too rude not to go down to dinner. Jon looks at her nervously when she walks in, but she can barely hold his glance. She feels so bad that she's having to let him think it was all one-sided. She knows he'll be feeling like shit, embarrassed and guilty and foolish, and all she really wants to do is go and put her arms round him and tell him that he was right. There definitely was something going on between them. But she can't. For Cleo's sake she has to keep up the pretence and hope that it will all just go away in time. Luckily the girls are chattering on as usual. Jon, it seems, managed to persuade them into going to the zoo, after all. The minute the dinner things are cleared Abi claims a migraine and heads back upstairs. She has no intention of coming down before she has to go to work in the morning.

'We missed you today,' Megan says, giving her a hug goodnight. 'It wasn't as much fun without you.'

Tara hugs her too. 'She's right for once.'

'Oh, Abi,' Jon says, following her out into the hall just as she is heading upstairs. She stops. 'I've got the evenings covered.'

Abi looks at him, not understanding what he's getting at.

'If you're seeing Richard or whatever. You do enough looking after the girls all day. The least I can do is make sure I'm here every evening so that you don't have to be.'

She forces a smile. 'Thanks. I'm staying in tonight; I feel like shit.'

Great, so now she's going to have to find somewhere to go every night otherwise Jon is never going to believe her relationship is real. She spends the rest of the evening sitting in her room, too distracted to even turn on the TV. Dreading that Jon might come up and try to speak to her again. Dreading it and longing for it at the same time. Fearing and hoping in equal measures that he might repeat some of the things he said to her last night.

She has to put some distance between them, so on Tuesday night she takes herself off to the cinema, the Everyman in Belsize Park, where she lies back in her comfy armchair and snoozes through a worthy indie film about death and love.

Wednesday evening is hot and humid, so she climbs up to the top of the hill with a sandwich and two cans of lager and does her best impersonation of a homeless person, sitting on a bench staring off into space. At one point someone actually gives her two pounds, and she's so taken aback she doesn't have a chance to protest before they're gone. Several customers from the shop walk by with their dogs and say hello or even stop for a chat. It's actually quite sociable. She keeps her fingers crossed that Jon doesn't look out of one of the windows and see her there. At about nine o'clock she looks over at the house and thinks she can see him pottering round the front room on his own. It nearly breaks both her heart and her resolve.

Thursday she is too tired to come up with a plan. Richard is taking Stella out to dinner at The Square so he can't even offer her the traditional two glasses of wine in the pub. She asks him if she can stay late cleaning and tidying the shop and he sweetly agrees – she can tell he knows why she is asking – and even offers to pay her for it. She starts to protest but he insists, so she backs down. She's not in a position to turn down money.

In the end she falls asleep in the stock room at the shop and doesn't wake up till one in the morning, and creeps into the house, being careful to make just enough noise to let Jon know how late she is returning but not enough to wake the girls.

Friday evening she sits in the pub on her own, nursing a glass of wine and trying to ignore the flirty stares of a group of inebriated office managers.

By Saturday she has completely run out of ideas, but she has managed to avoid seeing Jon pretty much all week. There's one more minefield of an evening to get through before Cleo comes back and everything can – hopefully – go back to what now seems the sane normality of them all tiptoeing round each other carefully trying not to say anything that might offend. She kills the day going out before anyone else is up and walking for miles and then, in desperation, she phones Stella and offers to babysit if she wants an evening out, but Stella tells her that she has strict rules about only going out a maximum of a couple of nights a week – born, Stella tells her, out of having a mother who went out every night leaving young Stella with whomever she could find – and that she has those nights organized already for this week. Abi tells her she's a good mum and is about to hang up when Stella asks if she'd like to spend the evening round at hers anyway.

'It'd be lovely to have the company, actually,' she says, and she sounds like she means it so Abi agrees, promising to pick up a bottle of wine on the way. Stella tells her not to eat before she gets there so that they can order a delivery from You Me Sushi on the Marylebone Road. Frankly that couldn't suit Abi better (both the not having to eat dinner at home and the fact that Stella is suggesting sushi, her favourite food in the world) so she makes a note of the address and promises to be there by seven. Coward that she is, she has a shower and gets ready and only stops by the kitchen on her way out of the front door to tell Jon and the girls that she's out again for the evening. It suits her story, obviously, to have him believe she is seeing Richard, so she doesn't mention where she's really going.

'You're never here any more,' Megan whines, and Jon tells her to leave Auntie Abi alone – she's entitled to have some fun after spending all day with you. Abi hugs both girls and promises them all kinds of adventures next week. As soon as Cleo gets back she is intending to announce the demise of her relationship, if anything just so she can have a few nights in. Once that farce is over with, she fully intends to devote all her time to her nieces again.

'Have a good time,' Jon says, smiling although it looks like it hurts.

She feels like a complete bitch.

Stella's flat is in Marylebone – a twenty-minute walk across Regent's Park – in a large, probably Edwardian, redbrick mansion block that stretches along the main road and down several of the side streets leading back from it. Abi eventually finds the right entrance and Stella buzzes her up to the fourth floor where it takes her another five minutes of taking wrong turns to discover Flat 451. When she gets there, Stella is standing at the open door laughing, because, she says, it's always a gamble to see whether her guests will actually persevere or whether the rabbit warren of corridors will defeat them and they'll go back down to the front door and ring her entry phone again demanding more specific directions.

'I'm glad I passed the test.' Abi hands over the bottle of Pinot Grigio that she bought in an off-licence round the corner and Stella gives her a hug hello.

'Thanks. The sushi's on me.'

Stella shows her through the hall into the small living room, a mix of stylish furniture and scattered children's toys. Abi's surprised actually that her place isn't bigger. Only because she remembers Stella saying that her husband went off with the au pair, which led Abi to assume they had a certain kind of lifestyle. Not that this place isn't lovely. It is. Stella obviously has good taste and it's surprisingly quiet up here considering the location.

Stella must read Abi's mind because as she opens the wine she says, 'I didn't want anything from the divorce. He pays maintenance for the kids, but I wanted to buy my own place with my own money.' Abi kicks herself for having given away what she was thinking.

'It's lovely, though.'

'Lovely but small.'

'It's still bigger than my house,' Abi says, which thankfully Stella takes for the genuine comment it is. Abi would hate her to think she was being judgemental. On the contrary, she admires Stella's independence. She never took anything from Phoebe's dad either. Mind you, he never offered her anything. He gave her gonorrhea once before she got pregnant, but that was about the extent of his generosity. And actually he gave her Phoebe, so she probably shouldn't complain.

Baby Rhys and his three-year-old brother, Sean, are looking unbearably cute in their little SpongeBob pyjamas with their faces rosy, scrubbed clean and with that gorgeous smell that only comes from small-child-meets-bubble-bath. They play with their toys on the floor like models of good behaviour while Stella and Abi peruse the menu from You Me Sushi, and then Stella asks her if she minds calling the restaurant while she gets the boys ready for bed. When neither of them protests, Abi can't help expressing her surprise and Stella tells her that she followed some rigid regime or other that she read about in a book from when they were both born and consequently their routine runs like clockwork. Abi gets the impression everything in Stella's life probably runs like clockwork. She's one of those people with enormous willpower who thrives on self-imposed timetables and discipline. In fact, she's one of those people Abi has always fiercely wanted to be, but she's never quite managed it.

'You're scary,' she says, and Stella laughs.

'I have two settings, order or chaos. To avoid the one necessitates being obsessive about the other.'

'Will you come and organize my life? It's a mess.'

'Don't ask me because I just might. Let me get these two to sleep and then you can tell me all the gory details.'

Sean, who has known Abi for all of twenty minutes,

comes over to kiss her goodnight in a way that makes her stomach flip, because it's such a visceral reminder of Phoebe when she was that age. Fifteen minutes later Stella's back refilling their glasses, the flat is quiet and Abi is dividing the sushi – she'd swear the delivery boy rang the doorbell before she'd even put the phone down – between two plates.

'So,' Stella says, curling her legs up under her on the sofa, 'what's going on?'

Abi's reluctant to bang on about herself and her own problems so they chat about other stuff for a while. Stella tells her about her ex-husband who worked in the City and who was, by all accounts, a bit of a flash bastard.

'I've never been impressed by men with money,' she says. 'In fact, honestly, the ones who don't have so much are usually nicer.'

Abi couldn't agree more. Wealth, power, status, she's never found any of those things an aphrodisiac. Now she comes to think about it, maybe she could have made her life easier if she did. She likes the fact that she and Stella have the same priorities when it comes to men: funny, smart, loyal, good with kids. Not that Abi has actually managed to ensnare a man who had all those attributes in living memory, but if you asked her who her ideal mate was on paper those are the boxes she'd tick.

Later on Stella presses her again so Abi fills her in with the whole sorry story, leaving nothing out, because actually she's decided that she can trust Stella and she would genuinely value her insight. She starts way back on that day in Covent Garden in 1985 and brings her right up to date with what's happening at the house right now.

'But don't tell Richard. Not the bit about Jon telling me he's in love with me.' She doesn't think she could handle the teasing, let alone the fear of what Richard might say to Jon in the name of humour if he ever bumped into him again.

'Of course I won't. Can you imagine how merciless he'd be?'

'And I'm sorry again for getting you both involved in my mess. I was put on the spot and I just didn't know what else to do.'

'I won't pretend I'm thrilled about it, but I completely understand. And, for the record, good on you for doing whatever you had to do to stop this thing with Jon in its tracks. It must have been incredibly difficult given how you feel about him.'

'That would be an understatement.'

'Not to mention how you feel about your Cleo.'

'That's the thing. She may be a nightmare, but she's still my sister. The only one I've got. I would never hurt her like that.'

'And that's exactly why she should appreciate you more.'

'It's complicated.'

Is it? Abi's not sure it is, actually. Stella's right —

Cleo could do with recognizing that in her sister she has a loyal and supportive ally a bit more. But, cathartic as it is offloading on Stella like this and as much as Abi truly thinks she can trust her, she's not about to stick the knife deep into Cleo yet. And do you know why? Because she's exactly the loyal and supportive sister Cleo doesn't appreciate she has.

'You shouldn't let her treat you the way she does,' Stella is saying, and Abi starts to worry that she's told her too much. She's pretty much filled her in on the whole story of her and Cleo's relationship since she was thirteen. It felt like a relief saying it out loud.

'I hate to say it, but I always thought she seemed like a bit of a bitch,' Stella continues, and Abi immediately snaps into defence mode. It's OK for her to think that Cleo is mean and self-obsessed and, sometimes, downright unpleasant, because she's also hardwired to love her unconditionally. This always happens. On the rare occasions when Abi offers up her whole personal story, warts and all, she begins to backtrack as soon as the person she's speaking to has got the message that Cleo is a bit of a monster. It's like she wants them to know, but she doesn't ever want them to acknowledge it. Because someone else voicing out loud what Abi knows in her heart makes it real. And once it's made real it's difficult to justify why she doesn't do anything about it. Stand up for herself. Have it out with her. Stop kidding herself that she can force Cleo into a normal sisterly relationship, whatever that is. It's a step too far for Abi to deal with. Once this conversation is over, she wants to be able to retreat into her own little world of pretending everything is fine when it suits her.

'No,' she says, 'she just has a funny way of showing affection, that's all. I feel sorry for her, really. She's been on show her whole adult life. Everyone treats her differently because of who she is. It's hard for her to know what normal relationships are.'

Luckily Stella takes the hint that Abi doesn't really want to talk about her sister any more. 'If you say so,' she says, yawning as she fills Abi's glass up again. 'Although I'm beginning to wonder whether you should just go for it with Jon anyway. Not that I'd ever recommend a woman try to steal another woman's man, but in this case I think everyone would understand.'

Abi knows she's half joking, but she can't let it lie. 'I'd never do that. Never.'

She looks at her watch. It's nearly ten thirty and she has no idea where the time went.

'Oh god, I should go. Sorry. You have to get up early.'

Stella, Abi found out this evening, has a consultancy business. After her seven-thirty run in the morning, she'll drop the boys off at nursery and then dress up in a power suit and go around advising big corporations on productivity and streamlining operations. Tomorrow she will be addressing a room full of pharmaceutical executives on a weekend retreat. It couldn't sound like a more fantastically high-powered or scary occupation to Abi if it tried. Of course, being Stella, she has it all worked out beautifully, and she crams five days' worth of work into three so that she can spend more time with her kids while still raking the money in. Aside from buying her flat she is ploughing most of the money she makes back into the business. She has a long-term strategy for expansion and probably world domination, and Abi has no doubt she'll succeed.

'No, don't rush off. Drink your drink first and then I can call you a cab.' Stella looks as if she's going to fall asleep on the spot. Abi hopes she hasn't bored her to tears with her personal worries, but, to be fair, Stella did keep asking her questions.

'Tell you what, give me the cab number and I'll call then finish my wine while I'm waiting for it to arrive.'

When Abi leaves, Stella says, 'Let's do this again. I've had a really nice time. Apart from the nights I see Richard, I don't get much adult company outside of work.'

In the taxi on the way home Abi realizes she is smiling to herself. It feels good to have made a friend. She feels pleasantly tipsy. When she gets home, the house is dark and quiet. She tiptoes up the stairs, holding her breath as she crosses the landing outside Jon and Cleo's bedroom. When she reaches her own little attic, she brushes her teeth and then locks her door again before she gets into bed. Just in case. She can't even lie to herself; she knows it's to keep herself in more than to keep Jon out.

17

Cleo's return is as much of a production number as
you might imagine. Firstly Elena is roped in for an
extra few hours to clean the house from top to bottom. Abi insists that the girls do their own rooms and
they agree without too much fuss when she tells them
that Elena almost certainly had plans to have breakfast with her own family this morning, but she
couldn't say no to coming in for fear of losing her
job. And all because they're too lazy to clean up
after themselves. She almost reduces them to tears,
actually, so convincing are her descriptions of Elena's
humble home and her sick husband and skinny,
undernourished children. She's making it all up, of
course. She has no idea if Elena is even married, but
she always wears a very nice line in cashmere cardi-
gans so Abi thinks she does OK and she seems
perfectly happy to have signed up for an extra shift.
Plus the chances of her having children under the
age of about eighteen are pretty slim and, if she
does, she'd be in the *Guinness Book of Records*. Despite
Abi's misgivings about having someone wait on her
hand and foot she has no doubt Elena is well com-
pensated and that this is a pretty good gig as far as

unskilled labour goes. Still, it doesn't hurt to try to instil the beginnings of a social conscience into her two nieces.

Jon left at the crack of dawn to go and get the car checked over before heading off to Heathrow, or so the girls tell Abi. She suspects he's probably hiding in a café somewhere, keeping out of her way until he returns with her sister as ballast. She's grateful to him. The less they are alone together the better. She and the girls do a quick sortie down to the deli to stock up on all Cleo's favourite essentials and then there's nothing to do but wait for them to return. Abi tries to keep occupied to stop herself from imagining their reunion, Jon kissing Cleo hello, telling her how much he missed her. Despite his profession of love for Abi, he has never said that he didn't still have feelings for Cleo. And she wouldn't have wanted him to. What kind of a person would she be if she did?

They finally turn up at about quarter past one, hours late because the flight was delayed. Cleo is her usual brittle, bright self. A little too desperate to have them all believe how wonderful everything was. The hotel may have been in Midtown, but it's the new hip young place to be seen, she and the other 'girls' ate at Le Caprice and the Park Avenue Café and A Voce and drank cocktails on the roof terrace at 60 Thompson, she even got papped when they were filming on the High Line, which just goes to show she's still got it.

Cleo has an old habit, by the way, that she thinks

Abi doesn't know about, of having one of her people tip the paparazzi off about where she is going to be and when. In her heyday she even cut a deal with one of them to give him exclusives and split the profits. The photographer once gave this away to Abi after he had seemingly randomly popped up outside a café in which they'd been having lunch. Cleo had made a big show of being annoyed, but as she had climbed into a cab ahead of Abi he had tapped Abi on the shoulder and said, 'Tell her to give me a call later and I'll let her know where I've placed them.'

She didn't say anything to Cleo then and needless to say she doesn't bring it up now, but she's a little suspicious that the New York wandering paparazzi brigade have nothing better to do than amble around Manhattan randomly in the hope of bumping into a washed-up former supermodel. Still, she's glad Cleo's in a good mood and seemingly completely oblivious to the rampaging hormones that are infecting the air. Plus the girls are clearly thrilled that she's back, which makes it fine by Abi.

They settle down to lunch. She can tell that Jon has gone into overdrive to show both her and Cleo that everything is fine, business as usual. He chatters away about all the stuff that's happened in the days she's been away (with one notable exception), making them sound like the Brady Bunch's slightly more whole-some cousins. Abi starts to wonder if, in fact, she's living in a parallel universe, one where this man didn't declare his love for her only days ago. She's even less prepared for what he says next.

'So, Abi's got a new boyfriend.' As he says this, he looks round at the others triumphantly.

'Abigail!' Cleo says, amazed, and why wouldn't she be?

Tara and Megan start giggling. 'Who is he?' Tara says. 'Is it Richard?'

Great. Still, Richard is the only man other than their father that Tara and Megan have seen her speak to since she's been here, so it could have been a lot worse. She shrugs.

'Who's Richard?' Cleo will be delighted at the prospect of Abi, her weird loner sister, dating.

'It is, isn't it? It's Richard!' Megan squeals.

Oh god, is she really going to have to keep this up?

Jon turns his manic grin on her. 'That's right. Abi is going out with Richard.'

'Who is Richard?' Cleo laughs, and looks at Abi. 'Tell me!'

'He's Abi's boss at the bookshop, isn't he, Abi?'

She nods miserably.

'We've met him. He's nice,' Megan says.

'He's hot,' Tara adds helpfully. 'Considering he's so ancient.'

Abi can't help it; she looks at Jon. He doesn't look at her.

'So,' Cleo says. 'Tell me everything.'

This is torture. 'There's really nothing to tell.'

'That is so typically you. I go away for less than two weeks and when I come back you're seeing someone, but you try to make out there's nothing to tell. There must be a story behind it. Did your eyes meet across a pile of books? Did he seduce you in the stock room after you closed up one night? What?'

'Yuk, Mum!' Megan pulls a disgusted face.

'No,' Abi says. 'Of course not.'

'Well, what then? Something must have happened. God, I can't believe you've met someone.'

Abi feels a prick of resentment. Why is it so hard to believe? She tells herself not to pick a fight with Cleo on her first day back.

'I don't want to talk about it. It's early days. It'll probably come to nothing.'

'Naturally, because that's your default way of approaching a relationship. Write it off before it's even properly begun. Save yourself the heartache later on.'

She's right, of course. Except for the fact that this time it's not Richard she's scared of getting too close to. 'That is so unfair.'

'But not untrue. Tell you what, why don't you invite him over for dinner one evening? Not tonight because I'm jet-lagged and I'll probably fall asleep in my food at about eight o'clock, but later in the week? That way we all get to scrutinize him. Make sure his intentions are honourable.' She laughs to show she's joking, but Abi knows that the part about inviting him over was deadly serious.

'I don't know . . .' Actually, she does. She knows that it's not going to happen. In fact, she's not even going to mention it to Richard because knowing his obsession with all things Cleo he would say yes like a shot. And she also knows that she couldn't trust him to just get through the evening without her deception being detected. He wouldn't be able to help himself. He'd say or do something stupid just so he had a funny story to tell down the pub later on.

'It's a good idea – you should,' Jon says, looking sort of at her but through her at the same time. It's like if he doesn't focus on her then she's not quite there. If they don't make eye contact, it's as if nothing ever happened.

'Let me think about it,' Abi says. 'Now can we talk about something else?'

Later, when she goes up to her room to read she hears Megan in her bedroom singing loudly enough so that Abi can hear: 'Auntie Abi and Richard sitting in a tree. K.I.S.S.I.N.G.'

Thankfully Jon goes back to work on Monday and Abi resumes her solo childcare routine while Cleo drops right back onto her punishing gym/nails/hair/casting treadmill. The atmosphere in the house is, to say the least, forced. Cleo is desperate for them to believe that her trip was a huge success and that her career has been successfully relaunched – and, who knows, maybe it has. Abi has no evidence to the contrary, Jon is manically trying to act like he doesn't have a care in the world while at the same time refusing to look her in the eye and she is exhausted from trying to pretend that everything is fine, that they're all as happy as can be. That's always been the way in her family. So long as no one ever acknowledges there's a problem out loud, then they are all experts at pretending that there isn't. They suppress things, bury their resentments and irritations deep enough so they never see the light of day, but not so deep that they can't feel them festering away in the depths. It can't be healthy, but it's the Attwood way. She wonders if Jon has picked up symptoms over the years.

He is studiously avoiding being alone with her, which can only be a good thing, although she occasionally catches him looking at her or, just as often, finds herself looking at him. For just a moment too long.

The hint of hurt that she thinks she can see in his eyes tears at her stomach every time. She wonders if he can see the same in her, because she can't imagine she is disguising it well. It's all she can do not to reach out to touch his arm when he walks by her and, at one point, she almost stretches out a hand to stroke his head when she passes behind his chair. There's a point where the hair stands up from his crown rebelliously – a cowlick she thinks it's called – and it's all Abi can do to stop herself smoothing it down.

On the surface, though, everything is just as it

should be. If they can just keep this up for another few weeks they'll be home and dry. She might have an ulcer, but that seems like a small price to pay. She can go back to seeing Cleo once or twice a year and Jon almost never. She'll miss the girls, though. They've definitely bonded, so she'll invite them down to stay with her in Kent once in a while. She finds herself daydreaming little scenarios whereby Tara, Megan and Phoebe are all running in and out of the house on a beautiful sunny summer's day. OK, she knows that Phoebe, at eighteen, is too old to be playing like a child and, anyway, the house is sold and the fantasy doesn't work quite so well with an above-ground-level flat, but she indulges herself anyway.

This, by the way, has been one of her more successful coping mechanisms throughout her life: if things aren't going well, inhabit a whole other existence in your head that you can control. It's a bit like playing Second Life, but you don't even need a DS. Tragically, even in her daydreams, she holds herself back. She can't just imagine she is successful or rich or happily in love. She gets bogged down by the detail. She has to rationalize each step. How did she become successful? What qualifications did she get? Did she work her way up from the bottom and, if so, how did she get her foot in the door? It's exhausting. It still works as a distraction, but as escapism it's doomed.

Somehow she gets through to the relative sanctuary of work on Tuesday. Word seems to have got round the neighbourhood about Richard and Stella, because all day there's a steady stream of distraught-looking young mums giving him disappointed looks across the bookshelves. Almost no one buys any-thing. They just stare mournfully, waiting for him to come and tell them it isn't so, which, of course, he doesn't. He soldiers on regardless, greeting them in the same way he always does, relentlessly flirtatious and friendly while they make Bambi eyes and sigh miserably. Richard steadfastly refuses to acknow-ledge their pain. Abi is grateful that in deference to Stella he doesn't play out the charade of her and him in front of them, but when they're on their own he's merciless.

'Darling,' he says, sidling up to her during a brief quiet period. 'Are you sure you don't want to pop out back for a quickie while the shop's empty?'

'Fuck off, Richard.'

'What's wrong? Don't you love me any more? Have you gone off me already? I'm devastated!'

'Not funny,' she says, shaking off the arm he has snaked round her.

'Oh, come on, it is. And, besides, you have to be nice to me or I might be compelled to go round and tell your handsome brother-in-law the truth.'

She knows he's only joking and, to be honest, usu-ally she'd laugh. She definitely would if it concerned anyone except her. But she seems to have had a sense-of-humour failure. Richard must be able to tell that from her expression, because he drops both his arm and the joke.

'God, you have got it bad, haven't you?'

'No . . . yes, OK, I have. But can we just pretend I haven't? Please?'

'You only had to ask,' he says, and Abi smiles for the first time today.

'Yeah, right.'

'OK, well, you only had to ask in that miserable tone of voice and look suicidal, how's that?'

She grants him a quick peck on the cheek. She really is fond of him and she tells herself she has to remember that he is doing her an enormous favour. 'Thank you.'

She is sticking to her resolution not to tell him about Cleo's dinner invitation, though. Her plan is to keep up the pretence at home while fighting off all attempts to integrate him into the family, and then in a week or so, once the equilibrium is restored at home and she thinks Jon has firmly got the message that she's not interested, she can announce that it's all over – she and Richard have broken up. She can cry pitifully for a couple of days, which shouldn't be too much of a stretch, and then announce her intention to swear off men for the foreseeable future. There's no reason for them not to believe her; they are both aware of her tragic track record. She's just allowing herself to think that everything might work out OK when the door opens and Tara and Megan come running in, followed by Cleo at a more stately pace, who gazes around the shop with an amused expression on her face. Abi moves forward to greet them, hoping that she can head them off at the pass and, maybe, suggest that they all go straight out for something to eat when Megan points a finger across the room and shouts, 'That's him!'

Too late. Richard looks up from whatever he's doing. Abi sees the brief moment of delighted recognition when he spots Cleo and then he turns his charm straight on to the girls, welcoming them as if they were members of his own family.

'So . . . back again so soon. Did you enjoy the books? How was the Jacqueline Wilson, Megan?'

'Fab,' she says, and then she turns to her mother. 'This is Richard. This is Auntie Abi's boyfriend.'

'Pleased to meet you. I'm Cleo,' Cleo says, and holds out a hand for him to shake. Richard does a phony double take.

'I know who you are,' he says, charm offensive back on. 'It's a pleasure to meet you.'

Abi finds herself getting annoyed. He's supposed to be pretending to be her boyfriend. What's he doing flirting with her sister? Now Cleo will think she's a complete loser whose new beau is already looking around to see who's next.

'And you,' Cleo says. Is she flirting right back at him? Does no one have any morals today? Abi needs to save the situation. She links her arm with Richard's.

'Cleo is my sister.'

'Your sister? I had no idea,' he says disingenuously. 'You don't look alike.'

Abi pinches his arm where she's hanging on to it. He flinches then remembers who they are all meant to be playing in this little drama, and puts the arm round Abi's shoulders proprietorially.

'What I mean is you're both beautiful, just different. Actually, now I look closer, I can see some similarities.' Nice try, but he's fooling no one. Abi and Cleo both know that he was bowled over by seeing her in the flesh. She's used to having that reaction from men and Abi is used to her having it too.

'She's our mummy,' Megan says conspiratorially.

'Well, I can see that, because you're just as gorgeous,' he says, and half of Abi hates him for still going on about the way Cleo looks even though it's in a roundabout way, while the other half is happy for Megan that she's been given a compliment while she's still young enough to take it at face value. Maybe if anyone had ever told Abi she was as beautiful as Cleo when she was seven she wouldn't have grown up to be such a fuck-up.

'So, what brings you in here? Checking up on me and Abi?'

'She wanted to get a look at you,' Tara says.

'She said most of Auntie Abi's boyfriends always sounded as dull as dishwater, but we told her you weren't like that, so she wanted to see you for herself.'

'I don't think I said that, Megan . . .'

'Yes you did. You said that exact thing, dull as dish-water, because I had to ask you what it meant and —'

Cleo, to give her credit, blushes a little. 'I think you've got confused. What I said was we should go and see Auntie Abi and see if she's remembered to ask Richard to come to dinner yet.'

'No, you didn't . . .'

Tara, realizing that things aren't quite going to plan, jumps in. 'Yes, she did, Meg. Stop being stupid.'

Abi looks at Richard, trying to communicate 'don't even think about it' with her eyes, which is harder than you might imagine, but he's got a smirk on his face and she knows she's lost him. The kudos to be earned from having gone round to Cleo's house for dinner far outweighs his feelings of loyalty towards her.

Before she can stop him he's saying, 'That would be amazing. Thank you. And, no, Abi hadn't men-tioned it . . .'

He looks at her, mock scolding. She looks back at him like she hates him, which at the moment she feels like she does.

'I didn't think you'd want to,' Abi says with what she hopes is the right amount of threat in her voice. 'It seems a bit early to be meeting the family and all that.'

'Nonsense, darling. You know I've been dying to meet your family.' He turns to Cleo. 'When would you like me?'

'Well . . . how about tonight? That is unless you have other plans?'

Abi has one last-ditch attempt. 'Weren't we going to go and see *On the Waterfront* tonight? He's never seen *On the Waterfront* and it's on at the South Bank somewhere. A Marlon Brando retrospective.' She realizes she is sounding slightly desperate and forces herself to shut up.

'Were we? I don't remember us deciding that. We can do that another night.'

'Yes, come to dinner,' Megan chips in. 'I can show you my room.'

'And mine,' Tara adds. 'It's much better than hers.'

'Well, I think that settles it,' Richard says. 'What time?'

When they've gone, having agreed that Richard will show up at the house at seven thirty, Abi turns on him even though she knows she has no right to.

'What the fuck? Why didn't you say we were busy?'

'Listen,' he says, 'you want them to believe we're going out together, this'll convince them, OK?'

'But we can't keep it up all evening. Not with them all looking at us . . .'

'This whole thing was your idea. I didn't ask you to involve me in your domestic dramas.'

He's right. She knows he is. 'I know you didn't. I'm sorry. I just . . . You don't know what she's like. She'll see through it in a moment.'

'Well, I'm clearly a cut above all your other boy-friends,' he says, and he raises one eyebrow James Bond style. 'I mean, what was it she said? Dull as dishwater. All of them?'

'Yes. All six of them. Well, since Phoebe's father, anyway.'

'And she's . . . what? Eighteen? Wow, you've lived an exciting life.'

'I'm not looking for excitement. I'm looking for reliability and responsibility.'

'Dullness . . .'

'Excitement's overrated, OK? And, anyway, I'm fine on my own.'

He gets her in a bear hug. 'Well, don't worry, you've got me now. I'll save you!'

'Just behave tonight. Please.'

Richard holds her at arm's length, a hammy look of horror on his face. 'I'm devastated you could even doubt it. Don't you know I love you?'

OK, he's got her. She can't help herself. She laughs.

18

Tara and Megan are fussing like two hormonal teen-agers over the fact that Auntie Abi's 'boyfriend' is coming to dinner. If she really had found herself a boyfriend, Abi thinks she would be insulted by the momentous importance this event seems to have assumed. Auntie Abi has a boyfriend! Some poor sap has somehow been conned into thinking our dried-up old spinster aunt is a catch! Get the bunting out! Let's celebrate!

They have tried on at least three outfits each and now Megan is sporting some of her mother's red Chanel lipstick that makes her look more like a malevolent doll than the sophisticated young lady she's hoping for. You would think that they were the ones gearing up for a date, not Abi. Although, of course, in reality, she's not, but she's having to make the effort to look as if she is. In fact, she is making far more of an effort than if she was going on a real date, because on a real date she makes precious little effort at all. She puts on heels with her jeans, and proper make-up, not just mascara, and she ties her hair back in a high ponytail. It's a shame there's no one to really appreciate it.

Jon is crashing around in the kitchen, somehow managing to make cooking dinner sound like a contact sport. Abi wonders if he's sneakily spitting in the soup when no one's watching or slyly tossing in some peanuts in the hope that Richard has a nut allergy and will go into anaphylaxis at the table. Cleo, when Abi eventually comes downstairs, is dressed to kill in a short black backless dress that she tells her sister is by Martin Grant, no doubt eager to show off her fabulousness to someone who couldn't quite disguise that he was an admirer, despite the fact that he is meant to be Abi's boyfriend.

Abi sheepishly asks Jon if there's anything she can do to help and he gives her that forced grin he's taken to wearing in her presence over the past few days and says, no, he has it under control. It all smells fantastic and she feels her heart go out to him for making such an effort when she knows how much it must be costing him. He's wearing old combat trousers and a faded army green T-shirt that she thinks are his way of trying to say he's not bothered about looking good. Why should he be? It's not like Richard is the competition. But if he's hoping to play down his attractiveness his ensemble is actually having the opposite effect. Well, on Abi at least. It makes him look vulnerable. A confused boy in a room full of power players. She feels a lump rise up in her throat and she backs out of the room.

At exactly seven thirty the doorbell rings and

there's Richard, bottle of champagne in hand and a big self-satisfied smile on his face.

'Hi, darling,' he says theatrically, even though there's no one else in the hall so for all he knows his performance is just for her. She, of course, knows that Jon is in earshot in the kitchen. Richard leans in and gives her a noisy kiss on the lips. She recoils. She knows they have to be convincing as a couple, but there are limits.

'Behave,' she hisses at him.

'Just getting into character,' he whispers back. 'Where is everyone?'

'In here.' Abi leads him through to the living room where Tara and Megan greet him like he's their long-lost brother and Cleo offers him her hand like it was a precious gift. Richard is looking around, taking it all in, no doubt so that he can report every detail to the others in the pub. Abi wonders how he's squared this evening with Stella.

'Wow,' Richard says as he takes a seat on the sofa. 'This place is incredible.'

Cleo laughs a forced little laugh, which Abi knows is meant to mean: Oh, this old thing? I just knocked it up in my spare time. 'Thank you.'

'That's interior designers for you,' Abi says, and Cleo gives her a look. Immediately Abi feels petty and mean-spirited. What does she care if her sister wants to give the impression that she did the house up herself?

She tries to smooth things over. 'What I mean is

you had a bit of help, didn't you. You weren't literally wallpapering the walls yourself.'

'Of course not,' Cleo snaps. 'I didn't say I was.'

This is going well, then.

They all sit down and there's a bit of an awkward silence. Even the girls are lost for words. Wine, Abi thinks. That'll help.

'Do you want a drink?' As she says it, as if he was waiting right outside the door for his cue, Jon appears brandishing a bottle of white and a bottle of red.

'Merlot or Gavi di Gavi? Hi, Richard.' Richard stands up and goes to shake Jon's hand, but Jon is holding the bottles so he's left hanging at first and then Jon offers him a couple of spare fingers so he shakes those.

'Merlot, please. Hi, mate, how are you doing?'

'Good, yes. Couldn't be better.' Jon's megawatt rictus smile nearly blinds Abi as he turns to her. 'I know that you'll have white.'

'Yes. White. Thank you.' She knocks back the glass he gives her almost in one. She has to stop herself holding it out for a second one straight away. OK, so she doesn't actually stop herself at all. She doesn't look Jon in the eye as he refills her glass.

'Something smells good,' Richard says.

'It's only coq au vin. I didn't have much notice, I'm afraid.' Jon gives Abi a slightly accusatory look as he says this and she wants to say 'it wasn't my idea, don't blame me', but, of course, she doesn't.

'Perfect,' Richard says. 'One of my favourites. And, listen, I hope this hasn't put you to too much trouble. Honestly, I'd have been OK with a takeaway.' You have to say it for Richard – it's hard not to be charmed when he wants you to be.

'Don't be silly,' Cleo chips in. 'It's no trouble. We invited you for selfish reasons, actually. We wanted to get a closer look at Abi's boyfriend.'

Richard laughs and, as if remembering why he's here, puts his arm round Abi. She knows she should relax into him as if they sit like this all the time, but, however hard she asks her muscles to oblige, they refuse. 'Well, I hope I pass the inspection.'

She smiles weakly at Jon who is standing rigid, looking at the happy couple as if they were a – not very appealing – exhibit. Abi resists the urge to shrug Richard's arm away.

'I'd better get back to it. Dinner'll be about twenty minutes. Girls, do you want to set the table?' Tara and Megan get up without complaint and Cleo watches them, eyebrows raised.

'That's a first. They must be trying to impress you, Richard.'

Abi doesn't bother to tell her that, in fact, the girls have made some considerable headway in the field of domestic science during their mother's short absence; she'll see for herself soon enough.

Richard is at his personable best, asking all the right questions about Cleo's career and showing appropriate amounts of, genuine, fascination with the answers. She laps it up and, Abi's surprised to find, it's actually quite interesting because she's always deliberately avoided talking to Cleo about it as much as she's been able to over the years, so she hasn't heard half of the stories before. Some of them are pretty funny and the atmosphere lightens tangibly as Cleo talks, Richard listens and Abi keeps an eye on the clock and wills the evening to be over.

Exactly twenty minutes later Megan comes through and announces that dinner is ready. Abi's relieved that they're eating in the kitchen as usual and not in the 'formal' dining room, which she finds intimidating at the best of times. Her plan is to set the girls off talking about something and hope that they don't stop until they have finished eating and she can pack Richard off home as early as possible.

Tara helps Jon distribute the starters of homemade mushroom pâté and little slivers of crispy toast.

'This looks amazing,' Richard says.

'He makes it himself,' Cleo says with an almost imperceptible eye roll. 'Although we have a perfectly lovely little deli up the road who do just as good a job and with none of the effort.' Abi hates that Cleo is belittling Jon's passion, even if she's not aware that she's doing so.

'Amazing,' Richard says appreciatively. 'That's really impressive, Jon. I wouldn't know where to start.'

Jon grunts his thanks.

'So, girls,' Abi jumps in. 'What else did you do today besides come into the shop?'

'I had street dance,' Tara says. 'My teacher said —'

She doesn't get to finish because Cleo interrupts. 'You can tell Auntie Abigail about it later. Don't think you're getting away without the third degree,' she says, turning to Richard and smiling. 'It's not often I get to interrogate one of my sister's boyfriends.'

Abi would just like to say here that if the ground opened up and swallowed her at this point it wouldn't be a moment too soon.

'Honestly, Cleo, don't embarrass Richard.'

'Who's embarrassing him? I'm just going to ask him a few questions. You don't mind, do you, Richard?'

She turns the full force of her A-list smile onto Richard, who basks in its supernova glow.

'Of course I don't. Abi, you should be pleased that your sister's so protective.' Abi shoots him a dirty look, but he's oblivious, seduced by the heady mix of good wine and the proximity of a real live celebrity. 'Ask away.'

'So,' she says, leaning forward on her hands like a TV journalist interviewing a politician. 'You run a book-shop?'

'I own the bookshop,' he says casually. 'But it's true that I do run it as well.'

'Ah, you own the bookshop. How long have you been there?'

'About nine years.'

'And before?'

Abi can't stand this any longer. It could only be worse if Richard really were her boyfriend and she wanted him to stay that way.

'Cleo, for god's sake. Stop being so nosy.'

Cleo laughs. She's loving this. 'It's my prerogative as your older sister. I have to check his prospects.'

How could Richard object to all this attention from a supermodel no less? Clearly he doesn't. 'Tell you what, I'll give you a quick rundown of my CV and then, if you think I'm not worthy of Abi's attentions, I can leave before the main course. Although if it's as delicious as the starter I'll be loath to go. You might have to kick me out.'

Oh, the hilarity. Throughout all this Abi can't even look at Jon. She just concentrates on eating far more of the pâté and toast than is healthy. Richard gives Cleo a brief precis of his life, all of which is news to Abi. He's forty-four as it turns out, divorced eleven years ago and has had a fair few relationships since, but nothing serious.

'Not until I met Abi,' he says, overdoing it enormously and putting his hand over hers at the same time. She withdraws her own quickly, trying to make it look as if she was going for the bread all along. Briefly she catches Jon's eye and he looks away.

'He's joking, of course,' she says. 'We've only known each other a couple of weeks, as you know. It's early days.'

Richard soldiers on with his personal history. He worked as a sub-editor on various newspapers for several years, then got sick of the rush-hour tubes and the nine to five and took voluntary redundancy to open his own business instead. Hence Regent's Park Road Books was born.

'It's a lovely shop,' Jon says, making an effort. Abi wants to hug him. Let's face it, she'd want to hug him even if he wasn't making an effort. She just wants to hug him generally. All day, every day.

'It is,' Cleo is saying. 'I don't think I've ever been in there before today.' And therein, Abi thinks, lies the difference between her and her sister in a nutshell. Cleo has lived within five minutes' walk of a beautiful independent bookshop for six years and never been inside. Abi supposes she should at least be grateful that Cleo hasn't been in there every day mooning over Richard like the other local ladies.

Jon and the girls start clearing the table and dishing up the main course, so Abi gets up to help, leaving Cleo and Richard to entertain each other. Over the coq au vin Cleo decides to up the ante.

'So how did you two get together?' Richard and Abi look at each other. They spent a bit of time this afternoon coming up with a fake history for this very eventuality, but she's struggling to remember it now. She made him promise not to offer up too many gory details.

'Oh, you know. I liked her right from the off, but she wasn't having any of it, so I took her down the pub and plied her with a few drinks.'

Cleo and the girls laugh, and Jon does a good approximation of it.

'He's joking about the getting-me-drunk bit,' Abi says, turning to Tara and Megan. 'Never let a boy get you drunk.'

'Yuk,' Megan says. Abi doesn't know whether she means boys or drink, but either way she's pleased that's the reaction.

'Anyway, there's no big dramatic getting-together story. We just thought we'd give it a go and see what happens.'

'She's such an old romantic, your sister,' Richard says, and Cleo says, 'Tell me about it.'

Luckily that seems to have exhausted the topic of Abi's relationship so they talk about other things. Richard asks Cleo all about her trip and he makes appropriately flattering noises about her decision to stage a comeback. At one point he asks her what the product is and Abi holds her breath, waiting to see what Cleo will say.

'It's made by La Vie En Rose,' she says, naming a medium- to high-end cosmetics company. This is more than she has told Abi or, as far as Abi knows, Jon before. 'Some new moisturizer or other.' Abi looks at Jon to see if he is registering any reaction and he catches her eye briefly. She raises one eyebrow and he mirrors her action. It's the first normal interaction they've had for days.

Then Richard turns his charms on Jon and they

chat about advertising in general and onehitcompari-son.com in particular. Under different circumstances Abi can see that they would get on like a house on fire, because they laugh at the same things and that even though Jon is clearly predisposed to dislike Richard he seems to be being won round despite himself.

Meal over and girls dispatched to bed, Abi starts to wonder how soon she can suggest to Richard that it's time to go home. She looks at her watch – it's only ten o'clock. To be honest, she feels absolutely exhausted from having to keep up the pretence of not-so-young love with the wrong person. She yawns loudly and they all look at her.

'Are we keeping you up?' Cleo says.

'Sorry, I'm knackered. And don't you have to get up early tomorrow, Richard? That . . . um . . . that delivery's coming.'

Richard looks at her as if she's insane. He's having a lovely time, why should he want to cut it short?

He looks at his watch. 'It's only just gone ten.'

'I know but, remember, you said to me to make sure you didn't stay late because you had an early start . . .'

Thankfully he gets the hint. 'Oh. Yes. The delivery. Of course.' He puts down his glass and gets up. 'Thank you so much for dinner . . .'

'Why don't you stay here? It seems mad you having to leave when Abi's got a double bed upstairs. And it's very private up there, isn't it, Abi? You've got your own bathroom.'

Oh. Good. God. Of course, it hadn't occurred to Abi that people would be expecting her and Richard to want to spend the night together — although it begs the question why they clearly haven't so far. Cleo and Jon must think they keep themselves going with afternoon sessions and just let the shop run itself. She could try to protest that she's saving herself, but that might have more weight if she was sixteen instead of a thirty-eight-year-old mother of one.

'No! No. Because then you'd have to get up and get dressed to go and let the delivery thing in whereas if you're at home you can just fall out of bed . . .'

'Abi's right. I'm not very good at getting up at the best of times.'

She knows that if she doesn't go with him the others are going to think that the relationship has lost its magic already, but there's no way she is going to head off into the night to sleep on Richard's sofa. What would Stella think, for one thing?

'And, you know what, I'm so tired I'm just going to crash out so there's no point me coming with you. You don't mind, do you?' she says, making an effort to cosy up to him a bit.

Richard kisses her on the top of the head. 'No. You get some sleep. Come round in the morning, though, won't you?'

She agrees and he says his goodbyes. Cleo and he, new best friends, hug.

'We must do this again,' Abi hears Richard say.

What? That wasn't part of the plan. Cleo, of course, purrs and says, 'How about this Saturday? We could go to the Ivy Club. It's so much more exclusive than the restaurant these days. And the food's fantastic.'

Abi has to butt in. 'Oh, I'm not sure we can. Weren't we going to go to the theatre this Saturday?'

Richard stubbornly refuses to take the hint this time. 'Well, we haven't got the tickets yet and it's probably sold out anyway. Dinner's so much more fun, don't you think? And you keep saying how much you're loving spending time with Cleo. We can go to the theatre any time.'

'I was looking forward to it,' Abi says firmly.

'What were you going to see?' Jon asks, and of course Abi has no idea what's even on in the West End so she just looks at Richard who says, '*Priscilla, Queen of the Desert*,' and somehow manages to keep a straight face.

'Oh,' Jon says, because, really, what else is there to say.

Abi is looking daggers at Richard, but he is steadfastly refusing to take any notice.

'It was me who wanted to see it, really. Abi wasn't that fussed. So let's do dinner instead.'

She knows what he's doing. This is her punishment for involving him in her little mess in the first place. He gets to hang out with Cleo and go to the Ivy Club and do whatever fabulous things he wants while Abi has no right to complain.

Jon shakes his hand. 'See you Saturday, then?'

He's being so nice to Richard, so friendly, Abi could kiss him. (Yes, yes, we know.)

'Lovely,' Richard says, smiling.

'I'll see you out,' Abi says, and she follows him to the front step where they agree to wait for a couple of minutes so the others will think they are having some kind of teenage snog fest. At one point Richard makes a sort of strangled moaning noise followed by a loud slurp and Abi has to hit him to shut him up.

'How was I?' he says in a stage whisper, when they're alone.

Even though his unabashed hero worship of Cleo drove her to distraction, Abi is still aware that this whole evening was above and beyond the call of duty. She knows that pulling him up for his suggestion of dinner wouldn't help her cause any. 'You were great. Thank you. And don't worry. In a couple of days I'll tell them we're no more and it'll all be over.'

'Oh, no rush. Your sister's lovely,' he says. 'Not at all like I imagined her to be from the way you've talked about her.'

Abi heads back inside before she says something she'll regret.

19

French conversation, street dance, gymnastics, violin practice, bookshop. The next few days go past without incident or event. Abi takes herself off to the cinema on her own again one night just so she can claim to have spent the evening with Richard.

'Has he got a secret wife stashed away at home, or something?' Cleo says the next morning. 'I mean, why won't he let you stay over?'

'I wanted to wake up in my own bed,' Abi says.

'Then tell Richard he can stay here. I'm not sure you're giving this relationship a chance.'

Ah, of course, Abi thinks, my fault. Abi sabotages her own love life as per usual.

She refuses to rise to the bait. 'Honestly, Cleo, it's all fine. Don't worry about me.'

Abi has insisted that they meet Jon and Cleo at the Ivy Club on Saturday to save them all having to share a cosy cab ride. She's had to pretend that she and Richard are going straight there from somewhere else. In reality, she has been hiding out in the stock room at the shop for a few hours like a fugitive. To pass more time they have a quick one in the pub before they go.

There's no sign of Stella, and Richard tells Abi that

she's taken the kids up to see her parents for a few days. Despite the fact that they are, in reality, doing nothing wrong, Abi feels guilty that the other people in the pub might think she has succumbed to Richard's charms while his girlfriend is out of town. She sits as far away from him as she can while still sharing the same table. Richard is dressed very smartly in a suit with an open-neck shirt and Abi too has pushed the boat out, pulling a dress from the depths of her backpack, and her one and only pair of high heels are making another appearance. They make a handsome couple if she says so herself.

'If I wasn't taken . . .' Richard twinkles when he first sees her.

'Don't even joke about it,' Abi says.

They get to the Ivy Club – The Ivy's younger, more elitist sister – at about twenty to eight. Cleo is a member, for some reason, although Abi has no idea when she goes. Maybe she just likes to know she could if she wanted to. They head up to the bar in the impressive glass lift and announce themselves to the woman behind the desk who leads them to a table surrounded by four cosy-looking armchairs. Cleo and Jon aren't there yet, so they order a drink. Richard immediately starts to scour the bar for famous faces.

'Look,' he hisses, 'there's Nigel Lythgoe. And is that Sylvester Stallone?'

Abi has to admit that part of her loves sitting in the opulent surroundings, glass of champagne in hand (what the hell, Cleo's paying, she assumes, and she's developed a taste for it over the past few weeks), star spotting. She just wishes it was under different circumstances. When Cleo and Jon walk in, there's a tiny little ripple of recognition from a few of the other non-celebrity customers – the ones who Abi noticed seemed disappointed when they looked up to see her and Richard arrive. Cleo surveys the room, keen to see what sort of reaction her entrance has provoked, waves her hand at a couple of people and then grants both Richard and Abi a stagey hug. Jon and Richard shake hands matily, and Jon and Abi sort of smile and say, 'Hi.' It's all a bit awkward, a bit formal.

After another glass – well, Cleo and Jon were ordering one and she didn't want to sit there empty handed – their table is ready and they move on up to the restaurant and order all manner of delicious-sounding things. Abi plumps for the smoked swordfish followed by cod with chorizo. She spots the sticky-toffee pudding on the dessert part of the menu and tells herself she has to try to leave room. Richard and Cleo are chatting away – he's asking her about all the other supermodels from her era and she's entertaining him with horror stories of which one was the worst diva and who was anorexic and who just stayed thin because they were a coke-head.

It's all horribly indiscreet and Abi keeps looking around to check if anyone else is listening. There's no point trying to change the course of the conversation because Cleo's loving holding court and Richard is lapping it up. It's not that it's not entertaining, it is, but after a while Abi starts to wish Cleo would let someone else get a word in now and again.

Richard is oohing and aahing as if on cue. He barely takes his eyes off Cleo, even when the starters arrive (seared scallops for Richard, onion-and-parsnip soup for Jon and chargrilled octopus for Cleo), and at one point he lays his hand on her arm and she lets him. Abi realizes with a sickening feeling that he's flirting with her again. In front of her, his supposed girl-friend. Never mind that the whole thing is a sham, the sole purpose of tonight was to hammer home the fact that Abi is unavailable because she is in a new and exciting relationship. Not that she has got together with a man who really is more interested in her sister. And let's not forget – far worse, if truth be told, because as far as Richard knows her crush on Jon was entirely one-sided – that this display is going on in front of Jon, Cleo's husband, without any regard for the way it might be making him feel. It occurs to Abi that Richard is not a man's man. In fact, if an attract-ive woman is in the room, he probably barely even registers if a man is there. Even if the woman he's chatting up happens to be married to them.

There's no doubt that Cleo has picked up Richard's signals – you'd have to be blind not to. She basks in the rosy spotlight. At one point, after something particu-larly banal that Richard has said to her, she gives a fake little girly giggle and says, 'You want to watch him, Abigail. He's a terrible flirt,' and Abi feels thirteen again, swimming blindly along in her sister's wake.

She can't even look at Jon. She's afraid if she sees his pity she'll burst out crying. Out of frustration, obviously, not because she cares what Richard is doing, but because Jon must think she does.

When she manages to make eye contact with Richard – which takes longer than you might imagine – she tries to indicate that she wants to speak to him in private. He steadfastly ignores her, so in the end she kicks him on the shin and he yelps in pain.

'I'm going to nip out on the terrace for a cigarette,' Abi says.

'I didn't know you smoked,' Cleo says. 'I thought you gave up.'

'Yes, well, Richard's got me started again. Coming?' she says to Richard. He looks confused. In reality, neither of them have smoked for years, so she's not surprised.

'Oh. Yes. Of course.'

Out on the little roof terrace they stand by the heater inhaling the smoke from the cigarette of another exiled diner. He looks quizzically at them when neither of them lights up. He's probably scared they're going to ask him for a spare.

'Passive smoking,' Abi says, smiling at him. 'I love it since I gave up.'

'What's going on?' Richard hisses at her.

She waits a moment in the hope that the smoker will decide to go inside, but when he finishes his cigarette and lights another from the butt she realizes he's there for the long haul. She hasn't really worked out what she's going to say, so it all comes out in a big inarticulate tumble.

'You're flirting with Cleo, what are you doing that for because now they won't believe that we're real and they'll just feel sorry for me like my boyfriend's got the hots for her. As usual.'

The smoking man is now a captive audience. Damned if he's going to miss this show. Abi is past caring. Richard is looking at her, mouth open.

'You're having a go at me because I'm being friendly to your sister? What do you want me to do? I didn't ask to be here in the first place if you remember.'

Well, strictly speaking, he did. He was the one who so readily accepted the first dinner invitation. The one who actually suggested the second. In fact, it's only down to him that they are here now. She decides not to go there.

'I'm sorry. I know you're doing me a huge favour, but the whole point is for it to look like we're a couple. Like we're in that first-flush-of-love thing.'

'Fine,' Richard says, his tone making it clear that it's anything but. 'My mistake. I thought if your sister liked me, then she'd be more convinced that our relationship was real. How you've misinterpreted that as me flirting I have no idea, but I can ignore Cleo from now on and play the devoted husband to you if that's what you want. Then she'll just think I'm rude, but anyway . . .'

'Don't be stupid. I'm not asking you to ignore her . . .'

'What then?' he says, petulantly.

'Just . . . tone it down a bit. Include me and Jon in the conversation sometimes. I'm not asking you to go over the top . . .'

'Whatever you want,' he says angrily, and he stalks off. Conversation over.

Back at the table it seems to Abi that both Cleo and Jon look at them like they know the relationship is a disaster and that she and Richard have been off for a fight. People feeling pity for her is one thing Abi just cannot stand. She is so worked up that she is barely capable of making conversation even when Richard makes a big show of asking her opinion on something. He goes over the top, holding her hand, stroking her knee, at one point even nuzzling her neck. She knows he's doing it to get back at her. He knows that she'll be totally uncomfortable with the displays of physical affection. She goes along with it, though. It's all she's got.

On the way home – there's no getting out of sharing a taxi this time – Cleo says, 'Now, of course you're going to stay tonight, Richard. It's Sunday tomorrow so I know you can't be getting up for a delivery.'

'Well, the shop does open on a Sunday,' Abi says, looking at the floor.

'Yes, but not till twelve. I checked.' Cleo laughs as if to say, 'Look how clever I am.'

So that's that settled.

They have a nightcap and because Abi and Jon pretty much sit there in silence – Abi just sick of the whole thing and Jon, no doubt, dreading knowing – or thinking that he knows – that she and Richard are about to be getting it on right above his head – Cleo and Richard resume their love-in. Cleo, Abi notices, is practically purring so ecstatic is she with the attention. She lays a hand on Richard's knee momentarily as if to put emphasis on whatever she is saying. Their body language implies they're oblivious to anyone else in the room.

Abi still can't look at Jon, but now she doesn't know if it's him or herself that she feels more humiliated for. She is trying not to drink too much for fear that she'll say or do something she shouldn't, so she drowns her brandy in Diet Coke and sips it slowly.

After an hour or so of more Cleo stories, she stands up and announces she's ready for bed.

'See you at breakfast,' Richard twinkles at Cleo as he follows Abi out. She can't get out of there fast enough.

On the way up Richard practically takes notes, keeping up a running commentary about how fabulous everything is. Abi knows he wants to store as much information in his memory as he can to share with whomever he thinks he can impress tomorrow. ('So I had dinner with Cleo at the Ivy Club. Remember her? Her house is just incredible.') She's beyond irritated with him. When they reach her room, he makes a joke about bouncing up and down on the bed so that Jon and Cleo think 'we're at it' and she can't even laugh.

'They're two floors down,' she says huffily. 'And the girls are staying at their friends' so no one would even hear it.'

She tells him he can sleep in her bed. She's only slept in the sheets once. And then she goes off to the other little bedroom next door and lies on the unmade bed under a fake fur throw that she finds on a chair. This has gone far enough.

In the morning she smooths down the covers to hide the evidence and then she goes next door and wakes Richard up at about half past eight, safe in the knowledge that Cleo won't even have thought about surfacing yet after a late night. She shoves him into the bathroom for a quick shower while she gets dressed hastily and then she practically drags him out of the front door. She can tell Cleo and Jon that they decided to go for an early morning walk and that Richard thought he might as well head home afterwards. She's not going to go through a repeat of last night's performance over breakfast. She can barely speak to Richard as they walk down the street side by side and when she leaves him at the end of his road she just says, 'See you on Tuesday.' She doesn't trust herself to say anything else.

She walks across Primrose Hill, having got herself a large coffee on the way. She needs time to think. She's building up to her big revelation that it's all over, which, she's decided, needs to happen sooner rather than later. She can't quite decide what reason to tell them. She doesn't want to give Cleo any more ammunition to back up her theory that Abi is incapable of having a healthy love life. Telling them that Richard has dumped her would on the one hand make it look as if she had messed up somehow, but it would also make her the victim and keep alive the myth that she had feelings for Richard and not Jon. She decides to give it a couple more days. That'll be long enough, surely. Long enough for them to believe it was real – just – but not so long that it becomes a family tragedy that it's over. Cleo won't have bought a hat for the wedding.

Once her head feels clear she starts to walk through Regent's Park into town. She'll spend the day at the Royal Academy of Arts on Piccadilly, studying the Summer Exhibition, the traditional open-to-all-comers annual event. She can't face going home.

Monday brings more of the same old routine. Cleo is off doing whatever it is she does and Abi ferries the girls around. It's got easier, though, because both

Tara and Megan have decided to drop some of their more arduous coaching sessions in favour of time spent playing like normal children. Cleo doesn't seem to object although Abi thinks that may be because she hasn't clocked it yet. She knows that Jon would approve, but as she's still avoiding spending any more time with him than she has to she can't confirm that. Cleo has been banging on about how great Richard is ever since Saturday and Abi is still having trouble looking at Jon, let alone speaking to him.

She feels better now she has a plan, which is to announce the sad demise of Richard and Abi tomorrow evening when she gets home from work. Knowing that she can see the end in sight makes her feel guilty that she has become so snappy with Richard – he has been doing her an enormous favour, after all, and, despite his Lothario tendencies, he is still the best friend she has in London, so she decides to stop by the shop with Tara and Megan in tow to say hi. If it seems as if he's noticed how offhand she's been with him, she can apologize. She'll play it by ear.

There's no sign of him as she goes in. Miranda, the assistant on the days when Abi's not there, looks up from the book she's reading, sitting behind the till, and jumps, startled. Abi laughs.

'Asleep on the job?'

Miranda doesn't say anything, smiles nervously. Abi's only met her once before, so she assumes this is just her usual demeanour.

'Is he in the back room?' Abi asks, and it seems to her that Miranda reddens although all she says is, 'Um . . .' Slightly bemused and wondering if, maybe, Miranda isn't just a little slow, Abi waves her hand over at the children's section. 'Go and choose something, girls. I'll only be a minute.'

She heads on back behind the counter and through to the small office-cum-staff-room-cum-kitchen. Miranda stands as she passes. 'Um . . . I think he might be busy,' she tells Abi in a quavery voice.

'Oh, I'll only be a sec,' Abi says, smiling. 'Would you keep an eye on the girls?'

The back room is through a door, down a little corridor, past the toilet. The hallway is practically impassable because new stock is piled up along the walls from floor to ceiling in places. Richard would never be able to employ any obese assistants or, if he did, they would have to go to the pub over the road if they needed to use the loo. Abi assumes he'll be in there doing the accounts or the orders. She's flattered that when she's working he tends to do both those things in the shop so they can chat, but he's told her before that he finds Miranda mind-numbingly irritating and that when she's on duty he uses every excuse he can think of to keep out of the way. Or maybe he's sneaked off for a nap because there's no noise coming from the staff room, not even the radio, which is rarely turned off, Richard being a devotee of Radio 4. She decides to creep up on him in the hope of catching him snoozing. If she jumps out on him, hopefully he'll laugh and any atmosphere between them, if there is one, will be broken. She pushes the door handle down tentatively and it makes the tiniest creaking noise, which in the end is probably just as well because it means that when Abi pushes the door open and prepares to leap in shouting, 'Caught you!' the two people inside have a split second's notice that someone's coming in. Just time to take a pace back from one another and attempt to look as if standing there together in a dingy back room in the half dark with the door shut is an utterly normal occurrence. Abi stops dead in her tracks.

'What's . . . what are you doing here?'

'Abigail. Hi. We were just . . . well, I just needed to ask Richard something . . .' Cleo trails off, clearly unsure how to continue. There's an almost tangible atmosphere in the room; the air feels heavy and full of sexual tension.

Richard tries to adopt a breezy tone. 'I . . . I left something at the house yesterday morning. Cleo just brought it round.'

'Yes,' Cleo says, attempting a smile. 'I did.'

Abi knows they're lying. She can feel it.

'Nice try,' she says. She turns to leave.

'Abigail, this isn't . . . well, whatever you think this is, it isn't that.' Cleo reaches out to touch her arm, but Abi moves away. She can't even bring herself to think about how many wrongs are being committed here.

She looks at Cleo. 'The girls are in the shop. I'd wait here for a few minutes if I were you and I'll take them home.'

'Abigail . . . Abi . . . wait. Don't be like this.'

Abi knows there's something else she needs to say. She loves her job. It's the only thing keeping her sane at the moment, but she can't see herself coming back here tomorrow. She turns to Richard. 'I don't want to let you down, but you'll have to find yourself another part-time assistant.'

Richard shakes his head. 'Abi, come on. Nothing happened,' he says.

'It's really none of my business,' Abi says, and then she walks out. She doesn't want to hear any more.

20

The wait while she pays for the books the girls have chosen is agonizing. Abi can hardly look Miranda in the eye. She just wants to get out of there as soon as possible. She tries – and fails – to act as if everything is normal, move along, nothing to see here. When they finally get out of the shop, she exhales loudly and realizes she has been holding her breath.

'Are you OK?' Megan says, taking hold of her hand and looking so worried that Abi plasters a smile on her face and reaches down to give her a hug.

'I'm fine. I just felt a bit funny for a second. I think maybe I'm getting a migraine.'

They walk home with Megan rubbing one of Abi's arms and Tara the other, as if that might help. It's such a sweet gesture and Abi feels so outraged on behalf of her nieces (not to mention their father, Richard's girlfriend, herself) that she feels her eyes welling up. She manages to hold herself together just long enough for them to reach home. She can hear Jon in the kitchen. She knows she can't see him now, he'd know immediately that something was wrong and she doesn't think she'd be able to stop herself from telling him exactly what it was. Megan runs on into the kitchen to show her father the book Abi has bought for her. Abi touches Tara's arm gently to get her attention.

'I think I'm just going to go upstairs and lie down. Could you tell your dad I don't want any dinner?'

Tara looks concerned, a tiny frown line etched on her smooth forehead. 'Shall we bring you up something later?'

'I'm going to try to go to sleep,' Abi says, hating having to lie to her niece. 'That way I should be fine by the morning.'

'OK . . .' Tara says. 'But if you wake up and decide you're hungry I can make you a sandwich.'

Abi kisses the top of her head. 'Thank you.'

She heads upstairs and tries to distract herself for a few minutes by looking at Phoebe's Facebook page. She doesn't want to have to think. She hasn't spoken to her daughter for a couple of days and, although she loves to keep track of her as much as she can, she always finds her Facebook entries a bit too revealing. She almost always sees something she wishes she hadn't and this time is no exception.

'Hungover and knackered from too little sleep (thanks Jimmy!)' Phoebe's status, last updated four days ago, reads. Abi has no idea who Jimmy is and why he is responsible for her daughter's lack of sleep and, to be honest, she doesn't wish to know. Phoebe is a grown woman; what she does now is her business. Yeah, right. Reluctantly Abi turns her computer off. What you don't know can't hurt you. Suddenly that saying seems very apt. An hour ago she didn't know whatever it is she thinks she might know now and she'd felt fine. Now that she does know, though, there's no ignoring it.

She lies back on the bed and forces herself to confront the issue head-on. She walked through to the back room, opened the door and . . . what? There were two people standing in the room. They weren't touching. They were fully clothed. They looked surprised to see her, but, by her own admission, she had crept up on them. That's the whole case, m'lud. Circumstantial evidence. It's hard to put her finger on exactly why the situation was so compromising. Why she *knows* something wasn't right.

The prosecution asks that the jury take the following into consideration:

The fact that Cleo was there at all, shut in the back room with Richard, a man she has only met a couple of times and flirted with excessively (circumstantial).

The silence (circumstantial).

The heavy atmosphere (circumstantial).

The fact that they couldn't quite get their stories straight (actually, this piece of evidence might just be admissible).

The look in both Cleo and Richard's eyes (circumstantial, but she doesn't care. This one most of all told her all she needed to know).

Cleo and Richard? They'd been flirting, of course

they had, but surely that was just how both of them operated? Just because someone was a flirt didn't mean that they would cross the line given the opportunity. After all, Richard seemed to have been having no problem remaining faithful to Stella despite his full-on love-ins with the local ladies. Abi pushes the thought of Stella to the back of her mind. She'll deal with that one later. And Cleo, of course, had Jon. Could she really be cheating on Jon? Sweet, kind, funny Jon. There were cracks in their relationship, that much was obvious, otherwise Abi didn't believe Jon would ever have thought – let alone admitted – that he had feelings for her. But underneath it all Abi had firmly believed there was something solid, something real, something worth saving in her sister's marriage.

She presses rewind and brings up the image of Cleo and Richard again. Not touching, but too close to each other to have been just having a casual exchange. If Cleo really had just been returning something Richard had left at the house (what? Where had he left it? Why not just give whatever it was to Abi to give to him?) then why were they shut in the room? Why were they standing so close? Why did they look so guilty?

Whatever is going on can't have been going on for long, Abi thinks. That's some small consolation at least. In fact, she has no doubt that today was the first assignation. Did they set this up on Saturday night somewhere in the middle of their flirty banter? Did one of them call the other? Or did Cleo just show up at the shop uninvited and insist on seeing Richard in private? Miranda had clearly known something amiss was happening back there.

The question that haunts Abi most of all is did she arrive after the event or before? Were they fully clothed because they hadn't got as far undressing each other yet or had they just finished putting their clothes back on?

Her head is genuinely beginning to hurt from the rush of images fighting for space in her brain. She closes her eyes, willing it all to go away. She doesn't know how long she lies there. Smells from dinner waft up from four floors below and she pictures the happy family sitting round the kitchen table, none the wiser. Well, three of them anyway. The other one is presumably living in fear that her secret will be exposed. That's if she cares and Abi has to believe that she does. Her sister may be a monster, but she loves her children; she's a good mother. Her twelve-year marriage has to mean something. Abi doesn't feel hungry even though she hasn't eaten since lunch. She couldn't eat now if her life depended on it. Great, you might lose some weight, some joker in her sub-conscious says.

Some time later, she doesn't know how long, she hears footsteps on the stairs. She locked the door behind her when she came in and now she's silently grateful. There's no way she's going to give Cleo the satisfaction of being able to explain herself. If anyone knocks, she'll ignore it, claim in the morning that she took a sleeping pill in an effort to sleep off her migraine. She lies as still as she can and waits. There's a tentative tap and then another a little louder. Abi doesn't respond. Then she hears voices, loud whispers, a ten- and seven-year-old's attempts to talk quietly.

'Let's just leave it outside. She can eat it when she wakes up.' This from Megan.

'No, stupid. It'll go cold.'

The girls must have brought her up dinner despite her protestations. She tries to ignore them, but it's more than she can do. She waits just long enough to make sure it's just the two of them and not either of their parents, and then she opens the door, feigning just-woken-up sleepiness.

'Oh no, did we wake you up?' Megan says. 'Dad said we mustn't.'

Abi gives her a hug. 'No. I'd just woken up anyway and I was starving so this is a real treat.'

Tara is bearing a plate covered in silver foil. She offers it up. 'We knew you'd be hungry,' she says smugly.

Abi takes the plate from them and Megan pro- duces a knife and fork from somewhere and some salt from her pocket.

'That's really thoughtful, girls. Thank you.' Abi's worried they might want to stay because even though the food smells delicious she has no intention of eating it. The girls hover in the doorway. 'Are you coming in?' Abi says eventually.

Tara grabs Megan by the hand. 'Dad said we weren't to disturb you.'

Abi kisses them both and says goodnight then freezes as she hears someone else coming up the stairs. Whichever of them it is, Jon or Cleo, she doesn't want to have to talk to them now, but short of bundling the girls out and locking the door again she doesn't know what she can do. She's backing into her room, thinking she might just have got away with it, when she hears Cleo's voice. This is the last thing she needs.

'I'm just going to chat to Auntie Abigail for a bit.' The girls obviously think this is the cue for them to stay put because then Abi hears Cleo say, 'On my own. I'll be down in a little while.' Tara and Megan moan and whine, but they comply and the next thing Abi knows there's Cleo in the doorway and there's nothing Abi can do short of telling her to go away. Actually, that's a plan.

'I don't want to talk to you at the moment, Cleo. Sorry.'

Cleo, never one to be told what to do, comes on into the room and shuts the door behind her.

'Abigail, listen to me. There is absolutely nothing going on between me and Richard. It's ridiculous that you would even think it.'

Abi sighs and turns away. She's not interested in Cleo's self-justifications. She knows what she saw — or at least, what she felt — and she also knows that

Cleo has nothing to gain by being upfront and honest with her.

'As if I would ever do that to you – with your boyfriend . . . I was so happy for you that you'd found someone,' Cleo says, and Abi thinks, Of course, in Cleo's mind she's not just been cheating on her husband but she's stolen my boyfriend too. The fact that the relationship is a scam and Abi couldn't care less about Richard except on Stella's behalf is neither here nor there. Cleo believed he was Abi's boyfriend and she still went after him anyway. It isn't lost on Abi that while she held herself back, rebuffing Jon's longed-for advances out of loyalty to her sister, Cleo seems to have no such scruples. Family, blood or otherwise, means nothing to her.

And suddenly it's as if Abi sees things clearly for the first time. Cleo hasn't changed; she's always been the same. Of course Gary Parsons had betrayed her and asked Caroline out. Abi can picture it now: Caroline had made sure that he would by smiling at him in class, taking notice of him, giving him just enough attention to allow him to get up the courage to ask so that she could go home and tell her sister that was what had happened. Of course she had insisted that she and Abigail wear the same outfits that summer, not because she wanted to show solidarity with her little sister, but because she had just realized the power of her looks and she knew they would be shown off to their best advantage when placed in direct comparison with Abigail's dumpier proportions. Of course she threw herself at Richard because, Abi now sees, she has to win. Life for Cleo has been one big competition that Abi didn't even realize she was part of. Caroline wasn't ever her protector, her mentor, her friend. She was her rival. Just as Cleo still apparently is. No one is permitted to be more desirable, more sexy, more beautiful than Cleo. It is simply not allowed.

She fights back tears. It makes no sense. Surely Cleo must know that she had already won? She had the looks, the career (even if it was going through a rough patch), the gorgeous husband, not to mention all the material things that Abi couldn't really give a toss about, but which she knows mean a lot to her sister. Why couldn't she leave Abi this one little thing that she believed was real?

Abi thinks about how much more devastating this would be if Richard really was her boyfriend, if she really cared about him. And that makes her think how much worse this truly is for Jon.

'Forget about me and Richard,' she hisses at Cleo. 'What about your husband? What about Jon?'

'I told you it was entirely innocent,' Cleo says, all big eyes.

'Right,' Abi says. 'So what were you doing in there with the door shut?'

'We were just talking. You really think I'd make a play for your boyfriend?'

'I'm not bothered about Richard,' Abi says,

exasperated. Actually, she is, on Stella's behalf, but Cleo knows nothing about Stella. 'I've known him five minutes. You're married. You have kids. Why do you always have to be so fucking selfish?'

Cleo looks at her and Abi thinks she can actually see the cogs turning as her sister decides which tack to take, what will cause the least damage to herself. She knows that whatever comes out of Cleo's mouth next will be self-justifying bullshit.

Cleo has conjured up tears from somewhere. Probably, Abi thinks, because of the fear of being found out. She blinks deliberately, forcing them out, and then looks at Abi pathetically, as if to say, 'See, you've made me cry.'

Abi waits.

'I . . . don't be cross with me. I can't bear it.' Cleo bats her eyelashes and a couple more tears roll down her cheeks. Abi nearly laughs. Cleo's performance is so hammy it reminds her of Scarlett O'Hara in *Gone With the Wind*. All she needs is a fan and a southern-belle accent. She won't step in and bail her out. At the very least Cleo owes her an explanation. Cleo doesn't seem to know how to continue in the face of Abi offering up no response. She's used to her sister giving in immediately, always wanting to make things right between them. Not this time, Abi thinks.

'OK.' Cleo takes a deep breath. 'We kissed. I'm really, really sorry. I don't know what came over me. But that's all. Nothing else happened.'

'Because I interrupted you.' Abi doesn't know whether to believe her or not. The fact that Cleo has admitted any guilt at all makes her inclined to think she might be telling the truth, but it's impossible to know.

'No. I don't know.'

'So why did you go there in the first place? And don't tell me Richard left something behind.'

'It wasn't premeditated. I admit I was attracted to him and I just had this ridiculous idea to stop by the shop to say hello. He invited me into the back room and it just sort of happened. It was stupid.'

'And?'

'And nothing. And then you came in.'

'What if I hadn't?'

'I don't know. God, it doesn't bear thinking about. I should be grateful to you. It was a moment of madness and it'll never happen again, I promise.'

Abi looks at her and feels . . . nothing. She ought to be angry, on Jon's behalf, Stella's, her own, but instead she just feels cold. Cleo reaches out and takes her hand.

'Please don't say anything to Jon.'

Abi pulls her hand away. 'Do you care?'

'Of course I care. He's my life, him and the girls . . .'

'Then why did you –'

Cleo cuts her off. 'Jesus, Abigail, have you never made a mistake?'

Abi ignores the question. 'You told me yourself that you didn't find Jon very … exciting … any more.'

'We've been together for fourteen years. We've been married for twelve. Of course there are times when you don't find each other very exciting any more, but there's other stuff that's way more important. I was just sounding off the other day, it didn't mean anything. Everyone moans about their partner sometimes. I adore Jon.'

If I had Jon, I would never moan about him, Abi thinks. But she knows that what Cleo's saying is right. She thinks back over exactly what Cleo said about Jon – was it really that damning? She said she was a little bored, that their relationship had become a bit stale. It was hardly a declaration of intent that she wanted a divorce. But then there's this thing, whatever it is, with Richard. Cleo is looking at her fixedly and Abi no longer has any idea whether or not she's being played. If Cleo is being honest – for once in her life, Abi thinks, and then tries to push that thought out of her head – then what would Abi have to gain by telling Jon what she thinks happened? He'd be hurt and humiliated. What if she told him something that caused their marriage to break up, but she was wrong? The girls would lose their family. She'd never forgive herself.

In a split second she decides that she has to give Cleo the benefit of the doubt. She betrayed Jon with a kiss, but nothing else. It'll never happen again. After all, who is she to judge? If Cleo is to be believed, she has only done what Abi herself did just days ago. Granted Abi pulled away from Jon, made sure he understood she was never going to take things further, while who knows what might have happened between Cleo and Richard if Abi hadn't walked in. But the crime, the intent, the betrayal is the same.

Cleo reaches for her hand again and this time Abi lets her.

'Please, Abigail . . . Abi . . . my marriage is the only thing in my life that I've done right. It's the only thing I can really be proud of. You have to believe I'm telling the truth.'

'I don't know what to believe,' Abi says, but not harshly.

'You know what?' Cleo says. 'Everyone thinks I'm such a success, but my comeback is a joke. Do you know what my great new campaign in America is?'

She looks at Abi for a reaction.

Abi shrugs. 'La Vie En Rose?' she says disingenuously. Is Cleo really about to reveal why she's been so vague about her new job?

'It's Satin Silk. You know what that means, don't you?'

Abi does. Now she understands exactly what Cleo's problem is. La Vie En Rose makes a fairly high-end eponymous line. They also make Satin Silk. Satin Silk is a brand whose USP is to appeal to 'real' women. They famously don't use models in their campaigns;

they feature an assortment of females of all shapes and sizes. Well, they say all shapes and sizes. Abi would put money on there being no one in any of their ads who is larger than a size 16 or smaller than a 10. They do use women of all ages, but they're always good-looking women of all ages. You never get any Picassos in there. There's not much cellulite or many stretch marks on show. But that's not the point. The point is that we're not talking about an elite modelling job here. We're talking something altogether more down-market. Beauty it may be, but not as we know it.

Abi is momentarily knocked sideways by the thought that this – Satin Silk – is the great break-through job that Cleo has been going on about for weeks. That this is what Cleo thinks is going to launch her back onto her adoring public. She's stunned that Cleo even went for the job, let alone took it. Actually, Abi thinks it's a great campaign. She'd far rather look at women who looked a bit like her on a good day rubbing lotion into their thighs than be confronted with an impossibly tall, skinny, beautiful creature who would make her feel both old and inadequate (although there is another kind of inadequacy that comes from seeing a sixty-five-year-old on your screen who seems to be in better shape than you are ever likely to be).

But this is Cleo. Status is everything. It's not like the campaign is for Azerbaijan or somewhere where there was maybe an outside chance that no one would get round to uploading any of it onto the internet and she could keep up a pretence that it had all been impossibly glamorous. It's not like she wasn't going to have to tell them at some point that her comeback was slightly (for that read totally) nonexistent. Like now, for example. Abi doesn't know what to say.

'Right . . .'

'It's about as low end as you can get in modelling terms. I think Falco just felt sorry for me. He certainly didn't cast me because they wanted Cleo to be the face of the product. Far from it.'

Abi knows this is a momentous admission. Even though she had worked out for herself that something was wrong with Cleo's tales of her fabulous comeback, for Cleo to own up to it herself is a whole different thing.

'And do you know what? I haven't even told Jon that because I was afraid it would make him see me in a different light. Like he'd be embarrassed for me or ashamed of me, or something. I couldn't bear for him to think I'm past it or a failure.'

'Jon would never think that,' Abi says, and she knows that what she's saying is true. 'I don't think that kind of thing is important to him. He just wants you to be happy.'

'I'd never want to lose him,' Cleo says, and the tears start again and, this time, Abi is convinced they're real.

'I won't say anything to him,' she says.

'And I know you're saying you don't care about Richard, but I want you to know I'm really sorry. It was an unforgivable thing to do.'

'Cleo,' Abi says. 'Do you remember Gary Parsons?'

Cleo looks confused. 'That boy who was in my class?'

'Do you remember when he asked me out and I said yes but then he suddenly asked you out instead?'

'No. Should I?' Cleo says, but she looks away as she says it, as if she's afraid to catch Abi's eye.

'No. No reason. I just wondered.'

'I was always jealous of you, you know.'

Abi can't help herself; she snorts. 'Yeah, right.'

'Of course I was. You were the funny one, the clever one. You always had an answer for everything. All I had was what I looked like.'

'I spent my whole life watching Mum boast about you and how you got your looks from her,' Abi says, incensed.

'Only when I wasn't there,' Cleo says. 'When you weren't around, she used to go on to people about how clever you were and how you were going to go to university. And how you inherited your brains from her, of course.'

Abi is floored. 'Really?'

'It used to drive me mad. I felt like all that mattered to her was how well I did in my exams. And however hard I worked I knew I was never going to do well, because that's not who I was.'

'I had no idea.'

'That's just what parents do. They don't want to spoil you so they praise you behind your back. Only sometimes they forget to do it to your face too.'

'I never thought you cared about not being academic. You always used to make a big joke of it.'

'Because I couldn't change it. I had to embrace what I had, what was me. It didn't mean I wasn't envious of what I didn't have, though. And you know what? Did I deliberately flirt with Gary Parsons to get him to ask me out? Yes, I did. I'm ashamed to admit to it, but I did, because I thought that if suddenly you weren't just the smart one but you were also the one getting the attention from the boys, then who was I? What did I have left? I was shallow and scared and insecure, OK? And I apologize for that and for all the other times I've treated you badly. God, I'm actually amazed you even want to have a relationship with me at all.'

Abi feels as if something's lifted, as if all the resentments and injustices and jealousies she's been nursing over the years have not completely gone – that's not going to happen overnight – but they're fading.

Another memory fills her head. The stained first-communion dress lying on the floor, Caroline standing over it triumphantly. She tries to see the angle, to work out what Caroline might have had to gain by sticking up for her, but she can't find anything. Just the altruistic, protective gesture of an older sister who cared about her younger sibling so much she didn't want her to get into trouble. 'Thank you,' she says.

'I'm really glad you're here,' Cleo says. 'I mean it. And I'll keep away from Richard. You don't have to worry about that.'

21

Cleo is making a big effort – Abi has no doubt about it. She still spends a lot of time at the gym or the beautician or occasionally at castings, but in the evenings she stays home and they spend time like a normal family, all together, watching TV or playing games. She sits through countless tweenage performances and fashion shows and allows herself to be a guinea pig for make-up and hair-styling sessions. Tara and Megan bask in the extra attention and even Jon seems to visibly relax.

It seems to Abi that Cleo's brittle defensive mask is weakening by the day. Not completely cracking, not yet, but the fault lines are widening. Something between the two of them has changed; it's as if a switch has been flicked and the stiffness, the polite formality, has gone. They're bordering on something like a normal, friendly relationship. Abi knows it's too soon to hope they're going to morph into the Waltons, but it feels like progress. Bizarrely whatever happened between Cleo and Richard may turn out to be the best thing for Cleo and Abi. Cleo is being extra nice to Jon too, which both pleases and upsets Abi. She wants their marriage to work, she really does, but seeing Cleo with her hand on his arm or her arms thrown round his shoulders is almost more than she can bear.

One evening they're playing Trivial Pursuit on the PlayStation, the five of them holed up in the cosy family room, the adults sharing their second bottle of wine, and Megan and Abi munching through a bag of microwaved popcorn. It's Megan's turn. She chooses entertainment, reads the question aloud.

'Who first presented *The Tonight Show* on NBC in 1992?'

She looks clueless, looks around the room for any help that might be coming her way.

'Don't give her any clues,' Tara says, looking accusingly at her father. 'It's not fair.'

Jon looks at Megan struggling, takes pity on her.

'Jay . . .' he offers up.

Megan looks none the wiser for a moment, then a big smile crosses her face. She's got it.

'JLS.'

Jon tries to keep a straight face. 'Um . . . not JLS, no.'

Cleo's face starts to twitch and then she snorts, which makes both Abi and then Jon start laughing in turn.

'Sorry, Meggy. I'm not laughing at you,' Cleo manages to say. Megan knows she's lying, looks indignant.

'JLS,' Cleo says, wiping her eyes. 'JLS! I don't know why that's so funny, but it is. Sorry, Megan.'

She lies back on the sofa giggling helplessly, one hand covering her mouth, and Abi thinks, Finally, there she is; there's Caroline.

'Is that a homeless person sitting on our steps?'

Megan, Tara and Abi are on their way home from a trip to Somerset House where Abi left the girls in the courtyard running in and out of the fountains with all the other kids while she had a quick art fix in the Courtauld Gallery. Now they're walking home from the tube station (sorry, Cleo, your girls are now old hands at getting the underground) and Megan is pointing to where, indeed, there is a scruffy young woman with long dark hair sitting on their front porch. Something in the way she brushes her long fringe away from her eyes strikes a chord and Abi's heart begins to beat like there's no tomorrow. She breaks into what – for her – counts as a run. By which she means she starts to walk fast.

'Phoebe? Phoebs?'

Phoebe stands up and practically throws herself at her mother. 'Mum!'

Tara and Megan – who haven't seen their cousin for a couple of years – stand open-mouthed as Abi hugs her daughter who, judging by the general air of her, not to mention the smell, may not have had a bath for several days. She's sure that Tara must be dying a few 'What will the neighbours think?' deaths but Abi doesn't care. Her little girl needs her.

Well, not exactly little. Phoebe towers above her. She has her aunt's height.

'What's happened? What are you doing here?'

Phoebe looks at her – Abi thinks she's lost weight in the few weeks she's been away, something she could ill afford to do in Abi's opinion – and immediately bursts into tears.

'Everyone hates me,' she wails.

Inside they sit Phoebe down in the living room and Abi sends Tara off to make her a cup of tea. Phoebe tells Abi a long tale about how she has fallen out with her two friends because one of them liked Jimmy but Phoebe got off with him (lovely, just what Abi wants to hear) and then her other friend accused her of doing it deliberately just to show off that he liked her best and then Jimmy didn't want to see her again anyway because it turns out he has a long-term girlfriend back home.

Abi waits for the big sting at the end – 'and now I'm pregnant' or 'and he gave me herpes,' but of course it never comes. In Phoebe's only just post-adolescent world, falling out with her friends is enough of an international incident to send her fleeing back across Europe into her mother's arms. While Abi feels for her, of course she does, she is so relieved that nothing more serious has happened that she almost laughs. She lets Phoebe cry herself out noisily like she used to when she was little, occasionally stroking her hair and telling her it'll all be OK. Eventually it seems Phoebe has got it all out of her system because she suddenly sits up and says, 'I'm starving.'

'Why don't I take you upstairs and you can have a quick bath while I fix you something to eat? Pasta? Pizza? I'm not sure what we have.'

Phoebe sniffs at herself. 'Do I smell? I smell, don't I?'

Abi shrugs and Megan says, 'You do a bit,' which makes Phoebe laugh.

'Hi, girls, by the way. Remember me? I probably wasn't this much of a mess last time you saw me.'

Tara wrinkles her nose. 'Definitely.'

'Actually, girls, why don't you show Phoebe up to my room? That way I can get some food on. Twenty minutes, OK?'

Phoebe nods, managing a smile. Tara and Megan edge round her like she's electrified and then beckon her to follow them out to the hall. Abi imagines they'd be behaving in the same way if she'd brought home a mangy old dog she'd found in the street. Interested but wary. Needing to make sure it wasn't going to bite before they get too close.

'Wow, you've grown, both of you,' Phoebe says as she follows them, a guaranteed crowd-pleaser for pre-teenagers.

'I'm the same height as my mum was at my age,' Tara says proudly.

'Bring your washing down,' Abi shouts after them.

'And use anything of mine you want.' She realizes that the idea of having someone to look after again is making her feel euphoric.

Twenty-five minutes later, just as Abi is worrying that the bean chilli she's rustled up is going to be dried out, Phoebe reappears, looking like the after photo in an advert for a miracle beauty product. She's wearing a dress of Abi's, which, while too big in one way (width-wise, obviously) is also too small in another, so that what, on Abi, is a run-of-the-mill knee-length sun dress has become a stunning mini, belted in at the waist, on her gazelle-like daughter. She looks tanned and glowy and a lot happier than she did half an hour ago.

'How are you feeling?'

'Better,' she says, and gives Abi a hug. Her hair is wet and smells of Abi's mint shampoo. 'Stupid. I think I overreacted. I just got an email from Carly saying sorry and that they're worried about me.'

'Well, you can always go back and join them later in the summer if you feel like it. But first you're going to stay here for a bit and I'm going to feed you up.'

'Great,' Phoebe says, and she sets about the chilli as if she hasn't eaten for weeks. Tara and Megan sit at the other side of the table and stare at her in awe.

'How tall are you?' Tara says after a while, and Phoebe says, 'About five nine.'

'You should be a model,' Tara says, and Abi imagines that's the highest compliment she can pay anyone.

'Why would I want to do that?' Phoebe says between mouthfuls, and Abi says, 'Phoebe . . .' to remind her where she is.

'I mean not that there's anything wrong with it. I just wouldn't fancy it, that's all. Thinking about what you look like all the time and never being able to eat what you want. Doing what you're told and never being in charge? Boring.'

'But . . .' Tara starts to say. In her world no one who was physically suited to being a model would ever want to do anything else. She's been brought up to think it's the pinnacle of existence.

'I'd rather be a fashion designer and make the clothes all the models want to wear,' Phoebe continues. 'That way I can get old and fat and still be rich and successful.'

'I want to be a nurse,' Megan says.

'Wow. Good for you,' Phoebe says. 'I really admire people who want to be nurses. I don't think I could do it myself. I'm not brave enough.'

Megan beams. 'Or an architect. I haven't decided.'

'Well. Either would be brilliant,' Phoebe says.

'Last week she wanted to be a vet,' Tara says dismissively. 'She keeps changing her mind.'

'How about you? What do you want to be?'

'A model,' Tara says as if it's obvious.

'Right. What if you don't grow tall enough, though?'

'I will.'

'Well,' Phoebe says, 'you might not. I mean look at

me, I inherited my height from Auntie Cleo. You might get yours from my mum.'

Tara shoots Abi an accusatory look.

'Sorry,' Abi mumbles apologetically.

'I'm just saying,' Phoebe says. 'You should come up with a back-up plan. Just in case.'

If she hadn't grown so fond of Tara, the look on her niece's face probably would have made Abi laugh.

'Do you want anything else?' Abi says to Phoebe. 'I think there's frozen yoghurt? Or would you rather go off to bed for a bit? You must be exhausted.'

Phoebe reaches up and takes her hand. 'Mum, stop fussing. I'm fine.'

'I know you are, but you have to let me fuss. It gives me a purpose in life.'

Phoebe stands up and kisses Abi on the top of the head. 'You need to get out more.'

Abi doesn't say anything, but she thinks Phoebe might have a point.

By the time Jon and then Cleo get home Abi has washed all of Phoebe's stuff and it's chuntering around in the dryer in the basement. The house smells like laundry, one of Abi's all-time favourite smells. Phoebe, Tara and Megan are sitting round the big table making necklaces out of things Phoebe has found in the kitchen like macaroni and chillis and red lentils which they are piercing with safety pins. It all looks a bit lethal but Abi trusts Phoebe not to let the girls do anything too potentially dangerous. She has been quizzing her about her weeks away and, to be fair, it all sounds like fun apart from the last few days. There's definitely no lasting damage done and it seems like really Phoebe just wanted to come home for a bit of TLC. Abi has no doubt she'll rejoin her friends sometime soon.

Jon and Cleo make a fuss of her, and they both just seem to assume she'll stay, which Abi is grateful for. Cleo looks Phoebe up and down and says, 'Gosh, you turned out pretty,' as if that's a major surprise considering who her mother is. Phoebe, who seems oblivious to compliments generally, just rolls her eyes and manages to mutter a thank you. She goes off to make up the bed in the room next to her mother's, and Tara and Megan who — now she is scrubbed up and looking less like a hobo — seemingly can't take their eyes off their grown-up cousin, follow her upstairs where, Abi has no doubt, she will put them to work.

'Thanks for saying she can stay,' Abi says to Jon once the girls are out of earshot. Cleo has gone to get changed and Abi and Jon and find themselves unexpectedly alone. 'Sorry we couldn't give you any notice.'

'Don't be silly,' he says, and he hands her a bag of carrots and the peeler. She is so grateful for the gesture, which to her says, 'Let's try to go back to our normal, friendly way of getting along,' as much as it says, 'Can you help me prepare the veg?' that she practically grabs the peeler out of his hand and sets to in record time. Its seems like a year since she and Jon used to prepare the dinner together every night. 'She's family. She's always welcome. Is she OK? Did something happen?'

'She fell out with her friends. Over a boy. I get the impression it's all blown over already. She just wanted to make a grand gesture, I think. Storm off and hope they felt bad. It worked. I must try it sometime.'

'I can't imagine you're the grand-gesture type.'

'No. I'm more your put-up-with-it-silently-for-years-then-go-mad-with-an-AK47 kind of woman.' Jon laughs as he's meant to. 'Actually, I was never given to histrionics. Even with Phoebe's father I let him off pretty lightly when he said he wanted out. I just didn't see the point of trying to force him to change his mind. You can't make someone do something they don't want to do.'

'No,' Jon says with a hint of resignation in his voice. 'I suppose you can't.'

Oops. Abi has inadvertently torn a tiny puncture in the easy atmosphere that they have so carefully constructed around them. She needs to patch it up quickly before too much of the stuff they've tried so hard to suppress leaks out. She has to get the conversation back onto a light and unthreatening topic, so that they can keep up the front that everything is fine between them. She has gathered from Jon during one of their – very general – chats as they eat dinner that the onehitcomparison.com campaign is all done and dusted. That they went with the inspired slogan 'The one-hit wonder' in the end. She has been waiting with baited breath for the finished article to pop up on some cable channel somewhere, in between *Most Haunted* and *Britain's Worst Parents*. Jon and his team have now shifted their attention to a chain of discount shops called Bargain Hunters whose USP seems to be that everything they sell is damaged in some way and therefore ridiculously cheap. Abi misses the fun easy conversations they used to have where they made each other laugh trying to come up with slogans as they diced vegetables.

'How's Bargain Hunters coming on?'

'Why pay for perfect packaging?'

'Right. That's good. To the point. What's the story going to be?'

'Normal mum next door with two adorable kids, in the supermarket picking up beautifully packaged produce. Looks in her purse; she doesn't have enough money for what she wants to buy. Voiceover says, "Why pay extra for the stuff on the outside?" Cut to the woman going into Bargain Hunters, filling her basket with the same stuff she was looking at in the supermarket, but it's all damaged and torn. Voiceover says, "When it's what's on the inside that counts." Woman at the till, paying with coins, big smile on her face. Turns to the camera, "Why pay for perfect packaging?" The end.'

Not much she can say to that. It's hardly genius, it's not going to win awards but it's a hundred per cent product appropriate. Which is surely all that really matters with advertising.

'Sounds good.'

'It is what it is,' he says, and that pretty much kills that conversation. Thankfully there's a noisy clatter on the stairs and the three girls appear to fill the kitchen with life again.

'Mum,' Phoebe says accusingly almost before she's through the door, 'Tara and Megan said you've got a boyfriend. And a job.'

Great.

'Actually,' Abi says. 'I don't really have either any more.' She keeps her gaze well away from Jon as she says this.

'You've left your job?' she hears him say, but luckily Phoebe is on a roll. 'But . . . why didn't you tell me?'

'I think I did mention the job,' Abi says sheepishly. 'In the bookshop, remember?' In fact, she knows she did, but Phoebe, being a teenager, probably didn't listen.

'But a boyfriend? I can't believe you kept that to yourself.'

'Well, it wasn't serious. And it's all over now.' She can see Jon looking at her, knife held motionless in one hand, out of the corner of her eye.

Megan is looking crestfallen. 'Richard dumped you?'

'No,' Abi says, somewhat huffily. Why is that the first conclusion anyone would come to? 'Actually it was me who finished it, if you must know.'

'Wow, Mum, I'm seriously impressed.'

Is she? 'Are you?'

'Yes. You finally got a boyfriend. It's about time.'

Abi always thought Phoebe would be upset at the thought of her seeing someone. She doesn't know why. That's why she never told her about any of the others. It never occurred to her that Phoebe might actually be happy for her, relieved even. That maybe it would make her daughter feel less responsible for her.

'So . . .' Phoebe says, looking at her expectantly, 'what happened?'

This time Abi can't help herself. She glances at Jon, who busies himself at the sink.

'It just sort of fizzled out, you know. Nothing dramatic.' She so wants to change the subject, but she suspects Phoebe would have none of it.

'No, but before. How did you get together? What was he like? Tara said he's totally hot.'

'For an old man,' Tara says hurriedly.

Jon coughs and wipes his hands. 'I'll be in the living room if anyone wants me.'

He's gone before anyone can stop him, so Abi gives in and tells Phoebe as much about Richard as she has to to make it sound convincing. She leaves out the bit about Richard supposedly cheating on her, obviously, and just brings their relationship to a very pedestrian conclusion. She tells Phoebe that she left her job voluntarily, because she didn't want things to be awkward between them.

'Good old Mum,' Phoebe says when Abi gets to the end. 'Back in the saddle after eighteen years.'

'I'm sorry it didn't work out for you and Richard,' Jon says quietly to her later when she passes him in the hall. 'But you shouldn't have to leave your job because of it. Do you want me to go down there and talk to him?'

Abi doesn't know why, but she lays her hand on his arm and they both nearly jump from the shock of the physical contact. She withdraws it quickly, looking to see if it has left an imprint, a burn.

'No. Thank you, but it's fine. It was my idea to leave,' she whispers and then she runs upstairs to the safety of her room.

22

Cleo's advert is out in America, so she tells them at dinner one evening, and the feedback her new agent has been getting has been fantastic. She doesn't make eye contact with Abi when she says this, and Abi knows that Cleo is hoping she will keep up the charade that Cleo is now the face of something high-end and glamorous. She will. She has nothing to gain from telling anyone what she knows. Jon asks Cleo if she has seen any of the artwork for the print campaign and she says she has, in her agent's office, and it's fabulous. Megan asks if she can see it and Cleo says she'll try to remember to bring a copy home next time she goes into town. Abi wonders why no one suggests Cleo ask the agent to email it, but luckily they don't, and she stays quiet. The whole thing has become this ridiculous farce of Cleo pretending everything is amazing and Abi blindly colluding with her in that lie. Head in the sand; it's the Attwood way.

Actually, Satin Silk aside, Cleo genuinely does seem to have been a different person since she and Abi had their heart to heart. Underneath it all she's still the old Cleo, of course, with all her ridiculous self-aggrandizement and sense of entitlement, but now there's something else Abi can see there too. Something more real. Plus she seems to be trying, really trying, to reconnect with her family, Abi included. It's definitely progress, a big step forward, a giant leap for mankind.

Now she doesn't have a job to go to Abi can spend her days having fun (although without spending any money) with her daughter and her two nieces. Tara and Megan are so enamoured with Phoebe that they agree to do all sorts of things that would have been branded uncool before. On fine days they play pitch and putt or softball or just take a picnic to Regent's Park or down to the river somewhere. When it rains, they do a tour of the charity shops in Camden (Tara is getting into the spirit of it with the rest of them now, although she always still has a cursory glance around in the street first to check none of her friends are watching) and dress up and put on plays and fashion shows with their newfound bargains. On the day when Tara announces at dinner that she no longer wants to be a model, but that she's planning on a career in fashion design just like her cousin, Abi almost cries with pride. She casts a sneaky look at Jon and he's beaming with pleasure too.

'Really? Are you sure?' Cleo looks confused. Not want to be a model? Her daughter? That can't be right. Why wouldn't she want to be just like her fabulous mother?

'Shoes,' Tara says. 'I'm going to design shoes.'

'You know you'll have to work hard. You'll have to go to college,' Jon says quickly, keen to keep the conversation on track.

'I know that, stupid,' Tara says. 'Like Phoebe. She's going to show me round the London College of Fashion when she starts her course.'

'How about you, Megan?' Abi asks. 'You changed your mind again?'

She nods. 'I want to work in the Marie Curie Hospice shop,' she says proudly, mentioning the shop where most of their clothing bargains are discovered, and they all tell her that's a great ambition and none of them mention the fact that she'll have to get another job somewhere else too to earn some money.

Jon still comes home to cook every night and the three of them all help. Even Cleo has been known to lift a perfectly manicured finger on the odd occasion. Phoebe announces to Abi that she thinks Jon is both 'hot' and 'cool', two very high accolades, and, cornered, Abi stammers that, yes, he has turned out to be very nice after all.

The day is rapidly approaching when Abi's new home will be all hers and ready to move into. While part of her is aching to go back to Kent and her new little flat and undemanding job, another part would like to put the move off indefinitely. She's on the verge of having the relationship she's always wanted with her sister. Every day things seem more relaxed between them. She's worried that when she leaves the momentum will be lost and the next time they see one another they'll have to start all over again. Not only that, but she has got used to living in a house full of people and life. She's not sure how she'll cope with being on her own full time – Phoebe has already announced her plans to rejoin her friends once they reach India in September. And, to be honest, Abi's not sure how she'll deal with not being around Jon. He was almost certainly more hurt and embarrassed by her rejection of him than he let on. They have still not completely regained their old easy way of being together. Even when she does ever meet up with Cleo again in the future – and Abi's now allowing herself to think when, not if – it's doubtful he'd come along. Honestly? Abi is scared she might never see him again.

'I hope the girls can come and stay with me sometimes after I go back,' she says to him one evening as she's washing the leaves for the salad. This is a genuine request, by the way. She loves the girls now, properly loves them in an unconditional way, not just because she thinks she should, and she's going to miss them. She's not asking just because she's hoping that if they ever did come to visit then their father would bring them down. That would be a – huge – bonus, but it's not her prime motivation. Tara and Megan both squeal with excitement.

Jon gives Abi a warm smile that makes her go weak at the knees. 'Of course they can.'

'Maybe at half-term?' Abi says, and she spends most of the next hour or so fending off questions about what her new flat is like and how near the sea is it and can they go out on a boat?

'I might get a dog when I get back,' Abi says at one point for no other reason than the idea has just popped into her head that a pet really might be a good idea and a cat for a single middle-aged lonely lady is just too much of a cliché. They argue for most of the evening about which breed would be good and whether a big or a small dog is more trouble.

'Mum, have you seen this?' Phoebe calls from her little bedroom one evening when Abi heads upstairs at about eleven. She's sitting on her bed looking at her laptop. Abi's heart sinks because she just knows what Phoebe's going to show her and, indeed, she's right because there on YouTube is Abi's sister, barely visible in the middle of a crowd of other women, in an advertisement for Satin Silk Body Moisturizer.

'I'm not imagining it, am I?' Phoebe says. 'They're the ones who make all those boasts about using real women and not models in their campaigns?'

Abi exhales. Knows she should be feigning surprise, but can't quite get up the energy. 'They are. But, who knows, this is a new campaign. Maybe they've changed tack?'

'Doesn't really look like it, does it? Still, I actually really like the ethos behind the ads. I just can't believe that Auntie Cleo would think the same. You know what she's like.'

Abi does. She could write a book about it. Instead she just says, 'I know.'

Phoebe pulls a face. 'I just got curious to see what it was. I put in Auntie Cleo's name and this came up.'

Without thinking, Abi scrolls down to the comments below. Luckily the ad has not had many viewers online so there aren't too many posts, because the ones that are there are all pretty awful. Basically along the lines of 'is that Cleo third from the left and if so she's clearly desperate or broke or both to be participating in a campaign like this'. A few are downright mean about the way she looks or what a bitch they've heard she is, so it's no wonder she can't get any proper work. One claims to have inside knowledge that she slept her way to the top in the first place, so what does she expect?

'We can't tell her we've seen this,' Abi says, and Phoebe looks at her as if she's simple and says, 'Well, obviously.'

Abi sits down on the bed. 'Let's just try and forget about it. Don't even say anything to Uncle Jon.'

'Of course not,' Phoebe says. 'Though I don't really understand what all the fuss is about.'

'It's important to your aunt, OK?'

She finds it hard to sleep. It's ridiculous, really. Abi would bet that all the other women in that advertisement were bursting with pride to be chosen. She'd bet they trawled YouTube, sat their families down as soon as they could find it and made them watch it over and over again. But, then again, she'd also bet their families aren't anything like her own.

What's so stupid is that if Cleo had come home that day and just said, 'Oh, I've got a job advertising Satin Silk,' Abi would probably have said, 'I love Satin Silk,' and left it at that. She might have thought it a little strange that Cleo would take a job like that. Actually, she almost certainly would have thought, Good on her. But instead Cleo built it up into the comeback of the century and now they are all being forced to collude in her delusion.

She's ridiculous, Abi thinks, irritated now, but then she feels sorry for her all over again. How sad to have to live your life pretending to be something you're not, because you think that you have to impress the people around you. The people who love you uncon-ditionally, even if sometimes they don't actually like you. The people who really wouldn't care either way if you were a famous supermodel or not. Maybe that's what being so successful at a young age does to you. You become defined by your success. There's no time to put a back-up plan into place or even to fully develop a personality that's not shaped by being rich and famous and spoilt. Maybe it's better to be the one no one has any expectations of. Better to be a nobody than a failed somebody. At least Abi can't disappoint.

*

She finds herself counting off the days. Not only until she has to leave London but until Phoebe – who has agreed to accompany her back to Kent for a few days – will be heading off into the unknown again on a bargain flight generously paid for by her aunt and uncle.

In her preoccupation about her daughter's imminent departure, Abi has forgotten that she was trying not to be left on her own with Jon if she could help it and one evening when she's been reading in the living room while everyone else is off doing other things she suddenly looks up and there he is.

'Are you OK?' he asks nervously.

Abi nods anxiously, looks for an escape.

'Abi . . . I've been wanting to talk to you.'

That's not good. Someone saying that can never be a good thing.

'What I said to you that time about Cleo and I having problems, I should never . . . well, the truth is of course we have problems now and again – what couple doesn't? I wouldn't want you to think I was being disloyal.'

'It's OK . . .'

'What happened between us – well, I'm sorry.' He raises his eyes to the door as if checking no one is in earshot. 'I should never have kissed you. I wouldn't want you to think I go around hitting on women behind your sister's back. Because I don't. It's never happened before. There's no excuse except that I temporarily lost my mind.'

'It's fine,' Abi says, and although she knows that it's good they're clearing the air she feels like a little bit of her has died. Even though she didn't want Jon to fall in love with her, knowing he thought he had had made her feel incredible.

'I have to be there for Cleo. I want to . . . And I would never have put the girls through . . . well, you know . . .'

He runs out of steam.

'Of course,' she says, thinking that at this precise moment she'd rather be anywhere but here. 'It's forgotten. I've forgotten it.'

She just wants the subject closed. Upstairs in her room she has been regularly indulging herself in an alternative-universe fantasy where she doesn't break away from Jon's embrace, where she thinks, Sod it, and throws herself into his arms, reciprocating his declarations of love. (Of course, she has to spend the first five minutes each time establishing a narrative in her head that takes Cleo out of the picture, but leaves her happy, healthy and, in the end, delighted that her ex and her sister have found love. In Abi's favourite version she goes off and marries Richard and everyone, Jon, Stella, the girls are all delighted for them.) Abi and Jon's relationship always progresses in the same way: the sex is amazing, a revelation; they move in together into a beautiful house that is neither too big nor too small; the girls couldn't be happier; Abi is pregnant again; the dog is there. It kind of peters out after that into an un-dramatic but most definitely satisfying happy-ever-after that leaves her basking in its comforting glow. Now she presses erase. Delete. Move to trash. It's gone.

She takes a deep breath. Tries to stay focused.

'But the truth is,' Jon says, 'I'm worried about her.'

Abi doesn't know what to say. The Satin Silk secret is not hers to give away. And the other secret, the Richard secret, is most certainly not one she's about to share.

Jon sighs. 'Has she said much about New York? The job?'

'Honestly?'

He nods.

She can't do it. 'Not really. I . . . maybe it wasn't quite the comeback she wanted.'

There's a moment where neither of them says anything, because they're both waiting to see what the other one knows.

Finally Jon says, 'It was Satin Silk by the way.'

'I know. Did she tell you?'

'No,' he says. 'I found it on the internet. I still haven't told her I know.'

'What do you make of it?'

He shrugs. 'It's a job.'

He sits down in the chair furthest from her. He looks tired and miserable. Worn out with trying to live with the mess that is her sister. 'What shall I do? Should I tell her I know and force her to confront the fact that she's delusional or should I just hope that she quietly gives up on her comeback and things go back to normal?'

Cleo's self-imposed deadline of a return to fame, fortune and fabulousness by the end of the summer is rapidly approaching and it's clear that nothing much is happening. The press are not beating a path to her door, there are no paparazzi lined up on the pavement. The great comeback campaign doesn't seem to have brought a ship full of offers in its wake, which comes as no surprise to Abi. She hardly thinks Karl Lagerfeld is scanning Satin Silk adverts to see who he should use in his next runway show. She knows that before long Cleo is going to have to admit defeat.

'That one,' Abi says. 'Don't confront her with it. Just be there to pick up the pieces when she finally has to admit it's not happening. She can't keep this façade up forever.' She closes her eyes briefly, steadies her breath. 'And she's going to need you.'

'I know. And I'll be here.'

That's good. She knows it is. She does. 'Good.' The old atmosphere is back. You could cut the air with a knife. There are so many elephants in the room Abi feels as if she's at Billy Smart's.

'I'm going to miss you when you leave,' Jon says quietly. 'Really.'

'Me too,' Abi says, and then she goes and calls the girls downstairs on some spurious pretext or other. There's no point going back down that road.

*

She's walking up Regent's Park Road one morning – she's kept up her habit of going out early on fine days otherwise she worries that she is in danger of losing herself. She spends all day with the girls (although to her credit Phoebe now often offers to take the two younger ones out without her, but Abi worries about them going too far or for too long, so she doesn't often accept), and every evening tiptoeing around the various minefields at home and willing the hours to go by till bedtime. Walking on her own in the mornings at least gives her the illusion that she has a life away from her family, things to do and places to be. She's an independent, strong and still youngish woman in a big city. Buy, buy, buy. Sell, sell, sell. In reality, she generally just walks up the road and back, sometimes stopping off at the bakery or the newsagent, but it's a habit she clings to. It's the only thing that is uncomplicated and wholly her own. Actually, she has noticed that all her clothes feel a little looser, so there have been some positive physical effects as well as the mental ones.

Anyway, she's having her morning stroll one Wednesday, about to turn up the hill towards Belsize Park, when she sees Richard and Stella on the other side of the street. They're both dressed in workout gear and Stella has the two kids with her, both in a jogging-friendly buggy, although Sean, the older one, is clearly a little too big for it and trying to climb out. Abi knew that this would happen one day. London might have nine million people trampling its streets, but it's a small community she's staying in here and, although she has been carefully avoiding passing the bookshop during opening hours, it was inevitable their paths would cross at some point. She has been dreading seeing Stella. Richard on his own she can cope with. His proved to be a friendship not worth salvaging and now, when she thinks about him, she thinks he is rather sad – a middle-aged would-be playboy who defines himself by the calibre of woman he can pull. Stella, on the other hand, is a different prospect. Abi liked – no, likes – her, respects her, hates knowing more about her relationship than Stella knows herself. Would, in an ideal world, still be friends with her.

Richard and Stella haven't seen her and her instinct is to put her head down and pretend she hasn't seen them either. That way if Richard does look over he can look away again quickly and not feel obliged to acknowledge her. Stella, however, has no reason to think that she and Abi are on anything other than good terms still, although she must know that Abi no longer works at the bookshop and wonder why that is. Or why she hasn't called. Abi looks anywhere but the other side of the road, but to no avail.

'Abi!' Stella calls across to her. There's no way she can ignore her.

'Hi,' she calls back loudly. She waves and keeps on walking, hoping Stella will assume she's in a hurry. No such luck. Before she knows it Stella is bounding across the road towards her. Richard hangs back, making a pretence of fussing over the boys, not looking at her. Abi has no choice but to stop, and she and Stella have those awkward few seconds where they don't quite know why they've stopped or what they have to say to each other.

'Where have you been?' Stella says warmly. 'Richard says you left the shop and I didn't know how to get in touch with you.'

'Oh, you know. Phoebe came back . . .'

'No!' she says. 'Is she OK? What happened?'

Abi fills her in on Phoebe's story, wanting to get away as quickly as possible because there's a limit to how long Richard can pretend to be otherwise occupied without looking rude, and he's obviously as keen to avoid her as she is him. Stella looks over as if she has only just realized he's not by her side.

'Richard,' she calls, 'what are you doing?'

Richard looks up nervously. 'Oh . . . nothing. Hi, Abi. How are you?'

'Get over here! What's up with you?' Stella laughs.

Richard crosses the road reluctantly, pushing the buggy. He avoids making eye contact with Abi. Much as she doesn't want to see him, Abi feels she needs to put him out of his misery for Stella's sake. He's obviously terrified she's going to spill the beans about him and Cleo, which, to be honest, she finds a bit insulting, but anyway. She plasters on the warmest smile she can conjure up.

'I was just telling Stella how I had to abandon you in the shop because Phoebe came home unexpectedly.' She can almost see the fear leave Richard's eyes.

'Yes,' he says. 'I've got a sixteen-year-old part time now. Tiffany. She's a disaster.'

They exchange banalities for a couple of minutes and then Abi begins to move off. She's done her bit; there's a limit to how friendly she can pretend to be with Richard these days.

'Well, it was good to see you,' she says.

'Don't be a stranger,' Richard says, clearly not meaning it.

Abi's about to give Stella a hug and get the hell out of there when Stella asks her if she fancies a coffee sitting outside one of the cafés while Richard goes off to have a shower and then open up the shop. She's tempted to say she's busy, she has things to do. She knows that there's no future in their budding friendship. On the other hand, the thought of spending some time with someone who is an adult, but isn't part of her family – not to mention also bright and funny and good company – is irresistible. She finds herself accepting.

They gravitate to the nearest café and take a table outside. Stella releases three-year-old Sean from the confines of the buggy saying, 'Do you remember Abi?' Abi is gratified when he replies that he does and gives her the sweetest smile. They keep half an eye on him as he runs round and round the other tables, which are luckily unoccupied. Baby Rhys clearly wants to be allowed to cause havoc with his brother, but has to be content to sit and sip orange juice instead. They're both as cute as Abi remembers them and, despite the frantic circuits, well behaved.

'So things are better at home, then?' Stella says once they have ordered coffees. Abi racks her brain, has no idea which of the many complications in her life Stella is talking about.

Stella must pick up on her bemused expression. 'With your brother-in-law. You're not having to pretend to go out with Richard any more so I'm guessing that sorted itself out.'

Of course. 'Oh god, yes, it did. Thank goodness. It did the trick so, yes, I'm really grateful to Richard for that, and to you of course.' She's blathering. She forces herself to shut up.

'Well, I'm kind of relieved it didn't go on for too long, I must be honest.'

'I'm so sorry I put you in that position,' Abi says, but Stella cuts her off. 'Oh god, it's fine. Anyway, what else has been going on? How's the unpaid babysitting going?'

Stella is refreshingly upfront. She has no side to her. Abi really likes that about her; she's a breath of fresh air in comparison with the hidden agendas and unacknowledged tensions crowding the air at home. Abi has no desire to discuss Cleo with her, though, not under the circumstances, so she tells her about her new flat and the plans she has to decorate. They chat away happily – with Stella's attention occasionally being sidetracked by Sean wanting a drink or for them to watch him doing something or other – for almost an hour. Stella and Richard are getting more and more serious Stella tells her, although she tells Abi it's still hard for her to go out much because she only has one friend she trusts to babysit the kids and she can't expect her to be free three or four nights a week. Richard sometimes comes over to the flat, she says, but she won't let him stay because Sean often gets into bed with her in the middle of the night and she doesn't think it would be right for him to find someone else in there too.

Abi smiles and nods, tells Stella she's pleased for her and keeps her mouth firmly shut about everything else. If she's giving Cleo the benefit of the doubt, then she feels compelled to afford the same consideration to Richard too.

It's tempting to sit here all day, but she promised the girls they could all go to the zoo – Jon bought them both year-long memberships when they went last time and they're keen to use them as often as possible – and, even though Phoebe would quite happily take them without her, she's quite looking forward to it. Plus Stella is still sweating quietly after her run and in obvious need of a shower, and Sean is getting a bit fractious from lack of attention. So they split the bill and walk up the road together, agreeing to try to meet up and do the same thing again in a couple of days, but not actually making a definite date. She knows it probably won't happen. It wouldn't feel right pursuing a friendship with Stella that had a dirty black secret at the centre of it.

Back at the house she finds Elena flapping in the kitchen surrounded by the detritus of three young girls' attempts to make a packed lunch. She assumes they must have sneaked in there while Elena was off hoovering somewhere else, because they're looking very pleased with themselves and the kitchen is looking like a bomb's hit it. Abi is so touched by their sweet intentions that she doesn't even bother pulling them up on the mess; she just gets down to it and starts cleaning it up, ignoring Elena's protestations. In fact, what the hell, she gets a coffee from the machine and steers Elena over to the table where she puts the mug down and sort of wrestles her into a seat beside it. She's not sure that legally it's acceptable to manhandle the staff, but she's hoping Elena will accept her gesture in the spirit it was meant. She looks as if she's going to get straight up again, so Abi wags her finger at her like Elena's always doing to her and, in the end, Elena breaks into a smile and sits back down. She knocks back the drink in record time and then she's back up on her feet and helping Abi, but Abi still feels it's a bit of a breakthrough.

Once she's happy that the kitchen is its old spot-less self she gathers up the girls and they walk the five minutes to London Zoo, the picnic in two carrier bags. By the time they've walked through the gorilla kingdom, seen the warthogs and the penguins, edged warily around the insect world and walked through the tunnel to admire the meerkats and lemurs she's so hungry that even a cold mackerel-pâté-and-rocket sandwich seems palatable.

23

Jon has a proposition for her. He tells her this in the kitchen with the girls as human shields so that she can't get the wrong idea for even a second.

'What?' she says, happy that at least Jon is finally feeling able to talk to her about something other than what needs doing for dinner or the wellbeing of his wife. They have no middle ground these days, banal and everyday or full-on psychotherapy seem to be the only choices.

'We're shooting the ads for Bargain Hunters in a couple of weeks and I . . . well, I feel bad about you having to leave your job because of everything that happened with Richard and . . . anyway, we need to cast the woman in it. Young mum. Friendly, attractive, approachable, someone you can trust. I was thinking you'd be great.'

Abi is so taken aback she laughs. The girls on the other hand go from nought to sixty on the hysteria scale in under a second.

'Oh. My. God. Auntie Abi's going to be on TV.'

'Can I come and watch?'

'You have to do it, Mum. It'll be awesome.'

Jon shushes them and says, 'The money's not bad.

I mean it's not great either. The ads are for cable, but they'll be on a lot so after the first buyout runs out there's a chance you'll get repeat fees. Plus there's a bit of a print campaign so you'll get paid for that separately. Like I say, it's not a fortune, but . . .'

'I don't know,' she says. It's so sweet of him to think of her. He knows she's short of money and this is his way of trying to help her, trying to make up for her losing her job in the bookshop. She runs through the adjectives that describe the character, adjectives that Jon thinks apply to her: friendly, attractive, approachable, someone you can trust. Attractive. She says it over to herself in her head a couple of times, relishing the moment. She can't believe that she is conveniently the best woman for the job, though, and she really doesn't want Jon compromising Bargain Hunters' undoubted integrity by forcing her onto them. Not to mention the fact that she has never in her life wanted to push herself into the limelight, to be the focus of everyone's attention. She knows they're talking about a downmarket ad, which will be shown on various TV channels with a combined viewership of about six, but that's beside the point.

'Just let me put you forward,' Jon is saying as he puts the finishing touches onto a home-made pizza ready to go into the oven for the girls who have made their feelings very clear about the squid rings the adults are having. 'If you get it, it'll be a proper shoot in a studio with a full crew,' he adds as if she might be thinking he's trying to get her on her own so he can take dirty pictures of her. Now there's a thought. She waits for a blush and is rewarded with the tiniest flicker of one.

'Go on, Auntie Abi,' Tara insists.

Abi looks over at Phoebe and Phoebe gives her an encouraging smile.

'Oh, OK, then. I suppose so. Maybe.'

'If they like the look of you, you'd probably have to come in and meet with them for a few minutes,' he says casually, not looking at her, as if by making this remark throwaway she might not actually take it in.

'No. Jon . . . I'm not sure I could do that.'

'Of course you could,' he says briskly, and then he turns his attention to the girls as if to say subject closed.

Abi decides to push the whole thing to the back of her mind. It's not worth worrying about. The chances are so slim that the clients will pick her and, even if they do, there's no law that says she has to take the job. She wonders briefly if she should be scouring the area for another part-time position – even a full-time one, because she's sure Phoebe would happily entertain her cousins if Abi had to work – but she's going home in just over a week and she can't imagine who's going to take her on knowing that. Besides, once she's back in Kent she's always managed to keep her head above water perfectly well working part time in the library. There's even scope further down the line to go full time if she wanted. Money has just never been that important to her. As long as she can get by. She certainly doesn't want to turn into the family charity case.

'OK. I suppose so.'

'I'll just need a snapshot of you to show them.' God, this gets worse. 'Have you got anything?'

All the photos there are of her that aren't in the attic in Kent – actually, in storage now – are either pictures of her and Caroline when they were kids or the few jokey snaps Jon or the girls have taken since she's been here. 'Not really.'

Phoebe comes to her rescue. 'I've got my camera upstairs. I can take some.'

'After dinner, then,' Abi says. The last thing she wants is for Phoebe to bring it down here and for her to have to pose in front of Jon. She's bad enough at having her picture taken as it is. She doesn't know if it's a reaction to Cleo's job, but every time anyone points a camera at her she feels compelled to cross her eyes or stick her tongue out. She thinks it's the need to make it look as if it's a bad picture by design rather than that she tried her hardest to look good, but it came out rubbish anyway.

'Actually, let's get it over with.' The girls all follow her upstairs where they fuss about with her hair and Tara insists she put a bit more mascara on. The first couple of attempts run to type. At the last minute she can't stop herself pulling stupid faces. Megan doesn't help by laughing every time she does it, because Abi really can't resist an appreciative audience. Phoebe does her best to direct her, but she's a lost cause so after a while Phoebe resorts to snapping her when she's off guard and actually gets a couple of good shots, not that Abi would admit it.

'That'll do,' she says. 'It's not going to get any better than that. Thanks, girls.'

Phoebe emails the best two pictures to Jon. Excitement over, back to the real world.

Abi forgets all about Bargain Hunters until, two days later, when they're all sitting down for dinner – all six of them, Cleo is still spending every evening at home – and Jon says, 'So, the people at Bargain Hunters like the look of you, Abi.'

The girls all scream and Abi is sure she sees Cleo's ears prick up.

Abi feels sick. 'Oh god. Really?'

'They want to meet all the potentials on Thursday week. Can you do that?'

'What's this?' Cleo says. 'Meet for what?' She's all wide eyes and nervous tension and it suddenly occurs to Abi that Cleo might not like the idea of her going in to meet for an advert. Downmarket and shoddy as it is, she might see it as Abi encroaching on her territory.

'Oh, it's nothing.' Abi tries to brush the subject away, but, of course, the girls are having none of it.

'Auntie Abi's going to be in an advert,' Megan squeals, and Abi says, 'No, I'm not, not necessarily.'

'An advert?' Cleo says with all the haughty frostiness of Lady Bracknell.

'It's nothing,' Abi says. 'Just some silly thing that Jon's put me up for. It's very low rent and I won't get it anyway.'

'It's Bargain Hunters,' Jon chips in. Abi wonders if he's picked up on the icy atmosphere that's beginning to swirl around the kitchen. 'I showed them Abi's picture because they're looking for a young mum to front the campaign and I know she needs the money.'

Cleo ignores him, turning the full force of her steely gaze onto Abi. 'I didn't know you were interested in doing adverts.'

'I'm not. I mean I wasn't.' She desperately doesn't want to break the lighter atmosphere that has made the house such a different place recently, but she also doesn't want to give up this opportunity just because Cleo might not like it. Whether she wants to go up for the ad or not is immaterial. It's the principle. She should feel like it's her choice. 'But it can't hurt to go and meet them, I suppose. It might be a laugh.'

'I didn't know you were looking so close to home for casting, Jonty.' Cleo's voice contains a hint of accusation that Jon immediately picks up on.

'It's not something you would have been interested in.'

'How do you know if you didn't ask me?'

The three girls are looking between Jon and Cleo like they're watching an episode of Jerry Springer. Abi recognizes the signs: Cleo's imperious look, the flared nostrils, the pursed lips. She sighs, knows she has to sacrifice herself for the greater good. Like the Cheshire Cat, the new, improved Cleo is disappearing before her eyes.

'I was only kidding,' she says. 'Of course I'm not going to go for it.'

'Mum . . .' Phoebe says, but then she stops when Abi nudges her foot under the table.

'I thought you must be joking,' Cleo says, her tone implying that she thought anything but. 'So, Jonty, what did you say it was for?'

Abi can see that Jon can barely contain his anger, but she knows he'll do everything he can to hide it in front of the children. 'It's for Bargain Hunters. By all means I'll suggest you for it if you want, but you're completely wrong for it.'

'God, no,' Cleo says, secure she's won a victory. 'That doesn't sound like my kind of thing at all.' She laughs a dismissive laugh. As if I'd lower myself. I only do beauty, don't you know.

Abi finishes her meal in silence, can't bring herself to look at her sister.

Upstairs, later, Phoebe's indignant. 'She's pathetic,' she says, banging the pillows around as she makes her bed. 'It's so obvious she just didn't want you to go to the casting because she has to be the only star in the family. It's a few little ads for Bargain Hunters for fuck's sake . . .'

'Phoebe,' Abi says, although she's not so naive that she really thinks her daughter hasn't learned to swear yet.

'Sorry, Mum, she just makes me so angry. She's so . . . selfish.'

'She's just insecure,' Abi says. 'It was a stupid idea anyway.'

Cleo appears at her bedroom door again. Phoebe, sensing trouble, makes herself scarce.

'You weren't really interested in that thing, were you? Bargain Hunters?' Cleo says, sitting down on the bed without being invited. 'I suddenly thought I hope I didn't put you off going up for it if you really wanted to?'

Abi thinks about saying, 'Actually, yes you did. You sulked and pouted until I felt I had to back down,' but she decides she can't be bothered. She and Cleo have been getting on better than they have in years and, even though she knows that just below the surface her sister is still the same self-obsessed and spoilt madam that she's been her whole adult life, she also knows that this version, the one that will play family games and apologize when she's in the wrong, is a much enhanced model.

'No, of course not.'

Cleo leans back against the pillows. 'Do you know that when you got your place at Kent Mum wrote me a letter saying how proud she was that you were the first of the Attwoods ever to get into university?'

Did she? All Abi can remember is Philippa making a fuss about the fact that Abi wanted to move into halls rather than stay at home and commute, and telling her that they wouldn't be able to afford to top up her grant so she was going to have to think about getting a job the minute she got to Canterbury or she was never going to survive.

'Really?'

Cleo nods. 'I've probably still got it somewhere, buried in the attic. I remember thinking maybe she was having a dig at me for not being clever enough.'

'As if.'

Cleo smiles. 'Remind me to tell Tara and Megan they're both brilliant at everything tomorrow. You can help me make a list.'

'Maybe it's a good thing I only had the one,' Abi says. 'She has no one to be forced to compare herself with.'

'That's true. But no one to share all her memories with either. That's kind of sad. I always wanted my two to have what we had.'

Did she? 'Did you?'

'Of course,' Cleo says. 'Wouldn't you?'

24

The summer is over. August has turned into a wet and windy month of storms and floods. The hill is already papered with brown and orange leaves that turn slushy and treacherous underfoot. Abi feels like it's symbolic, an end or a beginning, she's not sure which. Both maybe. She forces herself to put her practical head on, making lists, emailing her solicitor, arranging for her furniture to be moved out of storage once her new home is hers. Her plan is to give the place a quick coat of paint, freshen it up before she moves anything in there. Phoebe has promised to help. Abi thinks that between them they can cover the whole flat in two days if they ignore the woodwork. She has already arranged a cheap deal with a friend who runs a B 'n' B up the road for the two of them to stay there for a couple of nights. On the third day her furniture will hopefully arrive and then her life can settle back into its normal routine again except that her daughter will be gone.

Entertaining small girls in rainy weather is a whole different ball game to keeping them occupied in the sunshine. To give her credit, Cleo tries to help when she's home. Although no one is really talking about it, her castings seem to have got fewer and further between, and they all spend wet mornings playing Monopoly or Mario Kart. They can't stay in all the time, though – there's a danger they'll all kill one another – so on the Tuesday before she's due to go home Abi decides to take the children on the train to Hampton Court where she's read they are staging reconstructions of one of Henry VIII's weddings and allowing kids to dress up in Tudor costumes to play the part of guests. It sounds like fun and the girls are fired up about doing anything so long as it gets them out of the house. Jon is at work and Cleo has a go see she seems very excited about, so Abi, Phoebe, Tara and Megan set out for Waterloo station and the short train ride to the suburbs.

Phoebe has been complaining of period pains all morning, but, dosed up on Feminax, she has elected to go on the trip rather than remain home alone. By the time they have negotiated the Northern Line, though, she is practically doubled over, clutching her stomach and moaning that she should have stayed in bed. Tara and Megan watch her in wide-eyed horror while Abi is torn between alerting them to the fact that this is their future or allowing them to think something is seriously wrong with their cousin and traumatizing them in a whole other way. In the end she decides that it's better to persuade Phoebe to cut her losses and head home. Phoebe graciously allows herself to be persuaded and manages to put on a big show of feeling much better before she leaves, which goes some way towards assuaging the girls' fears.

By the time they get off the train at the other end, and battle their way across the river in the driving rain, all of their umbrellas blowing inside out on the bridge, Phoebe has left a message that she's already home and that Elena is making her a cup of tea, a sandwich and a hot-water bottle for her to take up to her room. Abi breathes a sigh of relief, relays the good news to the two younger girls and then throws herself into giving them a fun day out at the palace.

Three and a half hours later they're all exhausted. The girls have dressed up in cloaks and pretended to be courtiers then joined in a group activity to help Katherine Parr choose her wedding dress, toasted the king and queen and watched the wedding procession. Somewhere in the middle of all that they each wolfed down a sandwich and a Coke, but they're all famished, so Abi takes them to an Italian by the station where they order enormous plates of pasta. By the time they get on the train back to Waterloo they can barely keep their eyes open. In fact, neither Tara nor Megan do. They sit either side of Abi on a seat made for two and snuggle up to her, wet and exhausted, both falling asleep almost immediately. Abi nuzzles into their hair, Tara's so straight and dark, Megan's wavy mouse. She feels an overwhelming rush of love for her two small nieces. She allows herself briefly to imagine that they're her own – hers and Jon's. She tries to slot that idea into her fantasy happy-ever-after that she still regularly plays out in her head, but this time the practicalities, the rationale, overwhelm her.

At home Cleo is back and reading the paper in the living room, but Abi just waves at the door and heads on up the stairs, pushing the girls in front of her.

'We're all having baths,' she calls. 'We're soaked through.'

'Was it fun?' Cleo shouts back.

'Yes,' all three say in unison.

'It was brilliant,' Megan adds. 'I wish Auntie Abi would never go home.'

'Me too,' Cleo shouts back, and even though Abi knows she doesn't mean it literally it gives her a warm glow to know that her sister really does seem to like having her around now.

Abi drops the girls off on the second floor and traipses on up to her attic. Her limbs feel heavy and exhausted, and all she can think about is a deep hot bath. Maybe with a glass of wine if she could summon up the strength to go back down to get one. She pushes open the door to her bedroom and there, sitting on the bed, is Phoebe.

'Hi. Are you feeling better? You missed a fun time actually . . .' She stops as she notices the look on Phoebe's face. Her daughter looks pale and strained. 'Phoebe? What's wrong?'

Phoebe looks at her, looks almost scared.

'Do you feel really bad?' Abi sits on the bed next to

her daughter and instinctively places a hand on her forehead, feeling for a temperature.

'No. Well, yes, but not like that.'

'What's happened?'

'Mum, you mustn't say anything . . .'

Abi's brain holds up flashcards of what might be wrong. Pregnancy and STDs feature heavily, as usual, joined by illness, debt, boyfriend trouble (she crosses her fingers and hopes for that one even though she knows Phoebe doesn't actually have a boyfriend at the moment). Maybe it's about her exams. Maybe Phoebe didn't get the two As and two Bs she proudly told the family she had gained last week. After all, Abi didn't actually see the letter. That wouldn't be so bad. OK, imaginary boyfriend trouble or failed A-levels, either of those would be dealable with. She takes a deep breath.

'Just tell me what it is, sweetheart.'

Phoebe looks at her, looks away. 'It's Auntie Cleo.'

Now Abi is really confused. 'Auntie Cleo?'

Phoebe nods. 'After I left you that message, I went back to bed and read, and then a while later Elena came up to bring me another cup of tea and say bye because she was going. Then I think I went to sleep for a bit . . .'

Abi nods, impatient.

'Anyway, I heard the front door go. I think it was about two o'clock. I knew it wouldn't be you lot or Uncle Jon, so I assumed it was Auntie Cleo. I was feeling a lot better so I thought I'd go downstairs and say hi, but when I got to the landing I heard voices, Auntie Cleo's voice and a man's one I didn't recognize. It definitely wasn't Uncle Jon. I didn't want to go down in my pyjamas, because I didn't know who it was, so I went back to my room to get dressed, but then I heard them coming up the stairs . . .'

Abi feels sick, knows without a doubt what's coming next.

'They were giggling a lot. And then I heard them go into Auntie Cleo's and Uncle Jon's bedroom and shut the door.'

Phoebe runs out of steam and sits staring at the duvet. Abi reaches out and rubs her daughter's arm. 'And then what?'

'I just stayed up here, but they were in there for about an hour and a half.'

'Jesus,' is all Abi can say.

'I watched him out of the window when I heard him leave. He's got really short hair, like cropped.'

Abi nods. 'I think I know who it is,' she says. 'I think it might be Richard, from the bookshop, you know.'

'The one you used to go out with?' Phoebe looks at her incredulous. 'Why?'

Abi knows she can't tell Phoebe the half of it. She at least has to keep up the pretence that she and Richard were once an item. 'I just had my suspicions, that's all. They were very flirty.'

'How could she do that?' Phoebe looks as if she might cry now she's got her big secret off her chest. Abi can't bear to think of her sitting there all afternoon all alone and weighed down by what she had discovered. 'Uncle Jon's so . . . lovely.'

Abi sighs. 'I know. Does she know you saw them?'

Phoebe shudders. 'No. I've stayed up here all afternoon. I don't think she's even got any idea I was home.'

'OK. I'm so sorry you had to witness that, sweetie. You must have felt awful.'

'That woman is a complete bitch. I can't even believe she's your sister.'

'No. Me neither,' Abi says.

Abi lies in the bath, warm water up around her chin, but it's anything but relaxing. So Cleo is still seeing Richard. All her begging and her apologies and her promises that it was nothing more than a foolish near miss have turned out to be lies. All her protestations that she loves Jon and couldn't imagine her life without him, worthless. The whole thing has been a smokescreen, a misdirection, a construct. All the 'I'm really glad you're here' and 'I always wanted my two to have what we had' was just part of the performance. Desperate, needy, fucked-up Abi, so eager for crumbs from the family table, was guaranteed to fall for any line, however clichéd. It was all just another modelling assignment for Cleo. Act like you care about your sister. *Click*. Try to make us believe you're pleased to see her. *Click*. Look at her like you love her. *Click*.

Downstairs, she has no doubt, Cleo is working her magic on Jon. Abi has seen for herself how touched he has been by her attentions over the past few days, how surprised but pleased he's looked when Cleo has unexpectedly put her hand on his arm or granted him one of her oh-so-special smiles. He's taken the fact that she's been home more as a sign that everything is going back to normal, Cleo is accepting that her comeback is over before it began and that she's philosophical, even happy, about returning to her role as devoted wife and mother. He has been as taken in by her as Abi has, even more so maybe because he still remains blissfully unaware of the truth about how she has been behaving. He has put up with her moods and her selfishness and her ego, and he's been beating himself up because for one split second he allowed himself to get carried away and kiss someone else. Cleo doesn't deserve him.

A thought jabs at Abi out of nowhere, cold and steely. If Cleo has still been seeing Richard then maybe he's told her what he knows about Abi and Jon. Maybe he's used that as justification for his and Cleo's behaviour: 'She's in love with him, you know. Something happened between them while you were in New York, I'm not quite sure what . . .'

Never mind that it came to nothing, that Abi

turned him down for Cleo's sake, Richard could have spun it any way he chose. She forces herself to think it through. Is Richard really that cruel? Wouldn't he have taken into account the fact that she has never betrayed him to Stella? Wouldn't Cleo have dropped the sisterly act immediately and confronted her, taunted her about her assumption of the moral high ground, her double standards? She breathes out again, slowly. She would know by now. Cleo wouldn't have been able to keep it to herself.

Abi ducks her head back into the water to rinse off her hair. She thinks about Stella, how she said that she and Richard were getting serious, even thinking about moving in together. She has an overwhelming urge to broadcast what she now knows. She can't bear the thought of Cleo and Richard getting away with it, hurting people she cares about, but she also knows that she can't, she won't. It's not up to her, not her secret to share.

All she can do is confront Cleo, talk to Richard, beg them to do the right thing – either end it for good or come clean – and then get the hell out of there, go home to Kent and leave them all to deal with the fall-out. Or she could just take the coward's way out and say nothing. She wonders whether she should offer to take the girls down to the coast for a couple of weeks, leaving the adults free to talk about the future if they so choose, but she knows they're due back at school next week, so it's not really practical. She'll just have to hope Cleo has enough decency left to protect them from the worst.

She tries not to think about the fact that if she did speak up in front of everyone, throw it all out in the open, then Jon would more than likely end up on his own, available, free to form a new attachment with someone who would never even consider cheating on him.

There's a knock at the bathroom door. She hears Phoebe's nervous voice. 'Mum, are you OK in there?'

Abi realizes she has been lying there for over half an hour. 'I'm fine, sweetie. I'm getting out now.'

She drags herself out, wraps herself in an oversize fluffy towel and opens the bathroom door. She doesn't want Phoebe to worry about her on top of everything else.

Phoebe appears in the doorway. 'What are we going to do?'

'Nothing. We're going to go down to dinner as if everything's normal, for Uncle Jon's sake. I'll talk to Cleo later. Maybe. I haven't decided.'

She puts her arm round her daughter. 'You OK?'

Phoebe nods. 'Shouldn't we tell Uncle Jon? It's so unfair on him.'

'I know. But it's not up to us to interfere in anyone else's relationship. The only thing I can do is let her know that I know and then it's up to her. I'm tired of trying to convince myself that there's a good person under there, and that we have a relationship worth saving. There isn't and we don't. I can move into my new flat in three days' time and forget all about her. She can mess up her life on her own from here on in.'

'I'm so sorry, Mum. Maybe I shouldn't have told you. I didn't know what to do.' Phoebe looks so young and troubled that it nearly breaks Abi's heart.

'You did exactly the right thing,' she says. 'Don't even think that you have anything to feel bad about.'

It takes all Abi's strength to go down to dinner rather than just crawl into her bed, put her head under the covers and hope it'll all go away. She's so angry she's not sure she can look Cleo in the face without giving herself away. At the sight of her sitting with Jon and the girls at the kitchen table chatting away happily she feels a wave of nausea, as if she's going backwards, too high, on a swing.

'We made pizza – you missed it,' Megan says. Indeed there are several misshapen pizzas on the table along with a big salad.

'Well, it looks lovely,' Abi says as she sits next to Phoebe who has come down with her. She forces herself to look over at her sister. Cleo is showing no obvious signs of guilt, no telltale hint of post-coital satisfaction. In fact, she's smiling and laughing as though nothing is out of the ordinary, nothing is wrong. Abi feels weak with disgust.

'Jon, I've been thinking,' she suddenly finds herself saying out loud. She's standing on a precipice fighting the urge to see how far forward she can lean. 'I've decided I am going to go in and meet for that advert, after all. What's the worst that can happen?'

Jon beams. 'Good for you.'

Out of the corner of her eye Abi can see Cleo's carefree mask fall. The old sour, disapproving look is back even though she is clearly trying to suppress it.

'Gosh, Abigail, really?'

'Why not?' Abi says faux brightly. She plasters a tight smile across her face. 'Not that modelling of any sort is something I'd ever really be interested in – it's way too shallow. But just this once the money would come in handy.' She's aware she must look a bit manic – she certainly feels it – but there doesn't seem to be much she can do about it. Phoebe is looking a bit panicked.

Cleo's nostrils flare. 'Shallow? Is that what you think?'

Abi feels Phoebe press against her leg under the table. Calm down. Don't give yourself away, not in front of Jon and the kids.

'Sorry, that came out wrong. I just meant I've never thought posing in front of a camera would be that challenging.' Oh good, well done, that's lightened the mood.

Cleo arches her perfectly groomed eyebrows. 'And working in a library is?'

Abi knows she should back down, quit while there's still a possibility that they can avoid a fight.

And not just any fight but one where undoubtedly when backed into a corner she will feel the need to launch her weapon of mass destruction. But the recklessness is intoxicating. She feels a sense of freedom and abandonment she hasn't felt for years. She could just explode the whole thing, blow apart everyone's lives once and for all. It would almost be a relief.

She can feel the tension in the air. She's vaguely aware that next to her Phoebe is fidgeting anxiously, but everything is fuzzy round the edges. It's as if she's watching them all on an old-fashioned black-and-white TV. This is it. This is the moment. Full-on nuclear war or unilateral disarmament.

'I'd love to work in a library.' A small voice pipes up from across the table. 'You could read all the books and you'd never have to pay for them.'

The mist clears as quickly as it came. Abi's eyes come back into focus and she sees Megan smiling sweetly at her. She looks at Tara happily eating her pizza, oblivious. Of course this is not the time. Of course she's not going to initiate the apocalypse with her nieces and her daughter sitting in the fallout zone. She squeezes Phoebe's hand under the table. Deactivate. Defuse. Surrender.

'It's not as much fun as it sounds,' she says, feigning a lightness she doesn't feel. 'Your mum's right. It's not very challenging.'

'Well, a bookshop, then,' Megan's not giving up. 'Maybe I could get Richard to give me a job.'

Abi can't help it. At the mention of Richard's name her eyes flick to her sister. Cleo doesn't even have the good grace to show a trace of guilt.

'What a good idea,' Cleo says, smiling. 'We should go in and ask him.'

Abi breathes deeply. Counts to ten. Tries to swallow her food. Fails.

25

Abi can't seem to find a moment to get her sister on her own, or maybe she could but she's not trying as hard as she should because she knows exactly how the conversation will go and she can't face having to listen to any more of Cleo's bullshit. She knows that she has to do something, though, because the sight of Cleo, dressed up to the nines at eleven in the morning, leaving the house claiming she is going to a casting, is almost more than she can stand. Now that she knows what Cleo has been up to it's impossible not to interpret her every move as calculated. For all she knows her sister could genuinely be going to meet for a job, but something in the way she's styled her hair, the perfume she's put on, the hint of a smile when she says goodbye, says otherwise.

Abi can't contain herself any longer. It's her last whole day in London and she's been pretending not to notice that Tara and Megan have been holed up in the kitchen all morning preparing a surprise farewell dinner for her and Phoebe. She could just let it go; after all, in less than twenty-four hours, she will be out of here for good but, hearing the front door close, knowing where Cleo is going, she decides she has to act now.

She risks a look at Phoebe as she goes and she can tell that her daughter knows exactly what she is going to do. Abi gives her a reassuring smile, tries to convey with her eyes that everything is going to be OK. Phoebe smiles back warily.

'I'll only be a minute,' Abi says quietly and, she hopes, reassuringly.

She catches up with Cleo outside Odette's, the fabulous-looking restaurant that she has yet to go into. Cleo jumps when she sees her and then makes a show of looking up and down the road as if she had really been on the lookout for a taxi the whole time. Abi knows she has to be quick. She's not prepared to have a showdown standing on Regent's Park Road; she just wants to drop her bomb and then go straight back home. There's nothing Cleo could say in justification of her actions that she would want to hear at this point.

'Abigail?'

Abi sees that Cleo is flustered, but is doing a fairly good job of covering it up, consummate professional that she is.

Abi dives off, head first, no safety net. 'I know you're still seeing Richard. I know he was at the house on Tuesday and all that stuff you told me about it being a one-off was bollocks.'

She barely even pauses for breath. She doesn't want to give Cleo the chance to respond. Doesn't want to risk being sucked back into her vortex.

'I'm just telling you this so you know I know. I'm still not about to say anything to Jon. I'm not going to tell you to finish it or else. It's nothing to do with me any more. You can fuck your life up as much as you like. It's all up to you now. If you decide to go ahead and carry on, then I hope you can learn to live with the consequences. You have a beautiful family. If you think that this . . . thing . . . with Richard is worth losing them for, then that's your own funeral. You don't deserve them anyway. You're a crap wife, a crap mother and a crap sister, for that matter. Oh, and you were a crap daughter too, by the way. Mum and Dad might have idolized you, but deep down they knew you didn't really care about them. You've only ever really cared about yourself. I hope you're happy, Cleo, I really do.'

She turns on her heel and starts to walk back towards the house. She feels light-headed, exhilarated almost. Braver than she has ever dared to be.

'Given that's how you feel about me, I'm amazed you wanted us to spend the whole summer together.'

Despite herself, Abi turns. Cleo is still standing where she left her. She's speaking too loudly given where and who she is. People are turning to look.

'But then I suppose being able to sponge off your family for a couple of months at least saves you having to get a proper job.'

On the other side of the road Abi can see a young man, phone held aloft, no doubt recording the whole

375

scene for YouTube. She takes a few steps back towards her sister. She speaks as quietly as she can.

'I thought you wanted to build bridges. I thought you wanted us to have a proper relationship. Like family.'

'Poor old Abigail, living her lonely dull life in the sticks, desperate for crumbs from the family table.'

'You invited me, remember. I didn't initiate this.'

'Mooning around after my husband. Don't think I haven't noticed you hanging on his every word, blushing like a teenager every time he speaks to you. It's pathetic.'

Abi is stung. Has her infatuation really been that obvious? 'Jon's a good man. You're lucky to have him.'

'Maybe I am, but do you know what? It's none of your business. What I choose to do with my life is up to me.'

Abi can see that the young man has given up and gone, hopefully frustrated that he couldn't hear what looked to be a juicy argument. People are still going about their business, walking their dogs, drinking coffees, chatting to their friends, oblivious, while her own world is blurring, melting around her.

'You know that's not true, though. You have a husband, children, responsibilities. It can't just be about you.'

'You know what, Abigail? When you have managed to make a half-decent life for yourself, then maybe you can comment on mine. You're jealous of me, my life, my career, even my husband. You always have been. And I've always had to feel guilty about that. As if it was my fault that I made something of myself and you didn't. You're pitiful actually. Do what you like, tell Jon about Richard if you want. That would suit you, wouldn't it? Throw a hand grenade into my life and then run away. Well, if you want to ruin Tara and Megan's lives you do just that. And then you can live with the consequences.'

'I'm not the one threatening to destroy your family. You're doing that all on your own.'

'You want to get revenge on me for being prettier, more popular, Mum and Dad's favourite? Here you go. Now's your chance. Although I should warn you that whatever you do it's unlikely Jon is going to notice you. You're really not his type.'

Abi is momentarily stopped in her tracks. She hates this Cleo, the one who will say anything, however cruel, to win an argument, the one she now knows is the genuine article. All the other versions were just smoke and mirrors. But she knows she won't do it. She does have a hand grenade, but she'll never pull the pin.

'Don't worry, I'm not going to say anything to Jon. I'll leave that to you and your conscience.'

'Gosh, thank you, I'm so grateful,' Cleo says disingenuously. 'Is it cold up there on your high horse?'

Abi tells herself not to rise to it, not to waste her breath. 'If the girls hadn't planned the dinner for tonight, then I'd leave now. As it is I'm going tomorrow anyway so I'd suggest we just keep up the pretence that everything's fine till then.'

She turns and walks away before she can say anything she truly regrets. Unfortunately Cleo has no such qualms. 'Oh, and, Abi, you know you thought I only invited you up here because the nanny had left? You were right. I needed someone to take care of the kids for the summer and then I thought of you.'

And Abi knows, unequivocally, that whatever remnants of the Caroline she remembers that were left are now dead and gone. Who knows, maybe that Caroline only existed for the one brief moment when Abi was seven and hated her first-communion dress. Maybe her sister was always a nightmare in the making, the chrysalis of a monster, and now she has simply completed her metamorphosis.

Abi spends the afternoon packing. Not that there's much to pack; she hasn't acquired anything that doesn't fit in the rucksack she arrived with. Phoebe has taken over from Elena in supervising the girls – she had to pretend to walk in on them unawares and then persuade them to let her in on their secret – who are now, she tells Abi when she pops upstairs to check she is OK, decorating the kitchen for the big event, so Abi gathers up whatever she can find of her daughter's that is clean and puts it in a pile beside her rucksack.

Her plan is to leave straight after breakfast tomorrow. She should be able to collect the keys to her new flat around lunchtime and then, after a quick trip round B&Q, start painting in the afternoon. Or at least cleaning the place from top to bottom, ready for decorating on Saturday. She focuses on thinking about her new home, how it will look, how she'll feel living there, how comforting it will be for her life to go back to a version of normal.

As she piles her things out of the chest of drawers and onto the floor, she comes across a bag she had stuffed in the back of one of them on the day she got here. She knows what it is. It's the gift she brought with her to give to Cleo and Jon when she left. A thank-you-for-having-me present. She pulls it out of the bag. It's a small ornate silver photo frame, made by her friend Kate who has a stall at a local market and who sold it to her at a rock-bottom price. Inside Abi has put her favourite photograph of her and Caroline when they were young, probably nine and six, grinning unselfconsciously for the camera, arms round one another, laughing. It was taken in Broadstairs one summer holiday. She can remember thinking that it would make Cleo laugh. She can remember imagining the moment when her sister opened the bag and took it out, the hug that would follow, the newfound closeness they would have developed over the summer enveloping them. She can remember how optimistic she felt.

It was a stupidly inappropriate present, she realizes

now. It's impossible to picture the little frame jostling for position with all the exquisite, expensive works of art that are so carefully placed around the house. No room for sentimental tat here. Plus she's hardly going to leave Cleo a thank-you gift now. It occurs to her that she has nothing for the girls. In anticipation, the summer had been all about Cleo; she had barely given the others a thought. And then in the last few days she has been too preoccupied to think about anything other than her own miseries.

She looks at her watch – quarter to three – she has time to go to one of the beautiful shops on Regent's Park Road and buy something she can't afford. She wants Tara and Megan to have something to remember her by.

'What's that?'

Abi jumps. Jon is standing in the doorway. She has no idea how long he's been there for.

She looks at the photo frame in her hand. 'Oh, nothing.'

'Lovely frame,' he says. 'Is that hand-made?'

Abi nods. She hands it over. She has no idea what he is doing up here.

'Is that you and Cleo?'

'I was going to give it to her as a leaving gift.' Saying it aloud Abi realizes how pathetic it sounds. *I've brought an apple for the teacher; it might make her like me.*

'She'll love it,' he laughs. Of course, Jon knows

nothing of her and Cleo's latest fallout. As far as he's aware, their relationship has been growing stronger every day.

'I don't know,' Abi says. 'Maybe . . .' She's not about to let him know there's anything wrong, because then he'd want to know what and why, and she knows she can never tell him.

She decides to change the subject. Injects a lightness into her tone. 'What brings you all the way up here?'

'I came to say goodbye,' he says. 'In case I don't get a chance to see you on your own tomorrow.'

Abi feels a lump in her throat, blinks back tears, looks at the floor. 'Thanks for putting me up all summer. And for putting up with me, come to that.'

'It's been really great having you around. Honestly it has. It's been fun.'

A big fat traitorous tear finds its way out and rolls down Abi's cheek. She looks at her piles of clothes, pretends to busy herself with them.

'And I wanted to thank you. Having you here has had a great effect on Cleo. And the girls, of course.'

She's powerless to stop another tear and then another from running down her cheek. She tries to keep her head turned away, not to let him see.

'Abi?' She can hear him behind her. She knows that if he touches her she'll start to bawl and probably never stop.

'Are you crying?'

She grunts something that is meant to mean 'no, I'm fine,' but before she knows it Jon has put his hand on her shoulder and she's turned round and buried her head in his T-shirt and is sobbing uncontrollably. He puts his arms round her, stroking her back, which only makes things worse.

'You can come back and stay any time,' he says, misinterpreting what it is that is making her cry. She knows she should pull away but the feel of his arms round her is so powerful. It's so unfair she thinks, not for the first time. Cleo has this amazing man and she doesn't even give him a second thought.

'You have to anyway because the girls are going to miss you like crazy. And I'm sure Cleo will want to bring them down to Kent to see your new flat as soon as you're settled in.'

She doesn't trust herself to speak. There's so much she wants to say to him, but she knows she never will. She has to pull herself together. Get out of here with her dignity intact at least. She forces herself to stand straight, wiping her tears.

'Sure,' she says, trying to smile.

For a split second Jon keeps his arms round her and then he drops them to his side and they take a step back from each other.

'And anyway you have to come back up for the audition next week.'

Shit, she does. Well, maybe. Perhaps she can just back out again at the last minute.

'Of course.' She smooths down her hair, rubs under her eyes where her mascara will have run.

They both stand there for a moment, unsure how to end the conversation.

'It goes without saying I'll miss you too,' Jon says finally.

Abi swallows, uses all her willpower to stop the tears starting again. 'Me too.'

'I guess I'd better help the girls with the big surprise,' he says after a moment, mercifully breaking the atmosphere.

'I've been practising my shocked face,' Abi says, trying to smile. 'It's pretty good, if I say so myself.'

Abi gets herself together, washes her face, reapplies her make-up and then heads up to the shops to find a parting gift for her nieces. She crosses the road to avoid Regent's Park Road Books. She has no idea whether Cleo is in there with Richard still. She tries not to care. In one of the stylish interiors shops she buys two similar but not identical wooden boxes, beautifully made from rough wood washed with white. In one she places a necklace she bought for herself in Accessorize, and which Tara, no longer fixated by designer labels, has admired, and in the other a bracelet from Camden Market that is a favourite of Megan's. Into both boxes she puts a print-out of a photo she has on her phone of the four of them, Abi, Phoebe, Tara and Megan, taken by Jon. She decides she will tell the girls these are their memory boxes, places to keep mementos that mean a lot to them. Somewhere to document their, hopefully, happy family history.

Cleo makes an appearance at the last supper. Abi manages to gasp in fake surprise and genuine awe when she sees the trouble Tara and Megan have gone to to decorate the kitchen and prepare something that's at least half edible. A home-made banner strung from the top of one of the cupboards to the hanging pot rack reads 'We'll miss you, Auntie Abi'. Abi actually cries although not quite for the reasons everyone thinks. Cleo makes a point of not looking at her, but in the excitement luckily no one else seems to notice. When Abi hears Jon ask her how her day has been and Cleo starts to hold forth on all the fabulous things she has done – with one notable exception – Abi turns her attention to the girls and forces herself not to listen.

After dinner Jon insists on doing all the clearing up so Abi takes Phoebe, Tara and Megan up to her room where they all camp out on the bed until far too late.

When they eventually, reluctantly, say goodnight Tara and Megan cling to her like they are never going to see her again and then all four of them start laughing and crying at the same time.

26

She leaves without saying goodbye to Cleo. Elena pats her on the arm sadly and then gives both her and Phoebe a hug.

'*Köszönöm*,' Phoebe says in perfectly accented Hungarian – she has been practising – and Elena beams and says, '*Köszönöm*,' back and then follows it up with a whole string of other words that make no sense to anybody except her. Everybody cries again, Tara and Megan most noisily. Abi can still hear them sobbing theatrically as she and Phoebe set off for the tube station, rucksacks in hand.

When they step off the train in Deal, Abi breathes an audible sigh of relief. Back to safety and security. Back to predictability and the mundane but comforting ordinariness of her normal day-to-day life. They're too early to pick up the keys so they stop by the library, where Abi is greeted like a prodigal family member, and ask if they can leave their belongings there for a couple of hours while they go round to the hardware store and stock up on paint and sugar soap and brushes and all the other things Abi needs to give both herself and her new flat a fresh start.

Abi tries to remember exactly what the flat is like

as they argue over colours, which rooms get the light and which need lifting. She keeps changing her mind, but in the end she settles on a deep magenta for the wall behind where her bed will go and a soft sage green for one wall of the living room. She's tempted by the wallpaper, but she knows that if she buys it then it will only live in the spare room – Phoebe's room – for months while she waits for someone to take pity on her and help her hang it. And she wants Phoebe's room to be perfect, ready and waiting for her any time she decides she wants to come home.

In the end they buy so much stuff – because white paint is on special offer so Abi picks up more than she thinks she needs, just in case – that they can't carry it all. They spend the next hour or so ferrying things from the shop to the library and then the library to the flat once they are given the word that the purchase has finally gone through.

The estate agent is standing on the doorstep waiting for them when they arrive with their first load, sweaty and out of breath. He hands over the keys with a flourish and Abi tries to give the act of unlocking the door for the first time some kind of ceremonial weight, but she feels numb. Inside, the flat is a little dingier than she remembers, a little smaller, a little rougher round the edges. She's immensely grateful that Phoebe and the agent are there because otherwise she thinks she would probably burst into tears.

'So, everything OK?' the agent says, not really caring now.

Abi takes a cursory look around. The vendors have left everything they said they'd leave — basically just the well-worn carpets and curtains, which she'll keep until she can afford new ones — and they have cleaned up after themselves, but there's something sad about the imprint of their heavy furniture still carving troughs out of the pile. The weight of someone else's life. It's depressing.

'Fine.' She forces a smile, keen for the agent to go and leave them to it. She feels overwhelmed by the amount there is to do.

'Right,' Phoebe says as soon as he's gone. 'I'm going to pick up another load of stuff from the library and I'll get some coffees on the way back then we can get down to it.'

Abi doesn't move, doesn't know where to start, doesn't want to be here.

'Mum!' Phoebe says, trying to shock her out of her torpor. 'Tell you what, we'll start in the living room. God, that carpet's awful. I wonder what's underneath.' She lifts up a corner of the threadbare carpet to reveal a scruffy but altogether more palatable parquet floor.

'Wow. Shall we?' She gives Abi a smile that says, 'I dare you,' and Abi feels a rush of love and gratitude. She needs to pull herself together for her daughter's sake. These are her last three days with Phoebe before she goes off again, and she owes it to her to make them enjoyable.

'Definitely.'

Once they've ripped up the carpet, which is so old that it practically comes apart in their hands, and revealed a floor that's worn and a bit patchy but definitely a thing of beauty compared to what was there before, the room starts to look entirely more welcoming and Abi is feeling like a new person. They do the same in the bedrooms and the hall, revealing more parquet and some passable 1970s wood-effect vinyl that has a certain retro charm. Abi has no idea how they are going to get rid of the carpet mountain that has sprung up in her bedroom but she doesn't care. By the time they lock up for the night and stagger, exhausted, round to the B 'n' B clutching a takeaway from the Indian restaurant on the corner, the living room is finished and Abi feels as if she must have lost at least five pounds. She's so tired that she falls asleep almost as soon as her (paper) plate is cleared, only vaguely aware of her daughter pulling the covers over her and kissing her goodnight.

When she wakes up, she doesn't know where she is or why she is pinned up against the wall, until she turns over and sees Phoebe sprawled out across the whole width of the double bed, just like she used to do when she was small and crawled into Abi's bed after she had nightmares. Abi lies back and savours the moment.

*

By the time Monday evening comes round the flat is transformed, one of Phoebe's friends has been round with his van and carted all the debris away, all of Abi's belongings have been brought out of storage and arranged neatly, and it's starting to feel like home. Primrose Hill feels both a long way away and a long time ago. Her first meal in her new home – at least the first one she cooks and doesn't eat out of a carton – is also Phoebe's last before she sets off again.

In the morning Abi sees her off at the train station, manages not to cry until she's left and feels inordinately proud of herself.

'Let me know what happens at the audition,' Phoebe says to her on the walk to the station.

'Oh, I don't think I'll bother going. It's a stupid idea,' Abi says. Now she is home she isn't sure she is ever going up to London again.

'You have to otherwise Auntie Cleo will have got her own way all over again.'

'I'll think about it,' Abi says. 'Now you're sure you have your passport and the address of where your friends are staying?'

Walking back now, trying to think about anything other than Phoebe, she thinks instead about the casting for the commercial. She decides to leave it to fate. Jon hasn't let her know what time the meeting would be. She has no intention of reminding him. If he gets in touch, she'll go; if not, she'll just forget all about it. As if she's willed it to, her phone beeps and there's a message from Tara:

> Say by 2 Phebe from us, Tara and Megan xxx Oh and dad says
> the casting is at 3 on thurs at his office. Is that ok? Love u xxx

Abi's heart flips. She is going to see Jon again. He wants her to come up to London. OK, so he didn't get in touch himself, but he has specifically asked Tara to text her. He thought about her. She was in his head. Before she allows herself to really think about it, she texts back:

> Tell dad that's fine.

She presses send before she can stop herself, and then remembers that she should reply to the rest of Tara's message. She texts:

> Phoebe says she'll miss you. Love you both too xxx

The girls don't need to know they've missed their cousin by a few minutes.

The library is the same as ever. It's as if she's never been away. All the regulars come in and sit at their usual seats and read the newspapers. Juliet fills her in with what has been happening, which isn't much. Abi's glad to see her. An uncomplicated work friendship is probably exactly what she needs right now.

After work they go to the local pub for a quick glass of wine before Juliet has to leave to go home and cook the dinner. Abi takes a detour on the way back to the flat so she can walk along the front, which is near deserted, all the tourists having already left to get back to normality. She passes the end of her old street and doesn't even feel the faintest pull back towards the house and all its years of memories. It feels like so much has happened since she lived there that it's no longer a real part of her life. She knows she should be glad to be home, but she feels on edge, uneasy, dissatisfied with the smallness of her life. It's not enough. It probably never was, but at least before she had motherhood and Phoebe to hide behind.

Thursday comes round too quickly and before she knows where she is she's standing by her open wardrobe agonizing about what to wear. She runs through the necessary attributes in her head: attractive, approachable, friendly young mum. Then she pushes those aside and thinks about the fact that Jon will be there. It's ridiculous, but she wants to look nice for him. While she would still never even contemplate trying to take him away from her sister (who is she kidding? Of course she would contemplate it – she thinks about it all the time. What she would never do is act on it; there's a difference), she wants him to think she looks good. She doesn't want him to ever look at her and wonder, What was I thinking?

In the end she settles on her most flattering but everyday outfit, a flowery print dress from Hobbs that is now a little loose on her – she has definitely lost weight over the summer and thinks she looks all the better for it – and ballet flats. Feminine but practical. Trying just enough, but not too hard.

As the train gets closer to Charing Cross, she starts to feel a bit sick. It's too soon to be coming back. Luckily Jon's office is in Holborn so she doesn't have to venture anywhere near Primrose Hill. She finds it easily, tucked in an alley behind the tube station, a kitschy swirly neon sign announcing 'MacMahon Fairchild' in the window. Inside it's a stylish but intimidating space, part office, part warehouse. Behind the ornate high-gloss white reception desk sits the equally stylish but intimidating receptionist: part human, part mannequin. She looks achingly cool in clothes and thick-framed glasses that on most normal people would be read as frumpy. Abi introduces herself, feeling ridiculous when she says she has come for a casting. The receptionist smiles, instantly transforming into something less frightening.

'Take a seat. There's coffee or mint tea if you want it. They'll call you when they're ready.'

Abi can tell that every piece of furniture has been carefully thought out. No job lot from Ikea here. There are four white Barcelona chairs round a low glass coffee table. All of them taken by women who could be described as attractive, approachable, friendly young mums. In the middle of the table are several retro-chic flasks and a handful of cute mismatched flowery china cups and saucers. It looks a bit like a sale in a Cath Kidston shop, but the effect is homely and fun. Just enough to take the edge off all the hard shiny surfaces.

Abi lurks on the periphery, feeling self-conscious because she's standing while everyone else is sitting. She'd kill for a strong coffee but, despite what the receptionist said, she's not entirely convinced the flasks are practical and not just part of a design feature, so she decides not to risk it.

None of the women are chatting. Two are reading newspapers, one is knitting and the other playing with her phone. From time to time they give one another sidelong glances, checking out the competition. Abi wonders if this is their life: they go from casting to casting hoping to win the Holy Grail that is a TV advertising campaign. It's a way to pass time, she supposes, although hardly stimulating.

After about two minutes a door opens and another attractive, approachable, friendly young mum is shown out by a woman in her fifties. One of the candidates waiting in reception is called in and Abi takes her seat, prepared for a long wait. It can't be more than another two or three minutes later, though, that the whole process happens again and another one of the seated women moves on through the door. Meanwhile several more attractive, approachable, friendly young mum types have arrived. It's a bit like a production line for *The Stepford Wives.*

Abi's not sure what she was expecting but it wasn't this. It's a long way to come for such a swift meeting. Still, she comforts herself with the fact that Jon is through that doorway somewhere. Even if she is only in the room for thirty seconds, it will be thirty seconds with Jon. Long enough to assess how he is, whether anything has changed, whether he has found out that his wife has been cheating on him. Long enough to take him all in.

Eventually it's her turn. She follows the older woman through the door and all the way across a huge open-plan room where several people seem to be working (if chatting, drawing on a large board and sitting with your feet up constitute working – she's not sure), and into a glass-walled side office at the end. There are three people sitting in the room. None of them is Jon. The older woman speaks.

'This is –' she glances down at a long list – 'Abi Attwood.'

The three people mutter hello.

'So, Abi,' the woman continues, 'you know what this is for . . .?'

Abi is barely listening. Jon isn't there. He had an opportunity to see her and he declined. In her head she had allowed herself to believe that that was what this was really all about. He had suggested she come for the casting because he wanted to know he was going to see her again. Now she has no idea what she's doing here.

She notices that the three people sitting down are all looking at her expectantly.

'Sorry?' she says.

'Have you heard of Bargain Hunters?' one of them says.

'Oh yes. I have.'

'Great, well, if you could just say this line –' she is handed a piece of paper – 'into that camera. Say your name first.'

A small camera is set up on a tripod in the corner. A young boy, probably on work experience, she decides, pops up from nowhere and presses a few buttons.

'Ready,' he says.

Abi has no time to even think about what she's doing. She glances down at the piece of paper, she already knows the slogan: 'Why pay for perfect packaging?', but they seem to have extended the line, added a few extra words.

She looks vaguely in the direction of the camera, unsure of whether that's what she should be doing or whether it's rude not to be addressing the people in the room.

'I'm Abi Attwood,' she says falteringly.

'Can you speak directly into the camera,' someone says.

Abi forces herself to stare down the lens. 'My name's

Abi Attwood.' She looks at the piece of paper in her hand. Suddenly it strikes her that the Bargain Hunters slogan might as well be some kind of metaphor for her life. She needs to get this over with and get out of there.

'Why pay for perfect packaging when it's what's on the inside that counts?'

'Good,' a man sitting on an orange chair says. 'Can you do it again with a bit more energy? Maybe do it like you're holding up a damaged box of something.'

Abi feels self-conscious, embarrassed, humiliated all at once. Why is she here? How did she get herself in this stupid situation?

She waves her hand around vaguely as if she's holding something. 'Why pay for perfect packaging when it's what's on the inside that counts?'

'And once more like you're happy about it.'

OK, so that really does require some acting skills. Abi feels she has two choices, burst into tears and run out of the room and straight to Charing Cross station, never to return, or say the stupid line one more time with as much dignity as she can muster and then put the whole experience behind her, but at least she won't have shamed herself too much. She chooses the latter, takes a deep breath.

'Why pay for perfect packaging when it's what's on the inside that counts?'

She waits. The older woman, obviously realizing that the others must be satisfied they've seen as much as they need to, jumps in, waving an iPhone.

'If I could just take a couple of pictures,' she says, taking them before she waits for an answer.

'Who's your agent?' the woman asks as she hustles Abi out.

Abi explains that she doesn't have one, that her brother-in-law just insisted on putting her forward, but the woman doesn't really seem interested, simply writes down Abi's mobile number as they walk and then calls in the next candidate without even saying goodbye, leaving Abi back in the reception area where she started. The whole excruciating episode has taken about four minutes.

On the way up she had thought that maybe she'd treat herself to a gallery or a walk along the river after the casting, but now she's here, now she's realized what an idiot she's been, travelling all the way up to London in the hope of getting a glimpse of her secret love object, like an adolescent, she just wants to get home as soon as she can, back to the safety of her day-to-day life. There are still things in the flat that need doing, boxes that aren't quite unpacked, cupboards that haven't been arranged to her liking. She can spend the evening taking care of that.

27

'How low can Cleo go?'

The headline screams out at her from the computer screen. Abi is almost afraid to read the accompanying article. She has got into the habit of googling her sister since she came home, something she had always steadfastly refused to do before. She wants to feel connected to Jon, to know whether their marriage is still in one piece. Apart from regular texts and emails from Tara and Megan, which mostly contain news about them and their friends, she has heard nothing, nor does she expect to.

She stares at the screen. Every day she expects to read an exposé that Cleo has been spotted with a man who is most definitely not her husband. Although for all she knows Cleo may have broken it off with Richard on the day Abi confronted her about it. She may have thrown herself back into her marriage and be doing everything she can to make it work. Richard and Stella might be planning a wedding or going through an acrimonious break-up. Or, worst of all, Cleo and Richard might still be seeing each other in secret, a hidden bomb waiting to explode. She's learned by now, though, that headlines for even the most mundane of stories are written for maximum impact; she's had heart-stopping moments before, waiting for a story to download. It's amazing how much still gets written about even the most forgotten celebrity. Every day there are pages of Cleo-related stuff to wade through. She double clicks and waits.

It turns out to be a blog, not even a newspaper article. Someone's bitter and bitchy personal opinion safely hidden behind a pseudonym. She breathes a sigh of relief when she realizes it's not the story she's been dreading, merely yet another 'look at poor old Cleo reduced to doing an advert for Satin Silk, well serves her right' opinion piece. She skim reads it, still surprised to be able to feel hurt on her sister's behalf.

On the days when she's not at the library she's finding that she's at a complete loose end. She can't remember what it was she used to do before. It can't all have been Phoebe-related, not in the last few years anyway. Her life had seemed so busy with . . . what? Somehow she'd managed to fill all her days with nothing very much and she can even remember moaning sometimes that she was too busy and that she never had any time to herself. She wonders whether she should go full time in the library just to give herself something to do, but that would officially make her a librarian and she's not sure that's what she wants to be for the next twenty years of her life. Not that there's anything wrong with that. It's a fine career.

Some people go to college with the sole aim of spending their days cataloguing books. It's what they want. It's just not her. It was only ever meant to be a part-time filler till she found her true calling.

She doesn't know why it comes as such a surprise, but she's suddenly realizing she's wasted her life. She deliberately sabotaged any chance she had of making something of herself, using Phoebe as an excuse. She hid behind her single-motherhood and her need to take care of her daughter, but now those smoke-screens have dissipated. It's time to find out who she really is.

Phoebe calls. As ever when her daughter's name comes up on her phone, Abi panics that it's going to be bad news, so she holds her breath until she hears Phoebe's upbeat, 'Hi!'

'Hi! How are you, sweetie?'

'Brilliant. We're in Phuket. How's things? Did you hear about the advert yet?'

'No. Nothing.' It's been less than a week, but Abi is assuming no news is bad news.

'You should ring Uncle Jon, find out what's going on.'

No. 'Mmm, maybe. I don't really care.'

Phoebe tells her about the job she's been doing, working a few shifts in a beach café.

'When we've got enough money, we're going to move on to Kuala Lumpur and try and get some work there for a few weeks. The plan is to get to Australia by Christmas.'

'Wow. That's amazing.' Christmas, thankfully, seems a long way away. Abi silently decides to check out if there is a local homeless charity who will be looking for volunteers for the big day.

They trade news of Tara and Megan gleaned from emails and texts, and then, all too soon, Phoebe has to go.

'I love you. Be careful.'

'Love you too, Mum. Bye.'

She's in the crime section straightening books on shelves when she feels her phone vibrate. Mobiles are strictly forbidden in the library, but most of the staff keep them in their pockets and it's not unusual to see something pulsing away in there as they move about their business. She has a surreptitious look at who is calling. It's a number she doesn't recognize. Five minutes later she's out the back in the staff room listening to a message;

'Hi. This is Felicity from MacMahon Fairchild. I hope this is Abi Attwood. Could you give me a call, please? It's about Bargain Hunters.'

Abi notes down the number Felicity leaves, feeling stupidly excited. It's not that she cares about the job – it's the idea that anyone might think she's the right person for any job. She's assuming Felicity wouldn't be asking her to ring back just to tell her she hadn't been chosen. There seemed to be so many women at the casting it would take days to let them all down that gently.

She tells Juliet she's going on her break and then takes her mobile outside to call. Felicity answers almost immediately, sounding relentlessly upbeat. Abi imagines Felicity always sounds relentlessly upbeat.

'So,' she says once Abi has introduced herself. 'We'd like to offer you the Bargain Hunters campaign.'

She doesn't even wait for Abi to respond. 'Now I see you don't have an agent so shall I just email all the details through to you? The shoot is next Monday and Tuesday morning for the TV ad and then Tuesday afternoon for the print campaign. I see you live in Kent, so we'll put you in a hotel for the night on Monday and pay your train fare. I'll need you to get back to me before then to confirm that the deal's OK. Don't cut your hair in the meantime. Don't get a fake tan. You'll also need to email me your measurements. OK? Does that sound good?'

Abi waits to see if Felicity has definitely finished speaking. She's completely unsure how to react. She has got the job. She, Abi Attwood, is going to be in the new adverts for Bargain Hunters. She knows it's ridiculous. All she has done is look the part (attractive, approachable, friendly young mum!) and say the line with something approximating sincerity. But the truth is they still chose her.

'Yes. Great. Thank you.'

She gives Felicity her email address, promising to get back to her once she has checked the details over. She knows there's only one person who will truly appreciate both the enormity and the hilarity of what has just happened, so she calls Phoebe. Once her daughter has finished screaming with delight, Abi says, 'I might get all up myself now. I might start referring to myself in the third person and demanding people leave a basket of kittens in my trailer.'

'Face it, Mum, they're never going to give you a trailer.'

Abi laughs.

'I wish I was there then I could come with you. I could pretend to be your assistant and tell them all they weren't allowed to look you in the eye or speak to you directly.'

'No, because then I'd have to pay you and I can't imagine they're going to be giving me a fortune.'

'Who cares? It's an experience.'

'Exactly,' Abi says firmly. 'And it's about time I had a few of those.'

She can hardly wait to get home to read Felicity's email. It has popped up enticingly on her phone, but the attachment wouldn't open so she's had an agonizing day of clock watching. She tells Juliet her news and she reacts as if Abi has just been cast as Lady Macbeth at the National, and announces it to everyone who comes up to get their books scanned. To be fair they're all very kind and no one says, 'What's Bargain Hunters?' or, 'That sounds ghastly,' although Abi is sure more than a few of them think it.

On her walk home (she refuses Juliet's offer of a celebratory drink in the pub, so keen is she to get home to her PC) it strikes her that Jon must have been involved in the decision-making process somehow. He is the boss, after all. She can't imagine he sat down and trawled through the tapes and photographs, but, presumably, at some point, one of the people in charge of the Bargain Hunters campaign would have said to him, 'This is the person we want to use,' and asked him to sanction that choice. Whether he had an opinion about their decision or not is irrelevant. There's no doubting he must have thought about her for a minute. There's no doubting she's occupied a space in his mind, however tiny, for a few moments. A nanosecond. She wonders if he's told Tara and Megan.

Felicity's email couldn't be more obtuse if it tried. Abi is blinded by Basic Studio Fees and TVRs and percentages for this and that. It looks like an algebra test paper. She sits staring at it for a while, wondering what she is meant to make of it. There's a whole separate sheet of figures that seem to relate to the print campaign for posters and point of sale. On the bottom of each sheet is a number that seems to be a total of sorts. It's not a huge amount of money – the whole thing comes to less than £1,500, but it still seems like a fortune to her for two days' work. She tries to think when she's ever had a spare £1,500. That would be never.

The second time she reads it, it makes no more sense than the first. She decides she should probably just accept whatever is on offer. There's no way they are going to be ripping her off. Well, not too badly anyway. She goes to get a large glass of wine and then reads through it all again carefully. Just in case there's a catch. A random clause that might mean she ends up with nothing. She potters around putting pasta on to boil and assembling a tomato and olive sauce. By the time she comes back to her computer with her meal in one hand and her glass in the other, there's a new email in her inbox. She looks at the sender's address: jon@ macmahon_fairchild.com. Her heart nearly stops.

She's almost afraid to open it. It's the first she's heard from Jon since she left London nearly two weeks ago. He must have asked the girls for her email address. Even though she knows it will have something to do with Bargain Hunters, the timing alone makes that clear, she can hardly bring herself to open it.

Congratulations! It's our standard deal, but we always try it on a bit with the first offer. Tell them you want the buyout to be for an agreed number of TVRs only and that you want a three-month restriction on the print campaign. They'll check with me and I'll say yes. That way you'll get paid again if we keep running them. But don't tell them I told you that. See you at the shoot. J

Abi laughs. So he has been thinking about her. He bothered to find out her email address and send her a message. Even better is the last line: 'See you at the shoot.' He's going to be there.

She sends a message back. She tries to keep it to the point, friendly but businesslike.

Thank you. I will. Very exciting. Hope you're all OK. Send the girls my love.

She composes another email, this time to Felicity, laying out, in as humble terms as she can – she doesn't want to piss her off – what Jon has told her to say. She briefly wonders what she'll reply if Felicity asks her what number of TVRs would be acceptable, because she doesn't even know what TVRs are. Hopefully they'll just suggest something and she's already decided she'll agree to whatever it is. She imagines they go through this with every offer, much more so when agents and managers are involved. She sends the email before she can change her mind.

Then she sits up way too late into the night waiting, just in case Jon replies to her message. (There's no reason for him to, there's nothing to reply to, but he might anyway. She chastises herself for not asking him a question that he would feel obligated to respond to.) He doesn't.

28

She can't remember when she's ever been up this early in her life, but here she is on the 5.08, oversize coffee in hand, trying to stay awake because there are works on the line and she has to change trains at Ashford. If all goes to plan, she should get to the Bargain Hunters shop in Hackney where they are filming for the day just in time for her call at eight. The train is deserted. No one else is foolish enough to be travelling at this hour.

Felicity came back with a counteroffer, following Abi's email to her, and didn't seem to have taken offence at all. There is now a cap on the mysterious TVRs (she looked it up and it means 'television ratings' and refers to the aggregated amount of people who might see the ad when it's shown on various different channels – she's still none the wiser, really), and a three-month limit on all print adverts, after which time she'll be paid more if the campaign is a success and still running. She accepted readily, sent her measurements (praying that there wouldn't be a reason for Jon to have to see those. She had thought about lying, shaving a few centimetres off her hips and thighs, but that would slightly defeat the object), and arranged to swap her days at the library. They are putting her up tonight at the Jury's Inn Hotel on Pentonville Road. She laughed when she saw that, imagining Cleo's outrage if anyone had suggested that she stay somewhere like that when she was on a job.

She arrives at the shop right on time, having splashed out on a taxi from Charing Cross. She hangs around outside watching people bustling about, all totally focused on what they're doing. Bargain Hunters in the flesh looks every bit as stylish and sophisticated as you might imagine. They already have two hundred shops nationwide, Felicity explained to her, with a strategy to open fifty more over the next couple of years. Abi has to admit it's a principle she approves of. She wonders where the nearest branch to Deal is.

Eventually someone appears from the crowd and says, 'Abi?'

Abi nods, smiles. The woman holds out her hand. Abi recognizes her from the casting although they never got as far as introductions then. 'I'm Carmel the director. I know you haven't done this before. Are you nervous?'

'Terrified.'

'Well, let's get you some breakfast and into make-up. It'll be a doddle, don't worry. Lisa! Lisa will look after you.'

Carmel hands Abi over to Lisa who turns out to be a runner and who takes her straight into a back room where a make-up artist has set up. She doesn't have a moment to even worry about what is happening, because by the time she's had her make-up done and scoffed down an egg roll it's time for wardrobe and then, once she's suitably dressed as an attractive, approachable, friendly young mum (in a pale pink T-shirt and A-line skirt) there's no getting out of it; it's time for her to go and do what she's being paid to do.

Everyone is so friendly, but Abi feels sick with nerves by the time she's taken out into the shop and shown her position at the till. Someone brings over the two kids playing her children, a boy and a girl aged about five and seven. They both seem far more at home than she is. What is she doing here? She's never felt comfortable being on show. She feels ridiculous standing there with the lights and the cameras and the huge crew of people all waiting to film her. Carmel introduces her to the woman playing the shop assistant and then says, 'Right, let's have a rehearsal.' Abi breathes deeply, tries to stop herself from passing out. She looks around, no sign of Jon. Thank god. Now she's here she doesn't think she could get through it if he was watching.

They run through the whole thirty-second scenario several times. Even to her untrained ears the lines coming out of her mouth sound fake and over-acted. Every time she messes up she stammers and blushes. She feels as if she might cry. Eventually Carmel takes her aside.

'None of them are taking a blind bit of notice of you,' she says, putting her arm round Abi. 'They're only thinking about their own little area, how do the lights look or do we have the microphones in the right place. You could say anything and I swear no one would even register it. So just try to relax. We cast you because you look the part and we believed you when you said the words and that's pretty much all that matters. Don't act – just be natural.'

Abi nods. Tells herself to concentrate. She's here now; she just needs to get through it. They do it again and again and it gets easier and easier when she realizes that what Carmel said is true. No one reacts when she messes up – they just throw in helpful suggestions about technical things she doesn't understand. They try different staging and moving the props around, and by the time Carmel announces it's time to do the final checks and actually start shooting the thing she feels, if not completely relaxed, at least able to get through it without making a fool of herself. So what if she looks ridiculous? Who cares?

By lunchtime she's dizzy from the lights and the heat and the amount of times she's said the same thing over and over, but at least it seems as if they're getting what they want. Carmel seems happy.

Abi is sitting on the shop floor eating a salad and chatting to the shop-assistant woman ('I was the woman in the plaster cast in the injuredatwork.com ad – did you see that one? Oh, and I was in one of the Iceland ads. Not featured, just in the background, eating profiteroles . . .') and actually quite enjoying herself – if nothing else it's going to make an entertaining anecdote to tell Phoebe – when Jon suddenly appears out of nowhere and starts making his way across the room towards her.

She stands up, praying she has no lettuce in her teeth, willing the shop-assistant women to go away and leave them on their own. She has a split second to take him in before he reaches her. He looks well. He looks like Jon. For which read, in Abi's mind, he looks gorgeous. She stutters a hello.

'Abi.' Jon holds out his arms and gives her a hug. 'How is it going? Are you hating it?'

She nods, smiling. 'Every minute.'

There's so much she wants to ask him that she doesn't know where to start.

'Thank you, by the way, for this.'

'Oh, it was nothing to do with me. Well, they showed me the tapes of three people they were interested in, you included, and I might just have nudged them towards you a little. But you got on their short list on your own.'

'Well, I appreciate it. How's . . .' she starts to say, but then she hears someone calling for her and it's time to go back and repeat the whole process all over again, only this time with the camera in a different place.

'Oh, you're coming to dinner tonight, by the way.'

She starts to protest. She has no desire to see Cleo. Ever again.

'Thanks, but I'm shattered . . .'

'The girls would be devastated if you didn't. It's all they've talked about for days.'

Shit. 'OK. Thanks. I don't know what time . . .'

'Whenever,' he says. 'You're family — you don't need to make an appointment.'

Even though it's only been a couple of weeks, Primrose Hill seems like a different place. It's not just that the trees are now almost completely bare or that the hill has lost most of its lush green carpet, it's as if she's looking at it from an outsider's point of view again, partly in awe, partly with a detached cynicism. It's hard to believe that for a few short weeks it felt like home.

She's barely touched the bell when the front door flies open and two pre-teenagers nearly flatten her with the force of their hugs. You'd think they hadn't seen her for months from the way both of them cling to her, gabbling away about school and where they've been and what they've done. She had half expected that when she saw them again Tara and Megan would have reverted to their world-weary, seen-and-done-it-all, pre-summer selves, but it's evident very quickly that her fears are unfounded. They lead her straight through to the kitchen where Jon greets her with another hug and hands her a glass of wine. There's no sign of Cleo.

'Sorry, am I too early?'

The shoot had finished for the day at five and, although Abi hadn't intended to get to the house before seven thirty, once she had checked in to her hotel it felt too depressing to sit there on her own for too long, staring at the walls.

'Not at all. Perfect timing. Cleo's in the bath, but she shouldn't be long.'

Abi notices that the girls set to laying the table without, it seems, anyone asking them to.

'So,' Jon says, indicating she should sit at the table. 'How did it go?'

She tells them all about the shoot and how, after her initial nervousness, it had been quite fun although exhausting.

'I've told all my friends you're going to be the Bargain Hunters woman,' Megan says, sidling up for another hug.

'What did you have to wear?' Tara asks.

'You wouldn't have liked it. The idea was I had to look as ordinary as possible. Like any woman you might see in the street, any day.'

'I bet you still looked pretty.'

Abi puts her arm round her niece, squeezes hard. 'Thank you.'

'And tomorrow you have the shoot in the other supermarket, which we're filming in a studio, and then it's the stills shoot,' Jon says. 'And then it's all over, which, I'm thinking, you might be glad about. Am I wrong?'

Abi traces the rim of her glass with her finger. 'It's been an experience, don't get me wrong. And I'm eternally grateful for the money. But I think that'll be my acting and modelling careers over. I'll dump them before they dump me.'

Jon laughs. Abi notices the wilful bit of hair is standing up on the rebellious spot on his crown. She thinks about smoothing it down.

'I can't believe how long everything takes,' she says instead. 'Nine hours and we've got, what, twenty seconds of the ad done?'

'You're lucky it was Bargain Hunters. If this was a high-end product what you shot today would probably have taken a week.'

'I knew there was an upside to being low rent,' Abi says, making him laugh again.

'It's really good to see you,' he says, and he gives her a smile that makes her stomach flip.

'So, girls,' she says, brightly, breaking the moment. 'I need a new career. Or I should say I need *a* career. I thought I could use the money I make from the advert to pay to train to do something. Any ideas?'

'Architect,' Megan says.

'Fashion designer,' Tara chips in.

'Vet.'

'Stylist.'

'Doctor.'

'Make-up artist.'

'OK, OK stop. I think I need something that plays to my strengths. What am I good at?'

They all look at her blankly. 'You're funny,' Tara says eventually.

'And kind,' Megan adds.

'Great,' Jon says. 'You could become a stand-up comedian who only does gigs for charity.'

'Well,' Abi says. 'If you have any bright ideas let me know because I'm clueless.'

At about seven o'clock Cleo wafts in, fragrant and perfectly made-up after her bath.

'Abigail! You're here already. Why didn't anybody tell me?'

Abi forces herself to smile. Tonight is for Tara and Megan; it's not about her and her sister.

'I haven't been here long.'

She tries to think of something to say, some conversation for her and Cleo to share, but the only thing that comes into her head is, 'Still seeing Richard?' so she just keeps quiet. Cleo seems to be making a big show of being affectionate towards Jon and, even though it hurts Abi to watch it, she's relieved that he seems to be enjoying the attention. They look the picture of a contented, loving nuclear family even if she knows the truth, that some of the paper over the cracks is stretched to tearing point.

Over seared tuna steaks and a second glass of wine

Cleo says, 'So, did Jonty tell you? I've decided I don't want to go back to modelling after all.'

Abi flicks a look at Jon and he nods, smiling.

'Right . . .'

'It's too much of a commitment and it's not fair when I have a family at home who need me.'

Abi is in no doubt that the modelling world has rejected Cleo, not the other way round, but she knows she would have nothing to gain from saying so. Let Cleo rewrite history if she wants. Who cares?

'Good for you,' she says.

Cleo, she notices, doesn't once ask her how the Bargain Hunters shoot is going. At nine thirty the girls are finally convinced by their father that they have to go to bed and Abi decides it's time for her to leave. Without her nieces chattering on she really isn't sure what they'll all talk about. When her cab arrives, she says goodbye to Jon in the kitchen with a sister/ brother-in-law-appropriate hug.

'I won't see you tomorrow,' he says, dashing her hopes. 'I've got meetings all day.'

Cleo insists on accompanying her to the front door.

'It's completely over between me and Richard,' she hisses into Abi's ear once they are out of Jon's earshot. 'I just want you to know that.'

'It's really none of my business,' Abi says, and she means it. She's tired of caring about how Cleo is living her life. It's time to move on.

29

Weeks go by. Abi's routine ticks along, a flat plain with no highs or lows. Days in the library, days pottering about doing not very much. She thinks again about getting a cat, a dog, anything that will make her flat seem more like a home. She goes on a date with a man she meets at Juliet's birthday party. He's nice enough, kind and smart, but she can't summon up the enthusiasm to see him again. The cheque for Bargain Hunters arrives and the money sits in her bank account waiting to be put to good use. She hears nothing from Cleo or from Jon.

She takes to going up to London on the train whenever she can. She tells herself she's getting her modern-art fix, pounding the floors at the Tate and the Saatchi, but a big, mostly unacknowledged, part of her just wants to be there soaking up the energy of the city, trying to feel a connection to her family. To Jon in particular.

At the beginning of November she's watching the TV late one night, a mindless home improvement programme on a small cable channel, when suddenly there she is, attractive, approachable, friendly young mum urging the viewers not to waste their money on perfect packaging. She goes through every emotion from embarrassment to pride to sadness that she has no one to share the moment with. She checks the time, calls Phoebe, risks getting her out of bed.

'It was just on,' she squeaks with adolescent levels of excitement when her daughter answers her mobile. Phoebe knows at once what 'it' is.

'Oh my god, Mum. I can't believe I missed it. Tell me everything.'

'It's awful,' Abi says laughing. 'I look a fright and I sound really odd, like I'm putting on a voice.'

'Who cares? You're a superstar.'

Phoebe sounds happy. The world she's inhabiting, the sun, the sea and the spontaneity, couldn't seem more alien to the damp and dark predictability of a Kent autumn. She tells Abi that she and her friends are still in Malaysia, soon to depart for Bali and then on to Sydney, Melbourne, Tasmania.

'Lovely.' Abi can't help but be relieved that Australia is on the horizon. It feels like a safer, more familiar place for her teenage daughter to be. A larger Britain, just with more sunshine and cuter animals.

Every now and then someone double takes or asks her if they know her from somewhere. One of her colleagues in the library tells her they saw her face on a poster at a train station. It's a strange feeling; she's not entirely sure she likes it. She's a million miles from Cleo territory – in fact, make that two million, five, ten – but she's no longer completely anonymous. On one of her days off she takes the train up to Ashford, seeks out the poster and takes a photo on her phone to email to Phoebe and then copies it to Tara and Megan. She feels rootless, restless, adrift. She scours the internet for inspiration, but every course she finds seems too daunting or too frivolous or just too uninspiring. The significance of her choice – the choice of what direction the rest of her life might take – suddenly seems too weighty. She's paralysed, unable to commit. She stops looking, allows herself to drift back to her routine. After a while it's like she never went away. Every now and then she catches sight of her advert, still running on some obscure cable channel or other. It doesn't feel like her.

At the end of January – after a quiet Christmas that she actually quite enjoys, watching bad TV, eating too much, walking on the beach – another cheque drops through her letterbox. Bargain Hunters have decided to keep up their campaign for world domination for another three months and have therefore had to pay out almost the same again for her services. She pays it into the bank, into her fund for her mythical future, and wishes she had any clearer idea of what that future might be. Actually she's tempted to just hand the money over to Phoebe, to go some way to paying off the loans she's going to need to get her through three years at the London College of Fashion, but she doesn't even get a chance to mention the idea before Phoebe is telling her, in no uncertain terms, that that's not an option.

'You have to use it on yourself,' Phoebe says, a slight upward twang creeping into her sentences courtesy of her weeks in Australia. 'And for something proper. Don't go frittering it away on rubbish.'

Abi smiles. 'That sounds like something I would say.'

'Well, you know who to blame, then. I mean it, though. When are you ever going to get this chance again?'

She's right, but it doesn't seem to be that simple. 'I know.'

In February she gives in, goes to the nearest shelter and comes home with a sad-looking tabby-and-white cat. He's old and cantankerous and spends most of his time sitting behind one of the armchairs, peering out at her mournfully, but she gets to like knowing he's there. She sends a photo to Tara and Megan, asking what she should call him, declines their suggestions of Justin and Aston and instead plumps for a more regal Henry. Grumpy as he is, he's company. She knows she's a cliché but now she also knows why that cliché has become so universal. It's nice to have something to come home to. Everyone needs to be loved, even if Henry has a funny way of showing it.

She's sitting at her computer, Henry behind his chair, one morning, when her request for news pages for Cleo suddenly throws up multiple results. It's been a while since anything new popped up; in terms of her career Cleo seems to have firmly stepped away from the radar. Now there are ten or so stories, each with a variation of the same headline. Abi stares at the screen, unable to believe what she's reading.

Cleo in marriage split.

She reads every one of the links, scouring them for more detail than the one before, but they all say the same. Cleo MacMahon Attwood, one time supermodel, has split from her husband of twelve years, advertising executive Jonty MacMahon. The couple who have two children, Tara ten and Megan seven, say they are saddened by the end of their marriage, but the split is amicable. They will continue to bring up the children together.

Abi sits back. She feels numb. Cleo and Jon have separated. It's agony not knowing the details. Did Jon find out about Cleo and Richard? Did he walk in on them? Or did she confess – no, Abi thinks, that would never happen. Or maybe Stella discovered what was going on and turned up on the doorstep – 'I think your wife is screwing my boyfriend.' What do Tara and Megan know? Have they been as protected as they should be? Forced to take sides? Whatever they have been told, she knows they'll be devastated. She wants to call them or email them, but it's almost impossible to think what to say. The story might not even be true. She can hardly write to her nieces offering her condolences for their parents' impending divorce if there's a possibility it might not be happening at all. Eventually she composes a short but heartfelt message:

Hi my gorgeous girls,

I hope you're both OK. I just wanted to say if you ever need to talk to me about anything I'm here. And you know you're always welcome to come and spend a few days down here in Kent if you want to. You can meet Henry.

Lots and lots of love,
Auntie Abi xxx

Two hours later she's at work and, feeling her mobile vibrating in her pocket, she heads out of the front door, onto the steps and answers. A tearful-sounding Tara is on the other end.

'Dad's moved out,' she says, sniffling.

Abi can hear the bustle of a school playground at break time behind her. She sits on the top step. 'Oh, sweetie, I'm so sorry.' She's not sure what to say, she can hardly ask why or what has happened between Jon and Cleo. 'Do you want me to ask them if you and Megan can come down here for a few days? When's half-term?'

'It's OK,' Tara says. 'I don't think we should leave Mum on her own. She's really upset.'

Of course she is. Abi can picture Cleo now, making herself the victim, courting sympathy, not even attempting to be strong for the sake of her girls.

'Well, you can come any time you like. You don't even have to give me any notice. So long as either your mum or your dad says it's OK, then I'll come up on the train and get you. Any time. I mean it.'

'Thank you.'

'How's Megan?'

'She keeps on crying. It's harder for her because she's so young,' Tara says, mustering all her ten-year-old sophistication.

'You can look after her, though, can't you? And she can look after you too even though she's younger?'

'Yes.'

'Where's your dad living?' Abi tries to ask the question casually. Not just because she doesn't want to give away how interested she is in the answer, but because she wants to try to make Tara feel like her father moving out doesn't have to be such a big deal.

'He's staying with Uncle Simon,' Tara says, naming Jon's Shepherd's Bush-based brother. 'But he's looking for a flat near us.'

'Well, then hopefully it won't be so bad. You'll still be able to see him every day.' Abi has no doubt that Jon will do everything he can to make the transition as painless as possible for his daughters. She wonders again what happened. Wonders if she'll ever even know. 'Are you going to be all right?'

Tara sniffles a yes.

'Call me whenever you want, day or night. I won't mind. And I'll phone you in a couple of days just to check you're doing OK. And give Megan a big kiss from me. I love you.'

Abi speaks to either Tara or Megan almost every day and Phoebe tells her she does the same. They compare notes, trying to piece together what's going on. Thankfully neither of the girls mentions anything about their parents fighting or shouting so she's hopeful that whatever is going on Cleo and Jon are behaving like parents first and a couple in crisis second. Arguing behind closed doors and in low voices, probably. Saving the big fights for when their children are at school. Frustratingly that also means there are no clues as to what exactly has gone wrong.

Abi thinks about contacting Cleo to find out the truth, but she has no desire to get caught up in her sister's melodrama. And, of course, she thinks almost constantly of calling Jon to find out whether he's OK and what his plans are. She tries to pretend to herself that it's anything other than wanting to hear his voice again, wanting to find out if he's hurting or embarrassed, or even relieved, but she knows herself too well. Hard as it is, she knows she has to stand back and just let things take their course. Be there for Tara and Megan if they need her.

Weeks later, it seems like years, Megan tells her that Jon has found somewhere to live in nearby St John's Wood.

'We can walk there,' she says, sounding more cheerful than she has done in ages. 'Well, we could if Mum would let us, but she doesn't like us going on our own.'

'You do see him, though?' Abi asks, concerned. She has already decided that the one thing which would make her get involved would be if she ever heard Cleo was being difficult about letting Jon have access to the children. If she was a judge, she knows which parent she'd be awarding custody to.

'He picks us up from school most days. And on the weekends he comes to get us. He waits outside, though; he never comes in,' she adds sadly.

'Is it nice, his flat?'

'It's OK. We have our own room, but we have to share, so that's a bit rubbish, but Dad got us a hamster so that makes it better.'

'A hamster! Henry would like him.'

'Henry would eat him and he's a girl.'

'OK, well, we won't introduce them, then. Maybe they can write to each other.'

Megan giggles and Abi feels a wave of relief.

'Or text. Henry likes to text.'

'Stupid,' Megan says, laughing.

*

One night Abi wakes up in a cold sweat. What if Cleo and Jon didn't break up because of Richard? What if Cleo broke it off with Richard all those months ago, but Jon left for another reason (he met someone else? No, she knows that would never happen) and Cleo's devastated? Abi has become so suspicious of her sister, so immune to her posturing, that she has never even considered that she might be genuinely hurting. She thinks about what Tara said – 'I don't want to leave her on her own; she's really upset.' She could be scared to reach out to Abi in case Abi rejects her. Abi has no desire to have any kind of relationship with Cleo any more, but she also knows that she has a duty to check that she's OK. If her sister needs her, she has to be there for her. Or at least offer to be there. That's what family is all about, after all. You have no choice; you're related to these people – you share their genes – you can't suddenly decide you're not, like them or hate them.

It's no good – she can't get back to sleep. She gets up and makes herself a mug of tea, sits at her computer. She'll send an email giving Cleo the opportunity to turn to her if she needs to. She has no other option.

Hi Cleo

Obviously I've heard about you and Jon. I'm so sorry. I hope you're doing OK. I just wanted to let you know I'm here if you need someone to talk to. Also, I'd be very happy to have the girls for half-term or any other time if

you need some space to sort things out. I can come up
and get them.

Abi x

She sends it off before she can stop herself, forces
herself to go back to bed.

The next evening when she gets home from work
there's a response. It's short and to the point and tells
Abi everything she needs to know about Cleo and
Jon's break-up.

Abigail, you made your feelings about me and my choices
very clear the last time we saw each other. I don't think
there's anything else we have to say to each other now. I
don't need someone so judgemental in my life.

Cleo

Abi stares at the screen. Reads the email again.
And again. Despite everything that has happened it
had never really sunk in that their estrangement was
final. That the sickness in their relationship was ter-
minal. She reads it again. It's not just that Cleo is
effectively saying her and Jon's marriage has indeed
ended because of her relationship with Richard.
(Why else would she worry that Abi would judge her
harshly?) Sadly, things like this happen all the time.
People fall in and out of love. They break up mar-
riages and families. They move on. You might not
approve of what they're doing, but if you love your

family member then you won't cut them off because of it.

No, it's what she says about not needing Abi in her life – 'I don't think there's anything else we have to say to each other now' – that makes it crystal clear that Cleo is closing the door on her. Saying goodbye. Don't call me, I won't call you.

30

It's spring. There's no denying it. The first few tentative tourists have started arriving for day trips on the weekends, sitting on the benches by the seafront, wrapped up in layers of clothing, picking at foil-encased sandwiches. Abi's little one-chair, one-table balcony turns out to be a sun trap in the late afternoons and she takes to sitting out there when she's not at work, book in hand, trying to lose herself.

She's avoiding thinking about anything if she can help it. She goes to the library, does her days, has an occasional drink with Juliet or Kate, her friend with the market stall, talks to Phoebe on the phone if she's lucky and then watches TV with a glass of wine until bedtime. On her days off she walks along the beach, makes soup and curries that she freezes and then never gets round to eating. She still goes up to London every few weeks, but not as often as she used to. Every now and then when she's flicking through the cable channels she comes across an attractive, approachable, friendly young mum that she thinks might be her in another life.

She has heard nothing from Cleo, obviously. Just as unsurprisingly nothing from Jon. Tara and Megan keep in touch sporadically. One or other of them mentions that their mum has told them she has a new boyfriend. Abi assumes it's Richard, knows she can't ask. Not for the first time Stella pops into her mind, but she can't go there. If it hadn't been for Abi, Richard never would have met Cleo and it follows that nothing else that happened would have happened. There's nothing she can say to Stella that she's going to want to hear, really. She's just going to have to let that one go.

One of the full-timers leaves the library and Abi is offered his job. She knows she shouldn't take it. Knows that if she does she will probably end up staying there forever. But it's tempting. There's something comforting about the safety and security it offers. It would be like coming in from the cold and diving under a big warm duvet. Not at all challenging, but maybe just what she needs right now. She ums and ahs about it, asks them if she can have a few days. Although in her head she's pretty much given up on the idea of an exciting new future, she's loath to take that final step. She knows that she could take the job and then leave when inspiration strikes, but she also knows that she won't. She'll bed in, settle down and the next thing she knows she'll be retirement age and she'll have been working in a library her whole adult life.

She's still putting it off, still stretching her boss's goodwill by avoiding giving her an answer, when she comes home from work one day in April to find a large brown envelope on the mat. It looks like junk, but she opens it anyway. Inside there's a brochure, folded open at one page. A large advert, ringed in red marker pen, reads 'Part-time vocational course in curating contemporary art'. Her heart starts beating out of her ears. She looks for a clue. There's no note, nothing. Just a London postmark and the red marker pen circle. But she knows who it's from. Knows it can only be Jon.

She studies the advert. The course is attached to one of the big art galleries in London. Two days a week for two years. She had no idea such things existed. She had no idea that she could somehow turn her passion into a career.

It crosses her mind that this could be a sign, a way for Jon to initiate contact. She's tempted to ring him, to say thank you. But her rational self tells her that if he wanted to talk to her he could just have picked up the phone himself. He wouldn't have waited on the off chance that he might happen across a course he thought she might like and then have sent the details on anonymously. It's enough that he's been thinking of her. She nearly cries when she thinks how well he knows her to understand that this particular course is so completely perfect in every way.

She looks the course up online. Her money from Bargain Hunters will just about cover the two years with a bit of help from the library to pay for the train up to London twice a week. She hasn't heard any more from them so she assumes that their campaign for world domination is finally over and her cash cow has died with it. If she stays at the library three days a week (the course info states that it's on a Monday and Thursday; she'll have to ask if she can swap one of her days), then the whole thing might just be possible. And then, who knows? She could get a job in a gallery, get involved in deciding what they might or might not exhibit, work her way up. She doesn't feel as if there's an upper age limit on curators.

She calls Phoebe, not even thinking what the time might be in Argentina or Brazil. Last time she talked to her daughter she was in the former trying to decide when to move on to the latter.

'I think I've found my vocation,' she says when Phoebe answers.

'I'm at work – hold on,' Phoebe hisses.

Abi waits.

'Hi, Mum. That's better. I'm being a cleaner in a hotel in Buenos Aires. I've just had to nip outside to talk to you.'

'Shall I call you later?' Abi says, worried. 'I don't want you to lose your job.'

'No, it's fine. What did you say? You've found your what?'

'Oh, it's nothing really. Just a course I want to do.'

'That's brilliant. What is it?'

Abi tells her, trying to keep the conversation brief, but Phoebe is having none of it.

'That's so perfect. Where did you find it? I thought you'd given up.'

'I nearly had . . .'

'And you'll be in the West End two days a week. We can meet for lunch.'

Abi laughs. 'Yeah, right. I think once you get there and make friends you might decide you have better things to do.'

'Well, you can take me shopping sometimes, then. I'll be an impoverished student.'

'Me too.'

'Honestly, Mum, you have to do it.'

'I really think I'm going to. At least, I'm going to apply.'

There's a picture in one of the papers. Abi has long since stopped googling her sister – she no longer cares what she's doing – but she's flicking through one of the tabloids one day and there she is, dressed up to the nines, skin-tight jeans showing she's clearly not eating any more than she used to, on the arm of one of the better-known young British film actors of the moment. He's thirteen years younger than she is, but his career is already in danger of stalling after a succession of so-so period dramas in which he specialized as the fey young heart-throb. Despite the fact that his hair is starting to recede prematurely (resulting in a somewhat alarming comb-forward), up against him Cleo still looks tired and strained. His youth magnifying her age. The text underneath implies – no, actually it all out says – that they are as desperate as each other to keep alive their fading careers. It's cynical about the relationship, speculating a fast track to marriage in the hope of magazine deals covering the engagement, setting up home together, the stag and hen dos, the wedding itself and the honeymoon. Not, it suggests cruelly, that anyone is going to offer to pay much for any of it.

Abi takes it in. Richard is already history, no doubt discarded when it became apparent that there was nothing he could offer in terms of social, financial or, most crucially, celebrity advancement. She hopes it was worth it for him. Or that maybe he somehow managed to salvage his relationship with Stella before it was too late. She hopes he's learned his lesson.

She lets them down gently at the library and three people immediately offer to swap days with her if she gets accepted on the course. The way all her colleagues are so excited on her behalf you'd think it was them who had decided to try a new direction in life. It reminds her why she has always loved it here so much, why she never made a break for it before.

She applies for the course before she can talk herself out of it, calling Phoebe at least five times for help with the application form. She emails Tara and

Megan to tell them about it, hoping that they might pass her news on to their father so that he'll know she's acted on what she's still sure was his suggestion. After a couple of weeks she's asked to go up for an interview. She feels sick, excited, nervous, energized, happy, everything. More alive than she's felt in a long time. She's stupidly grateful for the good-luck phone calls that reach her while she's on the train – Phoebe (who must have got up at about six in the morning to time it right), Juliet, Tara.

'Oh, and Dad says to say good luck too,' Tara says.

'Oh,' Abi says. 'Tell him thanks.'

She hears voices in the background. Obviously Tara is with Jon right now.

'And he says tell you he left his job.'

'He . . . what? Why on earth?'

More mumbling.

'He says tell you he sold the company.'

'Why?'

Tara sighs. 'You talk to him,' she says, and before Abi can protest she hears Jon's hesitant voice saying hi. Her knees go weak.

'Um . . . You sold the company?'

'I took a leaf out of your book. I'm going to follow my dream. Climb every mountain and all that.'

Abi laughs. 'And what is your dream exactly?'

'I'm not sure. Open a restaurant. I might go to culinary school. Or maybe I should just start at the bottom, washing pots and chopping carrots.'

'You could go on *MasterChef* — that might be easier.'

'But more humiliating. It's a toss-up.'

The train is pulling into Charing Cross station. Abi curses the timing.

'Jon, I . . . I have to go. I've just reached London and I don't want to be late.'

'Let me know how it goes,' he says. 'Call me later.'

Abi feels light-headed, breathless. 'I will.'

'Good luck,' Jon says. 'Not that you'll need it.'

'I . . .' she starts to say, but he's gone and Tara is back on the line.

'Good luck, Auntie Abi.'

'Thanks, sweetie. I'll let you know how I get on, OK?'

She pushes through the crowd trying to get to the tube station. She feels elated. If she gets accepted on the course, she will be in London for two days a week. A city where she feels a tie to her family at every turn. Her real family, the people who care about her unconditionally and she about them: Phoebe, Tara, Megan and Jon. She's realized it's not all about blood.

She gets there early, goes around the gallery one last time for luck — she's been here so many times before she knows exactly what paintings they have and where they are. By the time she is called in every part of her is sweating she wants this so much. In the waiting area she sits next to a girl who looks about twenty-two with a pierced eyebrow and ripped jeans.

Abi looks down at her best Hobbs dress and feels stupidly suburban and formal.

One hopeful is shown out and Abi is relieved to see he's a normal-looking middle-aged man. He's dressed in a suit as if he might have come from his job in the bank. He looks pale and anxious. The girl with the piercing is led in.

'This is terrifying,' she mutters to Abi as she passes. 'I feel sick.'

Abi smiles at her warmly. 'Good luck.' Who knows? This girl might end up as her new best friend, another surrogate daughter. The middle-aged man could turn out to be her soulmate. Anything could happen.

After about ten minutes a casually chic woman in her forties calls her in. There are two other people in the room, both of whom look intimidating just because they look so at home. One of them, a man in his fifties she would guess, with a shabby air, smiles at her, breaking the tension. He looks down at her application form, checks her name.

'So . . . Abi . . . do you want to tell us why you're interested in taking this course?'

Abi closes her eyes. Tell them how much you love modern art, Phoebe had said. Show them how much you know about it and what it makes you feel. That's all they'll be interested in.

She takes a deep breath. She can do this.

Acknowledgements

Thanks as ever to the whole team at Penguin, especially Louise Moore, Clare Pollock, Alice Shepherd, Liz Smith, John Hamilton and everyone else who works so hard on the books behind the scenes but who I never get to meet; Jonny Geller and everyone else at Curtis Brown, not least Betsy Robbins and Melissa Pimentel; and Peter McFarlane for helping me understand the structuring of TV advertising deals, Samantha Mackintosh for her attention to detail and Charlotte Willow Edwards for her usual invaluable help.

Jane Fallon

Families you wish you'd grown up in . . .

Little Women – Louisa M. Alcott (OK we'd all fight about who got to be Jo)

Spencer's Mountain – Earl Hamner (the Waltons no less)

Ballet Shoes – Noel Streatfeild (made me wish I was adopted)

To Kill a Mockingbird – Harper Lee (I loved my dad but Atticus Finch makes a close second)

And the ones you're glad you didn't . . .

Bleak House – Charles Dickens (the interminable interfamilial lawsuit, Jarndyce vs Jarndyce, the 'family curse')

The Godfather – Mario Puzo (there are some advantages, I suppose, but overall I think I'd rather not)

Fingersmith – Sarah Waters (pervy uncle or violent criminals, neither of the girls has the ideal family life)

More About Jane

I was born in Harrow, in north London, the youngest of five kids, four girls and a boy. We moved out to Buckinghamshire when I was about two or three, where we lived above my parents' newsagents. My mum and dad worked incredibly hard, getting up at 4.30 every morning, seven days a week, to mark up the papers for the boys and girls to do the rounds. Watching them instilled a real work ethic in me. I've always worked hard and assumed that if I don't earn my own living no one else would do it for me. From as young an age as I can remember, the idea of having a career was important to me. I never fantasized about getting married and having babies – I just wanted to do something fabulous. Not that I knew what I wanted that fabulous career to be.

I was a shy, socially awkward child, and I hid myself away in books. I read all the time (I still do). I harboured secret ambitions to be a novelist, but that seemed like an unattainable goal. My other interests – gymnastics, dance and animals – didn't really offer much hope either, especially once I realized that sciences were never going to be my strong point, so there was no point even thinking about becoming a vet. (Even if I had been able to stomach dissecting a rat in biology class – I couldn't; I took the day off school sick to avoid it.)

When I was about fourteen I fell in love with an American TV show called *The Paper Chase*. Set on a Yale-like college campus, it centred round a group of law students and their charismatic tutor. I started to have visions of myself, books under my arm, pushing a bicycle through a leafy autumnal courtyard, sitting under a tree earnestly discussing the rights and wrongs of the legal system with my attractive, witty and smart fellow students. I have always had an overactive imagination, so I managed to overlook the fact that I couldn't (and still can't) ride a bicycle or that as I was in England it would probably be raining most days, and I somehow convinced myself that law was for me. I made the mistake of mentioning this at school one day and I was never allowed to forget it (my school was a convent, not at all academic, and I think the teachers got carried away with the idea of one of their pupils going to law school). Before I really knew what I was doing I applied, and was accepted, to study law at University College London.

I knew almost as soon as I arrived that I'd made a terrible mistake. There were nine o'clock lectures every day. The work – in the first term at least – seemed to consist of learning historical cases by rote. It was all way too much like being at school and, besides, it soon struck me that I had absolutely no interest in becoming a solicitor, and neither the finances nor the social confidence to become a barrister. I lasted a term. Unwilling to leave my newfound friends behind, I shopped around for another department that would take me and within days I was part of the history department. With no compulsory lectures and only one tutorial group a week, this immediately felt like home.

After university I drifted for a while, half-heartedly applying for jobs here and there. I kept my head afloat working in a health-food shop and a gym and a concert ticket office. I knew that somewhere out there was the perfect career for me, but I just couldn't work out what it was. I was terrified of putting a foot on the bottom rung of the wrong ladder and then waking up, ten years later, deep in a career I hated but beyond the point where I could start at the bottom somewhere else. I was happy to work my way up, happy to work for next to nothing – I just needed to find out in what field.

Eventually my dad sent me an advert he'd cut out of the paper for a 'Girl Friday' in a theatrical and literary agency. I fell in love with the place as soon as I walked through the door. There were scripts piled up everywhere, theatre posters on the walls jostling with the actors' 10 by 8s. I ended up staying there for three years, making tea, answering the phones, reading scripts and eventually working closely with a few of the young writers they represented. It opened up a lot of doors for me. I still had my own writing

More About Jane

ambitions, but instead of pursuing it (I still wrote, but only in secret, starting and abandoning countless novels and screenplays) I channelled my love of fiction into working in TV drama first as a script reader then script editor and eventually producing. During my time as a freelance producer I produced shows like *This Life*, *Teachers* and *20 Things to do Before You're 30*. I was lucky enough to be nominated for four BAFTA awards (none of which I won!) and the shows – particularly *This Life* – gained many other plaudits.

By 2006, though, I was feeling burnt out with TV, desperate for a new challenge. When I had the idea for *Getting Rid of Matthew* it seemed like the perfect time to make the break and to try to fulfil my lifelong ambition to write a novel. I decided to take a year out from producing and see if I could make a go of it. If nothing happened, I could just go back to work later. I told all my friends and colleagues what I was intending to do in the hope that it would shame me into actually producing something on paper. I knew that they would be calling me up saying, 'So, have you written anything today? Have you finished it yet?' It worked. I still don't quite know how I actually got up the courage to go through with it, but I'm immensely thankful that I did.

Did you always want to be a writer?

It was one of my dreams for as long as I can remember. But it always felt like one of those things that would remain a dream, like being a champion Olympic gymnast (my other passion that I used to daydream about for hours as I practised Arab springs and back flips in the garden).

When I was young my parents had a newsagent's that had a small paperback stand in one corner. My earliest memory of wanting to write fiction is from when I was about eight and I used to write 'books' (a couple of pieces of foolscap folded into eight pages, complete with illustrations) and try to persuade my dad to sell them with the other novels in the shop. From what I can remember they were all about animals – the third big love of my life – and not much ever happened beyond them going round to each other's for tea or going to the seaside for the day. I truly thought they were works of genius though. My father declined to put them up for sale and so my ambition subsided for a while. I think I just didn't imagine being a novelist was something girls like me – from ordinary suburban families with no artistic connections and the absolute certainty that when you grew up you had to work hard to make a living, not indulge yourself in your creative passions because how else were you going to support yourself? – could ever do. I continued to write all the time though. English was my best, and favourite, subject at school and I was always praised for my imagination and storytelling. But I became very self-conscious about it. At home I would write down an idea, but then throw it away in case someone found my notes and sneered at them.

Working in TV drama was definitely an outlet for my ambition. As a script editor then producer I would often write on shows, but uncredited. So I had all the satisfaction of crafting stories, but without having to take the direct heat.

Q&A with Jane

Can you tell us about your daily routine, as a writer? When do you find it easiest to write?

If I don't get up early and write for a few hours before the rest of the world starts to intrude too much, then I'm done for. On an ideal day I get up around seven, write until about eleven or twelve (interspersed with breaks to get coffee/play Scrabble on the iPad/make soup. I have all manner of diversionary tactics to hand) and then have the rest of the day to do whatever else I need to do. Of course, it almost never works out like that. Either I get up too late, or I get up but only because I have to let in the person coming to fix the boiler/the washing machine/the Sky box at eight and once there's someone else in the house I find it impossible to concentrate. Or I get up but I have to go into town for a meeting, or it's a nice day so I decide to go for an early run and, before I know it, I've missed a whole day's work.

Writing *Getting Rid of Matthew*, my first book, I was very disciplined. I felt like I had something to prove. To myself and everyone else I knew. I had left my job announcing that I was off to write a novel – (that sounds more dramatic than it was. I had always been freelance and decided to take some time out. If nothing came of it I could return to work later). My thinking really was that if I told everyone about my ambitions (something I had kept secret from all but a handful of people for years) then I would be shamed into having to actually come up with the goods. I knew that my friends and ex-colleagues would be calling, asking how it was going, how much had I written, was anybody interested, so pride made me get up in the morning and treat writing like a job. Once Penguin had picked up the book (after I had written 30,000 words), I felt that responsibility even more keenly, so I set myself a deadline to deliver the finished product to them and made sure I stuck to it.

Since then my methods have become more and more haphazard with each book. *Got You Back* was written when I was travelling backwards and forwards to the US every ten days or so. Much of it was achieved in concentrated seven-hour bursts on long-haul flights. For some reason I find it quite inspiring writing on planes. Much of *Foursome* was written sitting in cafes in New York. I wrote *The Ugly Sister* during a period when I was home in London for a long stretch. It was a lovely warm summer and I would often walk down through Primrose Hill into Regent's Park in the afternoons. Walking seems to help immensely when I'm stuck for ideas or I have a tricky piece of plot to work through. The book was originally set in a different part of London, but as the summer went on I started to feel like Primrose Hill was the natural place Cleo would have ended up in and also that it was somewhere Abi could really fall in love with.

The Ugly Sister is your fourth novel. Have you found that anything has changed about your writing process since beginning your career as a writer?

The idea for *Getting Rid of Matthew* popped into my head, more or less fully formed one night. I'm a lifelong insomniac and I have learned to try to force myself to use the long hours when I'm awake at night to try to think of ideas rather than just dwell on the fact that I'm not sleeping and how tired I am going to be next day. So I spent a couple of hours, probably, thinking it through, coming up with all the twists and turns I could think of. I was really trying to come up with an idea for a new TV series, but the more I thought around the subject the more I realized that it should be a novel. I went off to sleep eventually and in the morning I tried to remember the idea and to write it down before I forgot what it was I'd liked about it, what I thought made it unique. Now, I should say, this happens to me often. I spend half the night coming up with stories and plots. They're brilliant. They're original and gripping and sophisticated. They're the best idea I've ever had. Then I get up next day and remember them and think, What was that load of old rubbish? Most of what you come up with in a half-asleep/half-awake state at four in the morning is nonsense. This time, however, I knew I had something.

Sadly the ideas process has never been as smooth or easy since. Partly, I am convinced, because an anti-migraine medication I now take every night means I actually tend to sleep for a few hours. I may not have blinding headaches any more, but I've crippled my creative process! These days it takes me about three months to come up with a plot that I'm completely happy with. Most of that time is spent gawping out of the window, wandering the streets of north London, having an occasional panicking fit that nothing is ever going to gel, getting very excited about an idea for a week or two before having to admit that it's too flimsy. I need to be satisfied that I have enough potential for plot twists to keep the story moving for 100,000-plus words before I start. I learned that the hard way when, before *Got You Back*, I embarked on my second book too quickly and was 40,000 words in before I realized that it wasn't going to work. The temptation to just plough on was immense. I had been working on it solidly for about two months and the idea of just throwing that work away was soul destroying. It was definitely the right decision though. And I've also discovered that nothing is ever wasted. I keep all my half thoughts and false starts in a file and they've come in very useful when I've needed ideas for short stories.

Actually writing the first draft takes me about nine months. I don't work every day during that period. Every now and then I feel like I need a break from it for a week or so and I know now that I just have to allow that to happen. I think sometimes your brain just needs to put stuff on the back burner for a while.

Your readers have often said that they appreciate the fact that you write about female characters whose priority is often not just finding or keeping a man. Was this a deliberate move on your part, and, if so, why did you decide to write about women in this way?

Absolutely. I think it's really important that you can imagine being friends, or at least that you empathize, with the central character in a novel. At the very least you need to find them interesting. If you don't care about them in some way, then why read on? And I have never found women who obsess about being in a relationship particularly good company. It's boring. My friends are all strong, funny women who have all kinds of different priorities. Some of them are single and probably do wish they could find a good relationship – after all, who doesn't want that? – but it's not the be-all and end-all for them. It's not the focus of their lives.

When I first sat down to write *Getting Rid of Matthew* it was a response to the fact that I was starting to find that a lot of women's fiction didn't really speak to me. Not only was the focus almost invariably on finding a man, but there always seemed to be a time clock – set at thirty – involved. I must get married by the time I'm thirty! I must have a baby before I'm thirty! What? Why? This was 2005. Women had discovered they could happily conceive well into their 30s and even 40s. The concept of the old maid, left on the shelf if she wasn't married off at a certain age, had long gone, but, for some reason, still lingered on in fiction. I decided I wanted to write books about women I recognized. I wouldn't necessarily approve of the way they were behaving, but I would feel like they had something to say. I would want to spend time with them and find out more.

As much as we sometimes dislike Cleo, it's hard not to feel slightly sorry for her, as she worries about getting older in a career that prioritizes youthful beauty. Is this something that you feel particularly strongly about?

Cleo is definitely a victim of her own beauty, if you like. She was plucked out of nowhere before she had a chance to fully develop a personality that wasn't warped by her being famous – plus she wasn't helped by having a mother who indulged her and seemed to find her looks as important as she did. Her story can only end in tears really because her looks are fading – in the way the modelling industry defines beauty anyway, and that is all that really matters to her – and she has nothing to back them up, no skills or talents to get her through the rest of her life. I do feel sorry for her, but only up to a point. She's a monster; she treats people terribly. She has always been absolutely convinced that she is some kind of superior being.

I don't know what will happen to her, but I don't think she has a happy future ahead. She'll probably try to attach herself to younger and younger men (I never get why women do that. Don't they just look old standing next to them? Why would you want to go out with someone who people thought was your son?). Without a doubt she'll have way too much plastic surgery and end up with those big fake cheeks, over exaggerated cat's eyes and rubber lips. She'll end up alone or being leeched on by some young D-lister trying to get his fifteen minutes. There are certainly people who will think that it's karma.

I've always found it interesting that we value beauty so highly when it's something which is just a given – the owners of it have contributed nothing; they just are.

The Ugly Sister explores the theme of sibling rivalry. Why does this subject interest you, and is it something you've always been interested in?

Sibling rivalry is a classic forum for drama and storytelling. We all have such conflicted and complex feelings about our families, even those of us who have grown up in a happy, loving, nuclear set-up. Family feelings run deep, both good and bad. I've always thought it must be especially tough to be one of two children. You're always held up in direct comparison – particularly if you're the same sex. If you're not the best at something, then by default you must be the worst. I think that sibling rivalry probably exists in every family to some extent. It's inevitable given that you grow up vying for your parents' approval and attention. But when there are just two of you there's nowhere to hide. I think that I was fortunate to grow up in a big family where you could melt into the crowd a bit.

　　Also, although we often feel closer to our friends than our siblings, we can never get away from the ties that a shared upbringing gives us. If you fall out badly with a friend, chances are that friendship may be over, but your sister is always going to be your sister whatever happens. For Abi that blood tie keeps her doggedly trying to rekindle her relationship with Cleo. She barely knows her sister any more – and doesn't particularly like what she does know – but, with both their parents gone, she feels the need to be close to her even more strongly. Cleo is her only link to her past.

The London setting of Primrose Hill gives the novel a very strong sense of place, and the other locations in the novel, New York and Deal, in Kent, provide a big contrast. As a writer, is a sense of place important to you?

It is. I like to set my stories in places I know, that I feel comfortable with. Apart from anything else, it removes the need for endless tiny bits of research (is there really a Waitrose on that corner? Could you conceivably walk to there from there?). Of course, you can then take liberties. Richard's bookshop in *The Ugly Sister* is obviously a fiction and is not based on any real establishment, but it feels like the kind of place that could be there; it fits with the kinds of small independent shops that exist in Primrose Hill. Cleo and Jon's house is a fictional house, but it wouldn't feel out of place if you dropped it down on to Regent's Park Road.

In *The Ugly Sister*, in particular, the sense of place was key. Abi's life in London is so completely different to her life in Kent. I really wanted the reader to experience London through her eyes, to feel the attachments she was forming to the place as well as the people. Primrose Hill is an area with a split personality. There are the huge terraced mansions that were notorious for being home to a small group of celebrities who were tabloid darlings for a while with their bed hopping and excesses. Cleo would absolutely want to be a part of that group. She sees herself as one of the 'beautiful people', the glitterati. But the area is also a thriving real community. There are gorgeous independent shops, cafes with tables on the street, the hill itself, which towers green and grassy above the surrounding streets and is home to joggers and dog walkers and mothers playing with their kids. From the top you can look out across London towards the City and feel part of it, but removed at the same time. It's one of my favourite places.

Cleo is a fantastic character; it's shocking to watch how manipulative she can be. Did anything in particular inspire you to create her as a character?

I had been thinking a lot about families and genetics, how sometimes siblings could look so different. It struck me that if that difference was quite extreme – one sibling inherited all the good physical stuff as it were – then two sisters, quite close in age, could have a very different view of the world despite the fact that they grew up together. Of course, the same could be true to an extent if one sibling inherited all the brains, but people don't stop you in the street and tell you how brainy you are – they don't feel obliged to comment on your IQ at every given moment as if it is a prized possession. For sisters especially it must be hard to grow up and constantly to be reminded of the fact that you're not the pretty one by people who seem to value that over anything.

The other thing that I'd been mulling over was the idea that if someone becomes famous at a young age it can warp their personality. To be treated as though you're so special, to be able to order adults around and get your own way before you have truly found out who you are as a human being, must have a corrupting effect. Why bother to develop social skills when everyone fawns all over you anyway? Click your fingers and something gets done; you don't have to earn it, don't have to negotiate. And if that early fame is based on something so surface as looks then you're on even shakier ground. Because your looks will fade – at least they will lose the ability to make people jump to your beck and call, the ability to make you a living even – but you don't realize that when you're young so you don't modify your behaviour to take that into account.

I started to see that a character combining those two ideas could be really fun – a monster – but at the same time there's a sadness there. Cleo knows she can no longer rely on her biggest weapon. Plus, whether she acknowledges it to herself or not, she has burned most of her bridges. She made the mistake of believing her own hype, thinking she was a star, and she treated everybody as if they were lesser beings, lucky to be working for her. Her sense of entitlement was out of control. Now she's not the face of the moment, she's going to find it hard to get any work at all because she has no favours to call in.

Q&A with Jane

Before being a writer, you were a television producer, responsible for programmes such as *Teachers* and *This Life*. Can you tell us about the differences and similarities between working on TV and writing novels?

It's basically all storytelling but they're actually very different disciplines. Obviously with TV you have the visual element to help you tell the tale. With a novel you have to create the world from scratch, trying to make sure that the reader will picture places and people in the way that you want them to. You also have the joy of being able to be inside the characters' heads. You can tell your readers exactly what a character is thinking. It allows you to be expositional in a way that simply having to rely on dialogue doesn't.

The tricky thing with TV writing is conveying everything you need to using dialogue, but keeping that dialogue real and convincing. You can't have a character suddenly articulate their thoughts and feelings for no reason. Bad TV writing is full of exposition. My favourite is always the line that starts something like 'You know your brother Jim, the one who's a doctor, who you fell out with . . .' No one talks like this. You can see the writer desperately wrestling with the fact that he needs the audience to know that this character has a doctor for a brother and that they are no longer in touch and then thinking, Oh, sod it, I'll just have one of the characters say it. It's lazy writing and it's insulting to the audience. A clever TV writer feeds the audience the background they need without them realizing it. It's a real skill.

The other joy with novel writing is that, as the writer, you hold all the cards. With TV you might write a great script, but the director or producer might not see it in the same way you do. You might not like the finished product. There's something that's equal amounts liberating, thrilling and terrifying about having the sole responsibility for what reaches your audience. I love that the book I write is exactly the book my readers get to read. Whether they love it or hate it, it's exactly how I wanted it to be.

Reading Group Discussion Questions

How did you interpret the title in relation to the two sisters in the novel?

Cleo and Abi are very different in most ways, but did you see any similarities between them?

The differences in Abi and Cleo's personalities are reflected in their external lives: whereabouts they live, the houses they inhabit, their families and the objects around them. What did you feel that each of these contrasts added to your understanding of both Abi and Cleo?

Jon's cooking is an important part of his personality, and provides an introduction to the 'real' Jon, as opposed to the one that Cleo has created. How did Jon's interest in cooking affect your perception of him? Did your perception of Jon change throughout the novel?

Cleo changes her name and also her childhood: Abi recalls how in interviews, Cleo presented herself as coming from a rather more deprived and difficult background than she had in reality. Do you think it's ever possible to completely reinvent yourself?

Cleo, used to being beautiful, obviously finds the ageing process traumatic, and we witness her having endless beauty treatments. Abi, however, doesn't have this concern, as she never thought of herself as beautiful. Do you think that beauty is always something to envy?

Loyalty emerges as key theme in the novel. For example, in a sense, Richard is a great friend to Abi until his loyalty is put to the test. Similarly, Abi is also conflicted once her own loyalty to her sister is put to the test, but she refuses to betray her sister. What conclusions about loyalty did you draw as the novel progressed?

Family is an important theme in the novel. To what extent are Cleo and Abi's current circumstances a result of their childhood relationship? How does Abi's perception of family change throughout the novel?

Discuss the relationship between character and appearance. How far can Abi's advertising slogan be seen to reflect this central theme: 'Why pay for perfect packaging when it's what's on the inside that counts?'

Careers are often talked about throughout the novel, from Cleo's attempted comeback to Tara and Megan's ideas of what they would like to be when they grow up. Can we see a relationship between wealth and happiness?

He just wanted a decent book to read ...

Not too much to ask, is it? It was in 1935 when Allen Lane, Managing
Director of Bodley Head Publishers, stood on a platform at Exeter railway
station looking for something good to read on his journey back to London.
His choice was limited to popular magazines and poor-quality paperbacks –
the same choice faced every day by the vast majority of readers, few of
whom could afford hardbacks. Lane's disappointment and subsequent anger
at the range of books generally available led him to found a company – and
change the world.

*'We believed in the existence in this country of a vast reading public for intelligent
books at a low price, and staked everything on it'*
Sir Allen Lane, 1902–1970, founder of Penguin Books

The quality paperback had arrived – and not just in bookshops. Lane was
adamant that his Penguins should appear in chain stores and tobacconists,
and should cost no more than a packet of cigarettes.

Reading habits (and cigarette prices) have changed since 1935, but
Penguin still believes in publishing the best books for everybody to
enjoy. We still believe that good design costs no more than bad design,
and we still believe that quality books published passionately and responsibly
make the world a better place.

So wherever you see the little bird – whether it's on a piece of
prize-winning literary fiction or a celebrity autobiography, political tour
de force or historical masterpiece, a serial-killer thriller, reference book,
world classic or a piece of pure escapism – you can bet that it represents
the very best that the genre has to offer.

Whatever you like to read – trust Penguin.